Great British Fictional Detectives

Great British Fictional Detectives

by
Russell James

First published in Great Britain in 2008 by
REMEMBER WHEN
An imprint of
Pen & Sword Books Ltd
47 Church Street
Barnsley
South Yorkshire
S70 2AS

ISBN 978 1 84468 026 9

Printed and bound in Thailand
by Kyodo Nation Printing Services Co., Ltd

Pen & Sword Books Ltd incorporates the imprints of Pen & Sword Aviation,
Pen & Sword Maritime, Pen & Sword Military, Wharncliffe Local History,
Pen & Sword Select, Pen & Sword Military Classics, Leo Cooper, Remember When,
Seaforth Publishing and Frontline Publishing
MMMDCCLXXVIII DCCLXIV CCIX

For a complete list of Pen & Sword titles please contact
PEN & SWORD BOOKS LIMITED
47 Church Street, Barnsley, South Yorkshire, S70 2AS, England
E-mail: enquiries@pen-and-sword.co.uk
Website: www.pen-and-sword.co.uk

CONTENTS

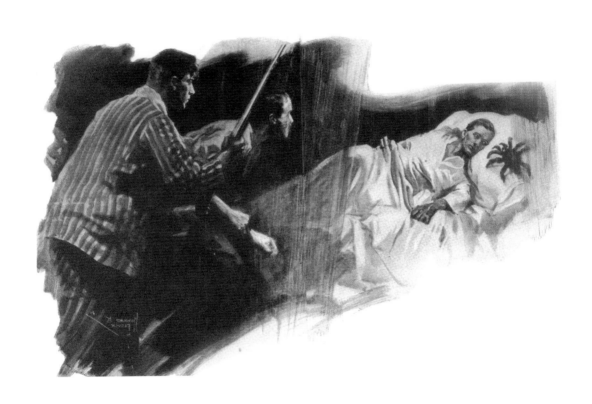

FOREWORD

By MARK BILLINGHAM

IT WAS ALL LEN BOWLES'S FAULT... Many people, especially those working in the creative arts, have a teacher to thank for that all-important encouragement early on: for providing a spark and helping it catch; for a nudge in the right direction or for the simple affirmation that an over-active imagination might, just might, be put to some good use. It's almost always an English teacher, but Len Bowles taught maths.

Len was a hugely eccentric and mercurial figure. He would juggle oranges and balance chairs on his chin if he was in a good mood, but was fearsome if crossed and utterly lethal with a heavy text book or a board duster, with which he could hit a the side of a small boy's head with unerring accuracy from 20 feet. Most importantly of all, as far as I was concerned, he got bored rather easily. Half way through a lesson, when quadratic equations were proving as tedious to him as they were to the rest of us, Len was prone to reach into a battered old leather bag, take out a well-thumbed copy of *The Adventures of Sherlock Holmes* and spend the rest of the lesson reading aloud to us.

And that was it…

Even then, transported far from Pythagoras and Pi's endless decimal places by *The Speckled Band* or *The Red-Headed League*, it was the character of the Great Detective that was so compelling. Of course I enjoyed the stories, outlandish and exciting, but it was Holmes himself, his mind like a 'racing engine tearing itself to pieces', that grabbed my interest and held it. Even then, I could easily appreciate how readers had been gripped to the extent that when he was killed off, many took to wearing black armbands on the streets of London. As a 12-old-boy of course, there were subtleties that I failed to appreciate, but as time went on I grew to relish Conan-Doyle's creation even more. Holmes was a man of science, a dynamic new force at the time the books were written and with more idiosyncrasies than most modern sleuths put together. The drug habit, the obsessive love of music and the tendency to fire guns into walls are enough to put even the edgiest of today's detectives to shame.

I have discovered and grown to love many fictional detectives since I first came across Sherlock Holmes, but those unconventional maths lessons were where it all began. Len Bowles is the reason I write detective fiction. He's also the reason why I can't add up.

Once I began to read for myself, after the joys of Alistair MacLean and popular blockbusters such as *Jaws* and *The Godfather*, I found myself increasingly drawn to rather more hard-boiled detectives. These were gumshoes whose creators flew in the face of RA Knox's infamous 'Decalogue', a set of rules for crime writers instructing them – among other things – to use no more than one secret passage per story and to avoid writing about Chinamen.

I devoured the works of Dashiell Hammett and Raymond Chandler, whose detectives moved through the real world, as opposed to that described by Chandler himself as 'stilted and artificial to the point of burlesque'. Hammett's Continental Op was distanced and ruthless and Sam Spade, although he appeared in only one novel, was the first hardboiled private eye, who had the famously cynical Dorothy Parker 'mooning around in a daze of love such as I had not known for any character in literature since I encountered Sir Launcelot'.

Chandler took the hardboiled detective to another level, and in Philip Marlowe, a hero 'neither tarnished nor afraid', he created a character who shaped my love of detective fiction every bit as much as Holmes had done. Chandler saw the detective as embodying the medieval conception of chivalry and it is no coincidence that his character's name echoes that of the man who wrote *Le Morte d'Arthur*.

Marlowe became a template. Any number of modern-day detectives, within their respective milieux, still behave as modern-day knights, Quixotic or otherwise, though their steeds are motorised and the maidens tend to be drop-dead gorgeous redheads. These are men (for the most part) who work in a 'world gone wrong' and answer to no higher power; not to God, like GK Chesterton's Father Brown, and certainly not to science, like Holmes or Nero Wolfe. They are characters who see the world from the perspective of the man on the street and, once Chandler had come along, the man on the street (and one particular student on the mean streets of Birmingham) couldn't get enough of them.

While feeding my addiction to mystery fiction at the library or local bookshop, I was also able to get plenty of cheaper fixes thanks to the glut of detective shows on TV in the 1970's. It's marvellous to finally see a book which acknowledges the role played by the small screen in moulding the iconic figure of the detective.

From its earliest days, the mass media played an important role in the popular perception of the detective. The gentler breed – The Saint, The Falcon, Mr Moto – were hugely popular in the Thirties, but their hardboiled descendants came to define the role on the big screen from the film noir movement of the Forties and beyond.

I have always enjoyed detective movies, with *Bullitt* and *Dirty Harry* as important to me in their way as any crime novel I have ever read, but the TV that I watched in my early teens was what truly cemented the figure of the detective in my imagination.

In the UK, the trend was towards ethnicity and regionalism. So I watched *Shoestring*, the Bristol-based radio detective; *Van Der Valk*, the Dutch detective; and David Yip as *The Chinese Detective*, flying solo in the face of one of RA Knox's sillier commandments. American television meanwhile produced a detective for everyone. It gave us McCloud, Kojak and Jim Rockford, together with a string of 'differently abled' detectives: Longstreet, who was blind; Ironside, who was a wheelchair-user; and Frank Cannon, who simply appeared to have eaten all the pies.

Above all, for me, it gave us the peerless Lieutenant Columbo, the homicide cop who dressed like Marlowe but had a mind like a Poirot. I adored and continue to adore this show, which not only broke the mould, dispensing with the traditional whodunit in favour of a *dance-a-deux* between cop and killer, but which proved to be a breeding ground for some of the finest talent in film and TV of the last thirty years. As my career has grown to include a certain amount of crime-fiction related broadcasting, I was privileged recently to present a documentary about the making of *Columbo*, interviewing the likes of Jonathan Demme, Steven Bochco and of course Peter Falk. Getting my first novel published was pretty great, and the kids being born…well, obviously, but hearing that gravelly voice say 'Just one more thing, Mr Billingham' was a thrill just about as great as any I have experienced.

The Booker Prize? Who needs it?

I remain today, as I was all those years ago in the classroom, most fascinated by the character of those detectives. For me it was what went on in Holmes's head that was so fascinating. In spite of the wisecracks and the gunplay, it was always the Philip Marlowe behind the black mask that I enjoyed getting to know; the one who went home and played chess and listened to music and felt insecure. This is why I have always preferred series characters, and it's also the reason I chose to write one. Most of the great detectives (Sam Spade being the notable exception) have grown and developed over a number of novels, TV series or movie adaptations, and we enjoy seeing that development. We enjoy watching the character change, while at the same time being able to count on the fact that some things, the important things, will always stay the same.

Some, dismissive of detective fiction, point to what they see as its clichés: to the battles with the booze and the problems with relationships and the tortured pasts. I'm sure that the majority of real detectives have no more than the occasional half of shandy and live in domestic bliss, and are not haunted by the victims of crimes they could not solve. The evidence would suggest, however, that people do not want to read about these characters, and I for one don't care to write about them. Who wants to know about a cowboy without a gun or a horse?

Like most of those who write modern detective fiction, I endeavour to make my central character stand out from the pack. I have tried to give him his own insecurities and passions. But at the same time, however much he is a character with unique drives and demons, he owes a debt to all those detectives created in the past 20 years, as they in turn honour those from previous eras, in the continuing evolution of one of fiction's most enduring archetypes.

As Columbo would have said…

"Just one more thing…"

Read on, and enjoy.

INTRODUCTION

Hercule Poirot rose to his feet. One hand caressed his moustache. He said: 'Mademoiselle, I am honoured! I will justify your faith in me. I will investigate your case of murder. I will search back into the events of sixteen years ago and I will find out the truth.'

FIVE LITTLE PIGS (1942) *by Agatha Christie*

HOW MANY DETECTIVES CAN YOU NAME? In this guide you'll find over four hundred. The bulk of the book is a comprehensive *A to Z* of fictional British detectives you can find in books, TV or film. By confining the selection to *British* detectives I have been able to bring you a far more detailed guide than you will find elsewhere, not only of the famous names – Sherlock Homes, John Rebus, Inspector Morse – but also of many equally fascinating but less well-known names. For example, can you name the book with the first woman detective, the first nurse detective, a blind detective, two Edwardian cycling detectives, the first transsexual sleuth and the dog that accompanied Valerie Drew?* Do you remember *Z-Cars* on TV? Here in these pages you will find not only the best-known TV detectives of today and yesterday but old favourites you thought you had forgotten. Older readers will remember Superintendent Lockhart – but what was the name of the programme? Anyone who watches TV today will know Morse and Rebus, but who are the starring actors in *Life on Mars* and *Mind to Kill*?

It's all here. The *A to Z* section lists over four hundred detectives, some of whom have only a line or two while the more interesting sleuths have two or three pages each. But there's far more here than that. You'll find quotes from books, plenty of illustrations and a wealth of inside information about detectives and crime fiction.

This is a book to dip into anywhere and any time you will. You can, of course, read through in sequence but you will probably prefer to skip straight to the sections that interest you most – a particular detective, the TV programmes, any of the essays shown in the *Contents*. This book is for keeping at your bedside or wherever you prefer to read detective stories – perhaps in your library, where the body lies foully murdered?

Even now I hear the butler knocking softly at your door...

Russell James
2008

*The first woman detective was **Mrs Paschal,** appearing in a short story collection in 1861. The first nurse detective was **Hilda Wade,** created by Grant Allen in *Strand* magazine, the best known blind detective was **Max Carrados,** while the two redoubtable cycling detectives are **Lois Cayley** created by Grant Allen again and MacDonald Bodkin's **Dora Myrl.** The first transvestite detctive story was *My Lady the Wolf* by Baron Skottowe written as far back as 1886, and Valerie Drew's trusty canine was called **Flash.** Now you know!

Exhibit One

Why We Love Detective Stories

Detective fiction is pre-eminently the literature of the sickroom and the railway carriage; even its admirers rarely argue that it is a serious art form.

THOSE WERE THE OPENING WORDS of *Bloodhounds of Heaven*, a study of early detective fiction by the noted critic Ian Ousby. I doubt it was true in 1976 when his book was published, and certainly many readers would argue with him now. Leaving aside a few dusty old literary critics, most readers today recognise that crime fiction is far more than an idle read; it can be as well-written as any non-genre novel, and can offer a sharper and more realistic portrait of modern life. Though we recognise this, our government does not: as recently as 2007 they refused to help save Undershaw, the house in which Conan Doyle wrote and created Sherlock Holmes. Holmes has been described as not only the most famous name in crime fiction but the most famous name in fiction – an extraordinarily impressive claim, even if it failed to impress Tessa Jowell, the misnamed Culture Secretary, when she was asked to upgrade Doyle's mansion to Grade 1 status to ensure its preservation. In her cultural myopia she replied that Sir Arthur Conan Doyle 'does not occupy a significant enough position in the nation's consciousness'. The pleas of several Scottish culture boards and of noted writers like Ian Rankin failed to move her. She presumably did not read Sherlock Holmes. Did she read at all, one wondered? The great author's house, which Doyle helped design, entertained many literary guests including Virginia Woolf and Bram Stoker (creator of Dracula: Ms Jowell must surely have heard of him?) but her government would not move. Interestingly, the fictional home of Holmes, 221B Baker Street, has more visitors each year than has either Jane Austen's or Charles Dickens', both of which are Grade 1 listed. As Ian Rankin said at the time: 'Around the world, more people know about and read Sherlock Holmes than read Jane Austen. He

The fictional home of Sherlock Holmes, 221B Baker Street, has been created as a popular tourist attraction.

created one of the most recognisable and archetypal figures in literature, and if his house is not worth saving, then I would say that no house is worth saving.' This was not the first time Ms Jowell found herself caught up in a controversy about house funding.

Visit practically any bookshop today and you will find a section devoted to crime fiction. For most people crime fiction means mystery, and mystery means detectives. The average reader who never commits a crime more serious than a road traffic offence loves to curl up with a tale of murder and skulduggery in which, despite every twist the cunning criminal can muster, there is a detective who is cannier. And what detectives! In thousands of splendid crime stories we meet detectives of astonishing variety – policemen and parsons, jockeys and journalists, aristocrats and artists, doctors and scientists, lawyers and lady cyclists, writers and rogues, old men, old ladies, schoolchildren, dogs – it's almost easier to list the few categories of people who haven't appeared as detectives. This book is full of them, from Johnny Ace the disk jockey to Aurelio Zen the Venetian, from a detective before Christ to 'Quint' in the 2020s yet to come.

Safe in our armchairs – actually, who reads in an armchair any more? Most of us read our detective stories on the beach or while travelling, or when we are snuggled up in bed late at night. Novelist Celia Brayfield once conducted a simple survey of a hundred regular readers: 60% read on long journeys, 77% in bed at night and 62% while doing something else. (*Bestseller* by Celia Brayfield, 1966.) But wherever we read – safely – we love the vicarious thrill of crime. We marvel at the ingenuity of the killer while we shudder at the horror. We pit our wits against the detective's and, perhaps more than in any other form of fiction, we transport ourselves into their world. We like to be part of the books we read, part of that magic land. The world of nineteenth century crime stories was exotic: far-off lands and strange peoples, country houses and city slums, gentlemen's clubs and opium dens. Even more exotic were the detectives. Auguste Dupin is often called the first detective (see more on this later) and he was as bizarre a hero as you could want: an aristocratic recluse who avoided daylight. Eugéne Vidocq was a thug turned lawman, Skinner was a Bow Street Runner, and two of the greatest novelists of the nineteenth century created their own immortals: Inspector Bucket and Sergeant Cuff. At that time, the middle of the century, the police were still something of a novelty, half mistrusted, rarely seen (little has changed, some say today) and, whether for that reason or for some deeper need, those stories of detection were seized upon by the public. They have remained popular ever since, and have become part of the bedrock of publishers and bookshops.

Stories have changed since Poe's Dupin. More than in other popular genres (romance, fantasy and humour), more than in mainstream 'serious' fiction, detective fiction reflects and comments on its time. Nineteenth century stories told of nineteenth century obsessions: the expanding police force (the CID wasn't formed until 1878); urban monsters (Jack the Ripper struck between August and November 1888); the newfangled use of science in detection (which contrasted with old-fashioned disdain for foreigners felt by the scions of the Empire).

After the horrors of the First World War, detective fiction grew less bloodthirsty: bodies shifted into the library. Later, in 1930s America, that country's pulp fiction writers would 'take the corpse out of the library and dump it in the gutter where it belonged', but the post-war generation in Europe had seen enough death at close hand. Readers sought a sense of detachment, with the body depersonalised and arranged in a stage set. Hence the library. Hence the 'locked room'. The emphasis in detective stories shifted from death to the puzzle. The murder itself could be quickly disposed of within the first two dozen pages, leaving the rest of the book for a civilised puzzling out, an academic game. Among the readers were a large number of intelligent, well-educated fans, many of whom approached the latest mystery much as they would approach a crossword puzzle or mathematical challenge. Plot became more important than character. Only the detective needed character; everyone else was part of the stage set, a lifeless prop. Many crime stories were just that, a story, a short story. All the great Sherlock Holmes tales were short stories, and none of the four novels, the 'long stories', were as taut and intriguing as Doyle's shorter tales. Writers hard on his heels – Hewitt, Chesterton, Bramah, Freeman – concentrated on short stories. Magazines and magazine readers lapped them up, and it is only in recent decades, as magazines have changed focus and content, that short stories, once the mainstay of the detective genre, have given way to novel-length stories.

If the aftermath of the First World War civilised the detective story, people's determination after the Second World War to sweep away the class-ridden, hidebound attitudes of the past saw a shift from the academic puzzle and country house mystery to a more American style action adventure. Not that the old world disappeared. Detecting favourites like Poirot and Inspector Appleby, the Doctors Fell and Fen, continued little changed, but others were jarred and altered by the war. Lord Peter Wimsey and Albert Campion represented much that the ordinary reader wanted done away with – and their authors duly changed them, making them move with the times, shedding their gentleman amateur twittishness for a more mature observer status. They were shoved aside by a new breed of realistic detective. Often as not these were working policemen, for in a British setting the American private

eye is not believable. The police detective, who in the nineteenth century had been eyed with suspicion and between the wars treated as little more than a bumpkin, now represented law and order and a peaceful society kept in check by the common man. Miss Marple kept her place, as did many like her, but only as a nostalgic fancy. The police were the detectives now. From Gideon and Inspector West in the Fifties through Inspectors Dalgliesh and Wexford, on to Rebus today the policeman detective has remained the most believable British detective. Private detectives came and went, struggling in our soil like foreign imports to a northern garden. Some survived; many wilted. The British detective could not remain a gentleman amateur – nor could he be an American tough guy. Detectives did not have to be male, and a modern Miss Marple would be a very different Miss to those who'd come before. Above all, a British private eye had to be quirky. As you will find in these pages.

We love exciting stories. We love mysteries – the stuff of myth and legend, and fairy tales. Let villains be unspeakably evil (think of the Minotaur, Bluebeard, dragons) the worse they are the more we love them – but we do want them caught. In the earliest myths the hero defeated the monster (in Homer's Odyssey, in Beowulf) just as happens in detective tales today. Our story begins with terror and monstrous evil. The hero enters, uncertain how to find the monster and defeat it. We, in comfort, share the dangerous journey, with its riddles and hopefully a race against time to stop more deaths. Perhaps there's a virtuous maiden who must be saved, perhaps the hero's life will almost be lost, but in the end the hero will crack the puzzle, confront the evil and set the world to rights. It's a glorious fiction, but it's what we want.

Exhibit Two

The First Detectives

WHO WROTE THE FIRST DETECTIVE STORY? No one knows. But some of the claims to push the start-line back are so far-fetched we can dismiss them. Dorothy L Sayers once claimed that the first detective story could be found in the Bible in the tale of Susanna and the Elders, and that when Aristotle in Poetics insisted a story should have a beginning, middle and an end, his demands were only truly met by the detective story. Far later, in 1747, Voltaire wrote an essay in detection in *Zadig*, where from a trail in the snow Zadig determined that it was left by a bitch (specifically a *female* dog) with an injured left foreleg and long ears, and that from various clues he could tell that the animal was accompanied by a horse having small hooves, a long tail and a height of at least five feet.

A more realistic credit is given to **Edgar Allan Poe**, who in 1841 created Auguste Dupin in *The Murders in the Rue Morgue*. Certainly Dupin was the first we in the West might recognise as a prototype, though even in Europe he had arguably been preceded by **William Godwin's** *Caleb Williams* (1794) who in his attempts to solve a murder mystery had to hide, spy, disguise himself and endure a term in jail. But *Caleb Williams* was not what we'd recognise today as a detective story, and wasn't alone among gothic thrillers of the time in having a resolute hero or heroine trying to solve or put right a crime. Poe's Dupin was different: he came as an outsider given the specific task of clearing up a mystery no one else could solve – the inexplicable murder of a young woman found in a room locked from the inside. In subsequent tales Auguste Dupin solved the murder of Marie Rogêt (based on a real-life New York murder which Poe reset in Paris), he discovered a purloined letter of international importance, he cracked a cipher which led to the discovery of buried treasure, and he solved each crime by logic – thus laying the groundwork for what we now think of as a detective story.

I am now awaiting a person who, although perhaps not the perpetrator of these butcheries, must have been in some measure implicated in their perpetration.

Auguste Dupin in *The Murders in the Rue Morgue*

But wasn't Dupin preceded in France by the big-selling memoirs of real-life crook-turned-investigator Eugène-Françoise **Vidocq**? This extraordinary man had been a thug and a notorious jail-breaker until in a real-life-is-stranger-than-fiction twist he became the head of the *Sûretè* in 1812. (The French had other things on their mind that year). As poacher turned gamekeeper he was supreme. He knew the crooks, he knew where to find them, and find them he did – with his soon to be immortalised cry: 'I am Vidocq, and I arrest you!' That cry and Vidocq's adventures were immortalised in four volumes of *Mémoires* in 1828 and 29. But even Vidocq was pipped to the post by Britain's **Thomas Skinner**, who a year earlier had brought out *Richmond: or, Scenes in the Life of a Bow Street Officer*, with a police detective as its hero. But the book did not sell well. It didn't have the magic of Vidocq who, like innumerable fictional successors, employed tricks and masterful disguises – or so he claimed, because the truth was probably more brutal. His books, like many modern celebrity memoirs, were ghost written. But their impact was colossal. Here was a policeman – a species formerly considered by most people as nothing more than a hated agent of the state – presented as hero and adventurer. The books sold well. And when books sell well, you can be sure other such books will follow.

Long before these books appeared in Europe – centuries before – the Chinese

anticipated them. Short detective stories in China can be traced back to the seventh century tales of **Magistrate Dee** – although as with many Chinese inventions they were unheard of in the West until the twentieth century, when in 1908 the first translation revealed hundreds of short tales by **Pu Sung Ling**. (Later so-called translations by Van Gulik are pastiche, says Julian Symons.) Further tales of an investigating **Magistrate Pao** survive from the eleventh century, but the legacy remained ignored outside China, as were seventeenth century detective stories from Japan like the charmingly entitled *Notes on Cases Heard Under a Cherry Tree* by **Saikaru Ihara** (1685).

In Britain in the nineteenth century came a revolutionary growth in reading – but working against it was the extraordinarily high price of printed books. A respectable novel at a guinea and a half cost more than a working man's weekly wage and was affordable only in monthly or weekly 'parts'. Cheap sensational literature was more easily purchased (or borrowed) in the form of pamphlets or single sheets. Following the success of broadsides in the eighteenth century telling of gruesome murders and the latest public hangings, the actual **Newgate Prison** sold pamphlets detailing the confessions of its condemned prisoners and their last words. From these cheap pamphlets came the *Newgate Calendar*, illustrated with dramatic and violent black and white etchings. Similarly lurid tales appeared in cheap magazines. *Recollections of a Detective Police-Officer* was serialised at length between 1849 and 1853, to be published in yellowback book form in 1856. The author, **William Russell** under the pseudonym of 'Waters', borrowed from Vidocq in staging dramatic confrontations and producing detectives who were masters of disguise.

His story ran concurrently with the far more important *Bleak House* (serialised 1852 and 53) in which Charles Dickens is said to have become the first British author to write a detective into a 'proper' novel – though this is to ignore his *Martin Chuzzlewit* which in 1843 introduced an agent for an insurance company, **Mr Nadgett**, who investigated the evil Jonas – all of which goes to show how hard it is to nail the first detective down. Let us stay with **Inspector Bucket**. He does not appear till a third of the way through the book; he is in truth a minor character, but as with so many of Dickens's minor characters he arrives on the page vividly realised. Dickens knew detectives; as a journalist he had walked among them, had accompanied them into vice dens, had gone out onto the river with them late at night as they fished for corpses and watched for thieves.

Although Inspector Bucket has a penchant for disguise and dramatic confrontation, he is more deductive than his melodramatic predecessors. He watches, observes. He insinuates himself among his suspects and tricks them into saying more than they mean to say. He even, in the unmasking of the murderess, stages a scene not unlike those of Hercule Poirot in the following century – though he doesn't go so far as to call the suspects into the library to hear the mystery explained. In truth, that section of the book, dramatic denouement though it is, is clumsily managed by Dickens; the sequence of scenes goes all awry. Dickens paid the price for writing in serial parts, making it up as he went along, rushing his pages to the press and finding himself unable to go back and change preceding episodes to fit with what he later realised must happen next. It was a problem Dickens faced in more than one book; he was a poor plotter (fatal for a crime writer!) and it was his friend Wilkie Collins who showed him how plotting should be done.

Wilkie Collins, Dickens's oft-while collaborator, is generally thought to have transformed the 'novel which contained a detective' into the 'detective novel'. Years had passed. Although Dickens often based his novels, dramas and short stories around a mystery, he seldom included a police detective. Only in his final unfinished *Edwin Drood* might he have brought a detective (Dick Datchery) to the fore. But Dickens died before the tale was finished, and no one knows how the tale might have been spun. Meanwhile, in 1859, Wilkie Collins had produced *The Woman in White*, a consummate mystery, brilliantly told, with enough red herrings and twists to satisfy a modern crime reader. But still there was no real detective – other than the reader who, like a detective, was presented with a series of personal and contradictory witness statements. For this reason some critics do not consider *The Woman in White* to be a detective story at all, yielding that accolade to *The Moonstone*. But *The Woman in White* is as fine a story of detection, pitting its two amateur sleuths (not a term they would use) Walter Hartright and Marian Halcombe (between whom there is no love affair, though there is some love interest) against the villainous Sir Percival Glyde and Count Fosco. The story itself is a splendid mystery with lashings of evil confronted by a plucky pair of heroes, and at its heart is a woman in peril. Quite simply, it has everything.

Except, insist the purists, a detective. It would take Collins almost a decade to introduce the man normally thought of as the first detective to appear in a full-length novel, **Sergeant Cuff**. But, carps R F Stewart in the magazine CADS (April 2006), Collins had, in fact, written detective stories before *The Moonstone*. In *Hide and Seek*, published in 1854, young Mat Grice searches to find the father of his dead sister's child. *A Stolen Letter* (a short story written in 1854) sets a lawyer and a young boy as his helper on the trail of the said letter – which is found to be in code! Another Collins short story, *The Biter Bit*, puts Inspector Theakstone, Sergeant Bulmer and a traineee detective, Mathew Sharpin, on the case of a mysterious and unexplained robbery. *A Plot in Private Life*, a Collins novella, sets Mr Dark, a lawyer's clerk, on the trail of an abscondee. Collins's 1866 novel *Armadale* (still in print) is an elaborately complex tale, but within it is a man Collins calls 'the necessary Detective' who is, says Collins, 'a man professionally ready on the merest suspicion (if the merest suspicion paid him) to get under our beds, and to look through gimlet-holes in our doors.' As Stewart points out, all of these stories appeared in print *before* the book often cited as the first British detective novel.

Meanwhile, in 1862, a little known author called **Charles Felix** had a story entitled *The Notting Hill Mystery* serialised in the magazine *Once A Week*, a tale which includes **Ralph Henderson**, insurance investigator, understandably suspicious of a widowed husband who had bought five life policies on his dead wife. Henderson is an investigator, that's his job, and he can make another claim to be the first fictional detective. (The book, sadly, is preposterous.) In 1863 the pseudonymous 'Andrew Forrester, Jr' brought out a fictional *Recollections of a Private Detective* and followed it with *Recollections of a City Detective* and *The Female Detective* both in 1864.

But all of these stories must stand aside for *The Moonstone* (1868), the book in which Collins introduced his fully-fledged detective, that unassuming but clear-headed **Sergeant Cuff**. This is a far better book than Felix's or Forrester's, as good as Dickens, and the whole plot revolves around the mystery and the detective. (There are two detectives in the book; Cuff is aided by **Ezra Jennings**, a doctor's assistant and amateur detective, and it is Jennings who really solves the mystery. But as happens in real life, credit is taken by the professional.) Where Inspector Bucket's investigations and discoveries take place largely off the page, those of Sergeant Cuff are shared with the reader. Like Bucket, he is not the central character, he does not have the largest part – but to the modern reader he is a recognisable detective. He investigates. He thinks things out. He shares clues with us. Dickens and Collins had sensed a popular mood: the public liked detective stories. They had always liked crime, and they enjoyed dramas in which innocent and helpless victims turned the tables on the guilty. Now came a character, the detective, to unmask villains credibly.

Detectives were not new in melodrama. Of particular note was *Ticket-of-Leave Man*, a **Tom Taylor** play of 1863 in which the eponymous Ticket-of-Leave Man (it means a convict released on parole) and his faithful sweetheart were no match for the dastardly villain. Only the strong and incorruptible detective **Hawkshaw** could stand up to him. Hawkshaw was a force for moral good, the saviour of the innocent. At the beginning of the nineteenth century the detective had been detested as a secret agent of the state. Now the tables had been turned. The new reading public hailed the fictional detective as its hero.

The Holmes Legacy

The popular success of Sherlock Holmes encouraged hundreds of writers to emulate Conan Doyle. While some copied, others began a trend that remains with crime writing to today – to take up a theme and improve it, to vary, to invert. The Holmes characteristics others picked up were his razor brain, bizarre habits, his notable – one might say trademark – clothes, and his less clever assistant stumbling in his wake to stand in for the reader. The most blatant copy – certainly the most successful – was **Sexton Blake** who, depending on who was drawing him at the time, might even appear garbed in a Holmes-like cloak and deerstalker hat from beneath which glint piercing eyes above an aquiline nose. Blake had a young lad (Tinker) as his assistant. The pair's adventures continued, largely in graphic form – weekly serials in story comics devoured by schoolboys for a hundred years – from Blake's 'birth' in 1893 until practically the present day. Blake was more a brand than the property of a single writer, and his stories were penned by countless hacks and by-the-line scribes. In the action-packed cartoon strip stories (they could hardly be called graphic novels), when Blake was drawn wearing that deerstalker hat, he was, in short, Sherlock Holmes drawn for children, although his were chase-and-fight adventures rather than tales of deduction.

Some Holmes copyists eschewed obvious imitation, and their heroes were conventionally dressed in contemporary fashion. Their creators saw that the appeal of Holmes lay less in his dress and specific habits than in his sharp observation and brilliant deduction.

> *'You have come in by train this morning, I see.'*
>
> *'You know me, then?'*
>
> *'No, but I observe the second half of a return ticket in the palm of your left glove. You must have started early and yet you had a good drive in a dog-cart along heavy roads, before you reached the station.'*
>
> *The lady gave a violent start, and stared in bewilderment at my companion. 'There is no mystery, my dear madam,' said he, smiling. 'The left arm of your jacket is spattered with mud in no less than seven places. The marks are perfectly fresh. There is no vehicle save a dog-cart which throws up mud in that way, and then only when you sit on the left-hand side of the driver.'*
>
> From *The Speckled Band* by Conan Doyle

The growing number of magazines in the 1890s and early years of the twentieth century was desperate for stories, short or serial: romantic, whimsical, ghostly, bizarre, adventurous or – the new craze – detective. Magazines were a hungry market; there was no radio, no TV, and short stories were an effective testing ground for characters who might be extended later into full-length novels. A writer could hone his craft, experiment, launch and test his characters. Short stories sold – especially detective stories; editors lapped them up because their readers wanted them, and what the reader wanted sold magazines. Many a writer dreamt of creating their own Sherlock Holmes: a detective differently dressed, from a different background – lacking, perhaps, Holmes's less acceptable habits like cocaine addiction and avoidance of women – but retaining his amazing ability to solve seemingly impossible and highly intriguing puzzle mysteries. Such a sleuth had to be more than a mere detective, he or she had to have their own unique characteristic, something to appeal and stick in the reader's memory: a gimmick. The hungry magazines called out for more detectives, for the new sensation who might out-sell Sherlock Holmes. Here are a few of them:

Paul Beck, created by M MacDonald Bodkin

A self-deprecating private detective who, although he claimed to have few skills (unlike Holmes) went on to demonstrate a formidable repertoire of abilities. He appeared mainly in short stories of the late 1890s and in the first decade of the twentieth century.

Max Carrados by Ernest Bramah

Coming a little late onto the scene (1914) the unique point about Carrados was that he was blind! Before he lost his sight (from amaurosis, which leaves no observable damage to the eye) he collected coins, which he judged later only by touch.

Dixon Druce by L T Meade

As a 'solvency inquiry agent' Druce has a better reason than most to investigate crimes. More usefully, he has access to countrywide network of specialist contacts to help solve his cases.

The Falcon by Michael Arlen

A fanciful adventurer, popular at the time. Best now avoided.

Inspector Hanaud by A E W Mason

Perhaps the only detective to be more arrogant than Holmes. Astonishingly athletic, despite being fat, French and deliberately infuriating.

Martin Hewitt by Arthur Morrison

Hewitt has no obvious quirks but is a straightforward and professional investigator, which when most writers were striving to make their detective odd made Hewitt different and Holmes's closest rival.

Kai Lung by Ernest Bramah

When Kai Lung first appeared (1900) wily Orientals were almost invariably villains, so Bramah created a Chinese gentleman who was an intelligent and thoughtful detective. He was impeccably honest.

Lady Molly of Scotland Yard by Baroness Orczy

The title tells it all. Where rival authors had their aristocratic characters look down on the police, Baroness Orczy placed her equally aristocratic lady inside the Yard itself.

Dora Myrl by M MacDonald Bodkin

An early example of the feisty female PI, as different from Sherlock as could be. She carries a gun and a lock pick, is tough and independent, but sacrifices her career to marry Bodkin's other 'tec Paul Beck.

The Old Man in the Corner by Baroness Orczy

Arguably the first 'Armchair Detective', the Old Man's gimmick was that he never left his chair in a Lyons ABC teashop but by deduction alone solved all the mysteries brought to him.

Francis Pettigrew by Cyril Hare

Pettigrew was a lawyer, no longer young, but disillusioned and avowedly uninterested in 'this business of detection', as he told the Chief Constable in *That Yew Tree's Shade*. Nevertheless, he became interested enough to spawn five detective novels.

Father Brown by G K Chesterton

Surely the most successful early twentieth century detective to follow Holmes – and the most different. A Roman Catholic priest who appeared to spend very little time in church (he must have sniffed less incense than Holmes sniffed cocaine), Father Brown had an astonishing knack of turning up at the scene of the crime and interpreting what he saw in ways that occurred to no one else.

Sherlock Holmes himself remains the one detective all crime fans know – with good reason. He has been filmed more often than his rivals and, more importantly, his books are better. One can enjoy reading any of the above but when you re-read Sherlock Holmes, especially in comparison with those near contemporaries, you are struck by the speed and efficiency of the tales. It may be less true of the four novels, but it is by the short stories that Holmes is known; those stories are clever, amusing and surprisingly modern, despite their period setting. Although we all know the setting, Conan Doyle himself devotes little time to its description; his are action tales, plunging straight into the story and whisking us along a step or two behind the great detective as he speeds to the denouement. Any of the rivals above are good (I hesitate at the Falcon) but Holmes was better. The only real debate is whether there has been a better since.

Into the Golden Age

Reading a Golden Age mystery nowadays is to transport oneself back to a dreamlike time when the sun shone on green fields and well-kept gardens, people knew their manners, and every house had its share of servants. Meals were taken in the dining room and tea out on the lawn. To travel by train was an adventure (it's still a challenge today) and a journey by car had that exciting edge of uncertainty akin to modern-day island-hopping in a local aeroplane with a propeller on its nose. Motoring enlivens many a golden age story, bringing speed and variety to a tale which might otherwise move at pedestrian pace. The first chapter of *The Nine Tailors*, when Lord Peter's car breaks down near a village he has never visited before, is the most exciting in the book. Another typical journey comes early in Edgar Wallace's *Big Foot* (of which more later) when Wallace, unaware that what he was describing would soon become outdated, tells of driving through the rain, 'cleaning the rain screen for the hundredth time'. (There were no automatic wipers then, simply a blade one worked by hand.) Roads were empty: 'The rain was pelting down, the lightning was so incessant that Jim had no need of his headlamps.' Headlamps were not compulsory; if the driver could see he didn't switch them on. The world encapsulated in these stories is long vanished, and one of the finest ways to recapture it without any of its discomfort and privations is in fiction of the time.

The best Golden Age mysteries are based on plots and puzzles cleverer than any written today. One can argue —often fairly – that their literary style is ordinary, the language stilted, the characters thin, but the mysteries are ingenious, and ingenuity is missing from crime stories today. Today's may be better written (some certainly are), they may have more carefully drawn characters and be more exciting, but they will not be based on plots of such astonishing complexity. In these classic stories it is not only a question of guessing who dunit, but how. How on earth. Because the crime seems impossible. Golden Age stories tell of murder victims found in rooms locked from inside, to which there are no other keys and no secret entrances; of victims killed in front of witnesses – none of whom saw the killer, and none of whom realised the victim had died; of secret codes and undetected poisons; of stopped clocks and dubious alibis.

Although the Golden Age was a golden age for puzzle mysteries, it was also a golden age for lightness of spirit. Many of the writers – and a surprising number of readers – were academics or had at least been educated at university, and the writers' donnish humour justified their dalliance with 'low-brow entertainment'. Crime novels were laced with literary quotes, classical allusions and intellectual jokes.

Many of the jokes were lame, but they appealed to intellectuals. Michael Innes's **Inspector Appleby** (over-fond of quotes) often quipped, **Campion** and **Wimsey** *et al* made asinine remarks (some of which are still amusing), authors H C Bailey and Anthony Berkeley (aka Francis Iles) could be very funny, Gladys Mitchell's **Mrs Bradley** stepped straight from farce. Humour was far more prevalent in Golden Age stories than it is today, and some of the novels – had critics not been dazzled by the mysteries – should have been more praised for their sparkling comedy. John Dickson Carr, master of the impossible crime in **Doctor Fell** stories, often piled incident upon incident to deliberate effect; no sooner did an impossible crime seem to have been partly illuminated by a ray of light than another character dashed in with a shock announcement to throw everything back into confusion. How on earth, one wondered, could all this be sorted out? One's enjoyment of these novels was often more in the journey than their terminus.

The cleverest humour came from Edmund Crispin and his *Gervase Fen*. At the heart of Crispin's finest novel, *The Moving Toyshop*, lies an extraordinary puzzle mystery but *en route* to solving it Crispin takes wonderful liberties with the novel's form. On several occasions he frankly acknowledges that he is writing and we are reading a piece of fiction, that this is *not* a real account – as when Fen chastises his friend Cadogan: 'Don't spurn coincidence in that casual way,' said Fen severely. 'I know your sort. You say the most innocent encounter in a detective novel is unfair, and yet you're always screaming out about having met someone abroad who lives in the next parish, and what a small world it is.'

Later, when Fen asks a student to act as decoy, the student objects that he doesn't think the plan will work. 'It will work,' Fen responded confidently, 'because no one expects this sort of trick outside a book.' Six pages later, as the pair drive out on what they hope is the villain's trail, they come to a fork in the road. 'Let's go left,' Cadogan suggested. 'After all, Gollancz is publishing this book.' (It's a reference, of course, to Gollancz being the publishers of the Left Book Club and other left-wing titles.) The jokes in *The Moving Teashop* – and there are just enough, not too many – transform what is already an ingenious mystery into one of the enduring classics of the Golden Age with an exuberance few writers try to match today. Crispin was by no means alone in mocking the seriousness with which some of his fellow writers (and critics) approached crime fiction. As early as 1913 E C Bentley had sent up the genre in his deliberately *outré* novel *Trent's Last Case* intended, as the title suggests, to be the only such novel he would write, in which the apparently brilliant but decidedly amateur detective made astonishing deductions but got everything wrong. (The unexpected joke was that the book was so successful Bentley had to write some more.) Two years before him, G K Chesterton had taken the crime novel into quite different territory with Father Brown, using the format of the short mystery story to create deft and amusing but moral – almost metaphysical – tales.

Barriers of Class

Things were not what they used to be. Dash it all, private detectives used to be private detectives – fellows you got to guard wedding presents at country receptions, fellows you went to – rather shamefacedly – when there was some dirty business afoot and you'd got to get the hang of it.

Five Little Pigs (1942) by Agatha Christie.

For many modern readers the novels of the Golden Age (broadly the Twenties and Thirties) read as irritatingly cosy and snobbish fables, telling of a world that never did exist and which bears no relation to today. The era when an 'umble lower class policeman touched his forelock to an insufferable twit has long disappeared. Perhaps there once was such a time – although in truth it had become archaic even in the Golden Age, having been dealt a mortal blow by the First World War. Before then, in late Victorian and Edwardian days, prattling 'knuts' from the upper classes were able to impose their half-remembered schoolboy manners on a browbeaten multitude: the unwashed mob (bathing on Fridays, if at all), more than half of whom were denied the vote (there were no votes at all for women, servants or servicemen), all of whom were forced into grudging servility to earn a meagre wage. In Edwardian days, visiting Americans were stunned at the rudeness with which the British upper classes addressed the unfortunates below them.

Mainstream fiction before the First World War was written by a relatively small and educated class. Many writers towards the bottom of that class, desperate to present themselves as dilettante rather than vulgar professionals, sprinkled Latin and Greek tags through their ramblings and wilfully refused to translate French paragraphs (because we all speak French, don't we, just as we all learnt Latin and Greek at our private school?) while adopting a gentleman's club, public school snobbishness in an endless stream of lightweight jottings on the amusing trivia of well-heeled life. The worst offenders were essayists who wrote for magazines, with some of their scribblings anthologised in hard covers later. Magazines in that far-off age filled the place of daytime TV today; they were of no importance but could be idly flicked through in the interminable hours of boredom before the servants brought tea.

Out of that vapid tradition gushed winsome novels, which if they seemed tolerable to Edwardians, would have been binned on sight by a post-war editor. The world had changed. The upper classes might still rule but they were no longer quite so necessary. True, a backward-looking gaggle of writers clung to their pre-war twitterings – perhaps because they couldn't understand the bright new world, perhaps because they spotted a new target: from the well-off book buyers of the Edwardian age they switched to the middle class *aspirants* of their day.

To historians of crime fiction, those interwar years (1919 to 1939) are called the 'Golden Age', although many novels of that time themselves looked back to a Golden Age of their own. It is one of mankind's timeless failings to imagine a Golden Age around its youth. Sayers, Christie and others imagined a wished-for Golden Age in which a kindly sun shone on English villages as church bells rang, vicars came to tea and the village bobby knew his place. Presiding over this pleasant land was a white-bearded patriarch in His Heaven and a Lord on earth who drove a drop-head Daimler Twin Six. God was Protestant, and the Lord was an Amateur Detective.

Everything about these sleuths was unconvincing. Beady-eyed spinsters, athletic poets and vacuous Drones like Peter Wimsey and Albert Campion stumbled daintily across corpses and contrived carnage – while policemen bowed to them. In the days of Sherlock Holmes such deference might have been credible. But Holmes had been more realistically drawn than were his post-war followers: Holmes was no quirky amateur, he was a specialist with a proven record and, crucially, he was professional; he worked for a fee. It was a legitimate device for Conan Doyle to have his Victorian police summon external expertise; the police had always done that, they do it now.

What they had never done and never would do is allow their investigations to be redirected and compromised by an interfering nincompoop who, as if things weren't bad enough already, turned out to be a friend of one of the suspects.

Class-ridden and unbelievable as many Golden Age stories are, with their remote manor houses, hosts of servants and cups of tea, they do have nostalgic charm. If charm was all they had the books would long ago have been consigned to the dustiest cellars of the county library. But the best of them – and that is quite a number – have one essential merit that redeems them and makes them enjoyable today: ingenious plots. The Second World War would bring another revolution in crime writing, replacing ingenuity of plot with action (even if in many novels the action was nothing more than police procedure).

Out went the genuinely inventive plots, the 'impossible' crimes, the 'locked room' mysteries, the unfathomable whodunits. They were the true legacy of the Golden Age, and are sorely missed. They are the entirely valid reason for reading the tales today. But to see the *society* pictured in those stories as being in any way real is as fanciful as to believe in fairy tales. That society – with its secluded country houses, eccentric servants and deferential bobbies, and its gay (in the old sense) world of academia – was an imagined potpourri from a never-never land. Even in their day the stories were shown up in all their falseness and complacency by brasher, realistic crime novels from America. American crime writers, and the few European ones who sensed the incoming tide, would indeed kick crime back to the gutter where it belonged.

The Golden Age has left a legacy

The Golden Age of Detective Fiction is too far back for most of us to remember. Its period is generally thought of as the Twenties and Thirties of the last century – although as soon as one begins to list the authors one finds that the Golden Age has spread out, like golden syrup, oozing back to late Edwardian days and running forward into the Forties. Best to define what the Golden Age comprised, its constituent parts. It was the age of puzzle mysteries and urbane detectives, where even criminals played by the rules. In a Golden Age novel there should be servants, a bumbling bobby, and a cast assembled in an isolated country house or

university. There should be a murder, although at a pinch a jewel heist might be acceptable, and the crime should be executed and discovered before the end of chapter four. The detective could be male or female, but if male was almost certainly university educated, even if only an Inspector from Scotland Yard. (Inspectors in the Golden Age all came from Scotland Yard.) If female, she would almost certainly be the wrong side of middle age and eccentric to the point of dottiness. Male or female, professional or amateur, the detective astounded the reader with flashes of brilliant inspiration.

Real life and police procedure had little place in the Golden Age. Policemen were either in awe of the detective or if they themselves were the hero they were learned, astute and knew exactly how to behave correctly in country houses or in the private apartment of a university dean.

> *It entailed, perhaps, some breach of the minor proprieties – but it was in a crisis in the college's history that justified the action fully. He took another glance at Appleby – the man was indubitably a gentleman – and plunged in finally. "Excellent," he said, "a most satisfactory arrangement. And you will of course dine with us now in hall."*

Inspector Appleby passes muster.
From *Death At The President's Lodging* by Michael Innes

Though the Golden Age novel duly delivered its corpse or several corpses it contained little unseemly violence. Violence, like sex, happened off the page. Indeed, in many books from the Golden Age, neither violence nor sex happened anywhere, nor could it be imagined happening between the characters. Few male heroes have ever have been as epicene as Albert Campion or Lord Peter Wimsey, and more than one woman reader has been heard to wonder: 'What on earth did they *do* in bed?' Violence too, though clearly necessary if murder was to occur, was presented bloodlessly. Women writers (unfairly caricaturised as smiling over their knitting while dreaming up yet another undetectable means of murder) seemed genuinely expert in obscure poisons, while men leant towards manipulation of clocks and timetables, self-closing doors and booby traps of all kinds.

If these were the weaknesses of Golden Age fiction, what were its strengths? Plot and ingenuity. The crime was seen as a puzzle – hence the detachment from reality and lack of violence. Someone died – they had to die – so we could get down to the mystery. Many of today's crime novels revel in sordidness and gore. Not so in the Golden Age: that was what made it shine. Today's crime

Male murderers would employ devices...

story dwells on death – we get pages and pages on both the killing and the autopsy – but in the Golden Age the killing usually occurred off stage. In a sense, the killing didn't matter – frequently the victim was unpopular – *solving* the crime was all. It was a shared experience, a puzzle we shared with the detective. The more complex the puzzle the better the book. Hence the popularity of these stories with people who enjoyed puzzles.

At the time it seemed odd to some that these supposedly simple stories, far from literature, were seized upon by intelligent readers. Looking back, we notice that a good many Golden Age stories were set in academia. Why? Because that was the world the readers lived in; if they weren't dons themselves they had at least attended university, and within these pages, larded with erudite references and scholarly jokes, they could be transported back to what in their fond memory was a golden age. An alternative setting of country house and minor aristocracy was an equally magic ground. Between the wars, when Golden Age novels were contemporary novels, readers wanted to be taken away from the real world, a world of unemployment and financial instability, into a gentler, more amusing world – a world that might have existed before the First World War: a golden age.

Most writers, then, while placing their intelligent middle and upper class characters in comfortable settings, assumed an equally intelligent and comfortable readership. It was all very British, of course, though a few British writers followed the American model. In 1927 Edgar Wallace wrote his memorable crime fantasy *Big Foot* in which the lugubrious 'Sooper' (Superintendent Minter) took a more down to earth attitude to his detection work:

> *"When I joined the force, reading' and writin' and figgerin' were all that a chap needed. If you pinched more burglars and tea-leaves than any other detective officer, you got promoted, and even though you mightn't know the least thing about the differentious – what's the word? Something about calculation – "*
>
> *"Differential calculus," suggested Jim.*
>
> *"That's the feller. No, you didn't need to know anythin' about bot'ny, or*

Females would favour poison. Demonstrating the poison ring ploy.

whatever department that diff'rential thing belongs to, or zoology or psychology or nothin'. The only thing you had to do was keep your eyes skinned and catch the lad in the act. If you pinched a feller that was bigger than you and he started somethin' rough, you were expected to know somethin' about anat'my, such as the proper place to hit him with your stick. But that was practically all the science there was in the old days. I never used a microscope except to examine my pay."

From Big Foot *by Edgar Wallace*

The Golden Age would end, as it was bound to end, with the cataclysmic Second World War in which brutal reality became everyday. After the war, in that grim austerity which dragged on for years, there was no returning to a lost world of servants and country houses, of village bobbies and visiting parsons. Some regretted that those days had gone; others rejoiced that the old class barriers had been swept away. Some readers clung to their favourites from the Golden Age while other readers, *most* readers, looked to the new world and what was to come. No time is as dated as is the previous decade and readers wanted books to reflect the new age. They wanted stories to be real. Julian Symons put it succinctly in his *Bloody Murder*: 'We can enjoy a certain degree of make-believe, but if the effect is wholly artificial, in the end we dissent from what is being offered us. The Golden Age was not the main highway of crime fiction that it looked at the time, but a minor road full of interesting twists and views which petered out in a dead end.'

The Second World War brought an abrupt end to The Golden Age as the experience of sudden death became commonplace. Below a victim of the London Blitz.

Exhibit Three

Puzzles and Mysteries

A MYSTERY, SAYS *Collins Dictionary*, is an unexplained or inexplicable event, whereas a puzzle is a problem that cannot be easily or readily solved. A mystery story, then, contains a puzzle. For many mystery readers, those who like detective stories more than thrillers, it is for the puzzle that they read the story. 'The puzzle addict,' wrote **Raymond Chandler** (in his *Twelve Notes on the Mystery Story*) 'regards the story as a contest of wits between himself and the writer; if he guesses the solution he has won, even though he could not document his guess or justify it by solid reasoning.' Chandler, who wrote thrillers rather than mysteries and who in one case couldn't remember who was the killer in his own story, went on to admit: 'I, in the role of reader, almost never try to guess the solution to a mystery. I simply don't regard the contest between the writer and myself as important. To be frank I regard it as the amusement of an inferior type of mind.'

Chandler didn't write Country House or Locked Room mysteries.

Country House mysteries, as the name suggests, are set in a country house – though this description can be extended to include any closed environment such as an isolated hotel, an ocean-going liner, a university, anywhere in fact where the cast of suspects can be credibly reduced to a small number of people, all known to the reader. In a country house murder, no tramp will have scaled the garden wall to effect the murder and disappear; nor will the murder have been committed by an irrelevant or minor character. Hence it cannot be that 'the butler did it.' You, the reader, will select from a small group of known suspects. In the hands of a master – **Agatha Christie** being queen of them all – you will never guess correctly. When she or any other mystery writer fairly defeats you, you never think it is because you have 'an inferior type of mind.'

A **Locked Room mystery** takes the puzzle a little further: not only must you guess who did it but, first and more importantly, how was it done? In the archetypal case the body will be discovered in a locked room – locked from the *inside* and probably with the only key left inside the room. Any windows will be closed and barred. The writer will have observed a further rule of the game in that there will be no hidden doors or secret passages. The method of death will make it almost certain that the victim was murdered and that it could not have been a case of suicide, cunningly concealed, nor accident nor natural causes. (It has to be said that this last rule has been broken several times) You, the reader, must rule nothing out, no matter how improbable. The solution, after all, will be improbable.

Edgar Allan Poe's The Murders in the Rue Morgue

The first 'locked room mystery' is usually said to be Edgar Allan Poe's *The Murders in the Rue Morgue* (1841) although a later nineteenth century author, Israel Zangwill, is sometimes given the credit. His short book *The Big Bow Mystery* (1892) is a locked room mystery more satisfying than Poe's, in that the reader can attempt to solve the mystery before having it explained by the author. (In Poe's story you can do nothing but observe as Dupin explains his reasoning; you have seen none of the clues before Dupin explains them.) Zangwill presented us with a scenario in which a man with his throat cut was found inside a room that had been locked, barred and bolted. Zangwill 'cheated' in his story, though, by making the detective the villain. (He committed the murder at the moment of discovery, dashing across the room and slitting the poor man's throat while he slept. Then he ushered in the witnesses.)

In Poe's *Mystery of the Rue Morgue* the solution was, for a modern reader, too bizarre. But he set a challenge to future crime writers: devise a crime where the question was not just who did it, but how? Crime writers love challenges, and in the early days of detective stories many writers tried to rise to Poe's, but many of their solutions were similarly melodramatic. Some were literally fantastic, with ghosts and spirit presences wantonly employed. Animals were used, to go where no man could go (think of Sherlock Holmes and *The Speckled Band*) but the real challenge was the challenge a magician faces, to create and solve something apparently impossible – by earthly means.

John Dickson Carr (1906 to 1977) can lay a fair claim to be the first great magician, the greatest exponent of the locked room mystery – although English as his settings were, Carr was in fact American. (He lived in England for many years.) And arguably the greatest deviser of impossible mysteries ever was another American, despite his name, **Jacques Futrelle**, born in 1875 and dying young in 1912 when he sank with the Titanic. Futrelle created the extraordinarily named Professor S F X Van Dusen, nicknamed The Thinking Machine – almost a dwarf, with a Mekon head, extended fingers and a thicket of yellow tangled hair – whose stories were collected in *The Thinking Machine* (1907) and *The Thinking Machine on the Case* (1908). Being American, Futrelle is outside the scope of this book, but his influence was considerable. Britain's **G K Chesterton** played with impossible mysteries in his Father Brown stories (some feel his solutions were equally impossible) when he set up situations such as having a killer everyone saw but who instantly vanished, a body with two heads, a disappearing bridegroom (who thus forsook a fortune), the lack of footprints in the snow, etc.

But no one in Britain could touch John Dickson Carr. His locked rooms would be literally that: locked doors and windows – locked from the inside, no secret passages, no possibility that the corpse inside could be a suicide. He wrote scores of locked room mysteries, he wrote a treatise on the subject (contained within a locked room novel *The Hollow Man*) and despite all who tried to emulate him Carr remains supreme. The Twenties and the Thirties were the heyday of these mysteries. Despite their complexity, many were short stories; to sustain a magician's trick for 180 pages is an ordeal. But Carr did it, Christie did it, and others have tried. Carr's main detective, Dr Gideon Fell, looking remarkably like Chesterton, was fantastical, if not as outrè as Van Dusen, but Carr's first locked room sleuth was a Frenchman, Henri Bencolin, who appeared in the splendidly titled *It Walks By Night* (1929).

John Dickson Carr, master of the locked room mystery.

'In short, there are no secret entrances; the murderer was not hiding anywhere in the room; he did not go out by the window; he did not go out by the salon door.'

Bencolin in *It Walks By Night*

Carr's position as Locked Room Supremo was confirmed when one of America's leading short story writers, Edward D Hoch (no one surely can have written as many stories as this indefatigable man) asked a panel of writers, critics and fans to help him compile a list of **the ten greatest locked room mysteries of all time**. American writers predominate (especially if one accepts that Carr was American) and the contributors delved back to include acknowledged if dated classics, but Hoch's list is still regarded as definitive. (He published it in the introduction to his *All But Impossible* in 1981.) This was his Top Ten:

1. *The Hollow Man* by John Dickson Carr (1935)
2. *Rim of the Pit* by Hake Talbot (1944)
3. *The Mystery of the Yellow Room* by Gaston Leroux (1907)
4. *The Crooked Hinge* by John Dickson Carr (1938)
5. *The Judas Window* by J D Carr writing as Carter Dickson (1938)
6. *The Big Bow Mystery* by Israel Zangwill (1892)
7. *Death from a Top Hat* by Clayton Rawson (1938)
8. *The Chinese Orange Mystery* by Ellery Queen (1934)
9. *Nine Times Nine* by Anthony Boucher writing as H H Holmes (1940)
10. *The Ten Teacups* by J D Carr writing as Carter Dickson (1937)

If you want to know more about locked room mysteries seek out *Locked Room Murders and Other Impossible Crimes* by Robert Adey (revised 1991). He mentions some two thousand stories including, inevitably, some by Edward Hoch.

Inverted Mysteries

There are only so many ways a crime can be explained: people have been saying that for a hundred years. Eventually writers either start repeating themselves or they change. Or they add a new twist to the detective story. Two of the greatest twists were conceived by the same man: **R Austin Freeman**. One, the Scientific Detective, is covered later, but his greatest was the revolutionary 'inverted' story. Freeman's *The Singing Bone* (1912) was described by Ellery Queen as 'one of the most important books of detective short stories ever written.' The normal detective story starts with a crime, introduces the detective, then takes the reader with the detective on a journey as the mystery is solved. Freeman turned the pattern on its head; he started with the crime, told the reader who had done it, then let the reader watch the detective flounder through the fog. Often the emphasis switched from an all-knowing detective to an equally clever culprit. The crime would appear perfect, the detectives baffled, and the joy of the story came in watching the whole plot fall apart.

From Ellery Queen again (in his introduction to *The Department of Dead Ends*): 'Doctor Freeman, a man of true scientific curiosity, posed to himself the interesting question: Would it be possible to write a detective story in which, from the outset, the reader was taken entirely into the author's confidence, was made an actual witness of the crime and furnished with every fact that could possibly be used in its detection? In other words, reverse the normal procedure: let the reader know everything, the detective nothing. Would the reader, in possession of all the facts, be able to foresee how the detective would solve the mystery?'

Notable examples of inverted stories are:

R Austin Freeman's *The Singing Bone* (1912)
Anthony Berkeley's *The Poisoned Chocolates Case* (1929)
Francis Iles's *Malice Aforethought* (1931) and *Before The Fact* (1932)
Roy Vickers's *The Department of Dead Ends* (1949)

Village Mysteries (and Cosies)

In the early decades of detective fiction all the discussion was about the detective – male or female, police or amateur, with or without astonishing idiosyncrasies – and few noticed the gradual creation of a small sub-genre, the village mystery. Early settings were generally upper-class: fine country houses, grand hotels, liners and resorts. An entirely different setting, the urban jungle, made little headway here and would not until the American hard-boiled novel muscled its way in to our all too cosy British scene. (When the urban patch did come in, it came as the hunting ground for police procedurals rather than as the hero's daily habitat.)

Writers seeking to set their stories away from the usual high-society circuit chose either an exciting location relevant to that particular story or they made up a village. (Unlike cities, villages are always created; the risk of libel is too great.) A village made a nice trip out for the detective and could be conveniently close to the country house in which (often in the library of which) a body had been found. No writer really latched on to the village as a series location, a setting that could be repeated, until Agatha Christie when she housed Miss **Jane Marple** in the fictional village of St Mary Mead in *Murder at the Vicarage* (1930). A village creates problems for a writer: it is small, hardly capable of infinite dissection, and unlikely to become a hotbed of crime. Christie saw this, and it was twelve years before she followed her first Miss Marple mystery with *The Body in the Library* (1942), after which her deceptive detective began to appear in print more often – even if she was sometimes taken away from St Mary Mead to journey in the Caribbean or on the *4:50 From Paddington*.

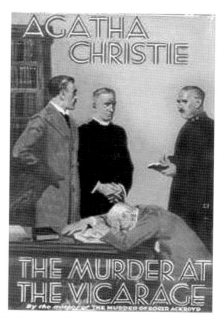

Other writers saw the village appeal: a murder in an English village is the ultimate 'cosy' mystery, one with attractions for the reader, being as displaced from everyday life and as apparently desirable as the high society settings of rival tales. The more sordid aspects of crime and modern life can be softened and shown through a rose-tinted haze.

Catherine Aird's **Inspector Sloan**, though attached to the CID, usually investigates village mysteries;

M C Beaton set **Hamish Macbeth** in the perfect Scottish village of Lochdubh;

Ann Cleeves has **Inspector Ramsay** investigate crimes in the former mining villages of Northumbria;

Hamilton Crane is the third writer to tackle the **Miss Seeton** series about crimes largely set in villages;

Elizabeth George has settled on no single village for her **Inspector Lynley** cosy mysteries;

Caroline Graham places **Tom Barnaby** in the village-strewn county of Midsomer;

John Buxton Hilton set his **Inspector Brunt** mysteries in and around the Derbyshire village of Margreave;

Nicholas Rhea created a long series of **Constable** novels set in the villages of North Yorkshire;

Phil Rickman's **Merrily Watkins** works in rural Herefordshire and Gloucestershire (but these are hardly cosy mysteries);

Betty Rowlands has her crime-writing amateur detective **Melissa Craig** living in a Cotswold village overlooking Gloucester;

Rebecca Tope sets her **Thea Osborne** stories in named and identifiable Cotswold villages.

Patricia Wentworth's Miss Marple-like **Miss Silver** investigates most of her crimes in villages though she doesn't live there.

But, nevertheless, **Miss Marple** remains the queen of them all, at St Mary Mead.

The Undead

'It was a freak of fancy in my friend (for what else shall I call it?) to be enamoured of the Night for her own sake.'

Dupin, in *The Murders in the Rue Morgue*

Along with the sagas, romances and travel tales that came before detective stories the most exciting to snuggle into bed with were gothic and supernatural mysteries. Walpole's *The Castle of Otranto* appeared in 1764, *Frankenstein* was written in 1818, *Castle Rackrent* in 1800 and Jane Austin's spoof gothic *Northanger Abbey* came out in 1818. The public had shown their taste for juicy horrors – a guilty taste, perhaps, but an appetite that demanded food. Serious improving fiction was all very well, but readers wanted something more succulent. Detective stories met the need, and were published alongside wildly fanciful Victorian shockers telling of exotic lands, fearsome foreigners, and a raft of unexplainable events. It was to the credit of detective stories that in them events were explained, and that the plots seemed more credible than in the wild tales of their competitors. But they were tales of mystery nevertheless, and for some writers the temptation to spice the mystery with help from 'the other side' was impossible to resist.

Notable examples are:

Guy Boothby's lurid adventures of the enigmatic mesmerist **Doctor Nicola**;

Conan Doyle's *apparent* ghost culprits in *Hound of the Baskervilles* and *The Speckled Band*, both of which, of course, turned out to have earthly explanations;

Carter Dickson's tales about his detective hero, the bulky **Sir Henry Merrivale**, who in *Lord of the Sorcerers* conducts a ghost-hunt.

In *The Burning Court* Dickson leaves the reader unsure whether the murder was perpetrated by a witch;

William Hope Hodgson (slain at the battle of Ypres, 1918) created *Carnacki the Ghost-Finder* (1913) in which **Carnacki** does exactly that. Most of the occult phenomena he investigates turn out to have earthly explanations.

Randall and Hopkirk (Deceased) was a delightful television series in which one of the two partners of a detective agency was killed in a hit-and-run incident but returned as a ghost to irritate his former friend and partner, interfere with his love-life and help bring his own murderers to book.

Sea of Souls and *Life on Mars* are two more recent TV detective series which have strayed into a similar domain. Only *Sea of Souls* took itself and the subject seriously.

The Rules of the Game

Back in the Golden Age, writers – despite their apparently light-hearted approach to crime – took their work seriously. Many of their readers were highly intelligent and took their reading equally seriously. They tackled their light reading, of mysteries, as battles of wits between themselves and the writer, and as in any battle of wits they required there to be fair play. In response to this, the writer and critic Ronald Knox (with his tongue pressed lightly in his cheek) devised this famous set of rules to be followed by every writer of detective stories:

1. *The criminal must be mentioned early in the story, but must not be anyone whose thoughts the reader has been allowed to follow.*
2. *All supernatural or preternatural agencies are ruled out as a matter of course.*
3. *Not more than one secret room or passage is allowable.*
4. *No hitherto undiscovered poisons may be used, nor any appliance which will need a long scientific explanation at the end.*
5. *No Chinaman must figure in the story.*
6. *No accident must ever help the detective, nor must he ever have an unaccountable intuition which proves to be right.*
7. *The detective himself must not commit the crime.*
8. *The detective is bound to declare any clues upon which he may happen to light.*
9. *The stupid friend of the detective, the Watson, must not conceal from the reader any thoughts which pass through his mind; his intelligence must be slightly, but very slightly, below that of the average reader.*
10. *Twin brothers, and doubles generally, must not appear unless we have been duly prepared for them.*

Ronald Knox's detective stories are almost forgotten now, but see **Miles Bredon.**

Exhitbit Four

The Procedural and The Scientific Investigator

He dipped into this bottle or that, drawing out a few drops of each with his glass pipette, and finally brought a test-tube containing a solution over to the table. In his right hand he had a slip of litmus paper.

'You come at a crisis, Watson,' said he. 'If this paper remains blue, all is well. If it turns red, it means a man's life.' He dipped it into the test-tube and it flushed at once into a dull, dirty crimson. 'Hum! I thought as much!' he cried. 'I shall be at your service in one instant, Watson. You will find tobacco in the Persian slipper.'

From The Naval Treaty by Conan Doyle

BRITAIN BROUGHT DETECTIVE FICTION to the world. Other countries can claim to have invented detective fiction (the Chinese, the Americans – see **First Detectives**) but it was a British writer, Sir Arthur Conan Doyle, who took an interesting but minor prototype and remoulded it into fiction's major genre. His detective, **Sherlock Holmes**, set a pattern we still follow: that of the detective as a lone figure, somewhat eccentric, driven by both a moral ethic and a genius for solving puzzles. The private detective generally lives alone but is granted a less skilled but loyal companion. The detective does not seek out cases; they are brought by clients. Most cases have an element of danger (without which there is little story) and every case requires the detective to solve a puzzle.

After that comes variation. The detective can be male or female, weak or strong, mature or young – working with or without police co-operation. Clients can be rich or poor. (Nowadays, if rich, they are as like as not to be the perpetrator.) The amount of variation is easily seen: read through a dozen entries in this guide and you will find that almost every detective has some unique feature. But for the British writer there is one insurmountable problem: having brought the detective into fiction's mainstream, Britain gifted him to America. In America, with its cowboy and frontier town history, its sheriffs and roving marshals, it is easy to believe in the strong lone hero, 'neither tarnished nor afraid' who walks the mean streets carrying a gun beneath his arm. In America's wide open spaces it is easy both to commit a murder and to hide the body. American criminals can cross a state line and re-establish themselves with ease a thousand miles away.

None of which applies in Britain.

Holmes supplied a model for many writers – that of the detective appearing like a doctor in his consulting room, engaged by anxious patients for a diagnosis – but the two great problems for later writers were first, that Holmes was unmatchable and second, that the form was limited. Holmes was reinvented by other writers as an insurance agent, a lady journalist, a priest, a doctor, as innumerable gentlemen of leisure, but however he metamorphosed he appeared cramped. Britain is so crowded and the gun laws so restrictive! In Britain everybody knows there is no real-life equivalent to the private eye. There are detectives here, certainly – I have met a few, I have even engaged one – but we British know that their tasks rarely amount to more than debt collection, credit reference and adultery. That is hardly Philip Marlowe, and far less Sherlock Holmes.

For two or three decades (effectively the Golden Age) readers closed their eyes and pretended they believed in amateur detectives. But it couldn't go on; it certainly couldn't survive the brutal reality check of the Second World War. America had already moved on: led by the gutsy stories in pulp magazines, their writers hardened their heroes and marched them off to places we couldn't go. Some British writers retreated into a false Britishness (largely a false *Englishness*) and continued to create detectives as little old ladies, witty dons and unemployed aristocrats. A few writers tried to import the American style. But many accepted what their public already knew: that the only credible British detective was a cop.

If the private detective was surrendered to America, the fictional *police* detective, fitted better here. The fact that a British policeman did not carry a gun (even if the criminal might) was an advantage: the reader didn't carry a gun either, so could identify with the detective. A police detective is credible; it's his job to investigate crime. (In the Forties and Fifties it was always a police man; the female cop then – leaving Miss Palmyra Pym aside – awaited her liberation.) In fictional terms the battle between the criminal and the forces of order was simple and fundamental: it was a battle between right and wrong; it was a battle in which readers had always known the rules.

Not British! At least in the early days.

> *The relative positions of a police-officer and a professed thief bear a different complexion according to circumstances. The most obvious simile of a hawk pouncing upon his prey is often least acceptable. Sometimes the guardian of justice has the air of a cat watching a mouse, and, while he suspends his purpose of springing upon the pilferer, takes care so to calculate his motions that he shall not get beyond his power. Sometimes, more passive still, he uses the art of fascination ascribed to the rattlesnake, and contents himself with glaring on the victim through all his devious flutterings; certain that his terror, confusion, and disorder of ideas will bring him into his jaws at last.*
>
> From The Heart of Midlothian *by Sir Walter Scott*

By the time the generation which fought in the war and learnt to cherish books in years of hardship gave way to a new generation to whom books were just another commodity, a new medium had emerged. In the Forties, **television** had had no more than a foothold, but in the Fifties TV ownership climbed steadily (legend has it that the Coronation was the catalyst). By the Sixties most households had a set. By the Seventies they had a colour one.

Television detectives are usually police detectives; private eyes seem less acceptable on screen than on the page. In the Fifties the great new British detectives were **Fabian** of the Yard, Inspector **Gideon**, Inspector **West** and the immortal **Dixon**

Dixon of Dock Green – *reassuring...*

of Dock Green, but it was in the Sixties that we first met some of the names still with us today. P D James brought us Inspector Adam **Dalgliesh** in 1962, while Ruth Rendell's Inspector **Wexford** first appeared in 1964. Sixties television introduced us to the ground-breaking *Z-Cars*, and the 1970s brought even more realistic shows such as ***The Sweeney***. The stream became a flood. Ground rules by then had been set so long they were like well-weathered concrete: make up a crime, as fanciful as you like, and solve it by good old fashioned police procedure. Leaven the mix with a large dollop of the copper's private life and you have a timeless and almost failsafe recipe.

On British television today the detective is increasingly likely to be a Detective Inspector or Detective Sergeant. There are plenty of exceptions in print ranging from the unlikely but companionable **Fitzroy Angel** to the totally realistic art investment specialist **Tim Simpson** – but despite the many civilian sleuths in books it is the police detective who dominates best-seller lists and has primetime slots on TV. Some writers, desperate not to write another PC Plod, place their hero in a halfway house as an expert working alongside the police. Hence the pathologists and psychological profilers, all of whose series become increasingly unlikely as the experts are dragged out of the workplaces to stand unprotected in the front line of one extraordinary case after another. Many writers, though, are content to give the market what it wants: police procedural detectives. Consider the variations within this theme:

...The Sweeny – *realistic.*

Dalziel and Pascoe	A wildly mismatched pair
Charmian Daniels	A working class Scot in middle England
Inspector Frost	Awkward and politically incorrect
Harpur and Iles	Deadpan comic dialogue
Inspector Lynley	A modern-day aristocrat cop
Detective Sergeant McRae	In his anarchic Aberdeen cop squad
Stella Mooney	A female cop with a complicated love life
Wesley Peterson	A black cop working in rural Devon
Inspector Purbright	Keeps order in the funniest books in crime fiction
Vera Stanhope	Plain and overweight, single and lonely

Some writers use a distinctive location to establish their detectives:

Amsterdam	Piet Van Der Valk
Channel Islands	DS Jim Bergerac
China	Inspector Wang
Cornwall	Charles Wycliffe
(not so) Cosy English villages	Inspector Sloan
Edinburgh	John Rebus
Essex	Inspector Finch
Galloway	Marjory Fleming
India	Inspector Ghote
Italy	Aurelio Zen
Lochdubh	Hamish MacBeth
'London' (the Second City of)	Inspector Coffin
'Midsomer'	Inspector Barnaby
Nottingham	Charlie Resnick
Oxford	Inspector Morse
Peak District	Ben Cooper
Rome	Nic Costa
Thames Valley	Superintendent Yeadings
Vale of York	Chief Inspector Hennessey
Yorkshire	Inspector Banks

The Scientific Detective

'Holmes is a little too scientific for my tastes,' declares Doctor Watson's friend Stamford at the start of *A Study in Scarlet*. 'I believe he is well up in anatomy, and he is a first-class chemist; but, as far as I know, he has never taken out any systematic medical classes.' It is the first Sherlock Holmes story, and Watson encounters Holmes in a hospital lab, 'lined and littered with countless bottles. Broad, low tables were scattered about, which bristled with retorts, test-tubes, and little Bunsen lamps, with their blue flickering flames ... At the sound of our steps he glanced round and sprang to his feet with a cry of pleasure. 'I've found it! I've found it,' he shouted to my companion, running towards us with a test-tube in his hand. 'I have found a reagent which is precipitated by haemoglobin, and by nothing else.'

But all this is a false introduction to Holmes, who relied on inspired deduction from observation rather than from any true scientific process. He was, in fact, dismissive of science, as practised by others, and what little science he used was sketched vaguely as if Conan Doyle, a trained doctor, were ignorant in such matters. In this,

Holmes and Doyle reflected the attitude of the real-life police of the day who, when the first Holmes books were written, were wary of fingerprints and, where they trusted science at all, prefered anthropometry, a complex system of head, limb and finger-length measurements. It wasn't until 1901 that the British police took up Francis Galton's recommendations on fingerprints.

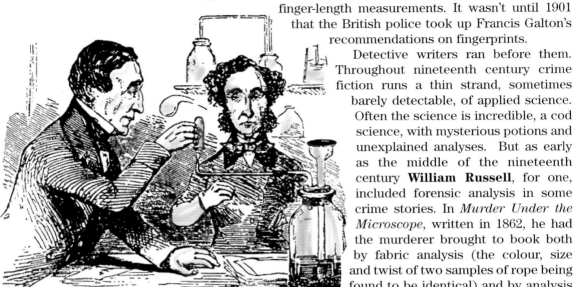

Early forensic detective work by two characters, doctors Taylor and Rees.

Detective writers ran before them. Throughout nineteenth century crime fiction runs a thin strand, sometimes barely detectable, of applied science. Often the science is incredible, a cod science, with mysterious potions and unexplained analyses. But as early as the middle of the nineteenth century **William Russell**, for one, included forensic analysis in some crime stories. In *Murder Under the Microscope*, written in 1862, he had the murderer brought to book both by fabric analysis (the colour, size and twist of two samples of rope being found to be identical) and by analysis of blood, where the blood on an axe was shown to be human while that on a billhook came from an animal. Thus was a murderer snared and an innocent man saved from wrongful conviction.

Sherlock Holmes might occasionally introduce a touch of science to his deductions but we had to wait for R Austin Freeman's **Doctor Thorndyke** MD, FRCP, before we met a detective who used real science to crack mysteries. Thorndyke was **detective fiction's first forensic scientist**, employed by the police on a semi-official basis. In the first book in which he appeared, *The Red Thumb Mark* (1907) Thorndyke used science to defeat science. The police had a thumbprint, clearly visible on a box from which diamonds belonging to the suspect's uncle had been stolen and were understandably confident. The use of fingerprints itself was new, the police having taken them up only six years before in 1901. So the police had a fingerprint, bang to rights – and here was Dr Thorndyke telling them their assumptions were wrong! This was cutting edge science and, in the stories which followed, the amazing Dr Thorndyke subjected ink to chemical analysis, detected poisons, broke ciphers, employed photomicrographics on soil residue, and put the full resources of his private laboratory at police service. What a laboratory: even his portable kit included test-tubes and reagent bottles, a tiny microscope, a spirit lamp, a crucible, a set of scales – all contained in his green Willesden canvas travelling case.

Freeman was something of a scientist himself – he had his own laboratory – but among crime writers he was a rare bird. Others were interested in fingerprints and poisons and would drop the names of impressive-sounding (often imaginary) analysis techniques, but their scientific backgrounds were slight. (One such was John Rhode, who wrote a long series featuring the sometimes almost supine **Dr Priestley**.

Given to enigmatic remarks and flashes of barely explained inspiration, Priestley is described to us as a scientist, but his actual experiments are not really explained.) Crime writers generally felt they didn't have the knowledge to write of science convincingly, and they knew that the moment a reader detected a single error the whole edifice of their plot would collapse.

For several decades an interest in real science flickered like the flame from a Bunsen beside a window, blazing briefly into flame in 1968 with the TV series *The Expert* in which the hero **John Hardy** was a Professor of Forensic Medicine and the storylines were supplied by real-life forensic experts (including crime writer Bernard Knight).

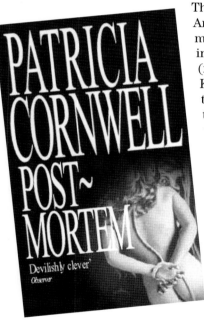

The flame spluttered feebly till 1990 when the American writer **Patricia D Cornwell** scooped major awards with *Post-Mortem*, the first novel in her ground-breaking series about the (fictional) Chief Medical Examiner for Virginia, Kay Scarpetta. Before long, other writers were tripping over each other (and occasionally tripping over their scientific procedures) in a tangle of copycat forensic thrillers. In parallel came other stories based on the loose semi-science of criminal profiling. All too soon, though, the emphasis shifted away again from science, from the grisly gore of the mortuary table to a more visceral obsession with torture and drawn-out death.

TV series about scientific detectives include:

The Expert (1968 to 71, and in 1976)
Cracker (1993 to 1996)
Silent Witness (1996 to date)

atoZ

JOHNNY ACE
by Ron Ellis

Ace doubles as a newly fledged private eye and a **Liverpool disc jockey** on local radio. In his agency he is partnered by an ex-CID Detective Inspector **Burrows**, who prior to that was a Merseybeat musician (as indeed was Johnny Ace). So the books are steeped in Liverpool – present and past, though the past is mainly 1960s. Thus we have memories of the Beatles and their contemporaries mingling with meetings with present-day 'names' such as Everton manager Dave Moyes and Alan Williams, one-time manager of those Beatles. One of the books, *The Singing Dead* revolves around some missing John Lennon tapes.

Ears of the City (1998), *Mean Streets* (1998), *Framed* (1999), *The Singing Dead* (2000), *Grave Mistake* (2001), *Single Shot* (2002), *City of Vultures* (2004)

LAURA ACKROYD
by Patricia Hall

No-nonsense investigative journalist who delves into a series of gritty cases in the company of Inspector **Michael Thackeray**. *Death By Election* (1993) began the series and as the title suggests was about corruption in local politics. *Dying Fall* followed in 1994. *Dead on Arrival* (1999), with apparent prescience of a real-life case later that year, told of illegal immigrants found suffocated in a lorry. *Deep Freeze* (2001) can be recommended also.

NIKKI ALEXANDER TV series *Silent Witness* which started 1996
(creator: Nigel McCrery)

As an apprentice archaeological pathologist introduced to the highly successful TV series ten years into its run, actress **Emilia Fox** lent life and glamour to what was often a dourly compelling series. She replaced the show's founding star **Amanda Burton** who had played Dr Sam Ryan from 1996, and like Sam Ryan she managed to spend plenty of screen time outside the lab. She had hardly arrived before slipping into a will-they-won't they relationship with fellow doctor Harry Cunningham (**Tom Ward**) and worse, being kidnapped by animal rights extremists.

DS KHALID ALI
(see *Handford & Ali*)

RODERICK ALLEYN *Inspector Alleyn Mysteries*
by Ngaio Marsh

A young lady dubs him 'The Handsome Inspector' in *Vintage Murder*, and certainly Alleyn appeals to the ladies. He is elegant in his first novel, *A Man Lay Dead* (1934) and remains svelte until his final appearance as late as 1982. Unfortunately his affairs don't always turn out happily – but it does mean that for the early part of the series he is alone and available

DEAD ON ARRIVAL

Patricia Hall

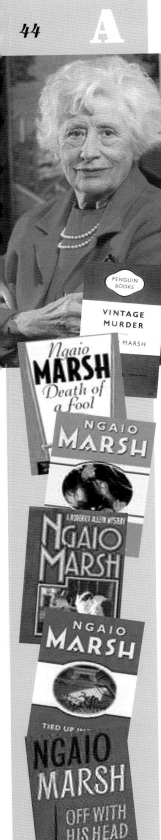

to female readers, even if he eventually succumbs to the chillingly named **Agatha Troy** (a society artist) in *Death in a White Tie* (1938). Alleyn meets Troy in **New Zealand**, where a number of the novels are set – unsurprisingly, as his creator comes from that country. (Marsh was a painter too.) Agatha's trade gives her access to high society settings, from where crime is seldom far, and her presence in gracious houses gives Alleyn access to high-born suspects. Not that he ought to need her help: he is tall, well-groomed and handsome, invariably well-mannered, has a double Oxford first in Classics (what else would a policeman need?), and is himself the son of Lady Alleyn of Danes Lodge.

Aristocrat that he may be, he is nevertheless down to earth enough to drink beer with his assistant **Inspector Fox** in a pub – and to eat cheese and pickles with him, to boot. But he is happiest with the gentry, as they no doubt are happier to have one of their own within the force. But the gentry should beware: his diffident manner conceals a sharp mind and he can be active when he must be. Alleyn is a decent and compassionate detective, if dated now – a Golden Age detective who stayed around beyond his period. He does have that Golden Age tendency to quote Shakespeare and drop French *bon mots* but at least he doesn't drift into Latin or ancient Greek, so he is Golden Age without the more tiresome quirks of that era. He is a more fully developed and, in truth, more interesting character than others from his period. He may be well-born and an Oxford graduate but he is a working policeman, and that is how he would define himself.

Usefully for the reader Alleyn is often allowed to share his thoughts with us; we hear him think and get to read his confidential correspondence. Helpfully, he is also given to drawing maps and sketches of the crime scene, as if to allow the reader a chance of beating him to the mystery's solution. Not that there's often a chance of that: Marsh is an ingenious crime writer. The stories are intricately wrought and for all their elegance can be deliberately misleading. It would take a good man to beat Inspector Alleyn. A good woman might manage it – but if they dared to try, they would first have to deal with the formidable Agatha Troy.

From a series of more than 30 books which ran from 1934 to 1982, one might choose *A Man Lay Dead* (1934), *Enter a Murderer* (1935), *Artists in Crime* (1938), *Death in a White Tie* (1938), *A Surfeit of Lampreys* (1941), *Final Curtain* (1947), *Swing, Brother, Swing* (1949), *Spinsters in Jeopardy* (1953), *Death of a Fool* aka *Off With His Head* (1956 – probably her best book), *Singing in the Shrouds* (1958), *Black As He's Painted* (1974), *Light Thickens* (1982)

Geoffrey Keen was an early television Alleyn when *Death in Ecstasy* was included in the 1964 series *Detective*. **Michael Allinson** played him also. In 1990 BBC TV brought out a pilot of *The Alleyn Mysteries* with **Simon Williams** as Alleyn, and **William Simons** (not an anagram of the same actor playing both parts!) as Inspector Fox, **Belinda Lang** as a rather cut-glass Agatha Troy and **Ursula Howells** as Lady Alleyn. But it was a curiously stilted production for its time (filmed in 1990 but set in 1948) in which the pleasantly diffident Williams was poorly served. When the idea was revived and a series of five episodes followed in 1993 the luckless Williams was replaced by **Patrick Malahide**. The series did at least clarify that Alleyn was pronounced 'Allen', but that seemed as disappointing as the series. Nevertheless, some one-off episodes were screened in 1994.

ENRIQUES ALVAREZ
by Roderic Jeffries
Balearic police inspector (the clever son of illiterate peasants) who appeared in a short series of novels – not written, as one might suspect, for the tourist trade but to explore the tensions between tourists and the islanders (also between the islanders and mainland Spanish). Somewhat ordinary mysteries but good novels. From several in the 1970s, *Mistakenly in Mallorca* (1974, the first in the series) is perhaps the best. It's a tangled tale of a chained inheritance (John inherits if Aunt Elvina outlives her ailing godfather *but* guess who actually dies first?) in which Alvarez dispenses justice, if not quite the letter of the law.

SIMON AMES
by Patricia Finney
Investigative courtier in the age of Elizabeth the First who appears in only two books. Along with his friend David Becket he counters an assassination plot and tangles (not romantically!) with both **Queen Elizabeth** and **Mary Queen of Scots**. Try *Firedrake's Eye* (1992) or *Unicorn's Blood* (1998)

AMISS & MILTON
by Ruth Dudley Edwards (1981 to date)
Civil servant Robert Amiss helps his friend Detective Chief Superintendent James Milton in a series of amusing but clever mysteries with an **Anglo-Irish** flavour. The first book *Corridors of Power* was short-listed for the John Creasey award (for best first crime novel) and two others, *Clubbed to Death* and *Ten Lords a-Leaping*, were short-listed for the CWA's Last Laugh award. The cast has grown as the series has developed but while Amiss continues to do most of the legwork, the unputdownable **Ida Troutbeck** steals the show. Books begin in 1981 with *Corridors of Death*. Apart from those above, *Matricide at St Martha's* (1994) and *Carnage on the Committee* (2000) are also worth a try.

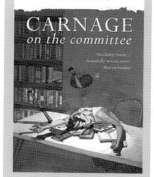

ANGEL
by Mike Ripley
Fitzroy Maclean Angel is the posh-sounding name of a decidedly unposh character, a dodgy geezer, half private eye, half amateur – half

Mike Ripley.

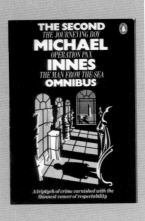

a lot of other things, he would tell you. Angel drives a black London cab, on the principle that when he's on a job his cab attracts little notice, and that it can wait on a double yellow line and avoid the congestion charge, and that the back is designed so that it can be cleaned out when things go wrong. As they often do for Angel. Called on for help by various friends (few of them innocents) Angel falls into a series of hilariously insane adventures and somehow (sometimes credibly) solves their problem. A page without a wisecrack is probably a page misplaced from another novel. The series began in 1998 with *Just Another Angel* and came out at the rate of around two books per three years till *Angel Underground* (2002). For a while it seemed that we might never see another angel, but Heaven relented, and in *Angel's Share* (2007), Angel settled down to working for a salary – with Rudgard & Blugden Confidential Investigations (had anyone checked their staff engagement policy?) – and in 2008 he was back again with *Angels Unaware*.

MICHAEL ANGEL
by Roger Silverwood

DI Angel is a hardworking serious copper from South Yorkshire, who thinks for himself and does his own thing while relying nevertheless on his regular team of four close colleagues. Off duty, he loves his wife, his cats and murder – but the only time he ever smiles is when a murderer gets Life. The series is set in the present day, in real time, with Angel currently in his mid-forties.

In The Midst of Life (2001), *Choker* (2002), *The Man in the Pink Suit* (2003), *Salamander* (2005), *Sham* (2006), *The Man Who Couldn't Lose* (2007), *The Curious Mind of Inspector Angel* (2007), *Find the Lady* (2008), *How to Murder a Man in Bare Feet* (2008).

INSPECTOR APPLEBY
by Michael Innes

The impeccably educated Inspector John Appleby (later to become Commissioner and finally Sir John Appleby) first appeared before the war (in 1936) in *Death at the President's Lodging*, when he investigated an ancient university where the President of a group of devious dons had been found dead, his body surrounded by small piles of human bones. University settings suit Appleby, often thought of as **the first of the 'donnish detectives'**, given to quotations, erudition and intellectual one-upmanship. (His creator, Innes, was a notable don himself, and under his own name J I M Stewart, wrote suitably donnish books.) Appleby appeared in over thirty novels, holding various ranks (the sequence with which he gained them amused some critics) and his final appearance came in 1986 in *Appleby and the Ospreys*. By this time he had been knighted.

Fifty years is an astonishingly long (fictional) career. Appleby grew and developed with the books, and one might say he lasted so long that he had to develop. He changed as the world about him changed, even if he never did quite get round to such everyday and mundane matters as fingerprints and pathology. (He left the examination of corpses to underlings.) Renowned for his wit and academic humour which, although they can seem arch and dated, remain the reason we still read him, the Appleby tales are rooted in the best traditions of **the classic police detective story**.

Selected titles: *Death at the President's Lodging* (1936), *Hamlet, Revenge!* (1937), *Appleby's End* (1945), *Appleby Talking* (short stories, 1954), *Death at the Chase* (1970), *The Ampersand Papers* (1978), *Appleby and the Ospreys* (1986).

OWEN ARCHER
by Candace Robb

Though his creator is American, Owen Archer is resolutely English – **fourteenth-century** English. Archer (as befits his name) is a captain of archers in the army but when he loses his left eye he has to quit military service. He becomes instead a spy for the Lord Chancellor of England and Archbishop of York. As a spy Archer is called in whenever there seems a suitable mystery for him to solve. The stories are well-researched (the author has an MA in medieval history) and from time to time they bring in real-life characters of the day, such as Geoffrey Chaucer. The plots combine history with both the spy and crime story.

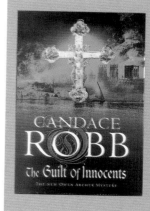

The *Apothecary Rose* came out in 1993 (and is the book in which Archer meets his future wife, at that time married to said apothecary) and was followed by a new book each year until 1999 (*A Spy for the Redeemer*). *The Cross-legged Knight* came out in 2002, *The Guilt of Innocents* in 2007, and *A Vigil of Spies* in 2008.

COMMISSIONER JAN ARGAND
by Julian Rathbone

In a European country invented by the author (Brabt) between Belgium and Holland, Police Commissioner Argand deals with refreshingly European problems of the day – not that such problems have gone today – such as corrupt businesses, fascism and ardent demonstrators. There are only three in this series, but any Rathbone book is worth reading. For example, *The Euro-Killers* (1979), *Base Case* (1981), *Watching the Detectives* (1983)

JONATHAN ARGYLL
by Iain Pears

Rome-based Argyll is by trade an art dealer – one of the few honest ones to appear in crime fiction. He is, in fact, affiliated to Italian National Art Theft Squad, which leaves him nicely placed to help investigate any number of **art crimes**, both in Italy or more often elsewhere, including England and America. It's a series concept practically without limit, and benefits from having a fine author (he wrote *An Instance of the Fingerpost* in 1997) who has written informed non-fiction works on art. The mysteries are complex and excitingly located.

Julian Rathbone.

The series starts with *The Raphael Affair* (1990). All are good, but try *The Immaculate Deception* (2000).

ISRAEL ARMSTRONG
by Ian Sansom
A Jewish travelling librarian who in the first novel *The Mobile Library* has an apparently undemanding day job driving his van in Northern Ireland. But who keeps stealing his books? Armstrong undertakes some amateur sleuthing to find out, and the results are hilarious enough to warrant the further books in the series. *The Mobile Library* (2006) begins the journey.

ASHENDEN
by Somerset Maugham
More a spy than a detective – the title of Maugham's short story collection is *The British Agent* – Ashenden is nevertheless **an important figure in the development of the modern investigator**. The stories are set in the First World War and are, in part, inspired by Maugham's own experiences in British Intelligence. Ashenden's cold amoral attitude prefigures that of later heroes and anti-heroes, and the stories give more of a spy's day-to-day routine than had been seen before in print. Nevertheless they are exciting and convincing enough for us to wish that Maugham had left us more.

Stories are collected in *Ashenden, or The British Agent* (1928), and Ashenden makes a cameo appearance in Maugham's *Cakes and Ale* (1930)

The Secret Agent is a curious and uneven Hitchcock film starring a young **John Gielgud** as Ashenden, **Peter Lorre** as the villain and **Madeleine Carroll** as the lady in peril.

Peter Lorre – the creepy villain.

BROTHER ATHELSTAN
by 'Paul Harding' aka Paul Doherty
Another ancient-times detective from this prolific writer, Athelstan was a **14th century clerk** to the Coroner of the City of London, and his series began with *The Nightingale Gallery* in 1991 and continued at the rate of almost one book a year. Selected from the series: *The Field of Blood* (1999)

(Doctor) DAVID AUDLEY
by Anthony Price
MOD detective (originally a backroom boy) who investigated a series of cases involving spies, traitors and espionage – and sometimes plain crime – in the post-war decades. There were nineteen Audley books, written from 1970 to 1989, beginning with *The Labyrinth Makers* and ending with *The Memory Trap*. Whereas in the first book Audley investigated the discovery of an RAF Dakota, presumed lost at sea in 1945 but now of great and deadly interest to the Russians, in the last book, when times had changed, he faced a world in which the familiar

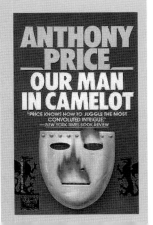

rules of the Cold War had been smashed for ever by modern-day terrorism.

David Hemmings played Audley in a TV series in the early 1980s.

DCI NOEL BAIN TV series *Mind to Kill*

A tough well-organised cop (played by **Philip Madoc**) who works on realistically down-to-earth cases and retains a sense of humour despite a tragic past (his wife was run down by a drunken driver, leaving him to bring up their daughter). *Mind to Kill* is an occasional series which has never taken off in the UK (probably because it has never been given prime channel air time) yet which sells well abroad. In later episodes Bain's daughter (**Ffion Wilkins**) joins the force and works along with him. Their relationship too is presented realistically.

INSPECTOR BANKS
by Peter Robinson

Popular and solid series featuring a **Yorkshire Dales** police inspector, originally a Londoner, in the fictional beat of Swainsdale. A far from cosy series, these well-written books include a number of vicious and harrowing crimes in which the solutions lie buried deep. Banks's own private life is put through the mangle too, and from the earliest books it seems inevitable that he will end up on his own, a lonely but fortunately unembittered man. At work he faces inevitable pressures from his colleagues, but as the series progresses and Banks becomes more entrenched in Yorkshire he builds his own network of people within and outside the force upon whom he can rely. Alan Banks has few, if any, of the idiosyncrasies of rival police detectives, and this serves to make him real. Five of Robinson's books have won awards.

Gallows View began the series in 1987. *In a Dry Season* (1999) is particularly recommended.

Peter Robinson.

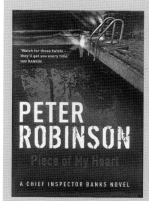

CHARLIE BARLOW

Lead character in BBC TV's *Z Cars* (1960 to 1978), then *Softly, Softly* (1966 to 1976) and the *Barlow* series in the early to mid-1970s, Barlow was memorably played by **Stratford Johns**. *Z Cars* was a ground-breaking TV series, showing the police more realistically than had been seen on British TV before. To some people, the portrayal was shockingly realistic: policeman sat in their Panda cars and *smoked!* (In today's sanitised world that might again seem shocking.) Barlow was tired, a little overweight, often grumpy – in short, human and believable. His relationship with Chief Inspector John Watt (played by **Frank Windsor**) was solidly professional, and made them one of the great double acts on 1960s television.

TOM BARNABY TV series *Midsomer Murders*
by Caroline Graham

The gloss of TV makes one think of Barnaby and his fictional county of **Midsomer** as lying at the heart of 'cosy' England, but the books have

Ground-breaking TV series Z-Cars.

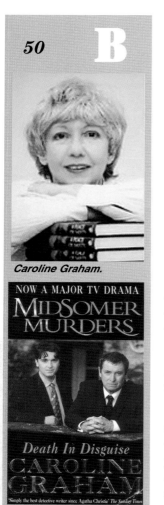

Caroline Graham.

NOW A MAJOR TV DRAMA

MIDSOMER MURDERS

Death In Disguise

CAROLINE GRAHAM

'Simply the best detective writer since Agatha Christie' *The Sunday Times*

more to them than that. DCI Barnaby is indeed a placid bobby well suited to his semi-rural patch, but Midsomer's villages and county town (Causton) are painted by Graham in faintly surreal colours and at times have a macabre tint. Agreeable as Barnaby is, the characters he comes across are less so (and that doesn't apply only to the criminals). Graham can't resist giving them amusing names: Fred Carboy the minicab driver; Mrs Grudge the cleaner; Mrs Sproat, mother in law to Barnaby's sidekick **Sergeant Troy**. (Sergeant Troy, of course, is manly, while their superior, CS Bateman, bates everyone.) Villages too have names like Midsomer Worthy, Morton Fendle, Forbes Abbot and (the subject of her first book) Badger's Drift.

The Killings at Badger's Drift (1987) was selected by the CWA as one of the best hundred crime novels of all time, and won a Macavity for best first novel. Five more titles followed in quick succession, leading to *Faithful Unto Death* in 1996. Then after three years came *Place of Safety* (1999) followed by another gap of five years, until *Ghost in the Machine* in 2004.

Meanwhile TV chugged along merrily, the series beginning in 1997. But the pace was gentle, almost soporific and the audience was kept awake only by the pleasant rural scenery and the quietly bizarre twists in the plots. **John Nettles** played Tom Barnaby, **Daniel Casey** played Gavin Troy.

THE BARON
by Anthony Morton (John Creasey)

Debonair jewel thief turned detective cum thief-taker in an astonishing 47 novels by this unbelievably prolific author. He belonged to the 1930s and 1940s, yet somehow managed to cling on with new titles in every decade till the Seventies.

Meet the Baron came first in 1937 and *The Baron, King-Maker* came out in 1975. *The Baron* appeared on British TV in 1965 to 1966, yet for some reason known only to the producers was given an American hero, **Steve Forrest**. The time period was also made more present-day.

BROTHER MATTHEW BARTHOLOMEW
by Susanna Gregory

Set in **medieval Cambridge** in learned communities who ought to know better, these gritty tales reek of the land and period. By no means are they standard detective stories transplanted to a different age; they are deeply researched and accurate tales which grow out of the specific times they are set in, and are of particular delight to anyone who wants a true portrait of the medieval period. Bartholomew is a mid-fourteenth century teacher and physician teaching medicine in what was to become Cambridge University. (Susanna Gregory earned her PhD there.) Bartholomew is also its Corpse Examiner, employed to investigate any sudden or suspicious deaths among scholars or on University property.

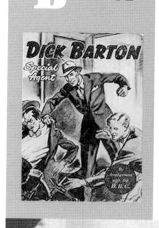

(The scholars were hated by the local population, even then.) On his investigations, which can be seen as early versions of modern-day forensic analyses, Matthew is assisted by his brother Michael.

A Plague on Both Your Houses (1996), *An Unholy Alliance* (1996), *A Bone of Contention* (1997), *A Deadly Brew* (1998), *A Wicked Deed* (1999), *A Masterly Murder* (2000), *An Order for Death* (2001), *A Summer of Discontent* (2002), *A Killer in Winter* (2003), *The Hand of Justice* (2004), *The Mark of a Murderer* (2005), *The Tarnished Chalice* (2006), *To Kill or Cure* (2007).

DICK BARTON

created by Norman Collins, but scripted by Geoffrey Webb & Edward J. Mason.

Dick Barton, Special Agent was the thrilling title rapped out on the BBC's Light Programme at a quarter to seven on the evening of 7 October 1946 – and each weekday evening after – by announcer Hamilton Humphries to the accompaniment of *The Devil's Gallop*, a signature tune even more famous than that of the radio serial that eventually replaced *Dick Barton*: *The Archers, An Everyday Story of Countryfolk*, the introduction of which showed that Mrs Grundy had won, and Aunty need never more disgrace herself by broadcasting programmes with street appeal. Only a nation cowed by post-war austerity could have allowed its favourite programme to be swept off the air.

The first series of *Dick Barton* ran from October 1946 to 30 May the following year, but was back in October. With intermissions it ran until the 30 March 1951, a night of infamy. Barton attracted 15 million listeners (an enormous audience) and delighted them nightly with wonderfully ludicrous tales of skulduggery and derring-do in which the eponymous agent tackled international criminals and spies with comic book bravado and a plethora of gadgets his audience could only dream of. Night after night the episodes ended on a cliff-hanger, his escapes from which were often hilarious, relying on 'one great leap' or a fabulous gadget or the help of his trusty friends **Jock** (Anderson) and **Snowy** White. In the original classic cast Barton was played by **Noel Johnson**, Jock by **Alex McCrindle** and Snowy White by **John Mann**. In September 1949 **Duncan Carse** took over as Barton, and from October 1950 he too was replaced by **Gordon Davies**. As part of the BBC's Jubilee in 1972, *Dick Barton* was revived for 10 nostalgic episodes with, as was only proper, Noel Johnson and John Mann in their rightful roles.

Various printed spin-offs in print are of no consequence. He was radio, pure and simple.

There were three low-budget films starring **Don Stannard** as Dick: *Dick Barton, Special Agent* (1948), *Dick Barton Strikes Back* (1949) and *Dick Barton at Bay* (1950).

Noel Johnson as Dick Barton.

COP KILLER THE MARTIN BECK SERIES

MAJ SJÖWALL & PER WAHLÖÖ

Walter Matthau.

The one attempt at a TV series was even less successful. **Tony Vogel** played Dick in a short-lived twice-weekly serial on ITV in 1979.

MARTIN BECK
by Maj Sjowall & Per Wahloo

This Swedish policeman is included because not only does he remains a favourite with many serious crime readers but because he is often cited as a favourite, if not an influence, by British crime *writers*. Beck appears in a finite series of ten books (Wahloo died when the tenth was written; Maj, his widow, did not continue the series) which laid the ground for Scandinavian crime fiction, both in terms of realism and of social comment. He is not the first fictional Swedish cop – there was *Stockholms-detektiven* in 1898 and, among others, a series of nineteen 'Commissioner O.P. Nillson' novels from Vic Suneson – but the Beck stories were an early template for realistic, detailed studies of police procedure such as **Henning Mankell**'s popular series on Kurt Wallander. It is notable how Beck changes through the series: he is a sickly, disenchanted, unhappily married and introverted cop in *Roseanna* (1967); he is almost killed but meets life-transforming **Rhea Nielsen** in *The Laughing Policeman* (1970); he works harder – only to discover the realities of cruel politically-driven justice-by-numbers in the final books. For this reason it is best if the books are read in sequence.

Roseanna (1967) starts the series. *The Terrorists* (1976) ends it.

The film *The Laughing Policeman* (1973) starred **Walter Matthau** as Beck, *The Man Who Went Up In Smoke* (1980) had **Derek Jacobi** as Beck, and all of the other Beck books have been made into Swedish films.

PAUL BECK
by Matthias McDonnell Bodkin

Influential early detective, made deliberately different from Holmes: 'I just go by rule of thumb, and muddle and puzzle out my cases as best I can,' he says in his first book *Paul Beck, the Rule of Thumb Detective* (1898), though he then goes on to demonstrate high intelligence, exceptional sporting and physical abilities and brilliance at disguise. Beck appears in a number of turn of the century stories, during which he meets and eventually marries the female sleuth **Dora Myrl**, thus adding continuity to what had been disconnected stories. A later Beck book, *Pigeon Blood Rubies*, again features Paul Beck – but opinions differ on whether this is Paul the father or Paul and Dora's son.

Stories began in 1897 and continue to 1911. *The Capture of Paul Beck* (1909) is of particular interest since the 'capture' is a romantic one, by Dora. *The Beck-Myrl Family Omnibus* (2005) is a useful modern anthology.

TOMMY & TUPPENCE BERESFORD

by Agatha Christie

Christie's most lightweight detectives – broadly amateur, though they invent 'Blunt's Brilliant Detectives' as a cover name in *Partners in Crime* – this merry pair of (originally) 1920s bright young things dive airily into a series of semi-comic adventures in which they solve baffling mysteries or unmask enemy agents and fifth-column rotters. Their first adventure results from their placing an advertisement, 'Two young adventurers for hire', and everything they do in subsequent books comes from this lust for fun. Lightweight, and untypical of Christie as they are, their off-and-on series persisted from 1922 to 1973. Tuppence, whose real name is Prudence, is far from prudent but her husband Tommy is a less unconventional dashing hero, propelled into one fling after another by his sometimes irritatingly reckless wife:

> *'We might be in a little railway accident on the way there,' said Tuppence, brightening up a little.*
> *'Why on earth do you want to be in a railway accident?'*
> *'Well, I don't really, of course. It was just... '*
> *'Just what?'*
> *'Well, it would be an adventure of some kind, wouldn't it?'*
> From *By the Pricking of my Thumbs 1968*

The Secret Adversary (1922), *Partners in Crime* (short stories, 1929), *N or M* (1941), *By the Pricking of my Thumbs* (1968), *Postern of Fate* (1973). The tales were made into a ten-part series by LWT in 1983–84 entitled *Agatha Christie's Partners in Crime*, starring **James Warwick** as Tommy and **Francesca Annis** as Tuppence. **Reece Dinsdale** played their film-mad assistant, Albert.

BERGERAC

created by Robert Banks Stewart

If one were uncharitable one might say that DS Jim Bergerac was stationed in the Channel islands because he wasn't up to a posting on the mainland: he is a recovered alcoholic, has a lame leg, and his wife has left him. And do criminals exist in the Channel Isles? You bet they do. Bergerac works for the *Bureau des Étrangers* (which investigates non-native criminals) and the wicked *étrangers* see the islands as a safe haven for ill-gotten gains – and perhaps also as a source of more ill-gotten gains. Island scenery made the series a visual treat, and many a shot featured Bergerac's trademark 1947 Triumph sports car – all of which, together with the general charm and good humour of the series – helped keep it on air for a decade (1981 to 1991). **John Nettles** who played Bergerac was joined by several long-running supporting actors, including **Terence Alexander** as dodgy one-time father-in-law Charlie Hungerford, **Sean Arnold** as Chief Inspector Barney Crozier, **Liza Goddard** as a sexy jewel thief, and **Cecile Paoli, Deborah Grant, Celia Imrie** and **Louise Jameson** as some of the women in his life.

Andrew Taylor wrote several novelisations based on the characters.

John Nettles

BERTIE
by Peter Lovesey

One of the least likely ideas for a detective ever: Queen Victoria's son, the Prince of Wales, later to become King Edward VII. Admittedly he lived a 'colourful' life and met many disreputable characters; admittedly also other authors have cast him as Jack the Ripper (to be alive then, male and famous was enough for some Ripper hunters); but Lovesey makes a decent fist of this, with three novels and two short stories. Lots of period atmosphere and guest appearances from actress Sarah Bernhardt among other names.

Bertie and the Tinman (1987), *Bertie and the Seven Bodies* (1990), *Bertie and the Crime of Passion* (1993).

INSPECTOR BEST
by Joan Lock

Joan Lock spent much of her working life in the police and has written copiously on the subject, so it's no surprise that her police procedurals are bang to rights on detail, even if Detective Inspector Ernest Best was working way back in the **1870s–80s**. Some of his cases are based on real-life disasters: the Regent's Park Explosion (1874), the tragic sinking of the *Princess Alice* pleasure steamer (1878) and the Fenian bombings which hit underground and railway stations and even Scotland Yard itself (1883–4). More murder and mayhem occur against the colourful backdrops of the Annual Police Fete at the Alexandra Palace, on stage during a melodrama, and even in the bedding department of Bainbridges, the world's first department store.

Dead Image (2000), *Dead Born* (2001), *Dead Letters* (2003), *Dead End* (2004), *Dead Fall* (2005), *Dead Loss* (2006).

BIRDSEYE & NEVKORINA
by Nancy Spain

The fact that Spain's two arch women detectives are summoned for their first case to a girls' school called Radcliff Hall is an obvious clue. The two women, Miriam Birdseye and Natasha Nevkorina, have forsaken the theatre to create a madcap detective agency, Birdseye et cie, in which they deploy theatrical skills – disguise, impersonation – to hunt down their quarry and have lots of larks. The tales are wildly extravagant and peppered with innuendo. In *Not Wanted on Voyage* (1951) when asked whether they catch men, Miriam loftily replies: 'Oh dear no. My partner quite often catches women... Or so she says.' Good fun, and by today's standards, good clean fun.

The 7 swiftly-written novels begin with *Poison for the Teacher* (1949) and end with *Out Damned Tot* (1952).

MODESTY BLAISE
by Peter O'Donnell

Born in 1962 as a cartoon strip character in the *Daily Express*, Modesty went on to star in her own series of books and as the title character in a camp 1960s film, but ended her life more graciously as a cartoon character again in the *Evening Standard*. She and her cockney friend **Willie Garvin** are retired criminals – she retired at twenty-six – tempted out of retirement by British Intelligence with the lure of an even more exciting life. Willie is strong, blond and handsome, devoted to Modesty, but his love remains brotherly. Since Modesty is a walking, breathing sex object – in one story she distracts the opposition by walking into a room topless – Willie's reticence seems strange. Modesty is also a superwoman, a master of unarmed or armed combat, a yoga supremo, a great brain, and has breasts to rival Jordan's. All of these assets are used to great effect. Her adventures, too, are a Superwoman's: tackling master criminals, potential world overlords and sundry manifestations of evil incarnate. She is frequently captured, but her budding torturers have barely time to salivate before 'with one kick she is free.' (Other weapons include her kongo or yarvana stick. Don't ask.)

> *Modesty Blaise threw herself sideways, firing as she fell. It was as if the single shot had hit both remaining men, for they both went down together, one spinning round, his reflex action loosing a brief burst of fire as he died. The other simply crumpled, clawing feebly at the three-inch haft protruding from his throat. Willie's second knife had found its mark.*
>
> From *Sabre-Tooth* by Peter O'Donnell

Daily Express cartoon strip from 1962; *Evening Standard* cartoon not long after (1963); books from 1965; cartoons syndicated worldwide. The first book was called merely *Modesty Blaise*, followed by *Sabre Tooth* (1966), *I, Lucifer* (1967), and a series of others including *The Impossible Virgin* (1971), *Last Day in Limbo* (1976), *The Xanadu Talisman* (1981) and *Dead Man's Handle* (1985).

Joseph Losey's *Modesty Blaise* (1966) infuriated her fans but wowed neutrals at the time, as it epitomised the worst excesses of 1960s cinema. Gorgeous **Monica Vitti**, heavily accented and eye-lined, played Modesty; the beautiful **Terence Stamp** played Willie Garvin; arch **Dirk Bogarde**, craggy **Harry Andrews** and others played cameos. Fun at times, it sure was different.

SEXTON BLAKE

by Hal Meredith and many others

Despite his numerous authors – often hack writers – and his several redesigns (especially of clothing) and despite the fact that no one, fan or writer, has claimed that his tales have any literary merit, it is likely that more words have been written about Sexton Blake and that he has had more adventures than any other fictional detective. He was created in 1893 and remained a stalwart (in every sense) of weekly serials for nearly a century. He was, in essence, a schoolboy's Sherlock Holmes, often presented in graphic form rather than text, usually in cheap comics and flimsy paperbacks. Drawn by different artists over the years, his costume changed from bowler hat and heavy coat to lounge

suit to Sherlockian garb complete with deerstalker, and on again to suit and tie. So attractive was his name that a cheap paperback *Sexton Blake Library* was created – initially for children (mainly boys) but later for adults also, and it ran for years, the adult series crammed with lurid tales of skulduggery penned by various writers under sometimes amusing pen-names. Not all of these stories featured Blake himself. His last appearance in the *Library* was in June 1963, but he has continued to reappear sporadically in hard and paperback.

His tales varied from crime and detection to spy stories (especially during and around the two world wars) and most were wildly fanciful. All were action-packed. Not for Blake the cerebral contemplation of Sherlock Holmes (though he did live in Baker Street). His companions changed; his enemies changed (among his adversaries were Zenith the Albino, Dr Huxton Rymer, Waldo the Wonder Man and Mademoiselle Yvonne). He had girlfriends (see *Yvonne Cartier*) and, in the days when such things were not only unquestioned but useful in order to sell more copies to schoolboys, he had a boy companion, **Tinker**, clad in shorts and with tousled hair. (Tinker first appeared in 1904 and like his master, never aged.)

No one will ever know all the authors of Sexton Blake. **Hal Meredith** and **Harry Blythe** are among the better known (and Hal wrote the first Blake story, *The Missing Millionaire* for *Halfpenny Marvel* magazine in 1893) but it has always been rumoured that famous names contributed under pseudonyms – assuming any author name was given at all, as it often wasn't in the comics. Soon after his debut in *Halfpenny Marvel* Blake was moved to Harmsworth's sister magazine *Union Jack*, which remained his home for years (despite guest appearances in other journals). Later, in his between-the-wars incarnation (1919-39) Blake was penned mainly by Anthony Skene, but Skene was one of many: it has been estimated that around 200 authors have contributed. *Union Jack* closed down in 1933, and Blake was seized by *Detective Weekly* and continued in his own *Sexton Blake Library*.

Blake's first appearance on radio came in 1939 when Ernest Dudley scripted *Enter Sexton Blake*, a serial, with **George Curzon** as Sexton Blake. Sexton Blake films date from 1914, and a series of silent movies in the Twenties starred **Langhorne Burton** in the role. By the Thirties **George Curzon** (who became the radio Blake) had taken over, to be followed in turn by **David Farrar** in the Forties.

ITV ran *Sexton Blake* from 1967 to 1971, with **Laurence Payne** as Blake, **Roger Foss** as boy wonder Tinker and **Dorothea Phillips** as their Baker Street landlady, Mrs Bardell. BBC TV serialised *Sexton Blake and the Demon God* in 1978, with **Jeremy Clyde** as Blake and **Philip Davis** as young Tinker. An indication of Blake's continuing ability to attract big names is shown by this series having been scripted by Simon Raven.

David Farrar.

SIR PERCY BLAKENEY
(see *The Scarlet Pimpernel*)

URSULA BLANCHARD
by Fiona Buckley

A lady in waiting to **Queen Elizabeth the First** may seem an unlikely sleuth, but those were troubled times and the virgin queen was at the heart of many conspiracies. The queen relies on Ursula for her cunning, and on a bevy of suitably able men for muscle, including Sir William Cecil who normally briefs our Ursula, while Ursula herself relies on tough man Roger Brockley and his less tough lover, Fran Dale. Forget the Spanish Armada, the main enemies here are Mary Stuart and her supporters. Slightly confusingly for a series, Ursula marries and becomes Ursula Stannard in the later books.

To Shield the Queen began the series in 1997. Notable titles since include *A Pawn for a Queen* (2002) and *The Siren Queen* (2004). The books can be found more easily in America than the UK.

JOHN BLIZZARD
by John Dean

DCI Blizzard works with Sergeant David Colley in the northern city of Hafton, whose affluent areas contrast with run-down council houses and neglected Victorian terraces. Blizzard, in his 40s, is a sour-faced chief inspector with a dry sense of humour and an instinctive approach to detective work. Colley is a laid-back, affable sergeant in his 30s sharp but more human in the way he deals with people.

A Flicker in the Night (1995) started the series, and the fifth *The Long Dead* came out in 2006.

SIR SIMON BOGNOR
by Tim Heald

In a long-running light-hearted series that first appeared in the 1970s, Bognor progressed from being a Special Investigator within the Board of Trade to become Head of Department of the Investigation Department (SIDBOT). Similarly, his girlfriend Monica progressed to become his wife, *Lady* Bognor. The books are set in real time, and thus run from the 1970s to date, and any one of the plots is wilder and more lively than would be a life spent in the real department's offices. One such plot, the theft by communists of a secret formula for honey, sets the tone.

Tim Heald.

Unbecoming Habits (1973) starts the series. *Blue Blood Will Out* (1974), *Deadline* (1975), *Red Herrings* (1985) and *Business As Usual* (1989) are all good reads.

Bognor was a Thames TV twice-weekly series in 1981, and a three-part mini-series *Just Desserts* followed in 1982, starring **David Horovitch** as Simon Bognor and **Joanna McCallum** as Monica.

NAPOLEON BONAPARTE
by Arthur Upfield

This Napoleon Bonaparte is an **Australian** Detective Inspector and he strides into my book of British detectives only because his creator was

Arthur Upfield.

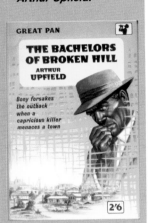

born in Britain. 'Bony' is of mixed race (half white, half aboriginal) and is a superb 'bush detective'. He is an intelligent but vain man, an MA of Brisbane university, married with three sons – and his knowledge of the boomerang, he tells us, is unsurpassed. He himself, despite his amusing vanity, comes across as charming, and his outback environment is extraordinary and exciting. It is the settings that make the stories; the outback is wild and superbly drawn, even if, as most admit, the humans including Bony himself tend to be rather wooden. But does that matter? Here's a detective who in *Man of Two Tribes*, for example, goes in search of a man in vast Nullarbor Plain accompanied only by two camels and a dog. You don't get that in Mayhem Parva.

I obey an order when it suits me,' Bony said, and Pavier marvelled that he could feel no ire. 'I am unique because I stand midway between the white and black races, having all the virtues of the white race and very few vices of the black race. I have mastered the art of taking pains, and I was born with the gift of observation. I never hurry in my hunt for a murderer, but I never delay my approach. You can find me a corner? There will be much research work to do'.

From *The Bachelors of Broken Hill*

There are around three dozen Bonaparte books, beginning with *The House of Cain* in 1928 and ending in 1966 with *The Lake Frome Monster* (which had to be completed by Upfield's wife after he died in 1964).

Boney was an Australian-made TV series, starring the New Zealand actor **James Larenson**, shown on TV in 1975.

SUPERINTENDENT BONE
by Staines and Storey

Robert Bone is a widower with an teenage daughter injured in the crash which killed his wife. This sombre background underpins a well-written series of classic crime puzzles in which both the crimes and the suspects veer towards the peculiar. The authors, Jill Staynes and Margaret Storey, were life-long friends and first worked together writing children's books. There is nothing childish about the Bone series.

Though the books stand alone the background story works best if read in sequence. *Goodbye, Nanny Gray* (1987), *A Knife at the Opera* (1988), *Body of Opinion* (1989), *Grave Responsibility* (1990), *The Late Lady* (1992), *Bone Idle* (1993), *Dead Serious* (1995), *Quarry* (1999).

NORMAN & HENRY BONES
Boy detectives who appeared on BBC's 'Children's Hour' in the 1940s. Spin-off books by Anthony C Wilson include the unimaginatively titled *Norman Bones, Detective* (1949) and *Norman and Henry Bones, the Boy Detectives* (1952).

JOHN BOTTRELL
by Kelvin Jones

A Chief Inspector in the Met, Bottrell retired following a breakdown caused by his wife's death in a car crash (for which he was responsible), and he went to Cornwall to brood on life. An introspective man, prone to depression, a heavy drinker (whisky) and a smoker, it's just as well that people drag him out of himself and into current investigations. A bit of an odd choice, you might think, though he does have a psychic ability which comes in handy on occasions.

   Stone Dead (2006), *Witch Jar* (2008), *Flowers of Evil* (2008).

DCI PETER BOYD TV series *Waking The Dead* (2000)

Boyd heads the Cold Case Squad, an old idea reinvigorated by opportunities created by recent breakthroughs in forensic science. Boyd himself, played by **Trevor Eve** (no stranger to oddball sleuth parts), has a disturbed past of his own and is given to sudden flashes of melodrama and upstaging of anyone else on set. Long into the series (and perhaps due to exasperation from its audience?) Boyd comes up with a reason for his irritating behaviour (a bereavement, as if he is the only person to have ever been bereaved) and makes some attempt to calm down. Filmed in a fashionable brooding darkness the show relies less on science than on flashes of illumination and Eve shouting in the dark.

NICHOLAS BRACEWELL
by Edward Marston

The Bracewell novels are set in the **late sixteenth-century Elizabethan theatre**, where Bracewell himself has the job of book holder. It ought to be a quiet job, suitable for a man (Bracewell is in his mid-thirties) who likes to keep his head down and pay close attention to the script. But he can't help getting involved in real-life dramas. Together with his actor friend **Lawrence Firethorn** he becomes embroiled in domestic and national issues of the day such as religious conspiracies and dodgy marriages. Elizabethan times were dangerous, and Bracewell's band of players have to fight and scramble their way through. But in *The Princess of Denmark* they get a trip to Elsinore – a highlight for any bunch of thespians.

   The many titles include *The Queen's Head* (1988), *The Merry Devils* (1989), *The Trip to Jerusalem* (1990), *The Mad Courtesan* (1992), *The Roaring Boy* (1995), *The Fair Maid of Bohemia* (1997), *The Bawdy Basket* (2002), *The Princess of Denmark* (2006).

MRS BRADLEY
by Gladys Mitchell

One of the longest running, if today almost forgotten, detectives, Mrs Bradley was not young when the series started, but Gladys Mitchell didn't realise the series would last more than fifty years. Mrs Bradley is a fiendishly intelligent psychiatrist and consultant to the Home Office who often uses psychological techniques to solve the cases presented to her. Her full name is Dame Beatrice Adela Lestrange Bradley, and she herself is a bizarre creation of almost witch-like appearance, given to shrieks and cackles, whose assistant **Laura Menzies** occasionally refers to her as Mrs Croc or The Old Trout. Her cases are suitably odd, with suspects ranging from modern-day witches to the Green Man and

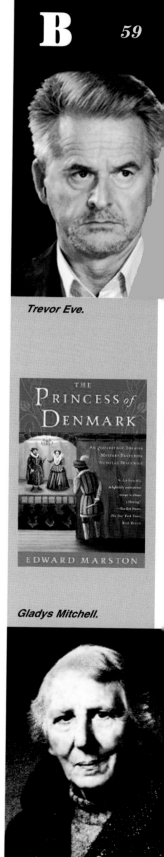

Trevor Eve.

Gladys Mitchell.

SPEEDY
DEATH
GLADYS
MITCHELL

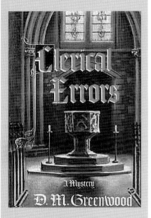

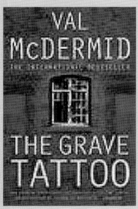

in one case to a cousin of the Loch Ness Monster. Of those who remember Mrs Bradley, some remember fondly and some could never stand her. Nevertheless, these were entertaining puzzle mysteries with clues and psychiatry cleverly interwoven.

Speedy Death (1929) began the series. Among many titles, *Laurels Are Poison* (1942), *Tom Brown's Body* (1949), *Watson's Choice* (1955) or *Dance to Your Daddy* (1969) might be chosen. *The Crozier Pharoahs* ended the series in 1984.

Diana Rigg played Adela Bradley (as she was termed in TV, for short) in a smartly-styled series on BBC in 2000, after a pilot in 1998.

THEODORA BRAITHWAITE
by D M Greenwood
Sharp and formidable deaconess who keeps getting drawn in to an extraordinary number of misdemeanours and worse that go on in the Church of England. Makes you think you should stay at home and watch *Songs of Praise* instead.

Clerical Orders started the series in 1991 and eight more followed annually with the regularity of church sermons every Sunday (though more enjoyably): *Unholy Ghosts* (1991), *Idol Bones* (1993), *Holy Terrors* (1994), *Every Deadly Sin* (1995), *Mortal Spoils* (1996), *Heavenly Vices* (1997), *A Grave Disturbance* (1998), *Foolish Ways* (1999).

KATE BRANNIGAN
by Val McDermid
Manchester-based female private investigator, and a match for any man. A redhead, of course, and an *alter ego* for any tomboy, Kate Brannigan takes on the nastiest of cases. Some of her clients are just as nasty. A curious feature of the cases is that they tend to start out quietly, almost cosily, with a complaint about a missing conservatory, for example, or a stolen painting, yet before long they descend into gangster feuds, child pornography and drugs. Strong stuff, from the creator of **Lindsay Gordon** and **Tony Hill**.

Dead Beat (1992), *Kick Back* (1993), *Crackdown* (1994), *Clean Break* (1995), *Blue Genes* (1996), *Star Struck* (1998). *Crackdown* is probably the best.

NELL BRAY
by Gillian Linscott
Where lawbreaking is concerned Edwardian suffragette Nell Bray has form. First encountered in *Sister Beneath the Sheet* (1991) she came fresh from Holloway prison where she had been held for throwing a half-brick through the window of Number 10 Downing Street. Nell's suffragist politics were central to the plots, in the first of which she was engaged by Mrs Pankhurst, no less, to collect a large sum of money from a murdered prostitute in Biarritz. Equally juicy plots followed at the rate of one a year culminating in 2003 with the last of the series, *Blood on the Wood*, and during the series Nell moved through suffragette history – the demonstrations, the First World War –

although the books themselves were written and published in a non-chronological sequence. (The penultimately published, *Dead Man Riding*, was set earliest, in 1900.) In Linscott's award-winning *Absent Friends* women had finally won the right to vote, and Nell stood as a candidate at the 1919 General Election. But the previous candidate had been murdered.

Sister Beneath the Sheet (1991), *Hanging on the Wire* (1992), *Stage Fright* (1993), *Widow's Peak* (1994), *Crown Witness* (1995), *Dead Man's Music* (1996), *Dance on Blood* (1998), *Absent Friends* (1999), which won both the Ellis Peters Historical Dagger and the Herodotus, *The Perfect Daughter* (2000), *Dead Man Riding* (2002), *Blood on the Wood* (2003).

MILES BREDON
by Ronald Knox

Insurance investigator for the (fictional) Indescribable Life Assurance Company, a name that indicates the seriousness of the books. Bredon and his wife Angela appeared in a brief series of amusing but rather clever mysteries set in Oxford, starting in 1927.

The Three Taps (1927), *The Footsteps at the Lock* (1928), *The Body in the Silo* (1929) and the final appearance: *Double Cross Purposes* (1937).

ROGER BROOK
by Dennis Wheatley

No one reads him now, but for young boys growing up in the 1940s and 1950s Wheatley was one of the great illicit pleasures (though not so illicit that he earned more than an indulgent smile from their parents). One of his daring protagonists was Roger Brook, adventurer and spy in the time of the Napoleonic wars. To a 10-year-old boy (at that time) his amorous episodes seemed erotic. And there was the fighting.

The Launching of Roger Brook kicked the stories off appropriately in 1947, followed by *Shadow of Tyburn Tree* (1948) et cetera (and which boy could resist *The Ravishing of Lady Mary Ware* in 1970?) until, in 1974, came the twelfth and final *Desperate Measures*.

LOVEDAY BROOKE
by Catherine Louise Parkis

Attractive young Victorian lady detective, early in the field, employed by a detective bureau in Lynch Court.

The Experiences of Loveday Brooke, Lady Detective (1894).

FATHER BROWN
by G.K. Chesterton

Father Brown was such an odd detective that Chesterton might have deliberately set out to create the opposite of Sherlock Holmes. Clad in black clerical garb, often laden with a precautionary umbrella and bulging parcel while peering amiably at the world through his round spectacles, Brown seemed the antithesis of an effective detective. Where Holmes had no time for God, Father Brown was a Catholic

G. K. Chesterton.

THE
COLONIAL RADIO THEATRE
ON THE AIR
PRESENTS

THE
FATHER BROWN
MYSTERIES

STARRING
J.T. TURNER
DRAMATIZED BY M.J. ELLIOTT
FROM THE STORIES BY
G.K. CHESTERTON

Alec Guinness.

priest. Where Homes was tall, lean and sinister, Father Brown was short, chubby and avuncular. Where Holmes was logical to the point of arrogance, Brown pottered amiably to his conclusions. He hailed from Essex, which was again the opposite of Baker Street.

> *There shambled into the room a shapeless little figure, which seemed to find its own hat and umbrella as unmanageable as a mass of luggage. The umbrella was a black and prosaic bundle long past repair; the hat was a broad-curved black hat, clerical but not common in England; the man was the very embodiment of all that is homely and helpless.*

From the story *The Absence of Mr Glass*.

Chesterton was a writer, an essayist and poet. His stories are literate and descriptive: 'It was one of those chilly and empty afternoons in early winter, when the daylight is silver rather than gold, and pewter rather than silver,' he writes in *The God of the Gongs*. He did not disparage his 'little stories'. Popular fiction, he thought, could do powerful work. Crime stories, declared this robust Roman Catholic, were moral tales; they could demonstrate 'that courage is splendid, that fidelity is noble, that distressed ladies should be rescued, and vanquished enemies spared'. Such would be the work of Father Brown.

In over sixty short stories he sought miscreants, not in the first instance to bring them to justice but to offer the chance of redemption, of forgiveness, of seeing the error of their ways and putting sins right. Brown was **the pastoral detective**. Yet while he worked his way with wrongdoers he worked a different spell on his readers. Less concerned with the stories' morals – often unaware a lesson was being preached – Brown's many fans read the tales for their neatness as mysteries. For they are unlike other stories. They contain few recognisable clues; indeed many break the rules of crime fiction in that they don't share information with the reader but allow Father Brown to pull off a fairy's masterstroke, sweeping away our bewilderment with a magical 'Hey presto!' A swish of the surplice, and all is revealed. None of us had seen it; only Father Brown knew, and he knew from the start. *What* Father Brown knew was often not merely how a clue was concealed but how a *personality* was concealed. He saw beyond what was presented to him, he saw beneath the skin to the real person. He saw their soul.

All of which, if you have never read Father Brown, might make these delightful stories sound like Sunday School fables, and in a way they are – but like the fables of Aesop it is not so much the moral we read for (though we do perhaps remember the moral) it is the story. Chesterton defended good stories. They meant more than literature: in his famous essay *A Defence of Penny Dreadfuls* he wrote: 'Literature is a luxury; fiction a necessity'. He explained that a story engrosses us and captures our thoughts for hours, perhaps for days, on end. Therefore, he said, an exciting story has a greater and longer impact than has a 'greater' piece of art. It is an unorthodox verdict, but he was an unorthodox writer. No surprise, then, that he should have created **one of the most unorthodox detectives in crime fiction**.

It cannot be denied that the Father Brown stories are uneven. At best

they are witty, deft and ingenious, but for every fine tale there follows an overly contrived fable, and occasionally, as in *The God of the Gongs*, an outburst of eye-watering racism that today would have publisher prosecuted. For the sake of decency and Chesterton's reputation, the worst of these stories should be removed from reissues. The Father Brown stories are collected in five volumes of short stories: *The Innocence of Father Brown* (1911), *The Wisdom of Father Brown* (1914), *The Incredulity of Father Brown* (1926), *The Secret of Father Brown* (1927), *The Scandal of Father Brown* (1935)

In the 1974 ITV series *Father Brown* the bumbling cleric was portrayed by *Doctor in the House* and *Genevieve* star **Kenneth More**.

The Detective was the American title for a splendid British film, *Father Brown*, made in 1954, starring the incomparable **Alec Guinness**, though there had been earlier efforts, of which the only notable version, *Father Brown, Detective* came out in 1934 with **Walter Connolly** in the role.

Kenneth More

INSPECTOR BRUNT
by John Buxton Hilton

Set in and around a **Peak District** village at the turn of the century (nineteenth to twentieth) these stories are, according to Mike Ashley, 'amongst the best historical detective stories of their day'. Accurately set and well plotted, with a real feel for the place and the time, the six books in the series are well worth tracking down.

Gamekeeper's Gallows (1975), *Rescue from the Rose* (1976), *Dead-Nettle* (1977), *Mr Fred* (1983), *The Quiet Stranger* (1985), *Slickensides* (1987).

INSPECTOR BRYANT & MAY
by Christopher Fowler

An amusing but clever series. As 'the longest serving detectives in London' Bryant and May (paired because their names match?) run the Peculiar Crimes Unit, which handles cases that may cause public unrest if the truth was ever made public. John May is the sauve senior officer, technologically literate and charming, while Arthur Bryant is irascible, curmudgeonly, rude and prone to exotic beliefs. They and their team solve classic crimes – often stetching far back in time – while fighting the bureaucracy of the Home Office as it tries to close them down.

Full Dark House (2003), *The Water Room* (2004), *Seventy-Seven Clocks* (2005), *Ten Second Staircase* (2006), *White Corridor* (2007), *The Victoria Vanishes* (2008).

INSPECTOR BUCKET
by Charles Dickens

Although a fairly minor character in *Bleak House* (1852), Bucket is **the first fictional detective to appear in a proper novel** and, minor though his role might be, it is pivotal. Bucket is introduced around the period when the relationship of police and detectives to the civilian population changed. Previously the police and their assistants had been seen as hostile agents of the state. The Bow Street Runners had existed

Player's Cigarettes

Inspector Bucket.

Bleak House

Charles Dickens.

and been grudgingly tolerated from 1749 to 1829, while the Metropolitan Police began to employ their first detectives in the 1840s. Bucket, in a novel written later but set just before that time, was a policeman engaged independently to undertake detection work on behalf of the lawyer Tulkinghorn. Though the lawyer's motives were malicious, Bucket (not above deviousness himself) was an honourable professional, concerned only to investigate the crime.

At first he worked to Tulkinghorn's brief, probing into the mysteries of Lady Dedlock's past but, when Tulkinghorn was murdered Bucket turned to investigate the murder and find the culprit. He did this by observation, interrogation and deduction – much as would almost all detectives who came to follow him. That his technique seems a little creaky today is hardly surprising given his period and the fact that he – or Dickens – was creating a prototype. Some of Bucket's investigation takes place off-stage – a practice which has come to be regarded as cheating by mystery writers but which, at that time, was a conventional technique for drama – and the Inspector's able accomplice Mrs Bucket is not introduced to us at all. But Bucket is sly and a cunning questioner, and both these facets *are* displayed to us. We see him at work and we enjoy watching him lay his snares. We see how he makes it impossible for those he is questioning to avoid his demands. We shiver slightly at his ability to slip unnoticed into a room and startle the occupants, immediately wrong-footing them as, while they struggle to answer his questions, they wonder how much he has already heard.

"Dear me, sir, I wasn't aware there was any other gentleman present!"

Mr Snagsby is dismayed to see, standing with an attentive face between himself and the lawyer, at a little distance from the table, a person with a hat and stick in his hand, who was not there when he himself came in, and has not since entered by the door or by either of the windows. There is a press in the room, but its hinges have not creaked, nor has a step been audible upon the floor. Yet this third person stands there, with his attentive face, and his hat and stick in his hands, and his hands behind him, a composed and quiet listener. He is a stoutly built, steady-looking, sharp-eyed man in black, of about the middle-age. Except that he looks at Mr Snagsby as if he were going to take his portrait, there is nothing remarkable about him at first sight but his ghostly manner of appearing.

"Don't mind this gentleman," says Mr Tulkinghorn, in his quiet way. "This is only Mr Bucket."

From *Bleak House* by Charles Dickens

The more pressure the suspects are under the more likely it is that Bucket will sit back and take his time, leisurely drawing them off into apparently unrelated side issues, thus confusing them further as they try not to be panicked into saying what they know they must not say. As they squirm beneath his tortuous questions Bucket is likely to step forward, smile understandingly, and place a friendly but heavy arm

From Bleak House.

around their shoulders. A gentle squeeze, and it all comes out.

As a journalist, Dickens had spent many a night watch with real-life policemen; he liked them, he was fascinated by their craft. This is easily seen in the magazine articles he wrote about the still-new Detective Department and its real-life Inspector Charles Field in 1850 and 1851, just a year before he created Field's fictional counterpart in *Bleak House*. How much of Field's character and techniques appear in Bucket we will never know, for Dickens could describe nothing without embellishing it. Bucket was an early prototype, sketched and not finished. The great climactic scene when Inspector Bucket reveals the culprit and explains his reasoning has in some later adaptations (notably the recent BBC success) seemed the forerunner of the 'library' scene that ended many Golden Age mysteries in later years. But in the book the detective does not reassemble the cast; the scene doesn't take place in the library. It is a trap and revelation, with Bucket reporting to the man who engaged him (Sir Lester Dedlock), revealing to both Sir Lester and the reader who was guilty of the crime. It may have been done better since, but Bucket's role in *Bleak House* is undoubtedly that of the great detective.

Bleak House has been a major TV drama three times. The first was in 1959 and the second ran for eight episodes in 1985 when **Ian Hogg** played Bucket, and **Diana Rigg** followed **Iris Russell** into the role of Lady Dedlock. In these first two adaptations Inspector Bucket's role was tiny. It was only in the sensational 2005 version with **Gillian Anderson** wowing the nation as Lady D that Bucket's role came to prominence. **Alun Armstrong** extracted every ounce from the part.

BULL-DOG DRUMMOND
see *Drummond*

INSPECTOR BURNLEY
by Freeman Wills Crofts
With Inspector Burnley it could be argued that Crofts created the **police procedural** crime novel. In his *The Cask* (1920) Crofts has Burley investigate the mysterious death of a Frenchwoman, part of whose body, together with a small cache of gold coins, is found in a packing cask at the London docks. Given this premise, previous tales would have embroidered fantastic patterns to explain how she and the gold coins got there; her very Frenchness would have signalled the exotic; the gold might have been cursed. But Burnley proceeded slowly, as a policeman would. He didn't work on his own; he used his whole department – and the way they worked was explained in meticulous detail. For today's tastes the detail is too meticulous, but it was an important change: it brought reality to what had before been fantasy. Burnley has no flashes of inspiration. He makes few jokes. But he seems real. Burnley led the way to Crofts's longer-lasting protagonist (hero would be an exaggeration) **Inspector French**.
The Cask (1920)

Freeman Wills Crofts.

KATE BURROWS
by Martina Cole

Essex hard-girl Detective Inspector who appears in two of Martina Cole's brutally realistic gangland stories. In the first, *The Ladykiller*, which is Cole's second book, Burrows has a gruelling time on the trail of The Grantley Ripper, a man who rapes the daughter of one of London's most feared criminals. Burrows finds herself defending the bad against the bad. In the second Kate Burrows novel, Cole's seventh overall, Kate has – incredibly – shacked up with said hard man from the first book and wants his help on a case concerning abandoned children. Not surprisingly, he has other things on his mind. Martina Cole's books sell in vast quantities but are not for those of delicate sensibilities.
The Ladykiller (1993), *Broken* (2000).

BROTHER CADFAEL
by Ellis Peters (Edith Pargeter)

Twelfth century monk cum (by necessity, for they were evil times) amateur detective, based in Shrewsbury Abbey. His ostensible task there was to tend the herb garden but, fortunately for the reader, his life was rather more exciting than that, as from time to time he was called upon to use his formidable powers of deduction to solve earthly mysteries. Though not the first detective to have stories set in 'olden times', Cadfael was the first to achieve real and international success; through him, what had been a tiny avenue of publishing became a thoroughfare. Not that Peters had expected that: her first Cadfael book, *A Morbid Taste for Bones* had been intended as a once-off, less a crime story than a historical novel. Peters, one should remember, was an already established author under her own name of Edith Pargetter (not to mention a less successful pseudonym, Jolyon Carr).

Cadfael himself is no young dashing hero. He is a monk, he is Welsh and in the first book he is over 60. He had fought his battles (overseas, in the Crusades) and he now looks forward to his retirement tending herbs. But one who specialises in herbs is likely to know quite a lot about poisons – since in the twelfth century it was from herbs that poisons came. Thus was Cadfael recruited by the local sheriff to help solve crimes. The third Cadfael novel, *Monk's-Hood* is a pun: monkshood is a poisonous herb. The novel won Peters the CWA Silver Dagger. By now the series and Cadfael had become popular. Refreshingly different, *respectable* crime stories with more than a dash of history thrown in, they appealed to a widespread fiction-reading audience. They benefited too from arriving early in the field and, during the 1980s, came out at the rate of one or two full-length novels every year. As other crime writers turned to the historical field, Ellis Peters was scampering ahead on the horizon.

Peters won the CWA Cartier Diamond Dagger in 1993 and was awarded the OBE in 1994. In 1999 a special award was created in her memory: the CWA Ellis Peters Award for the best historical crime novel of the year. It remains her testament.

A Morbid Taste for Bones began the series in 1977, followed by *One*

Corpse Too Many in 1979. From 1980 the books flowed: 15 in the 1980s and three more in the Nineties before her death. Cadfael's final appearance was in *Brother Cadfael's Penance* in 1994.

Cadfael was a series of occasional ninety minute once-offs running on ITV from 1994 to 1998. **Derek Jacobi** played Cadfael.

JACK CAFFERY
by Mo Hayder

Detective Inspector Jack Caffery is young, apparently unshockable and is firmly set on the Met's fast track for bright young officers. But that doesn't necessarily make him popular with fellow coppers who are coming up the traditional and slower way. For all his surface hardness Caffery has demons in his past that rise up to haunt him. The premise of the first book, *Birdman*, was startling enough to propel it into the top ten: Hayder is not the first author to write of young women sexually abused and ritualistically murdered, but she was the first to dream up a killer so warped that he cut his victims open and sewed live birds inside their chests, so that when the corpses were first discovered they appeared to still be breathing. The second Caffery book is almost as gruesome. *The Treatment* has a husband and wife badly beaten, then tied up and left without food or water in their own home while their assailant makes off with their young child. And Jack's own demons are still there. After *The Treatment* Hayder took time out to write stand-alone novels, no less gruesome
Birdman (2000), *The Treatment* (2001).

Derek Jacobi is Cadfael.

KEITH CALDER
by Gerald Hammond

Probably the only **gunsmith-detective**. An interesting choice of alternative profession even if, one suspects, it exists mainly to provide a basis for the author and Calder's campaign to set right current prejudices against traditional country sports and rural lifestyles.

Dead Game (1979) began a long series which ran to *Illegal Tender* in 2001, and Calder made a minor appearance in *Keeper Turned Poacher* (2006).

SLIM CALLAGHAN
by Peter Cheyney

Tough amoral private eye of the war years, written in Cheyney's cod American style which never works as well for Callaghan as it does for his other hero, the American agent **Lemmy Caution**. He has a touch of the Robin Hood in that he is likely to fleece his clients if he doesn't like them but, although the stories are characteristically lively, Callaghan's cases sit uneasily in a British setting, and to modern taste he is surprisingly violent. Nor does it help when he and his buddies lapse into a dubious American vernacular. Caution can do that because Caution is American. And Caution is a whole lot funnier, which allows him to get away with much that Callaghan cannot.

Callaghan was introduced two years after Caution in *The Urgent Hangman* (1938), and continued at yearly intervals with *Dangerous Curves, You Can't Keep The Change, It Couldn't Matter Less* etc. until *Uneasy Terms* in 1946.

Slim Callaghan's all-action approach appealed to French film makers, and he lit up the screen in *A Toi De Jour Callaghan, Plus De Whiskey Pour Callaghan* and *Callaghan Remet a*. He also appeared in two British movies, *Uneasy Terms* and *Meet Mr Callaghan*.

ALBERT CAMPION
by Margery Allingham

A unique character – because unlike many **Golden Age** detectives he does have a character – Campion progresses through the books from a raffish debonair hero of the 20s (or to be cruel, a silly young ass) into a more thoughtful and hardworking detective in the grim Thirties, on again to become almost a social commentator after the war, and on yet again in the 60s (as he himself was ageing) to become a knight of chivalry. One would not have expected this from the early books in which Campion, related in some unspecified way to the royal family, is at times unbearably asinine. His manservant is a reformed burglar, **Magersfontein Lugg**, an idea that must have seemed a great hoot when Allingham thought of it but which as the tales develop and become more serious seems increasingly silly (as does his increasingly dated accent). Campion has – indeed, for the sake of the stories he needs – high-up contacts in the police and, as the tales mature, he meets (*Sweet Danger*, 1933) and marries (*Traitor's Purse*, 1941) the more down-to-earth aircraft engineer (a spirit of the times) **Amanda Fitton**.

The fact that Campion aged was but one of his unusual characteristics. Fictional detectives around him did not change; they remained suspended in the deceptive haze of a timeless afternoon. For this and other reasons the Campion books, though each is quite separate, are best read in sequence, partly so we can live with the hero as he changes but also so we can watch the author refine her work. Allingham is more than competent to begin with, bringing us a young and merry Campion, carefree adventurer, who (assuming you like this sort of thing) glides through delightful reads such as the first book, *The Crime at Black Dudley* (1929), then into *Mystery Mile* (1930) and on again to *Look to the Lady* (1931). The mood darkens with *Dancers in Mourning* (1937). Few could regret its more sombre tone, for this is one of the finest books in the series. As Campion changes, so do his circumstances; he marries, he becomes a father. He also, to an extent, shrugs off and minimises the noble ancestry which had suited the Golden Age but which would not do for a post-war hero. But he retains his old-fashioned decency. In the final books it is his fundamental decency and refusal to run with the cynical nihilism of the age that, surprisingly, makes the Campion books as a series stand out against the slicker but shallower competitors of the time.

Margery Allingham's illustrator husband, Youngman Carter,

collaborated with her on many of the early stories and when she died in 1966 he completed her *Cargo of Eagles* (1968), then wrote *Mr Campion's Farthing* (1969) explaining that it was a book that he and his wife had devised before her death. It was a bizarre and convoluted thriller about the search for a man who has vanished with a 'diabolical formula'. (Carter went on to write another but the magic had gone.)

When considering the full Allingham output it remains true that the series is best approached in its entirety – but even a selection should be read in sequence. Of the earliest (and more frivolous) I recommend *The Crime at Black Dudley* (1929) and *Look to the Lady* (1931), then *Sweet Danger* (1933) and *Death of a Ghost* (1934), followed by *Flowers for the Judge* (1936). *Dancers in Mourning* (1937) is a must, as is *Coroner's Pidgin* (1945) and the essential thriller *The Tiger in the Smoke* (1952). Of the remaining volumes, perhaps *The Beckoning Lady* (1955) is the finest. There are also several short story collections, although not all the stories – especially in *The Allingham Minibus* (1973) – are about Campion.

Tiger in the Smoke was an evocative film (with **Donald Sinden** and **Muriel Pavlov**) which includes an extraordinary scene in which Pavlov, locked in a cupboard, acted more effectively with her eyes than many another actress managed with her entire body.

CANALETTO
by Janet Laurence
The historical record doesn't say much about Canaletto's abilities as a private eye, but the record is redressed in Laurence's brief series of **historical art mysteries** in which whenever the Italian artist pops across to Britain to push his wares he becomes involved in local skulduggery. In the first book, *Canaletto and the Case of Westminster Bridge*, set in 1746, the flamboyant artist visits Georgian London to meet, he hopes, his would-be collectors. Unfortunately the city is also home to folks who wish him dead. Undaunted, he comes back to London two years later for another dose, fails to learn his lesson and returns a third time to become embroiled in the schemes and build-up to a visit by Bonnie Prince Charlie.
Canaletto and the Case of Westminster Bridge (1997), *Canaletto and the Case of the Privy Garden* (1999), *Canaletto and the Case of Bonnie Prince Charlie* (2002).

SIR ROBERT CAREY
by P F Chisholm (aka Patricia Finney)
Deputy Warden of the Scottish Borders and more importantly cousin to **Elizabeth the First**, he can hardly fail to become caught up in the tussles between Scots and English. Responsible as he is for upholding law he also has to solve murders – and at times, fight for his life.
A Famine of Horses (1994), *A Season of Knives* (1995), *A Surfeit of Guns* (1996), *A Plague of Angels* (1998)

CARNABY

by Peter N Walker

Carnaby was the first series from this prolific author (in real life a lifelong police officer), another of whose characters inspired the popular TV series *Heartbeat*. Detective Sergeant James Aloysius Carnaby-King, to give him his full name, is a more flamboyant character than is **Nick Rowan** in *Heartbeat* and perhaps too flamboyant for a Yorkshire beat. Carnaby has a private income, so has a freer attitude to his work, and from time to time he becomes involved in cases which allow him to work undercover.

The first book was *Carnaby and the Hijackers* in 1967 and the eleventh and last was *Carnaby and the Campaigners* in 1984.

CARNACKI

by William Hope Hodgson

Psychic detective who solves cases that involve the supernatural via an interesting mix of ancient wisdom and modern science. The ideas are better than the writing. The original nine stories are collected in *Carnacki, the Ghost Finder* (1913).

MAX CARRADOS

by Ernest Bramah

While rival writers competed to devise more and more idiosyncratic private detectives Bramah hoped he'd scooped them all with the creation of a blind detective who had to solve his cases by reason alone. In the tales, Carrados is consulted by a sighted detective, **Louis Carlyle**, who turns to his old friend because he himself is unable to solve the mysteries. Carlyle becomes Watson to Max Carrados. He is himself an inquiry agent who changed his name and, to some extent his profession, when he was struck off as a solicitor for falsifying a trust account (with good intentions, one assumes). He is one of the more intelligent Watsons, as he needs to be, since he provides the eyes for Carrados. These are light-hearted but clever stories of their period. By no means all are murder stories; they include kidnap, jewel theft and missing persons. Even Carrados himself is kidnapped – and proves far from helpless. The stories are collected into *Max Carrados* (1914), *The Eyes of Max Carrados* (1923) and *The Max Carrados Mysteries* (1927). (Bramah also wrote the **Kai Lung** stories.)

DCI JAMES CARRICK

by Margaret Duffy

Carrick turns up in an occasional series of his own and also makes cameo appearances in some of Duffy's **Gillard & Langley** series. He is a Detective Chief Inspector in the CID, working in historic Bath, and during the series marries his one-time sergeant Joanna Mackenzie.

Dressed to Kill started the 4-book series in 1994, which appears not to have continued (on its own) since *A Fine Target* in 1998.

WEBB CARRICK

by Bill Knox

Carrick works for the **Scottish Fishery Protection Service**, investigating and at times hunting down nautical marauders. In different books he tackles gun-runners, spies, murderers and the inevitable smugglers. Action takes place both at sea and on various Scottish islands, and it is the locale that provides much of the interest.

The Scavengers came first in 1964, with a new adventure every two or three years until The Drowning Nets in 1991.

YVONNE CARTIER

by G. H. Teed, then several other authors

Cartier was a welcome addition to the **Sexton Blake** team, appearing first in 1913, and widening the appeal of the series from young boys to their fathers. An Australian adventuress, elegant but pugnacious, very intelligent, a mistress of disguise, she first embarked on her trail of retribution in Beyond Reach of the Law after being defrauded by business associates of her dead father. That crusade set her initially on the opposite side to Blake – and showed her superior to him: she kidnaps both Blake and Tinker, fools him with her disguise and escapes without help from a moorland prison. Though she is blonde and beautiful, Blake is struck by her beautiful mind! In many subsequent stories they work together – with Tinker panting dutifully behind – and their robustly chaste relationship continued till 1929.

Cartier appeared in many Sexton Blake stories, mainly in Union Jack magazine.

Yvonne Cartier joined the Sexton Blake team.

HENRI CASTANG

by Nicolas Freeling

French police detective operating out of Brussels, by the author of the more successful **Van der Valk** and similar to him in that he tackles specifically European cases. Castang was introduced around the time the Van der Valk series came to an end. There was a degree of overlap in that Van der Valk's wife **Arlette** appeared with Castang in Lady MacBeth, but Castang was too dry and European to appeal to British readers.

A series of 17 books, including the first, A Dressing of Diamond (1974), What are the Bugles Blowing For? (1975), Lake Isle (1976), The Night Lords (1978), The Back of the North Wind (1983), A City Solitary (1985), Lady MacBeth (1988), Not as Far as Velma (1989), You Who Know (1993), A Dwarf Kingdom (1996).

Eddie Constantine as Caution.

LEMMY CAUTION

by Peter Cheyney

Introduced in the 1930s and hugely popular through the '40s and '50s, Caution was a British-based, trench-coated, fedora-wearing FBI agent at a time when such men could be heroes. His **G-Man** status let him roam wartime Britain in pursuit of criminals and spies, ostensibly on

behalf of American Intelligence, though this thin excuse for his presence in Britain faded as Lemmy became assimilated and took on tasks for British masters. Caution seemed to be one of the few men at the time able to lay his hands on a fast car – and fuel – when he wanted it. He laid hands on a number of compliant 'dames' as well, and was unashamed about it:

'It is as dark as hell. The moon has scrammed an' a fine rain is fallin'. It is one of them nights when you oughta be discussin' the war with something' in a pink negligee an' a nice frame of mind.

Typical wisdom from Lemmy Caution.

Equally at home at Scotland Yard, the American Embassy, in low-life nightclubs and on romantically dangerous private boats moored offshore, Caution's two-fisted direct approach had everything his readers wished for. War was dreary, life was careful – but with Caution it could be fun.

This Man Is Dangerous (1936), starts this series and continues through twelve books until *I'll Say She Does* in 1945 and *G Man at the Yard* in 1946. They can be read in any sequence.

In the 1950s several *film noir* dramas were made starring **Eddie Constantine** as Caution. First came *La Mome Vert Des Gris* based on *Poison Ivy*, followed by *Cet Homme Est Dangerous* and five other Caution movies before the extraordinary Jean-Luc Goddard sci-fi film *Alphaville. Comment Qu'elle Est!* (1960) is perhaps the best of the films.

LOIS CAYLEY
by Grant Allen

'Nature had endowed me with a profusion of crisp, black hair, and plenty of high spirits.' Thus does Lois introduce herself, and thus does she show she was created by a man. **A breezy, bicycling, mountain-climbing, camel-riding, tiger-hunting ex-Girton girl** from the Victorian age, Lois sleuths her way through Europe secure in the knowledge that Britain is best and adventure is all. She outwits the foreigners and, not surprisingly, finds herself an attractive fiancé.

The Adventures of the Amateur Commission Agent (1898), *Miss Caley's Adventures* (1899) and various *Strand* magazine stories.

THOMAS CHALONER
by Susanna Gregory

In this fairly new series from a writer more famous for her **Brother Bartholomew** series, we meet Thomas Chaloner, an ex-Commonwealth spy trying to earn a living in the restoration London of **King Charles II**. His work for the Lord Chancellor takes him from the dangerous underworld in England's biggest city to crime and corruption at the highest levels.

A Conspiracy of Violence (2006), *Blood on the Strand* (2007).

DI PAT CHAPPEL TV series *The Vice* (1999)
by Barry Simner & Rob Pursey

Ken Stott established himself as Britain's top cop portrayer with his appearance in *The Vice* as crumpled, lived-in, battered and streetwise Pat Chappel, long-term member and now leader of the Met's Vice Squad, committed to his work, sympathetic to its victims and relentless against villains – even when found within the force. He blames the pimp, not the prostitute; the dealer, not the addict. Some of the victims become his friends. It's a mark of Stott's screen presence that we find it entirely credible that people at the bottom of the heap see this policeman as a friend and in some cases as rather more. They can rely on him. They can turn to him. Chappel has seen enough to know that while there is no depth to which men won't go, their victims are truly helpless. As each new case lumbers in we sense the effort with which he has to lift himself to face it. His private life is negligible, but this only adds to his believability, since no wife could bear his daily immersion in vice and iniquity. Even the viewer can find it tough, for this is a series which goes in hard, exposing but not exploiting the world of tawdry vice.

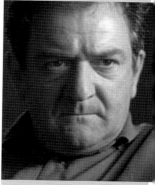

Ken Stott as Pat Chappel.

SIOBHAN CLARKE
(see **Rebus**)

SERGEANT CLUFF
by Gil North
Not to be confused with Wilkie Collins' Sergeant Cuff, Detective Sergeant Caleb Cluff is a modern-day small-town policeman in **Yorkshire** (perhaps in Skipton, though called Gunnarshaw here). Not your present-day smart cop, Cluff wears heavy country tweeds, carries a stick and wears a tweed hat with a feather in it. He even has a sheepdog called Clive – but then, he comes from Yorkshire, not Peckham. Curious mysteries, very Yorkshire.

Sergeant Cluff Stands Firm (1960) is the aptly-named first in the series which includes such titles as *Sergeant Cluff Goes Fishing* (1962), *More Deaths for Sergeant Cluff* (1963), *The Confounding of Sergeant Cluff* (1966), and *Sergeant Cluff Rings True* (1972)

Cluff appeared on BBC TV in 1964 and 1965. **Leslie Sands**, as Caleb Cluff, did well not to be upstaged by either Clive, his loyal collie, or by the stunning Yorkshire countryside. (We watched in black and white in those days).

INSPECTOR COFFIN
by Gwendoline Butler
The most extraordinary aspect of John Coffin is where he works. He works in London, but not a London that exists. The boroughs, especially those in which Coffin operates, sound and feel like real places but are in fact invented; they are subtly different from but almost... one is never

quite sure where. (Blackheath is the best guess. Almost.) Freed from the constraints of real geography and real people, Butler let her imagination loose; the London she presented was stranger than reality, almost Dickensian a century later. She herself described her books as Victorian gothic and her locale as the **Second City of London**. In *A Coffin from the Past* even her time sequence became ambiguous, and in *A Dark Coffin* that familiar plot device, the twin brother, was doubly ambiguous: we were told a character had a twin brother but as the tale unfolded we began to wonder: had he? The theatre and all of its illusions intrudes into more than one book. Even transvestism makes an appearance – and this too wrong-foots the reader, who has been lulled into believing that the book is a conventional crime story, almost a cosy police procedural. The effect is subtle, but bold. It doesn't always work. With the Coffin stories it's particularly important to start with one that does work. The first Coffin book, *Dead in a Row* came out in 1957, but had Inspector Coffin in a role secondary to another of Butler's occasional characters, **Inspector Winter**, who shared the limelight again with Coffin in *The Dull Dead* (1958) and *The Murdering Kind* (1958 also). Coffin soon outshone Winter and then continued to appear almost annually through the Sixties and Seventies. He slowed in the Eighties, only to return to annual appearances from 1987 to 2002. *A Coffin from the Past* (1970) is especially good, and *A Dark Coffin* (1995) showed that the magic hadn't faded. *Coffin on the Water* (1986) flipped back to Coffin's first ever case, just after he was demobbed from the war. *A Grave Coffin* (1998) and *A Coffin for the Canary* (1974) are interesting. Late in the series Coffin rises from Inspector to Commissioner. Practically all books have *Coffin* in the title.

ROBERT COLBECK
by Edward Marston
Detective Inspector Robert Colbeck is a **Victorian Railway Detective** in his 30s and on his cases is assisted by his colleague Detective Sergeant **Victor Leeming**. The series is set in the 1850s when the railway had opened up the land, making travel a reality for millions who had never before gone beyond the nearest market town. But fast and easy travel transformed crime – as did the fact that trains carried quantities of goods, mail and even bullion. It is a bullion robbery from a train that Colbeck and Leeming have to solve in their first adventure, *The Railway Detective*, set at the time of the Great Exhibition of 1851. Colbeck also has to rescue a female hostage. In *The Iron Horse* a train is unloaded in Crewe, a man's hatbox is dropped and a human head spills out, leading into an investigation that takes Colbeck first to Ireland and then into the stables of three main contenders for the 1854 Derby at Epsom. A neck-and-neck race to find the villain ensues.
The Railway Detective (2004), *The Excursion Train* (2005), *The Railway Viaduct* (2006), *The Iron Horse* (2007).

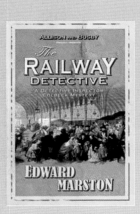

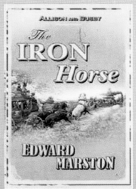

BEN COOPER

by Stephen Booth

Detective Constable Ben Cooper serves with Derbyshire Constabulary in England's **Peak District** and is the son of a sergeant killed on duty. As a 'local lad' he cares about the people he deals with, and the resulting conflict of loyalties and his uneasiness with some aspects of modern police work can lead him into trouble. In a pleasant change from the usual male cop / female cop partnership and its inevitable romantic interest, Ben Cooper has a rough time from his superior officer, the ambitious DS **Diane Fry**. (Some female readers have written to the author complaining about Cooper's treatment at her hands.) In 2003 Stephen Booth won the CWA's Dagger in the Library award for the author whose books gave readers most pleasure.

Ben Cooper first appeared in *Black Dog* (2000), which won the Barry Award for Best British Crime Novel in the USA, and in 2003 Ben was a finalist for the Sherlock Award for Best Detective created by a British author. The next Ben Cooper novel, *Dancing with the Virgins* (2001), won a second Barry Award. *Blood on the Tongue* (2002), *Blind to the Bones* (2003) and *One Last Breath* (2004) were all shortlisted for awards. They were followed by *The Dead Place* (2005), *Scared To Live* (2006) and *Dying to Sin* (2007).

DEN COOPER

by Rebecca Tope

Detective Constable Cooper (only a constable initially) works a rural patch and the crimes he deals with have a farming background. (The author runs her own small farm.) Cooper appears first in *A Dirty Death* (1999) and has to investigate the murder of a corpse found in a slurry pit. The second Den Cooper title is *Death of a Friend* and the third *A Death to Record*. In the fourth in this series, *The Sting of Death* (2002), Cooper meets and join forces with Rebecca Tope's other early hero, **Drew Slocombe**.

A Dirty Death (1999), *Death of a Friend* (2000), *A Death to Record* (2001), *The Sting of Death* (2002).

HUGH CORBETT

by Paul Doherty

A strong series from this astonishingly prolific author of historical crime novels, the Corbett novels feature a clerk of the King's Bench in the Court of Chancery, who finds plenty of time between scribing to solve classical puzzle mysteries, including in his first, a locked room mystery (the locked room being a church). Corbett is aided (and sometimes frustrated) in his quests by a semi-reformed felon, **Ranulfatte Newgate**, whose attitude to wrongdoers is rather more robust than is Corbett's. Corbett would bring a bad man to book; Newgate would kill him.

Satan in St Mary's (1986) starts the series and is where to begin.

C

CORINTH AND BROWN
by David Roberts

In a curious throwback to the aristocratic detective novels of the Golden Age, David Roberts has created Lord Edward Corinth and his journalist companion Verity Brown. The well-bred pair tackle much the same crimes their forbears did (which is hardly surprising, given that the stories are set in the Thirties and are a deliberate recreation of those times). They become involved in mysteries against backgrounds of elegant cruise liners, private aircraft, the French Riviera, country house parties and the turf. Much of the pleasure in these books comes from idling one's hours in times unlike our own:

> Edward had put Frank up for his club and thought he might like to meet some of the younger members he did not already know. He was pleased that the boy seemed uninterested in 'doing the season' – a ritual he had endured under protest, finding it demeaning – a marriage market in which deals were made with women hunting men down like frightened foxes.

From *A Grave Man*

Sweet Poison began the series (which can be read in any order). *A Grave Man* was the sixth, in 2005, followed by *The Quality of Mercy* in 2006, then *Something Wicked* in 2007.

MONTAGUE CORK
by Macdonald Hastings

Cork was general manager of the Anchor Insurance Company, a position which occasionally involved him in offbeat investigations. Old when the series started (about sixty and looking forward to retirement) he nevertheless managed to stalk grumpily through five rather old-fashioned but worthwhile books – worthwhile more for their setting and style than for the ingeniousness of their mysteries.

Cork on the Water (1951) came first, with Montague Cork in some pleasant if rainy country around the Scottish salmon rivers, but *Cork in Bottle* (1953, without *The*) sunk him in a macabre East Anglian village called Bottle. *Cork and the Serpent* (also 1953) involved him in horse racing and some fairly decorous prostitution. *Cork in the Doghouse* (1957) may have been his best book, and concerned illegal dog fighting, while *Cork on the Telly* (1966) plunged Cork into an environment his broadcasting author knew well.

Dr TUDOR CORNWALL
by Tim Heald

Head of the Criminal Investigations Dept, University of Wessex, and ably assisted by his Tasmanian friend **Elizabeth Burney**, Doctor Cornwall delves into curious problems from the present day and the past, often coming up against his adversary Professor Ashley Carpenter. This unusual mix of past and present, real and fictional, sees Cornwall and Burnley investigate a murder in a foreign university, the murder of Alec d'Urberville in Thomas Hardy's great novel *Tess*, and a real-life

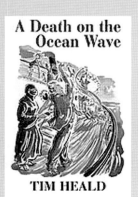

murder under his very nose when he is guest lecturer on a cruise liner. Which book is which is obvious: *Death and the Visiting Fellow* (2004), *Death and the d'Urbervilles* (2005), *A Death on the Ocean Wave* (2007).

NIC COSTA

by David Hewson

Maverick **Rome-based cop** whose career becomes more shaky with each new escapade. Initially idealistic until soured by corruption within the force, his initial battering in *A Season for the Dead* (2003) would have made a lesser man quit the force. Fortunately he stayed for this dark dense dramatic series. In the first Costa book a serial killer's imaginative approach to slaughter recreated the martyrdom of saints, while in the second book, *Villa of Mysteries*, a girl was found in a peat bog outside Rome with her throat cut. She wore a ceremonial dress and had a coin inside her mouth. Was it to ease her passage to the next world? *The Sacred Cut* moved on from these themes; set during the Christmas after the second Gulf War, it was permeated by the clamour around Iraq and the fallout it caused, sometimes among friends. But in *The Seventh Sacrament* Hewson returned to Rome's invaluable mix of religion and violent history. Human sacrifice, religions that pre-date Christianity, Rome's subterranean passages, and a 14-year-old T-shirt that begins to show fresh bloodstains... Add a father intent on vengeance and we have another darkly disturbing tale.

A Season for the Dead (2003), then *The Villa of Mysteries* (2004) a strong sequel. *The Lizard's Bite* (2005) and *The Sacred Cut* (2006) followed, and *The Seventh Sacrament* followed with cults and the Vatican again in *The Garden of of Evil* (2007) and *Dante's Numbers* (2008).

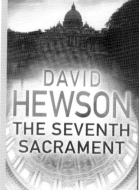

David Hewson.

DAVID
HEWSON
THE SEVENTH
SACRAMENT

MELISSA CRAIG

by Betty Rowlands

An amateur detective can seem credible in a stand-alone novel but becomes unlikely in a series. Rowlands overcomes this by making Melissa Craig a working crime novelist, attracted to scenes of crime. She also has friends such as a journalist boyfriend, a friendly police contact and a nearby doctor. The **Cotswold settings** and the titles of these books make them sound more cosy than they are, for the rural idyll is disturbed by drug smugglers, murderers and thieves. Melissa moves to her village in the first book, *A Little Gentle Sleuthing*, in the hope that little will disturb her writing – but before long receives a succession of mysterious telephone calls. And she has not quite escaped her previous, over-protective boyfriend. Settling in to her new environment in *Finishing Touch* she takes a part-time job teaching creative writing – but someone has been too creative, and the department secretary is found with her throat slashed. By the seventh, *Deadly Legacy*, Melissa's familiarity with murder makes her the obvious choice to complete the manuscript of a recently murdered crime

BETTY
ROWLANDS
SWEET VENOM
A MELISSA CRAIG MYSTERY

'A clearly gifted and knowledgeable writer, never less than engaging and readable'
Financial Times

novelist. When she reads it, she thinks it might hold the clue to a series of local sex murders. Then there are those recent burglaries. Could they be linked? By the time we reach *No Laughing Matter* even Melissa's mother isn't safe. In her nursing home two residents have been poisoned.

Titles include *A Little Gentle Sleuthing* (1990), *Finishing Touch* (1991), *Deadly Legacy* (1995), and *No Laughing Matter* (2003). They are best read in sequence.

THEA CRAWFORD
by Jessica Mann

Crawford might have inspired a series in her own right but in the event was shunted out by her protégée **Tamara Hoyland**. There were only two Crawford books, though she makes appearances in some Hoyland stories. Thea Crawford, a recently appointed professor of archaeology at Edinburgh, debuts in *The Only Security* (1973), follows up with *Captive Audience* (1975) and sends Tamara on her second adventure in *No Man's Island* (1983). Thea's own adventures are more cerebral and closer to home, more concerned with academic in-fighting at the university (even if, in her second tale, a corpse is discovered while the students are rioting).

The Only Security (1973), *Captive Audience* (1975), plus appearances in some Hoyland books.

DAVE CREEGAN TV series *Touching Evil* (1997)
(creator: Paul Abbott)

Before the series began DI Dave Creegan was shot in the head, which perhaps explains his unconventional approach to the job they gave him next, with the Organised and Serial Crime Unit, tracking down serial killers, child abusers and the like. A divorced father of two, intelligent, and with no further complications in his private life, **Robson Green** threw himself with relish into the action each story brought.

SERGEANT CRIBB
by Peter Lovesey

One of the most successful examples of a cop transplanted to a different era, Cribb personifies the Victorian age, in particular the 1880s. Cribb arrived fully realised in the first book, *Wobble To Death*, which was in fact the first (prize-winning) book from an as-then unpublished writer who has since gone on to become prolific, popular and a winner of more prizes. Cribb, with his faithful **Constable Thackeray**, is a solid, almost stolid, Victorian policeman, steady as a rock and a necessary bulwark against the weird and murky waters in which his author plunges him. Cribb stands fast against the tide when murder halts a marathon walking contest (*Wobble To Death*), when people hit below the belt (in the bare-knuckle boxing matches of *The Detective Wore Silk Drawers*), at the seaside (in *Mad Hatter's Holiday*) and against malevolent spirits from 'the other side' (in *A Case of Spirits*). The stories came out one a

Peter Lovesey.

year in the 1970s and then suddenly stopped. The author had moved on (see **Peter Diamond**) but had left a splendid legacy.

Wobble to Death (1970), *The Detective Wore Silk Drawers* (1971), *Abracadaver* (1972), *Mad Hatter's Holiday* (1973), *Invitation to a Dynamite Party* (1974), *A Case of Spirits* (1975), *Swing, Swing Together* (1976), *Waxwork* (1978)

After a pilot in 1979 *Cribb* became a television series on ITV in 1980 and 81, in which Cribb was played by **Alan Dobie** and Thackeray by **William Simons**. For once the detail and atmosphere of the TV episodes matched those of the original books.

Alan Dobie.

CROWNER JOHN
by Bernard Knight

Crowner John is the first coroner for Devon, in 1194, **Sir John de Wolfe** (the eponymous Crowner John, 'Crowner' meaning coroner) and his adventures are suffused with the events and colour of the twelfth century. When we meet him first, in *The Sanctuary Seeker*, Sir John, fresh back from the crusades, holds an inquest on an unidentified body. The dead man turns out to be a fellow crusader, and Sir John's own brother-in-law Sheriff **Richard de Revelle** is a deliberate obstacle to the investigation. In *The Poisoned Chalice* a businessman's daughter is raped, and Crowner John must bring the unknown assailant to justice. Meanwhile Lady Adele de Courcey dies after an illegal abortion, and John suspects the two events are related. The ninth book, *Figure of Hate* (2005), begins with a jousting day at which an altercation breaks out between Hugh Peverel, Lord of Sampford Peverel, and a stranger by the name of Reginald de Charterai. Two days later, Hugh's body is found in a barn. Is de Charterai to blame? Crowner John finds plenty of other suspects for the killing of the almost universally hated Hugh Peverel. All three of his brothers had a motive: two for the succession and the third to steal Hugh's attractive young wife, Beatrice. It's no secret that Beatrice herself detested her adulterous husband, as did his mother-in-law, Adelina. Another suspect is Godwin Thatcher, a Saxon villager whose two sons were hanged some months earlier, having been arbitrarily sentenced by Hugh at his manorial court. In *The Elixir of Death* medieval politics force their way through: Prince John wants to seize the throne from his brother, Richard the Lionheart, and is supported by Philip of France. Philip offers to help by sending John a mysterious alchemist, Nizam the Mohammedan, who claims to be able to turn base materials into gold. But the ship is found wrecked off the south Devon coast, its crew savagely slaughtered, while shortly afterwards a Norman knight named is foully murdered and his severed head is stuck on the rood screen of Exeter cathedral. Crowner John investigates, and finds Richard de Revelle once again involved.

The Sanctuary Seeker (1998), immediately followed by *The Poisoned Chalice* (1998), *Crowner's Quest* (1999) and a book a year including *The Elixir Of Death* (2006), *The Noble Outlaw* (2007) and *The Manor of Death* (2008).

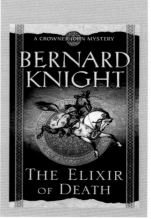

A CROWNER JOHN MYSTERY
BERNARD KNIGHT
THE ELIXIR OF DEATH

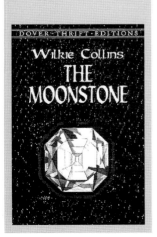

Wilkie Collins.

SERGEANT CUFF
by Wilkie Collins

The Moonstone (1868), often called **the first detective novel**, introduces Sergeant Cuff. In some ways, the book is more remarkable than its detective, as its technique of first setting up an intriguing mystery (the loss of a precious stone) and then telling the story through several narrators, while all the time maintaining a vigorous pace untypical for the nineteenth century, marks this book as one of the most significant of its day. For readers wary of Victorian novels, Collins's two masterpieces, *The Moonstone* and especially *The Woman in White*, are ideal places to start.

Sergeant Cuff is not the main character of *The Moonstone* but he is a true detective, and his search to discover who took the jewel and how forms the backbone of the story. Cuff is not a young man; grey-haired, clad in black, a hatchet-faced man with a love of roses, he interrogates, examines clues and uses inspired deduction to solve the crime. Nor is he a hero; Collins's description has all the ambivalence that the Victorians had toward these newfangled paid spies.

> *... a grizzled, elderly man, so miserably lean that he looked as if he had not got an ounce of flesh on his bones in any part of him. He was dressed all in decent black, with a white cravat round his neck. His face was as sharp as a hatchet, and the skin of it was as yellow and dry as an autumn leaf. His eyes, of a steely light grey, had a very disconcerting trick, when they encountered your eyes, of looking as if they expected something more of you than you were aware of yourself. His walk was soft; his voice was melancholy; his long lanky fingers were hooked like claws. He might have been a parson, or an undertaker, or anything else you like, except what he really was.*
>
> From *The Moonstone*, 1868 by Wilkie Collins.

Cuff is not a particularly interesting man – later writers would burden their detectives with a heavy mass of idiosyncrasies – but he never bores the reader, largely because Collins keeps him off the page for long chapters at a time. The book's several narrators come in their turn like witnesses in the box, and Cuff stands by as quietly as a judge. He is human too, sometimes making mistakes, and sharing those mistakes with the reader. Like **Inspector Bucket** Sergeant Cuff was based on an identifiable real policeman – in his case Inspector **Jonathan Whicher** of the Detective Department, well-known to readers of true-crime reports of the day for his role in the Constance Kent murder, after which he was labelled 'the Prince of Detectives'. Cuff, though, is a fictional creation, a character sharply drawn by Collins and, although not overburdened with peculiar traits, those that he does have are ones that later writers would re-use to flesh out their own detectives, such as his deliberate use of apparently irrelevant questions (a trick he could have learned from Inspector Bucket) and a habit of trimming his nails with a penknife to buy time. Cuff's patient manner leads nevertheless to an extraordinary denouement – an extraordinarily nineteenth-century

denouement – in which exotic opium plays a significant part. Collins later claimed that he had dictated much of the novel while under the influence of the drug.
The Moonstone (1868).

GIL CUNNINGHAM
by Pat McIntosh

Gil Cunningham is a notary – a recently qualified lawyer – in **medieval Scotland**, and the stories have him investigate mysteries in various kinds of religious institution: monasteries, cathedrals and lowly almshouses in and around fifteenth-century Glasgow. In *The Harper's Quine* he investigates the murder of a cruel nobleman's runaway wife; in *St Mungo's Robin* it is the murder of an almshouse warden. (Gil is short for Gilbert.)
The Harper's Quine (2004), *The Nicholas Feast* (2005), *The Merchant's Mark* (2006), *St Mungo's Robin* (2007), *The Rough Collier* (2008).

ADAM DALGLIESH
P. D. James

Dalgliesh is one of the most famous British policemen of modern times. But although he is a policeman the books he appears in are not police procedurals. Indeed, James has made it clear she writes *detective* stories, in which readers are presented with sufficient clues to work out the mystery for themselves – if they are clever enough. Set mainly in East Anglia and written with a fine sense of place, the books paint an accurate portrait of provincial – sometimes clerical – life, but at the same time they don't shirk giving details of dead bodies and pathological practice. The author knows her subject, having held senior positions both in hospital administration and in the Home Office; thus when James writes of pathologists and mortuaries she knows whereof she writes. She describes in detail. With her background she has no need to invent when, in her first book, *Cover Her Face*, she describes, sensitively but not sensationally, life in a home for unmarried mothers (this was back in 1962 when single motherhood carried a stigma). Her second, *Mind to Murder*, was set in a psychiatric clinic. In *The Black Tower* much of the story took place in a home for incurables, and in *Death of an Expert Witness* she described practices inside a forensic research laboratory. So it went on.

Adam Dalgliesh is a tall, sensitive but lonely man, son of a vicar, who lives both in London and East Anglia, where he owns a converted windmill. He is a professional cop, somewhat stolid and painstaking, though in his spare time he is a poet. In the early books he nurses the emotional wounds of bereavement, having lost both his wife and son within hours of the boy's birth, and he never quite gets over this. Gradually he thaws but, book on book, he remains a private, even introverted person whose life is in his work. He is rewarded for his successes, starting out as an Inspector, becoming Superintendent, and eventually rising to become Commander.

P. D. James.

Paul Johnston.

Tally looked across at the Commander. She thought of faces as being either softly moulded or carved. His was carved. It was a handsome authoritative face and the dark eyes that looked into hers were kindly. He had an attractive voice, and voices had always been important to her. And then she remembered Muriel's words.

The police believe nothing. That's the way they're trained to think.

From *The Murder Room*.

The provincial realism of Dalgliesh's work and private life takes the books well away from the hard edges of crime noir, but within their own more civilised world they are supreme. The stories run deep and the reasons for the crimes within them can be complex. Characters are carefully drawn, as are the landscapes, and over the years Adam Dalgliesh has gathered a large and loyal readership.

Books: *Cover Her Face* (1962), *A Mind to Murder* (1963), *Unnatural Causes* (1967), *Shroud for a Nightingale* (1971) won the CWA Silver Dagger, *The Black Tower* (1975) won a second CWA Silver Dagger, *Death of an Expert Witness* (1977), *A Taste for Death* (1986) won both the CWA Silver Dagger and a Macavity, *Devices and Desires* (1989), *Original Sin* (1994), *A Certain Justice* (1997), *Death in Holy Orders* (2001), *The Murder Room* (2003), *The Lighthouse* (2005).

The Dalgliesh adventures were televised by Anglia TV under individual book titles, rather than as a 'Dalgliesh series'. **Roy Marsden** played Dalgliesh (much to the author's approval) until in 2003 **Martin Shaw** took over the role. *Death of an Expert Witness* began the TV series and was shown in seven parts in 1983, to be followed by most of the other titles through the 1980s and 1990s, mostly again in serial form.

ISABEL DALHOUSIE
by Alexander McCall Smith
Introduced in *The Sunday Philosophy Club*, Isabel Dalhousie is an Edinburgh-based rich maiden lady from the creator of **Precious Ramotswe** (*No 1 Ladies Detective Agency*) in a series which could do almost as well. Equally unlikely as a detective – a description Isabel would dismiss as she edits the *Review of Applied Ethics* and is pedantic enough to protest at the use of adjectives as nouns – Isabel tries to concern herself with the improvement of other people's lives. That this sometimes leads her into their little mysteries is just too bad.
The Right Attitude to Rain (2006).

QUINT DALRYMPLE
by Paul Johnston
The oddly named Quintilian Dalrymple is a private detective in a surprisingly recognisable Edinburgh, given that the novels are set some twenty-five years into an imaginary future. Dalrymple and his sidekick, Davie the Guardsman, fight most of their battles against an all-encroaching, all-corroding bureaucratic state – a clear satire on today's bureaucratic oligarchy, in which neither Blair's nor Brown's Anglo-

Scottish Britain nor a post-devolution Scotland seemed to have much attraction for the author. Darkly comic mysteries, they were a critical and commercial success from the first. *Body Politic* won the CWA John Creasey Award for best first novel for 1997. Four subsequent novels continued the **futuristic crime theme**, each featuring the same maverick investigator, although quite who Dalrymple was investigating on behalf of whom seemed as much a mystery to the detective as it was to the reader.

Body Politic (1997), *The Bone Yard* (1998), *Water Of Death* (1999), *The Blood Tree* (2000), *The House of Dust* (2001).

DALZIEL & PASCOE
by Reginald Hill

Unlike each other as these two are, they must nevertheless be treated as a pair. Each *could* exist without the other – there are plenty of times when each wishes the other would disappear – but alone they might fade into mediocrity. Strong characters each, they need each other – for they are polar opposites, existing by contrast to each other. Dalziel (whose name television has taught us to pronounce Dee-ell) is overweight and coarse, deliberately rude and prejudiced, a northern male, while Pascoe, his sergeant, is neat and refined, intelligent, and dutifully married (for much of the series). Dalziel sneers at the label PC (whether for Politically Correct or Personal Computer, for neither of which he has time) while Peter Pascoe is fastidiously proper. If Pascoe ever slipped he'd face a stinging reprimand from his wife Ellie, who is more correct than he: straight-laced, a feminist, lacking humour. In the books one rather admires her (albeit reluctantly, if one is male) though on TV she became unbearable. Only Peter could have been sorry when they broke up – unless perhaps Dalziel mourned Ellie's passing; she had been a worthy opponent to him, snapping in his face, giving back anything the fat man hurled at her. Grudging respect, one felt, on both sides.

That Reginald Hill made either of these policemen likeable is an achievement. Dalziel is an intemperate hard-drinking bully who uses offensiveness as a weapon, while any description of Peter Pascoe (even his name) makes him sound far too goody-goody. Yet Dalziel is the roughest diamond, and beneath the boorish crust hides a man who cares deeply about fairness, justice and his job. 'Make 'em think you're a thick, racist, sexist pig,' Dalziel tells Peter in *A Killing Kindness*. 'Then they underestimate you and overreach themselves.' Pascoe can be sly, he can manipulate, he can even, when the chips are down, swing his fists and put the boot in. (Though Heaven help him if Ellie sees.) Thus do two monstrous caricatures become human. Hill is a skilful writer, good on description, a little too free with quotes occasionally, but excellent with jokes. It is the jokes, together with terse descriptions and artfully tangled plots, that even before television stepped in to wave its magic wand, had already made this series a solid and popular success.

Dalziel lay naked in the dead man's bed under half a dozen blankets. After stripping off his wet clothes and towelling himself down till his flabby and fat-corrugated skin glowed, suddenly a warm nap had seemed the best of all things.

From *An April Shroud*, 1975.

A Clubbable Woman (a typically non-PC pun) kicked off the series in 1970, followed by *An Advancement of Learning* (1971), *Ruling Passion* in 1973, *April Shroud* (1975) and *A Pinch of Snuff* in 1978, which despite its genteel title was about snuff and porno films. Five more titles came in the Eighties, then two in 1990: *Bones and Silence*, which many consider the finest in the series, and *One Small Step*. A further eight titles followed, beginning with *Recalled to Life* and recent titles including *Dialogues Of The Dead* (2001), *Good Morning, Midnight* (2004), *For Love Nor Money* (2005), *Secrets of the Dead* (2005), *Death Comes for the Fat Man*, aka *The Death of Dalziel* (2007) and *The Last National Serviceman* (2007).

Dalziel and Pascoe began on BBC TV in 1996 with **Warren Clarke** as Detective Superintendent Andy Dalziel, and **Colin Buchanan** as Detective Sergeant (later Detective Inspector) Peter Pascoe. **Susannah Corbett** played Ellie. The show ran to several series. There had been an initial three-part pilot, *A Pinch of Snuff* starring the comedians **Hale and Pace** in the title roles, but it is Clarke and Buchanan who have become identified with the characters.

CHARMIAN DANIELS
by Jennie Melville

Jennie Melville.

Though Charmian Daniels works in pleasant middle England – Deerham Hill, a new town in an invented patch around **Oxford and the Thames Valley** – she was born in Dundee and educated at Glasgow University. She is a tough no-nonsense Scot in middle-class England, and the books are a similarly contradictory mix of police procedural and modest feminism. Daniels needs to be tough, as much against institutional male prejudice as against villains. (She rises through the ranks in the series from Constable to Superintendent.) Some of her toughest villains are women too, as in *Murder Has A Pretty Face* where the pretty faces belong to a group of pretty but far from fair female criminals. Ambitious at work, she is less guarded in her private life, and in *Murderer's Houses* (1964) an act of untypical carelessness nearly costs Charmian her life. Daniels is described by Melville as having brown eyes and *yellow* hair, which must make her unique in the force.

This long series began back in 1962 with *Come Home and be Killed*, followed by *Burning is a Substitute for Loving* in 1963. Four more followed till *A New Kind of Killer, An Old Kind of Death* in 1970, then came a ten-year gap until *Murder Has A Pretty Face* in 1981, and another gap till *Windsor Red* (1988), after which the books came in a steady stream through the millennium. Melville's knack for great titles is shown by *The Morbid Kitchen* (1995) and *The Woman who was Not There* (1996).

PETER DARINGTON

by Douglas V. Duff

Plucky Peter is a Senior Seaman Cadet who, in the only book about him, fights his way through eight adventures with titles such as *The Rifled Strongroom*, *The Kidnapped Heiress* and *Terror By Night* – which despite their bloodthirsty sound, are stories for (older) children. Even more exciting than the stories are the seven paintings by Nat Long, the first of which is *Peter's Fist Crashed to the Man's Bearded Jaw*. Just the book to read beneath the blankets with a wonky torch.

Peter Darington, Seaman Detective (undated but late 1920s or early 1930s).

ARCHER DAWE

by Joseph Smith Fletcher

'The famous amateur detective, expert criminologist, a human ferret' is how Fletcher described his gruff and solid Yorkshire hero. Though around sixty years of age he had a useful pair of hands – as a handyman: he could cut a spy-hole, mask it, make an impression of a key, and generally foil a miscreant by dint of good old-fashioned Yorkshire craft and common sense. Dawe appeared in a number of short stories from this prolific (if now forgotten) writer, some of which werre collected in *The Adventures of Archer Dawe, Sleuth-Hound* (1909).

SAM DEAN

by Mike Phillips

Odd to think that when Phillips introduced his British-born black journalist cum detective at the end of the Eighties, Sam Dean's skin colour was considered unusual enough for him to be picked out for special attention – much as he was from time to time under the SUS laws. Philips used Dean to display and explore the parallel world of blacks in a country they nominally belonged to but in which they were only junior partners. Dean's cases, unsurprisingly, were in that separate country known as Black Britain. The picture he painted was not a happy one, with easy resource to crime, drugs and casual – literally care free – sex corroding too many lives. The result was to sadden rather than inflame the reader.

Blood Rights (1989), *The Late Candidate* (1990), *Point of Darkness* (1994), *An Image to Die For* (1995).

JUDGE DEE

by Robert van Gulik

Dee was a real-life seventh-century Chinese judge who was brought to the West in translation in 1908 (*Dee Goong An*), but the Gulik tales are recreations in which the author uses his genuine knowledge of **ancient China** (he was a historian) to paint a portrait of a wise detective who not only investigates but dispenses justice. Oh, and he's an expert swordfighter too.

The Chinese Bell Murders (1958), followed by *The Chinese Gold Murders*, *The Chinese Lake Murders*, *The Chinese Nail Murders*, then *The Chinese Maze Murders*, containing *The Murder in the Locked Room*, *The Concealed Will* and *The Girl with the Missing Head*.

The Chinese Gold Murders
Robert van Gulik
A Chinese Detective Story

Keith Miles writes under the pseudonym Edward Marston.

DELCHARD & BRET
by Edward Marston

In a series of books set in the eleventh century at the time of **William the Conqueror**, Ralph Delchard and Gervase Bret are Domesday Commissioners. Delchard, a Norman soldier, is the more senior man, in his thirties, while Bret is a Breton-Saxon lawyer in his twenties. Their work is to help with the compilation of a famous catalogue that will show all King William owns – for which reason many existing owners wish their own properties to be omitted from the survey. Delchard and Bret meet inevitable opposition and come across some highly medieval crimes – such as finding that their chief witness has been killed by a wolf (*The Wolves of Savernake*) or having to investigate a murder when two local barons vie for the hand of a beautiful young woman (*The Elephants of Norwich*).

The Wolves of Savernake (1993), *The Dragons of Archenfield* (1995), *The Lions of the North* (1996), *The Wildcats of Exeter* (1999), *The Elephants of Norwich* (2000)

DORCAS DENE
by George R. Sims

Early example of the female detective; an ex-actress who has to leave the stage for more remunerative work when her husband is blinded, she takes a job in a nearby detective agency. So good is she at her work that when the owner retires, as he soon does, she takes over the agency, advertising herself as 'a professional lady detective'. To help with some of her cases she drafts in her husband, his mother and their sturdy bulldog, **Toddlekins**. Having once been an actress, she is a mistress of disguise. *Dorcas Dene, Detective* (1897).

HARRY DEVLIN
by Martin Edwards

Liverpool solicitor who might have become nothing more were it not that (in the first book of the series) he is the chief suspect when his ex-wife is found murdered. Only amateur detection can save him! *All the Lonely People* is in fact a serious book, and it won the CWA's John Creasey Award for best first crime novel. Devlin books continued at the rate of about two per three years, all solid and well-informed – hardly surprising since the author has a first class degree in law, is a partner in the firm of solicitors that represents Liverpool Football Club (and less exalted clients), writes on the law and is editor to a number of fine crime collections by other hands. Though Devlin is not an alter ego for Martin Edwards, he might share the author's taste in music since, although the books are set in current time (or the time when they were written) they are given backing tracks of 1960s pop music. Those who lived in the 1960s can't forget it. Nor can Liverpool.

All the Lonely People (1991), *Suspicious Minds* (1992), *I Remember You* (1993), *Yesterday's Papers* (1994), *Eve of Destruction* (1996), *The Devil in Disguise* (1998), *The First Cut is the Deepest* (1999). 2008's title, *Waterloo Sunset*, begins with Devlin reading his own obituary!

Martin Edwards.

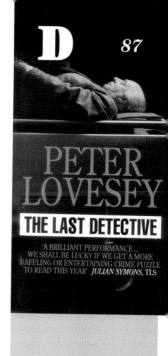

PETER DIAMOND
by Peter Lovesey

Diamond was the first modern-day serial detective from the pen of a writer previously known for his period heroes (**Sergeant Cribb** and other stand-alone novels). An old-style policeman (in that he believes in old-fashioned values), human, occasionally fallible – an engaging man who this clever author plunges into splendidly complex cases (old-style in their intricacy, but up to date in their telling) – based in and around the historic city of **Bath**. The series began in *The Last Detective* with Diamond's resignation from the force as a result of his reluctance to accept the modern and improved methods of policing he felt were being foisted upon him. In the next book *Diamond Solitaire* he had become a private eye but in the third book *The Summons*, to the surprise of many, Diamond moved back into the force (whose attitude changed when a man Diamond had arrested years ago escaped from jail and took a hostage.) *Bloodhounds* found him still in harness but, in a nod towards traditional detective stories, he had to solve a locked-room mystery. (This book won both a CWA Silver Dagger and an American Macavity.) *The Secret Hangman*, latest in the series, concerns exactly that: a serial murderer who hangs his victims. There is also an interesting reference back to *Bloodhounds*, telling why the dogs are no longer used in police work. Or did you think they were?

The Last Detective (1991), *Diamond Solitaire* (1992), *The Summons* (1995), *Bloodhounds* (1996), *Upon a Dark Night* (1997), *The Vault* (1999), *Diamond Dust* (2002), *The House Sitter* (2003), *The Secret Hangman* (2007).

AUGUSTE DIDIER
by Amy Myers

A little over a hundred years ago there lived (if we are to believe Miss Myers) an arrogant but infuriatingly skilful Anglo-French master chef named Auguste Didier, a man much in demand from top restaurants and the highest houses in the land. You wish to hold a grand banquet? Send for Didier. One in which nothing can go wrong? Ah... The problem is – otherwise there would be no stories – that things often do go wrong. Not in the kitchen; you can't blame the chef. But in the grand houses, on swish liners, even in restaurants frequented by the rich. Their valuable jewels may go missing, occasional corpses may be found. And if he is a master in the kitchen, Didier is equally adept in the field. Just as well, really, because in the first book, *Murder in Pug's Parlour*, he himself is the main suspect when the Duke's steward is found poisoned. (At such times you'd wonder about the chef.) In later books Didier runs his own restaurant, tangles with series character **Inspector Egbert Rose**, and serves generous helpings of entertainment every time.

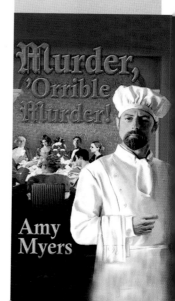

Murder in Pug's Parlour (1986) began a series which produced nearly a book a year until the final *Murder in the Queen's Boudoir* in 2000. The books can be read in any sequence, and perhaps 1989's *Murder at Plum's* is ... if not the plum, then the *pièce de résistance*.

GEORGE DILMAN
by Conrad Allen

In a series set upon the luxury liners of the Edwardian age George Porter Dillman is employed as a **ship's detective**. A former Pinkerton detective, he is a natural choice for the Cunard Line who want a capable man for the maiden voyage of the *Lusitania* in 1907. The murder of a journalist on board has international implications and while trying to sort it out Dillman gets unexpected help from **Genevieve Masefield**, a young woman emigrating to America, who he invites to work alongside him in future, thus setting up a series of crime-spun cruises. In *Murder on the Celtic* not only does their ship have a murderer on board but among the other passengers is one Arthur Conan Doyle.

Murder on the Lusitania (1999), *Murder on the Mauritania* (2000), *Murder on the Minnesota* (2002), et cetera till *Murder on the Celtic* (2007).

GEORGE DIXON
created by Ted Willis

Dixon of Dock Green originated unpromisingly in the film *The Blue Lamp* (1949) – unpromisingly because the film ended with him shot dead by the villainous Dirk Bogarde. But you can't keep a good man down, and George Dixon was as good a man, infuriatingly so to many, as you could find. Reliably honest and old-fashioned, the homely television policeman aged in twenty-one years of programming from middle age to elderly. (In late episodes the actor, **Jack Warner**, was so infirm he could hardly move. Most of his scenes were shot with him either behind the station desk or at some other piece of solid furniture he could use for support. By then he was 80-years-old.) The series was enormously popular, a national institution, and even for those who claimed they never watched it, something was lost when our night-time viewing no longer began with his familiar 'Evenin' all.'

Willis continued the character in *The Blue Lamp* (1950), *Dixon of Dock Green: My Life* (1960) which sounded like a Jewish joke and, as unvarying as George himself, *Dixon of Dock Green: A Novel* (1961).

The Blue Lamp (1949) was an Ealing Studios film starring **Jack Warner** as trainee policeman George Dixon, **Dirk Bogarde** as the callow young hoodlum, and a bevy of old British troupers including **Jimmy Hanley, Bernard Lee** and **Dora Bryan**, which tells you exactly what to expect from the film. Despite the title it was in black and white.

Jack Warner as trainee policeman George Dixon.

FABIAN DONOGHUE
by Peter Turnbull

Inspector Donoghue leads 'P' Division in the gritty heart of Glasgow. Despite the real-life city's generally successful attempt to throw off the 'No Mean City' image and to represent itself as a beacon of culture, Turnbull's Glasgow is a modern-day throwback to a violent past. 'P' Division rolls up its sleeves and tackles cases of murder, mutilation and incurable drug addiction. People don't just die in Turnbull books, they

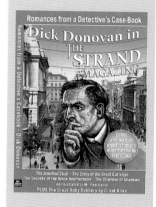

have their faces sliced off, have macabre clues tattooed in their groin and are tampered with after death. These are dark, worrying books. Donoghue heads 'P' Division but he is barely the star; Turnbull shines his grim light on the whole team.

Deep and Crisp and Even was the disarming title of the first, in 1981. Five more followed in the Eighties, and another four in the Nineties, ending in 1998 with *The Man With No Face*. Being Turnbull, he meant it literally. He then turned to his new series, featuring **Chief Inspector Hennessey**.

DICK DONOVAN
by Dick Donovan

> Of course, if I had been the impossible detective of fiction, endowed with the absurd attributes of being able to tell the story of a man's life from the way the tip of his nose was formed, or the number of hairs on his head, or by the shape and size of his teeth, or by the way he held his pipe when smoking, or from the kind of liquor he consumed, or the hundred and one ridiculous and burlesque signs which are so easily read by the detective prig of modern creation, I might have come to a different conclusion.

> From *The Problem of Dead Wood Hall* by Dick Donovan

Early rival to Holmes, in a long series of stories by the journalist Joyce Emmerson Muddock (male) calling himself Dick Donovan and often writing in the first person as if he himself were the detective. Some of the Donovan stories are about fellow detectives (all equally fictional) and are told in the more customary third person style. Despite their popularity, Muddock claimed not to like his own creation. He may have thought his own autobiography, *Pages From an Adventurous Life* (1914) more exciting.

Collections of stories included *The Man Hunter: Stories from the Notebook of a Detective* (1888), *Caught at Last! Leaves from the Notebook of a Detective* (1889), *Romances from a Detective's Notebook* (1892), *Found And Fettered* (1894), *Dark Deeds* (1895) and *Tales of Terror* (1899).

WILLIAM DOUGAL
by Andrew Taylor

High in the ranks of bizarre concepts comes William Dougal, who began life as a post-graduate student of history with a pressing need for money but, as time went by, evolved into a multi-murderer and a louche private investigator of low moral fibre. But, he might have reminded you, he was still good company and didn't really mean any harm. He was, some said then, Britain's answer to Highsmith's Ripley. Two constant figures in his life were the gentlemanly psychopath **James Hanbury**, and his once and future girlfriend **Celia** who became the mother of his daughter. The first in the series, *Caroline Miniscule*, won the CWA's John Creasey Award for the best first crime novel of 1982.

Caroline Miniscule (1982), *Waiting for the End of the World* (1984),

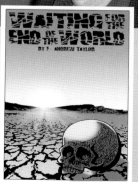

Our Father's Lies (1985), *An Old School Tie* (1986), *Freelance Death* (1987), *Blood Relation* (1990), *The Sleeping Policeman* (1992), *Odd Man Out* (1993).

INSPECTOR DOVER
by Joyce Porter

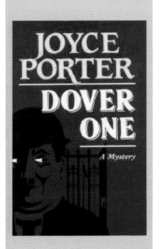

A comical detective, known as the '**Shame of Scotland Yard**' for his general inefficiency and lack of heroism – or indeed of any other quality his superiors expect from their officers. Fat and lazy, over-fond of beer, Dover leaves most of the legwork to his assistant **Sergeant MacGregor**, though, if he can stir himself, Dover is prepared to take the credit for MacGregor's work. The Yard's main way of dealing with him is to shunt him off to the provinces – the remoter the better. Dover doesn't mind; it gives him a chance to sample different ale. Earlier titles are the funniest.

Dover One (1964) was first and best. *Dovers Two* and *Three* followed in 1965 and 1966. *Dover and the Unkindest Cut of All* maintained the early standard but *Dover Goes to Pott* (1968) had begun to milk the joke. Five more titles followed, ending with *Dover Beats the Band* in 1980. There are about a dozen short stories too.

VALERIE DREW
by John W. Bobin and 'Isobel Norton'

Bobin had had a crack at creating at least two previous girl detectives before Valerie Drew. (See **Lila Lisle** and **Sylvia Silence**). Like her predecessors Valerie was sporty and beautiful, though a touch older (her career went on till she was in her late 20s) and her costumes were correspondingly more mature. Bobin died in 1935 but the series continued, at first anonymously and then as by Isobel Norton (presumably staff writers). One of the few detectives then to age in real time, Valerie first appeared aged 18 and went on to leave school, learn to pilot a plane, and take possession of a flat in Park Lane. Her adventures, nevertheless, often took her back into schools – pretending to be a student, and later as she aged, in the guise of a teacher. Multi-talented inevitably, she is made more human (and more in touch with her readers) by having a lovable Alsatian called **Flash** – not that he can't become aggressive in her defence. At times Flash seems even more intelligent than Valerie: he can understand English, interpret complex commands and, of course, track people down. Flash is not the first canine assistant but he was one of the more memorable and influential.

Flash.

Valerie appeared regularly in *Schoolgirls' Weekly* from 1933 till the magazine's closure in 1939, when she transferred for a short while to *Schoolgirl*. But even she had to succumb to Whitehall, when wartime paper shortages closed *Schoolgirl* down.

SIR CLINTON DRIFFIELD
by J. J. Connington (Alfred Walter Stewart)

Unjustly forgotten police detective of the Golden Age, a chief constable of an unnamed English county who, says Julian Symons, 'undoubtedly

has a claim to be considered among the outstanding detectives of the inter-war years.' A keen chess player who, wisely, collects books on crime, he at one point delivers a masterly put-down to his 'Watson', Mr Wendover JP: 'Masterly survey, squire,' said Sir Clinton cordially. 'Except that you've missed out most of the points of importance.'

Murder in the Maze (1927) began a series of 17 books stretching to the final *Commonsense is All You Need* (1947).

Tenderly Valerie removed the message from the injured pigeon. Then she stared at it in amazement. It was in code!

DIXON DRUCE
L. T. Meade

Druce heads 'Werner's Agency, the Solvency Inquiry Agency for all British Trade', but seems far too well-bred for such a task, having been educated at Harrow in the 1870s. In the one book I know of Druce (though the author was astoundingly prolific) Druce's clients were upper class too, as was his running villain, Madame Sara, a clever and beautiful extortioner in *The Sorceress of the Strand* (1903).

BULL-DOG DRUMMOND
by 'Sapper' (H. C. McNeile, then Gerald Fairlie)

Xenophobic and sadistic gentleman-adventurer of the kind who gave gentlemen a bad name, Bull-dog Drummond was in his time a hugely successful blood and thunder hero. Since his time he has been rightly excoriated for his views and behaviour, but his defenders would point out that he emerged from the sickening and largely pointless violence of the 'Great War' which itself climaxed three decades (some might say centuries) of British scorn and loathing of foreigners. Hugh Drummond himself had been an army captain and came out of the war in search of more excitement. Unsatiated by trench warfare he set out after enemy spies, crooks and dastardly villains of all kinds, preferably foreign and thus demonstrably foul. Where he himself is a club man, a gentleman, ex-public school, his opponents are 'Bolshevik Jews, dagos and wogs'. In the first book, *Bull-dog Drummond* (1920), his acts of violence include his forcing a villain into a bath of acid to extract a confession. In *The Black Gang* (1922) two suspected criminals whose Jewishness is uglily described are beaten by the masked Drummond 'to within an inch of their lives' with a cat-o'-nine-tails. And so it goes on. And on. One enemy to survive his encounters is **Carl Peterson**, who – perhaps – dies at the end of the fourth book *The Final Count* (1926), and whose confrontations are collected in an omnibus *Bull-dog Drummond: His Four Rounds With Carl Peterson*.

"I shall drop you down the stairs if you talk to me like that, you damned little microbe," said Hugh coldly, and the other got to his feet with a snarl. His eyes, glaring like those of an angry cat, were fixed on Drummond,

Jack Buchanan.

who suddenly put out a vast hand to screen the lower part of the hunchback's face. With a cry of fear he recoiled, and Hugh smiled grimly. So it had been Mr Atkinson himself who had flung the bomb the night before: the eyes that had glared at him through the crack in the door were unmistakably the same as those he had just looked into over his own hand.

From *The Black Gang.*

Bull-dog Drummond (1920) started a long series interrupted after *Challenge* (1937) when McNeile died and was replaced as 'Sapper' by Gerald Fairlie. *Bull-dog Drummond on Dartmoor* (1938) picked up where McNeile left off. *Bull-dog Drummond Attacks* was the inevitable title for 1939, though the books paused throughout the war, only to resume straight after with *Captain Bull-dog Drummond* in 1945. (He had been a captain in the First World War.) Five more books continued, ending with *Return of the Black Gang* in 1954.

Derided as he is now, Drummond was popular enough to spawn plenty of films. **Carlyle Blackwell** and **Jack Buchanan** stepped in early (1922 and 1925), followed by (the much better) **Ronald Colman** in *Bull-dog Drummond* (1929) and *Bull-dog Drummond Strikes Back* (1934). Later portrayals came from **Kenneth McKenna** (1930), **Ralph Richardson** (1934), **Jack Hulbert** (in a spoof *Bull-dog Jack*, 1935), **John Lodge** and **Ray Milland** (both 1937). **John Howard** carried the role for eight films starting in 1937, to be followed by **Ron Randell** (1947), **Tom Conway** (1948), **Walter Pidgeon** (1951), then **Richard Johnson** (1967 and 1969).

DUFFY
by Dan Kavanagh
First, an identity check. Dan Kavanagh is the pseudonym of top literary author and journalist **Julian Barnes**, used for the four novels concerning Nick Duffy, a bisexual cop turned private detective. They have a novelist's touch, in that they are well-written, expertly set, witty and inventive – but one has to say they lack the crime writer's touch. It is a novelist's London, not a crime writer's: too tidy, too tame, violent occasionally but in an apologetic way. That is not to say they're not good fun. And it was refreshing to move from the conventional environments of stale police stations and dusty back rooms and to peep instead into the behind-the-scenes world of the world's least favourite airport, a mangy dog track and a no-hope minor football club. If I tell you the first book was set in Soho, you can work the others out from the titles.
Duffy (1980), *Fiddle City* (1981), *Putting the Boot In* (1985), *Going to the Dogs* (1987).

PETER DULUTH
by Patrick Quentin
Investigator of 'puzzle' mysteries (many with the word 'puzzle' in their titles). The stories were light and bright and moderately popular in their

Some more Bull-dog Drummonds, from top to bottom,
Ronald Colman
Ray Milland
John Howard
Ron Randell
Walter Pidgeon

day and, although seldom read today, can surprise and engage with the deftness of their plotting. Though set in America, often on Broadway, their pseudonymous author was born in Britain.

Puzzle for Fools, Puzzle for Wantons, Puzzle for Pilgrims, et cetera.

Dr STEVEN DUNBAR
by Ken McClure

A **Medical Investigator** with the Sci-Med Inspectorate (a Home Office unit investigating crime and wrong-doing in the world of science and medicine) Dunbar is a tall, dark, athletic man in his late 30s. After serving in the Parachute Regiment and the SAS, Dunbar left to join Sci-Med whose investigations concentrate on reports and rumours of unusual events and possible crimes in hi-tech areas of medicine and science. Dunbar has been widowed and from that marriage has a young daughter, Jenny, who is looked after by his dead wife's sister. In the second book, *Deception,* Jenny is kidnapped, which is not the sort of thing Steve Dunbar takes lying down.

Donor (1998), *Deception* (2001), *Wildcard* (2002), *The Gulf Conspiracy* (2004), *Eye of the Raven* (2005), *The Lazarus Strain* (2007).

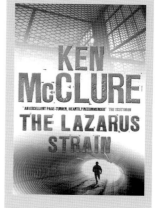

AUGUSTE DUPIN
by Edgar Allan Poe

Poe is American, Dupin is French, but since Dupin is acclaimed by many as **the first fictional detective** he deserves his place in this mainly British *vade mecum.* Poe's entire detective output stretches to only six titles (at most, only three of which include Auguste Dupin) but they introduce practically all the features we now expect from a detective story: Dupin was a loner, outside the police; he solved crimes by logic and observation; he saw what no one else saw and let tiny clues lead him to the perpetrator. Unfortunately, Poe also made Dupin an aristocrat – a Chevalier – who thus had the leisure to interest himself with other people's crimes; that concept, of the dilettante amateur, may have been responsible for the numerous wealthy and upper class gentlemen detectives who cluttered British crime fiction for several decades. It's the only disappointment from Poe's legacy.

The Murders in the Rue Morgue was the first and most ground-breaking story (each of the three is a longish short story, not a book) and is told by a 'Watson', Dupin's friend and nameless amateur amanuensis. We meet Dupin in his darkened room (he does not care for daylight) where he, like Holmes and others afterwards, has noticed a fascinating mystery in the newspaper: the brutal murder of a mother and daughter inside a **locked room** to which no one else had a key. Dupin visits the scene and swiftly discovers the gory truth. His second story, *The Mystery of Marie Rôget,* is more densely written, practically a treatise, and is a mechanism (frankly, a rather tedious mechanism) through which Poe gives his own explanation for a real-life crime in New York.

Edgar Allan Poe.

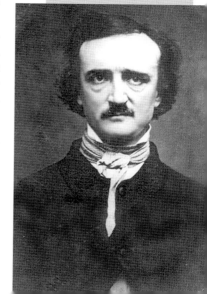

Auguste Dupin is acclaimed by many as the first fictional detective.

The third and final tale, *The Purloined Letter*, is famous mainly for the convincing simplicity of its solution. Despite their fame, the stories are not easy reads today. Heavy in style, dripping with Poe's obsessions, unlikely in the extreme, they nevertheless set a mould. Indeed, each of Poe's three other non-Dupin detective stories has its own ground-breaking element: *The Gold Bug* (1843) has a mysterious (yet ultimately, quite simple) **cipher** which, when cracked, leads to hidden treasure; in *Thou Art the Man* (1844) **the least likely person** turns out to be the culprit; in *The Man in the Crowd* (1845) a disinterested observer deduces **a stream of inferences** about a stranger (in the crowd) from nothing more than his clothes and how he behaves. Each of these devices has been reused by others in thousands of stories since. So has the concept of a disinterested observer outside the police, an eccentric obsessive whose drive and unique acuity solve a crime that baffles everyone else – and who shares and explains his deductions on the page. These combine to form a unique overall concept which makes Auguste Dupin crime fiction's first detective.

The three Dupin short stories are *The Murders in the Rue Morgue* (1841), *The Mystery of Marie Rôget* (1842) and *The Purloined Letter* (1844). *Murders in the Rue Morgue* was a Robert Florey film made in 1932 in which **Bela Lugosi** played the gorilla's keeper; *Phantom of the Rue Morgue* came out in 1954 with **Steve Forrest** as 'Professor *Paul*' Dupin; Gordon Hessler directed *Murders in the Rue Morgue* again in 1971 with **Jason Robarts** and **Herbert Lom** sharing acting honours. None of these films is worth seeking out.

MONTAGUE EGG
by Dorothy L Sayers
In contrast to the author's Lord Peter Wimsey, Montague Egg is vulgar and low-born. A travelling representative for Plummet and Rose, wine and spirit merchants, Egg lives much of his life in the dusty bedrooms and saloon bars of country hotels (middling standard) from which vantage points he becomes accidentally involved in assorted mysteries. He is, in fact, considerably more acute and perceptive than Lord Peter, even if his talents are less widely recognised.

There are only eleven Egg stories, six of which appear among the twelve in *Hangman's Holiday* (1933) and five among the seventeen in the collection *In the Teeth of the Evidence* (1939).

FRANK ELDER
by John Harvey
Retired Detective Inspector Frank Elder of the Serious Crimes Unit (he is in his 50s) made his debut in 2004 in *Flesh and Blood*, which won that year's CWA Silver Dagger award. Harvey maintained the standard in *Darkness and Light* two years later when he had Elder re-open one of his unsolved cases concerning a young girl's very particular, almost ritualistic murder because, eight years later, another body had been found murdered in a similar way. Why should Elder become involved?

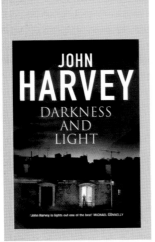

Because the woman's sister was a friend of Elder's estranged wife. Harvey has specialised in creating three-dimensional characters (he is more famous for his **Charlie Resnick**), and Elder, not entirely lost to bachelordom and unlikely to achieve his quiet ambition of reading his way through a retirement that clearly came too soon, looks no exception.

Flesh and Blood (2004), *Ash and Bone* (2005), *Darkness and Light* (2006)

FABIAN OF THE YARD
various writers

An early cops'n'robbers show on black and white TV which ran from November 1954 to March 1956. An air of realism came from the series being shot on film rather than being broadcast live from the studio, as was generally the case in those days. In a less successful attempt to add realism the real-life Inspector Fabian rather stiffly summarised each episode 'from his casebook' – but he was in curious contrast to the actor **Bruce Seton** who played him as a considerably more debonair character. Support came from **Robert Raglan** as DS Wyatt and **Isobel Dean** as Mrs Regis, and from London itself, which in Fabian's summary seemed a mere tourist attraction.

FALCO
by Lindsey Davis

Marcus Didio Falco is a **Roman rogue**, a streetwise informer cum detective whose eye for the man chance is diverted by his scruples. He tells his own stories in the books, chatting to the reader as if sitting beside him in the pub – though these stories are set in ancient Rome, in the time of Vespasian, and into the comedy and crime Davis slips lots of snippets of history and curious details of Roman life. Half of Falco's stories are actually set outside Rome on one or another of his various jaunts to the Provinces, and in these again we are fed tasty titbits about the Roman empire. But in no way is Davis dull or academic; her learning is worn so lightly it's a wonder it doesn't fall off. Falco's life is shot with problems we recognise today: his tax bill, having builders in to repair the house, errant tradesmen, naughty children, unruly teenagers, devious politicians, his relationship with his common law wife (Helena) – Falco's problems are so modern one wonders whether Davis doesn't simply take whatever has happened in her own life this year and transplant it to ancient Rome. If she does, it's to the delight of her large readership.

The Silver Pigs came first, in 1989, followed by *Shadows in Bronze*, *Venus in Copper* and a new book every year. *Two for the Lions* won the Ellis Peters Historical Dagger in 1999. *Saturnalia* came out in 2007.

THE FALCON
by Michael Arlen

Originally the 'Gay Falcon', a title perhaps wisely dropped, the Falcon (real name **Michael Waring**) was a gentleman rogue crime-buster from the end of the period when such a creature was believable, in fiction at

Tom
Conway

George
Sanders

John
Calvert

least. Though the stories are best forgotten (even assuming you can find them) the films (amazingly) did better, at least in America, where they believe anything of the English.

The first three films in 1941 and 1942 (*The Gay Falcon*, *A Date With the Falcon*, *The Falcon Takes Over*) starred **George Sanders**, who refused to play any more, so his real-life brother **Tom Conway** played *The Falcon's Brother* (1942) and then took over the part for a further nine films until a (poorer) final three efforts in 1948 and 1949 in which **John Calvert** dug the Falcon's grave.

WILLIAM FALCONER
by Ian Morson
Regent Master William Falconer works in the new Oxford University in the **thirteenth century** at the time of the civil war. Also at the university at that time is the real-life early scientist **Roger Bacon**. Although these are straightforward, almost simple tales, they are redolent of the period and supply plenty of medieval action and insights. Falconer himself, large and taciturn, intolerant of fools and believably thirteenth century, applies intelligent detection techniques to solve the mysteries set before him, but understands little about his own personal life.

Falconer's Crusade (1994), *Falconer's Judgement* (1995), *Falconer and the Face of God* (1996), *A Psalm for Falconer* (1997), *Falconer and the Great Beast* (1999). This last was shortlisted for the Ellis Peters Historical Dagger Award. Subsequent appearances have been in *Medieval Murderers* compilations *The Tainted Relic* (2005) and *House of Shadows* (2007).

JOE FARADAY
by Graham Hurley
Portsmouth-based Detective Inspector, a widower with a profoundly deaf son, he is something of a martinet – a perfectionist given to outbursts of temper. Against that he is a keen birdwatcher who can be found in his off-duty hours up to his ankles in the mud of nearby estuaries. Later books in the series see Faraday rely on one colleague he thinks he can trust – Detective Constable Winter. But the author likes the maverick **DC Winter** and, if Faraday doesn't watch out, his young assistant could oust him.
Turnstone (2000) The Take (2001), *Angels Passing* (2002), *Deadlight* (2003), *Cut to Black* (2004), *Blood and Honey* (2006), *One Under* (2007), *The Price of Darkness* (2008).

MIKE FARADAY
by Basil Copper
A hard-boiled detective based around Los Angeles who, despite having appeared in some 50 novels, never quite made it to the big time. Strange to think that the author lives in Sevenoaks, Kent. He writes the **Solar Pons** stories.

The Faraday series began with *The Dark Mirror* (1966).

INSPECTOR FARO
by Alanna Knight

Working in **nineteenth-century Edinburgh**, Jeremy Faro is a suitably pessimistic law officer whose cases sometimes reach back far into the past – in *Bloodline* he looks back three centuries to a crime involving royalty. All the stories have interest and Knight's Edinburgh is strongly drawn. Faro is usually assisted by his stepson Dr **Vincent Laurie**, but his daughter **Rose McQuinn** shows herself so able that from *The Inspector's Daughter* (2000) she begins a series of her own.

Faro books include the first *Enter Second Murderer* (1988), *Bloodline* (1989), *Deadly Beloved* (1990), *The Evil That Men Do* (1992), *Murder By Appointment* (1996), *The Coffin Lane Murders* (1998). Faro continued in parallel with Rose McQuinn: *Unholy Trinity* came out in 2004 and *Faro and the Royals* in 2005.

Dr GIDEON FELL
by John Dickson Carr

Fell is the supreme investigator of impossible crimes and locked room mysteries, and is a suitably impossible character: a huge swaggering thespian of a man with an actor's hair, he wears a flowing cloak and swings his glittering eyeglasses suspended on an unmissable black ribbon. Not a fit man, Doctor Fell walks with the aid of two canes, wheezing loudly as he goes. He drinks beer, not Burgundy as one might expect, and is permanently engaged on his magnum opus *The Drinking Customs of England from the Earliest Days*, a tome which he is doomed never to finish. About drinking, as about practically any subject suggested to him, Fell knows more than anyone else and, extraordinarily, this makes him all the more endearing. In his day, the 1930s, Fell would have been recognisable as a caricature of **G. K. Chesterton**.

The stories are far-fetched and at times over-complicated but at their best have an irreproachable inner logic; they are melodramatic, often they seem impossible – but they come from the author who is king of the 'impossible crime'. As Chesterton did in some of his own tales, Carr occasionally drags in whiffs of the supernatural – his first Fell novel, *Hag's Nook*, was positively gothic – but he brings in the fantastic only so that in the end he can sweep everything away with a peremptory swish of Fell's cane. In *The Hollow Man* (which contains Carr's famous essay on locked room mysteries) it is suggested there may be vampires; in *The Crooked Hinge* witches may exist – but these explanations won't do for Doctor Fell. His solutions may be incredible but they are at least of the real world. The corpses are real, even if they died in ways that seem unreal, and in such cases, we discover, there must be a real solution.

Some find the Fell novels poorer than the short stories – so there's less excuse to avoid the short stories. From his vast repertoire the best novels are probably *Hag's Nook* (the first Doctor Fell novel, 1933), *The Mad Hatter Mystery* (1933), *The Eight of Swords* (1934), *The Hollow Man* (1935), *The Ten Teacups* (1937), *The Judas Window* (1938), *The*

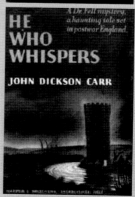

Crooked Hinge (1938), *The Black Spectacles* (1939), *The Seat of the Scornful* (1942) and perhaps the last great Fell story, *He Who Whispers* (1946). All the early novels are worth reading, but the seven that crept out after 1946 until 1967 are less effective. Of several short story collections, the most complete and therefore desirable, is *Dark of the Moon* (collected and issued in 1967).

INSPECTOR FELSE
Edith Pargetter (aka Ellis Peters)
Set in Pargetter's native **Shropshire** (unconvincingly renamed Midshire) the Inspector Felse novels are among the more 'domestic' crime stories around. They often concern members of Felse's own family, who become involved in crimes either as witnesses or as friends of the victims, and when his own family is not directly involved, the chances are that family issues (albeit of a different family) will lie at the heart of his investigation. Although this domestic slant makes the stories relatively quiet compared to other authors' crime books (especially to those written today) it does give them an interesting depth, because they are family novels which happen to include a crime. In addition, and of some interest, they show what it is like to be part of a policeman's family.

The first Felse book, *Fallen Into the Pit* (1951), when Felse was a sergeant, almost stood alone as it was to be ten years before the second, *Death and the Joyful Woman* in 1961. (Felse was now Inspector.) This book won an Edgar in America (for best crime novel). Seven more titles followed in the Sixties, notably *The Piper on the Mountain* (1966), partly set in Czechoslovakia, *Mourning Raga* (1969), partly set in India, and *The Grass-Widow's Tale* (1968). Four more titles brought the series to an end in 1978 with the appropriately named *Rainbow's End*.

Edith Pargetter, better known as Ellis Peters.

GERVASE FEN
by Edmund Crispin
One of several **Oxford don detectives** and modelled supposedly on Carr's **Gideon Fell** (although Fen is thinner, fitter and a tad less theatrical), Crispin's creation is wondrously old school. Given to expostulations, like 'Oh, my fur and whiskers!', Fen strides briskly from his scholastic corridors to solve a series of impossible crimes and fiendish puzzles. Clad in oversize raincoats and unbecoming hats he paces, bicycles or roars through the streets of Oxford in his wonderful if unreliable vintage car to hound villains down, sometimes by logic but just as likely with fists or pistol, scattering quotes and quips along the way – some literary, some more typical of a don in a world of students: 'Ah, Mr Hopkins,' he said to an undergraduate, who was perambulating with his arm round the waist of an attractive girl. 'Hard at it already, I see.' Like Fell again, Gervase Fen likes his beer, and a dreamy mist of alcohol wraps its spell around several of the tales. Again like Fell, he is the author of abstruse scholastic tomes such as, in his case, a definitive edition of Langland and a thesis on minor eighteenth-century satirists.

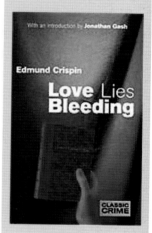

Time came in 1980 with seven more in the Eighties, then *Past Reckoning* (1990), *Foul Play* (1991), *Burden of Innocence* (1996) and *The Unquiet Grave* (2000). The twentieth Finch novel, *Going Home*, came out in 2006.

FIZZ AND BUCHANAN
by Joyce Holms

'Fizz' Fitzgerald is a lively young law student and Tam Buchanan an older and far less lively solicitor. Together they chase up the **Edinburgh** crimes Rebus hasn't noticed – though how he missed their first case is a mystery in itself: a woman's body is found impaled on railings, and both still drip with blood. Fizz and Buchanan are not lovers, although whenever a suitable woman shows an interest in Tam she soon sees Fizz and slips away. Romance plays little part in these books: they tell of a seamy Edinburgh brightened with mordant laughs.

   Payment Deferred came first in 1996, followed by others at yearly intervals, including recent titles *Hidden Depths*, *Hot Potato* and *Missing Link* (2006). They are best read in sequence.

FLASH the Alsatian
(see **Valerie Drew**)

DI MARJORY FLEMING
by Aline Templeton

DI Marjory Fleming is the sort of policewoman you wish you could still find at the local nick: tough, humorous, a farmer's wife, a mother and a daughter with ageing parents, she copes with all the pressures modern women face. Her patch is the beautiful rural area of **Galloway** in south-west Scotland, which at the start of the series (2001) is devastated by the foot-and-mouth epidemic. Her sergeant, **Tam MacNee**, is a wee Glasgow hard man with a flair for investigation and a passion for Robert Burns. He has history, too, which is bound to come back and 'greet' him some day. Meanwhile, they have murders to solve, and some particularly local crimes, such as the mysterious wrecking of the community lifeboat.

   Recent titles are *Cold in the Earth* (2005), *The Darkness and the Deep* (2006), *Lying Dead* (2007) *Lamb to the Slaughter* (2008).

Aline Templeton.

DR GRACE FOLEY TV series *Waking The Dead* (2000)
Sidekick to Peter Boyd who dominates the series, Foley is a criminal psychologist and profiler played with typical strength and conviction by **Sue Johnston**. Her concerned scientific approach contrasts well with Boyd's more impulsive intuition.

SIMON FORMAN
by Judith Cook

In the age of **Elizabeth I**, Forman was a real-life astrologer and physician treating and mingling among the highest in the land, which at

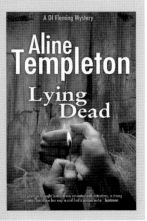

that particular point in English history was a dangerous place to be. The stories, though, are fictional.

Death of a Lady's Maid (1997), *Murder at the Rose* (1998), *Blood on the Borders* (1999), *Kill the Witch* (1999), *School of the Night* (2000).

REGGIE (& sometimes JOAN) FORTUNE
by H. C. Bailey

Largely forgotten today, Reggie Fortune was one of the most popular detectives during the Golden Age, and was arguably **the first gentleman amateur**. A pathologist cum investigator, often consulted (deferentially) by the police, his languid, almost somnolent attitude concealed a quick and inventive mind, although his rather patronising style will grate with many today. Get over that and the stories are a pleasant way to spend a nostalgic summer afternoon, even if, unlike Reggie, you don't have a chauffeur, maid and gardener.

Call Mr Fortune (1920) was the first of over 20 anthologies and novels including *Mr Fortune's Practice* (1923), *Mr Fortune Speaking* (1929), *Mr Fortune Objects* (1935) and the final *Shrouded Death* (1950).

CHARLIE FOX
by Zoë Sharp

The guy in the passenger seat was closest. He got out first, so I shot him first. Typical no-nonsense from *First Drop*.

Charlie Fox is as feminine as a tigress. Previously a Special Forces soldier, now out in civvy street and turned bodyguard, she works with her former army training instructor and sometime lover **Sean Meyer**, who runs his own close protection agency. Though recent books have been set in America, Sharp is a British author and her first two were set closer to home, in Lancaster and Morecambe, and the third switched between Yorkshire and a fictional town near Stuttgart, Germany. All these stories are out-and-out thrillers set in the present day, and come recommended by such as top thriller writer Lee Child, who said of Charlie Fox: 'Today's best action heroine ... Scarily good.'

Killer Instinct (2001), *Riot Act* (2002), *Hard Knocks* (2003), *First Drop* (2004), *Road Kill* (2005), *Second Shot* (2007), *Third Strike* (2008).

Zoë Sharp.

INSPECTOR FRENCH
by Freeman Wills Crofts

It seems little recommendation to say that French developed from the dull and painstaking **Inspector Burnley** but both were important in the early years of the police procedural crime novel. Crofts himself was painstaking; his novels were intricately plotted and his mysteries as devious as in many amateur detective stories, relying on apparently unbreakable alibis and, oddly for today, the reliability of railway timetables. (Crofts had been an engineer on the Belfast & Northern Counties Railway. He wrote his first novel *The Cask* while convalescing from illness.) French, like Burnley, was dull, but his mysteries were far from dull. Raymond Chandler called Crofts 'the soundest builder of

them all,' and one assumes that was a compliment. Oddly again by today's standards, Inspector French is a dutiful policeman enjoying good working relations with his colleagues, he is happily married, good mannered and has no problems with either drink or his digestion.

Inspector French's Greatest Case (1924) starts a long series in which either the second, *Inspector French and the Cheyne Mystery* (1926) or the mid-point *The Loss of the Jane Vosper* (1936) is the best. The railway connection may be guessed from titles like *12.30 From Croydon* (1934), *Fear Comes to Chalfont* (1942), *The Affair at Little Wokeham* (1943) and *Death of a Train* (1946). The series reached its terminus with *Anything to Declare?* in 1957.

INSPECTOR FROST
by R. D. Wingfield

Another example of the TV version being quite different from the author's. TV's is the more famous, having been prime time viewing for a decade, the fictional town of Denton's crumpled police detective is played by **David Jason**, but the original Frost had his characteristics written more dourly. Wingfield's Jack Frost is darkly drawn: he is put-upon but insubordinate, a chain smoker, frequently unpleasant, a gritty loner (he is a widower living alone) – much of which sounds like Jason's portrayal but is not. Wingfield's Frost is politically incorrect in ways that Jason could never be. He isn't even a great detective, in that his deductive powers are only moderate and he solves his cases more by dogged legwork and grim tenacity than by reasoning. (His full name, seldom used, is William Edward Frost; Jack is his inevitable nickname.)

Though Wingfield's are good straight-forward crime books, the first, written in 1972, had to wait twelve years to find a publisher. But

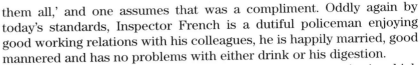

television has changed that, and Denton's workaday copper has become one of the nation's favourites. Jason can't help being the sort of man who attracts viewer sympathy; despite his talents he could no more play a villain than could Frankie Howerd. And if one wanted viewers to watch in their millions one would choose Jason rather than an actor who gave a more true-to-the-book portrayal. Viewers and readers may have to differ on which version they prefer.

The books are: *Frost at Christmas* (1984), *A Touch of Frost* (1987), *Night Frost* (1992), *Late Frost* (1995), *Winter Frost* (1999), *Autumn Frost* (2007).

ITV's television series goes out under the name of one of the books, *A Touch of Frost*, and has added a number of episodes merely based on Wingfield's characters. **David Jason** plays Inspector Frost, **Bruce Alexander** is a splendidly uptight

A TOUCH OF FROST
NOW A MAJOR NEW TV SERIES
STARRING DAVID JASON AS
D. I. JACK FROST

Mullett. Most of the remaining cast has come and gone since the show's inception in 1992.

DIANE FRY
(see **Ben Cooper**)

MATTHEW FURNIVAL
by Stella Phillips
In a long series of police procedurals Matthew rises from Detective Inspector to Chief Inspector while remaining, seemingly, stuck in his mid-30s. Given that his first appearance was in 1967 and he steamed effortlessly through the millennium, this may be his greatest achievement! He is accompanied throughout the series by Detective Sergeant **Reg King**.

   Down to Earth began the series in 1967, to be swiftly followed by *Hidden Wrath* (1968), *Death in Arcady* (1969), *Death Makes the Scene* (1970), *Death in Sheep's Clothing* (1971) etc. through to *Three May Keep a Secret* in 2005.

SIR BALDWIN DE FURNSHILL
by Michael Jecks
Sir Baldwin is the grandly titled Keeper of the King's Peace, in whose job description lurks the fact that he has to delve deep and dig the dirt on some disreputable medieval characters. Set as if in real time in the **fourteenth century**, Sir Baldwin's adventures began in 1316 when he was 43 and have progressed to 1325 (making him 52). Since the series shows no sign of ending he may soon bemoan the lack of a medieval old age pension. He or his younger colleagues, specifically **Simon Puttock**, should shortly enter the Hundred Years War. The tales may be light-hearted but they are thoroughly researched and accurate, giving a fine portrait of both the age and the area he works in (mainly Devon and London). Each is a detective story.

Michael Jecks.

The Last Templar (1995), *The Merchant's Partner* (1995), *A Moorland Hanging* (1996), *The Crediton Killings* (1996), *The Abbot's Gibbet* (1998), *The Leper's Return* (1998), *Squire Throwleigh's Heir* (1999), *Belladonna at Belstone* (1999), *The Traitor of St Giles* (2000), *The Boy-Bishop's Glovemaker* (2000), *The Tournament of Blood* (2001), *The Sticklepath Strangler* (2001), *The Devil's Acolyte* (2002), *The Mad Monk of Gidleigh* (2002), *The Templar's Penance* (2003), *The Outlaws of Ennor* (2003), *The Tolls of Death* (2004), *The Chapel of Bones* (2004), *The Butcher of St Peter's* (2005), *A Friar's Bloodfeud* (2005), *The Death Ship of Dartmouth* (2006), *The Malice of Unnatural Death* (2006), *The Dispensation of Death* (2007), *The Templar, The Queen and her Lover* (2007).

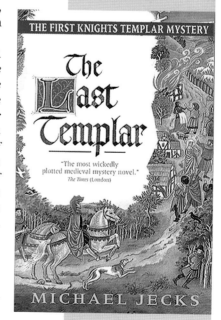

RILEY GAVIN
by Adrian Magson
An investigative journalist who in each book finds herself

Adrian Magson.

H. R. F. Keating.

sucked into tough all-action stories – anything from drug gangs to brushes with British Intelligence. Whatever the assignment Gavin doesn't flinch. She is often aided by former military policeman **Frank Palmer**, rather a misfit since he left the force but a useful man to know, given the situations Riley gets herself into. They're a working partnership, rather than a romantic one – though who knows what may happen as the series continues? Since Palmer seems to be shaping up as a private investigator, he may become the main man anyway.

No Peace for the Wicked (2004), *No Help for the Dying* (2005), *No Sleep for the Dead* (2006), *No Tears for the Lost* (2007), *No Kiss for the Devil* (2008).

INSPECTOR GHOTE
by H. R. F. Keating

Inspector Ganesh Ghote worked in the **Bombay CID** and his adventures were written by an English crime writer who when he began writing the series had famously never been to India, not that it seemed important at the time. Keating's search for different settings led him to set his fifth book – a one-off, he intended – in exotic India. This was *A Perfect Murder* and it won the CWA Gold Dagger. Although Keating had never been to India he researched thoroughly through films, books and newspaper articles (he had been a journalist) and he created an India so lifelike and lovable that much of his fan base was found in that sub-continent. But his famous lack of first-hand knowledge could not continue. In 1975 Air India offered him a free return flight and, having finally seen his adopted country, Keating returned there six months later with a TV crew to repay the favour.

His Inspector Ghote (pronounced 'hoe-tay', though practically no one outside India pronounces it correctly) is polite and diffident, if persistent, and has survived through twenty-five delightful books, ten in the first ten years, seven in the 1980s, and six more in the 1990s. Quite how he survived would seem a miracle to Ghote, who is timid, unadventurous and by no means a he-man. (The very idea would make his wife scream with laughter. Even his young son, the apple of his eye, might raise an indulgent smile.) Nor is Ghote a genius; he makes mistakes and indeed he accepts mistakes as a natural part of life. (Fortunately, several of his criminal adversaries are bunglers too.) In the course of a long series of cases Ghote has been helped by several assistants including **Axel Svenson**, a Swede, and an American, **Gregory Strongbow**. He also left India for a while to solve a case involving an Indian girl in London. In *Inspector Ghote Hunts the Peacock* he makes his first visit to London and is as awestruck and in love with it as his creator was with India when he finally went there – though, in a realistic touch, Ghote does come across colour prejudice, a feature of English life for which he is entirely unprepared. But unpreparedness is not new to him, and Ghote's recognisably human weaknesses endear him to his readers. Light and whimsical as the books appear, they examine and comment on society's structure and morality in ways that are relevant to both the Indian sub-continent and the West.

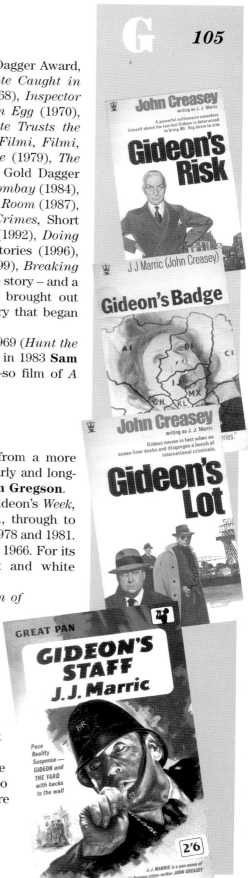

The Perfect Murder (1964) Winner of the CWA Gold Dagger Award, *Inspector Ghote's Good Crusade* (1966), *Inspector Ghote Caught in Meshes* (1967), *Inspector Ghote Hunts the Peacock* (1968), *Inspector Ghote Plays a Joker* (1969), *Inspector Ghote Breaks an Egg* (1970), *Inspector Ghote Goes by Train* (1971), *Inspector Ghote Trusts the Heart* (1972), *Bats Fly Up for Inspector Ghote* (1974), *Filmi, Filmi, Inspector Ghote* (1976), *Inspector Ghote Draws a Line* (1979), *The Murder of the Maharajah* (1980), winner of the CWA Gold Dagger Award, *Go West, Inspector Ghote* (1981), *The Sheriff of Bombay* (1984), *Under a Monsoon Cloud* (1986), *The Body in the Billiard Room* (1987), *Dead on Time* (1988), *Inspector Ghote, His Life and Crimes*, Short Stories (1989), *The Iciest Sin* (1990), *Cheating Death* (1992), *Doing Wrong* (1994), *The Inspector Ghote Mysteries*, Short Stories (1996), *Asking Questions* (1996), *Bribery, Corruption Also* (1999), *Breaking and Entering* (2000). This, we thought, was the last Ghote story – and a locked room mystery, to boot – until in 2008 Keating brought out *Inspector Ghote's First Case*, the now-it-can-be-told story that began Ghote's career.

The 1968 book was adapted for BBC TV as a serial in 1969 (*Hunt the Peacock*) with **Zia Mohyeddin** in the part of Ghote, and in 1983 **Sam Dastor** played him in *Inspector Ghote Moves In*. A so-so film of *A Perfect Murder* was made by Merchant Ivory in 1964.

INSPECTOR GIDEON
by J. J. Marric (John Creasey)
A strong but straightforward Scotland Yard Inspector from a more deferential age who inspired a series of books and an early and long-running 1960s TV series starring the then heart-throb **John Gregson**. *Gideon's Day* was the first book, in 1955, followed by Gideon's *Week*, *Night*, and *Month*. Then came his *Staff*, *Risk*, *Fire*, etc., through to *Gideon's Drive* in 1976, with follow-ups by W V Butler in 1978 and 1981. On TV *Gideon's Way* starred **John Gregson** from 1964 to 1966. For its day it seemed a grainy and realistic series. (Black and white photography helped.)

The Film *Gideon's Day* (1958) – or in America, *Gideon of Scotland Yard* – preceded the TV series. It was directed by John Ford and starred **Jack Hawkins**, but was dull.

GILLARD & LANGLEY
by Margaret Duffy
Patrick Gillard and his wife Ingrid, née Langley, are ex-MI5 agents who later become consultants to the police. Their stories therefore combine counter-insurgency with crime. They sometimes overlap with Duffy's other series, about **DCI James Carrick**.

A Murder of Crows introduces the couple, when they are both still with MI5, and from the subsequent series of 10 (so far) *Dead Trouble* (2004) and *Tainted Ground* (2006) are recommended.

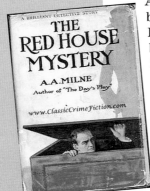

ANTONY GILLINGHAM
by A. A. Milne

If it seems odd to find the author of *Winnie the Pooh* (1926) in this book it is on the strength of his one essay into crime fiction, introducing a 'gentleman of independent means', Antony Gillingham, who tackles a typically Golden Age mystery in which a relatively modern house turns out to hide a secret passage. Raymond Chandler hated this book and, in the 1940s, wrote a vitriolic piece saying so.

The Red House Mystery (1922).

DCI WALTER GLASS
by Ron Ellis

Scotland Yard Detective Chief Inspector in his mid-50s who often works with his son-in-law **Robin Knox**. Compared to Knox (indeed compared to most people), Glass is resolutely old-fashioned. He drives a wooden-framed Morris Traveller, stalks about dressed in an Oxfam greatcoat and trilby, and has old-fashioned attitudes to match. The books mix excitement with dark humour.

Murder First Glass (1980), *Snort of Kings* (1989), *Murder on the Internet* (2004).

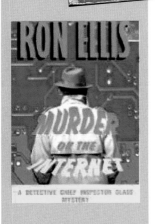

LINDSAY GORDON
by Val McDermid

Scottish investigative journalist, notably lesbian, socialist, loud and hard-drinking (all but the last two of which traits she shares with her creator), Gordon rocked the boat of British detective fiction when she barged on to the scene in 1987. The last person, you might think, to have probe the darker secrets of an all-girls' boarding school. Yet that's just what McDermid had her do in the first book (*Report for Murder*) where a dead girl was discovered in – wait for it – a **locked room**. Gordon was dispatched to what might seem more congenial territory for her second outing, a women's peace camp, where the title (*Common Murder*) tells it all, and parts of that story spill over into the third, *Final Edition*, in 1991. Two more titles followed before McDermid abandoned Gordon and turned her affections to her other heroine **Kate Brannigan** and to the man in her life, Dr **Tony Hill**.

Report for Murder (1987), *Common Murder* (1989), *Final Edition* (1991), *Union Jack* (1993), *Booked for Murder* (1996).

Val McDermid.

ROY GRACE
by Peter James

Detective Superintendent Roy Grace comes from the pen of film producer cum script and thriller writer Peter James. (He produced the award-winning *Dead of the Night* and wrote the best-selling *Possession*.) His **Sussex**-based policeman is a man troubled with demons and plagued with doubt. What happened to his wife Sandy, who simply (or was it simply?) disappeared nine years ago and has never

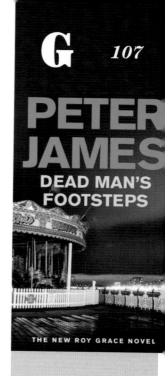

been heard of since. In the first novels this is introduced as a background thread, but it clearly can't remain so. The lonely Grace meanwhile has buried himself in his work, although he still trawls the occasional antique market as he used to do with his lost wife. In his office is his sad collection of three dozen vintage cigarette lighters. Despite this, the books are absolutely up-to-date American-style crime thrillers, with capital letters, strong language and an awful lot of short chapters.

Dead Simple began the series: an all-action puzzle mystery of greed, seduction and betrayal. *Looking Good Dead* (2006) followed, in which a murder witness is told that if he speaks not only will he and his wife be targeted but their deaths have already been posted on the internet. In 2007's *Not Dead Enough* Grace investigates a man who, it seems, murdered his wife while being sound asleep in bed 60 miles away! This peculiar case starts to stray closer to Grace's own concerns. The 2008 story, *Dead Man's Footsteps*, links 9/11 with 2006 Brighton.

ALAN GRANT
by Josephine Tey

A quiet understated policeman who appears in only a few books. Indeed, his quietest appearance (where if you weren't looking for him you'd barely remember he was there) comes in *The Franchise Affair* which, if it doesn't allow Grant to shine, is a superb and classic suspense mystery. Grant, a slight, dapper man and well-off bachelor, debuts in Tey's first crime story, *The Man in the Queue*, written for a competition supposedly in a fortnight and under the pseudonym Gordon Daviot. His intermittent but long career climaxes for some readers in *The Daughter of Time*, in which Grant, even less active than usual after having been immobilised after a fall, helps a student solve the centuries-old mystery of the Princes in the Tower. He is a quietly obsessive detective, and in his self-effacing way, just as quietly convincing. Tey is a fine writer.

The Man in the Queue (1929), *A Shilling for Candles* (1936), *The Franchise Affair* (1948), *To Love and be Wise* (1950), *The Daughter of Time* (1951), *The Singing Sands* (1952).

PATRICK GRANT
by Margaret Yorke

It seems curious that Grant should have made his appearance in the 1970s when at first sight he seems a **Golden Age** detective – a handsome **Oxford don** who can't help becoming embroiled in other people's mysteries – because Margaret Yorke is one of the country's finest crime writers, not given to nostalgic pastiche. She herself has said she made Grant an amateur because, at the time, she knew nothing about police procedures. Well, she certainly does now; in 1999 she was awarded the CWA Cartier Diamond Dagger for her lifetime achievement in crime writing.

Most of Margaret Yorke's novels are stand-alones, but the five Patrick

Grant stories are *Dead in the Morning* (1970), *Silent Witness* (1972), *Grave Matters* (1973), *Mortal Remains* (1974), and *Cast for Death* (1976).

CORDELIA GRAY
by P. D. James

P. D. JAMES

An Unsuitable
Job for a Woman

In her early 20s Cordelia became sole proprietor of Pryde's Detective Agency in Soho (motto: We Take A Pride In Our Work) and it was this employment which provided the title for the first book: *An Unsuitable Job For A Woman*. Small and wiry, not particularly attractive, randomly dressed, there was nothing about Cordelia to attract the eye – which, as any true detective will tell you, is a professional advantage. She was neat and tidy, eminently practical, and these were further reasons to believe in her as a sleuth. Her lack of looks did not bother her; she'd rather curl up with a good book than with a man, and was, in truth, rather a prude. As female sleuths go, therefore, she had everything going for her, which made it all the more surprising that her creator was reluctant to stay with her.

An Unsuitable Job For A Woman* (1972) stood alone for ten years until the warmly received *The Skull Beneath the Skin* came out in 1982. But despite the praise, P. D. James remained faithful to her main man, **Adam Dalgleish**.

An Unsuitable Job For A Woman appeared first on television in 1985 as a stand-alone TV movie starring **Pippa Guard** as Cordelia, and became a TV series of further adventures based on the character from 1997 to 2001. In this series, which began with a three-part story, Cordelia was played by **Helen Baxendale**. Greatly expanded from the original books, her detective agency was renamed Gray's Detective Agency and Cordelia herself became pregnant, something the original Cordelia would never have done. But she had to: Helen Baxendale had become pregnant in real life. By the time plump Helen/Cordelia took to waddling after suspects it really did begin to look a most unsuitable job for her. It was a popular programme, though.

MARSHAL GUARNACCI
by Magdalen Nabb

Italian policeman in the **Florence Carabinieri**. Though written by a British writer (permanently resident in Florence), the persistent and likeable Guarnacci is thoroughly European in outlook, more contemplative than the usual image of Italian cops might lead one to expect. The Florence presented by Nabb is a secretive, sometimes sinister, coolly beautiful place – Florentine, in fact. And the Tuscan countryside cannot fail.

Only the first book concentrates on the English in Florence. After *Death of an Englishman* (1981), Nabb shifted her gaze – first to the giveaway target in *Death of a Dutchman* (1982) and then to the city and the Italians themselves in titles from *Death in Springtime* (1983)

onwards. By the time of *The Marshal and the Madwoman* (1988) the plots had become thoroughly Italian. The series continues today.

BERNIE GUNTHER
by Philip Kerr

> *I checked my appearance in the bedroom mirror and then picked up my best hat. It's a wide-brimmed hat of dark-grey felt, and is encircled by a black barathea band. Common enough. But like the Gestapo, I wear my hat differently from other men, with the brim lower in front than at the back. This has the effect of hiding my eyes of course, which makes it more difficult for people to recognize me. It's a style that originated with the Berlin Criminal Police, the Kripo, which is where I acquired it.*
>
> Gunther, in *March Violets*, 1989.

Bernie Gunther is the anti-Nazi detective hero of Kerr's 'Berlin Noir' trilogy, which attracted much interest and critical favour at the time, until despite that enthusiastic reception Kerr abandoned crime fiction for mainstream thriller writing and eventually children's fiction. In the original triology, beginning in Berlin in the late 1930s, Gunther is an ex-policeman turned freelance – even Göring hires him! – but is understandably troubled by his conscience. It's no place for an honest cop. The first two books see Gunther's growing distaste for himself and those about him as they rely on an increasingly Nazified state for their income, and in the third book, set in 1947, he looks back across the horrors to cast his verdict – his final verdict, it seemed, until a fourth book appeared in 2007, swiftly followed by another in 2008.

March Violets (1989), *The Pale Criminal* (1990), *A German Requiem* (1991). Penguin published the three as a trilogy, *Berlin Noir*, in 1993. Then came *The One From The Other* (2007) in which Bernie, now in post war Munich, is invited to help former Nazis on the run. 2008 brought *A Quiet Flame*.

MICK HABERGHAM
by Colin Campbell

Curiously, the first in the Habergham series, set in the present day, had him about to retire from the force, while the second was set back in 1976 when he was a new cop on probation. (The author hadn't intended to write a series.) In *Midnight*, intended as a stand-alone, Habergham ('Ham' for short) is contemplating the impending end to his long marriage and seeks comfort on the night shift, life is quiet. But there's a mad knifeman about. *One Legged Man* leaps back to cover his early learning curve, and set as it is, thirty years before Ham's likely retirement, where it plenty of time for a proper series, in which Ham's sidekick, **PC Andy Scott**, will play a large part. Books so far are *Through the Ruins of Midnight* (2004), *Ballad of the One-Legged Man* (2006). *Midnight* has been adapted for TV.

HAGAR (or HAGAR THE GYPSEY) see Hagar **STANLEY**

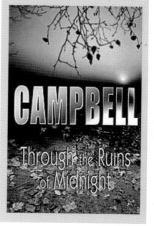

Dennis Neilson-Terry was Inspector Hanaud in 1930.

INSPECTOR HANAUD
by A. E. W. Mason

Fat, French and deliberately infuriating, though popular in his day, Hanaud was an exaggerated version of Holmes himself, but more arrogant and more athletic, surprisingly given his girth. Penned by Mason, an Englishman, the French cop appeared in six widely-spaced but entertaining crime books alongside his amusing companion **Julius Ricardo**, wine-lover and patron of the arts.

'Of course I see something. Always I see something. Am I not Hanaud?' is a typically arrogant remark from *The House of the Arrow.* (1924).

At The Villa Rose (1910) was followed by nothing until *The House of the Arrow* in 1924, *The Prisoner in the Opal* in 1928, then *They Wouldn't Be Chessmen* (1935). A novella, *The Affair at the Semiramis Hotel*, and a final book, *The House in Lordship Lane* came out in 1946.

At The Villa Rose and *The House of the Arrow* were both early films in the 1920s and 1930s, but you are unlikely to catch them now. *At the Villa Rose* starred **Teddy Arundel** as Hanaud in 1920, **Austin Trevor** in 1930, and **Kenneth Kent** in 1939. *The House of the Arrow* starred **Dennis Neilson Terry** in 1930 and **Kent** again in 1940.

FRANCIS HANCOCK
by Barbara Nadel

In novels set in the Second World War Francis Hancock is a strictly amateur sleuth, an Anglo-Indian undertaker in the London Borough of **West Ham**,whose cases arise from his work. Still shell-shocked from his time in the trenches of the First World War and disillusioned with life thereafter, he regards the dead he deals with as having been placed in his care. Where he suspects foul play he acts. He has a girlfriend, **Hannah Jacobs**, who sometimes helps with his investigations. She is single, in her forties, and works as a prostitute in the dockside community of Canning Town. She doesn't trust men and even Francis is not allowed to get too close. The pair follow up crimes committed in blitzes and in the worst times of the war.

Last Rights (2005), *After the Mourning* (2006), *Ashes to Ashes* (2008).

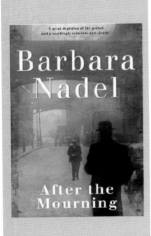

HANDFORD & ALI
by Lesley Horton

DI John Handford and DS Khalid Ali are a Bradford-based pair whose cases normally involve racial and cultural issues – hence the **Bradford** setting. The two cops were an uneasy partnership at first, as Handford had recently been accused – though exonerated – of racism and Ali considered himself a token Asian detective sent into any subdivision with a crime involving the Asian community. Suspicious of each other initially, as the series progresses we see them learn to respect each other, both as detectives and as people. These tough and realistic stories subject the complexities of multiculturism to an unflinching gaze.

Snares of Guilt (2002), *On Dangerous Ground* (2003), *Devils in the Mirror* (2005), *The Hollow Core* (2006), *Twisted Tacks* (2008).

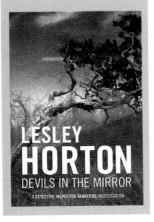

RICHARD HANNAY

by John Buchan

Gentleman-adventurer from the days when Britain still believed she ruled the world. (Her empire was the largest *in* the world.) Hannay's plucky self-confidence can sometimes tip over into xenophobia or facile contempt for his enemies, but it is that same self-confidence which drives the stories and makes them exciting adventure books. As befits the right sort of fellow, Richard Hannay has been privately educated, is rich (from his own efforts in South Africa) and has had a distinguished military career. Of all the gung-ho stories which abounded at the time, Buchan's are among the finest.

The famous book *The Thirty-nine Steps* came first, in 1915, although many Buchan fans feel that the following year's *Greenmantle* was better. Certainly its plot about Britain's enemies trying to use the Islamic prophet Greenmantle for military purposes has modern resonances. Straight after the war came *Mr Standfast* (1919) followed by *The Three Hostages* (1924) and *The Courts of Morning* (1926). Hannay also appeared in some of the short stories of *The Runagates Club* (1928) but had to wait for his final appearance (he was now *Sir* Richard Hannay) in *The Island of Sheep* (1936).

Only *The Thirty-nine Steps* has been filmed – three times: first in 1935, directed by Alfred Hitchcock, when **Robert Donat** played Hannay; then in 1959 when **Kenneth More** played him; and finally in 1978 when it was the turn of **Robert Powell**. (There was also a TV movie starring **Barry Foster**.) As ever, none of the remakes was a patch on the original.

John Buchan

FRAN HARMAN

by Judith Cutler

In this present-day series, Detective Chief Superintendent Harman is in her mid-50s, working with Assistant Chief Constable (Crime) **Mark Turner**. Fran works out of Kent Police Headquarters in **Maidstone**. Although she appears tough and impregnable she is in fact battling with a trio of personal problems: middle age, a constantly changing job and senile parents. Against this she can set her new – hopefully long-term – romantic relationship with a colleague, but even that brings problems. A policewoman's lot is not a happy one.
Life Sentence(2005), Running Deep (2008).

HARPUR & ILES

by Bill James

Detective Chief Superintendent Harpur and Assistant Chief Constable Iles make up a much-admired duo of diametrically opposed companions whose dry but witty dialogue is the main attraction in a long series of superior police procedurals. Harpur is the down-to-earth, no-holds-barred cop contrasted with the loftily egocentric Iles. For some readers it is the humour in their dialogue that is the main appeal of the series but the books are in fact tougher and more cynical than newcomers to the

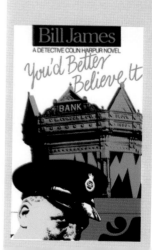

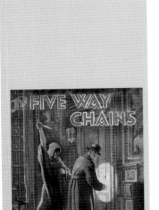

series might suspect. Harpur and Iles are dedicated to their job – so much so that they will stoop to illegality themselves to bring criminals to book. So it's particularly ironic that in later novels they are given the task of uncovering corruption elsewhere within the force. But for all their professional shortcomings the pair are not conventionally corrupt; they bend the rules into an entirely different shape but only to do what they agree is right. They are the ultimate vigilantes. It is notable how many crime writers (though by no means *all* crime writers; Julian Symons was a notable exception) place this series among their favourites.

You'd Better Believe It (1985) began the series. Apart from a slight falling-off in the most recent titles, the standard remains fairly consistent throughout the rest of the series, among which are *The Lolita Man* (1986), *Come Clean* (1989), *Astride a Grave* (1991), *Roses, Roses* (1992), *In Good Hands* (1994), *Top Banana* (1996), *Lovely Mover* (1998), *Eton Crop* (1999), *Pay Days* (2001).

DIXON HAWKE
by Edwy Searles Brooks and others
Comic paper detective in the **Sexton Blake** mould whose essential boy companion was **Tommy Burke**, Tinker being otherwise engaged. (See **Nelson Lee**.)
Appeared first in *Adventure* comic in the 1920s and faded out by the start of the Second World War.

JOHNNY HAWKE
(see **Johnny One Eye**)

DAN HAWKER
by Martin Inigo (Keith Miles)
Dan Hawker is a sports journalist in his 30s who appeared in a pair of crime novels, the first of which concerned the murder of an American star tennis player during the Monaco Open Tennis Tournament, while the second saw Dan investigate the death of an American found in a slurry lagoon near his hotel while he is covering a Ryder Cup golf match at the Belfry.
Touch Play (1991), *Stone Dead* (also 1991).

HAWKSHAW
by Tom Taylor
Detective in the trend-setting play of 1863, *Ticket of Leave Man* (see **First Detectives**), whose name became a generic term for private detective in the States where 'Hawkshaw' for private detective was later shortened to 'Hawk'. An unrelated *Hawkshaw the Detective* ran as an American cartoon drawn by Gus Mager from around 1913 into the 1940s.

HAZELL
by P. B. Yuill (Gordon Williams and Terry Venables)
James Hazell was a smart and tricky Cockney private eye (and ex-cop and ex-alcoholic) who, despite the success of the books, appeared in only three, each of which is still worth reading. Williams was an established writer (Scottish) and Venables a useful footballer who went on to become England manager.

Hazell was played by **Nicholas Ball** in the 1978 ITV series. Books: *Hazell Plays Solomon* (1974), *Hazell and the Three-Card Trick* (1975), *Hazell and the Menacing Jester* (1976).

THORPE HAZELL
by V. L. Whitechurch

A **railway detective**, in that he has a fairly common late Victorian obsession with railway timetables. He is so expert on timetables, signals, points and branch lines that he is frequently consulted by railway companies and the police for help with crimes committed on trains, or where train journeys may have played a significant part. He is as eccentric as his hobby would suggest, being practically vegan, a bibiophile and a nut. Most of his exercises were reported in magazine short stories but there was one collection:
Thrilling Stories of the Railway (1912).

CHIEF INSPECTOR HAZLERIGG
by Michael Gilbert
A meticulous and nit-picking detective who never really sparkles on the page, even though one of the books, *Smallbone Deceased*, is regarded as a minor classic. But it is a classic because of its plot, not its detective, and even Michael Gilbert admitted that he preferred his other detective **DI Petrella**. The fault, such as it is, lies with the fact that Gilbert chose to prepare a deliberately realistic portrait of his police detective; the stories themselves are well-constructed, thoroughly researched and reasonably witty.
Close Quarters (1947), *They Never Looked Inside* (1948), *The Doors Open* (1949), *Smallbone Deceased* (1950), *Death Has Deep Roots* (1951), *Fear to Tread* (1953).

ABBESS HELEWISE
by Alys Clare
A sturdy medieval abbess who, though meant to be confined within Hawkenlye Abbey, finds herself confronted by a series of God-given mysteries to solve. She manages much without His help. The series began with *Fortune Like the Moon*, though one can start anywhere e.g: *The Chatter of Maidens* (2001).

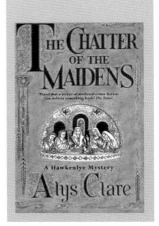

CHIEF INSPECTOR HENNESSEY
by Peter Turnbull

Based in the **Vale of York** where the author lives, this is a follow-up to Turnbull's dark 'P' Division series (see **Fabian Donoghue**) and, if not quite as dark as that series – and certainly not as dark as his deliberately shocking 1996 stand-alone novel about child abuse, *Embracing Skeletons* – these tales won't go down well with the Vale of York Tourist Board, but fans of hard-hitting modern police procedurals should enjoy them. Hennessey and his work companion **Sergeant Yellich** find nasty stuff beneath York stones.

The Hennessey books rushed out at the rate of more than one a year. *Fear of Drowning* came first, in 2000, followed by *Deathtrap* (2000), *Perils and Dangers* (2001), *The Return* (2001), *After the Flood* (2002), *Dark Secrets* (2002), *All Roads Leadeth* (2003), *The Dance Master* (2004), *False Knight* (2006), *Fire Burn* (2006), *Chelsea Smile* (2007).

MARTIN HEWITT
by Arthur Morrison

The stranger started and frowned. "You've the advantage of me, sir," he said; "you seem to know my name, but I don't know yours."

Hewitt smiled pleasantly. "My name," he said, "is Hewitt – Martin Hewitt, and it is my business to know a great many things."

From *The Case of the Flitterbat Lancers* (1896).

Among late Victorian writers, Arthur Morrison is one of the most readable – perhaps no surprise, given that he also wrote *Tales of Mean Streets* (1894) and *A Child of the Jago* (1896) – and his private investigator Hewitt is one of the most believable. Although, like all detectives of the period, he finds himself, from time to time, creeping into manor houses and investigating mysterious fraudsters, his cases are more down to earth and realistic than those of his peers. Even his career is realistic, as before becoming an investigator Hewitt started out as a solicitor's clerk. (His first cases are in that role.) Like his creator, Hewitt hails from the East End, and although he has bettered himself he remains an ordinary man, with all the advantages that brings when dealing with witnesses and ordinary criminals. Most of the stories, with the exception of the later ones in *The Red Triangle*, remain genuinely readable.

As soon as she had left, Hewitt turned to the pedestal table and probed the keyhole of the locked drawer with the small stiletto attached to his penknife. "This seems to be a common sort of lock," he said. "I could probably open it with a bent nail."

Just like that; from *The Case of Mr Gellard's Elopement, (1896)* Stories appeared in *Windsor* and *Strand* magazines etc., and the best collections were *Martin Hewitt, Investigator* (1894) and *The Adventures of Martin Hewitt* (1896)

HILDEGARD OF MEAUX
by Cassandra Clark

Hildegard is the Abbess of Meaux in the series set in the reign of Richard II and Chaucer, who becomes involved in detection initially during the aftermath of the people's rising in 1381 when there is a plot to murder the local lord, Roger de Hutton. Her less than scrupulous motives for taking holy orders are that with her husband believed dead in France, her young son in the Bishop of Norwich's army, and her daughter recently married to a Lollard knight, she decides that by joining the powerful order of Cistercians she can acquire political influence and personal independence, as well as a measure of safety in dangerous times.
Hangman Blind (2008), *The Red Velvet Turn-Shoe* (2008).

TONY HILL TV series *Wire in the Blood* (2002)
by Val McDermid

Introduced in McDermid's book *The Mermaids Singing* (1995) which actually preceded *The Wire in the Blood* (1998), Doctor Tony Hill is a clinical psychologist and profiler working closely with the police on a series of generally gruesome cases – though not too gruesome to stop its TV audience growing to a healthy 8 million per episode. Each of McDermid's books was used as a basis for TV but the series kept coming back and, as often happens, had to commission stories 'based on' her characters.

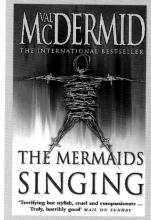

    The Mermaids Singing (1995) is where to start, although *The Wire in the Blood* (1998) and *The Last Temptation* (2002) won't disappoint.

    Wire in the Blood has had solid viewing figures since its first series in 2002. Hill is played by **Robson Green** and Carol Jordan by **Hermione Norris** till she was surprisingly replaced in series 4 (2006).

JOHN HO
by Ian Kennedy Martin

Detective Sergeant John Ho was *The Chinese Detective* from the TV series of that name. The show was the first drama to have a Chinese lead (**David Yip**) and benefited enormously from doing so. Sergeant Ho was a **London-born Chinese cop** working for the Met; his accent was near-cockney and his attitude was cockney-maverick, showing none of the 'quaint' or 'comic' Chinese traits of yesteryear, and with few politically correct concessions on his part. He is a cop who happens to be of Chinese origin. His family is more traditionally Chinese, though they have lived in London for many years, and the series shows John Ho span the gap between their lifestyle and the world he works in. But this was background; the series never let that aspect dominate what was essentially a strong and up to date police drama.

    The Chinese Detective was screened on BBC in 1981 and 1982, to good reviews and not too small an audience. It's disappointing that little followed in the quarter century since. **David Yip** played John Ho.

David Yip.

DIDO HOARE
by Marianne Macdonald
An **antiquarian book dealer** for whom crimes stroll in off the street. Disturbing the peace per volume have been a car bomb in her ex-husband's car, an escaped monkey who caused more than the usual havoc, and a book scout who had no sooner sold her a share in a medieval manuscript than he was killed. Dido suffers from a raging curiosity and can't stop from piling in – much to the annoyance of the police – and in her efforts she is aided by her father, a retired Oxford professor, and a computer geek working his way through university. How her customers put up with all the noise is another mystery.

The series began with *Death's Autograph* in 1996. *Three Monkeys* (2005) and *Faking It* (2006) are recommended.

MISS HOGG
by Austin Lee (aka John Austwick)
Forthright lady detective who specialises in crimes committed in ecclesiastical circles, about whom in *Miss Hogg Flies High* (1958) was made the famous comment, 'A curious career for a woman'. In the Golden Age tradition of the body in the baptistery and the corpse in the crypt, the stories are far-fetched but well constructed puzzle mysteries which also raise a smile.

> *"It's all due to the idiotic taboos inflicted on us by men," Miss Hogg said. "Women never had a hand in making the laws. I must say I think most men who have been bumped off by women deserved it."*
>
> *"What about Lizzie Borden's father?" asked Parker. "And I hope you don't hold a brief for Mary Blandy."*
>
> *"Of course there are exceptions," said Miss Hogg airily.*
>
> From *Miss Hogg Flies High*

Sheep's Clothing began the series, which ran to 9 titles including *Miss Hogg and the Bronte Murders* (1956), *Miss Hogg and the Dead Dean* (1957) and the final *Miss Hogg's Last Case* (1963).

SHERLOCK HOLMES
by Arthur Conan Doyle
> *"And the murderer?"*
>
> *"Is a tall man, left-handed, limps with the right leg, wears thick-soled shooting-boots and a grey cloak, smokes Indian cigars, uses a cigar holder, and carries a blunt penknife in his pocket. There are several other indications, but these may be enough to aid us in our search.'*
>
> From *The Boscombe Valley Mystery*

Conan Doyle's first Sherlock Holmes story, *A Study in Scarlet*, was rejected by two publishers and sold outright by him to Ward, Lock for a mere £25. On publication in *Beeton's Christmas Annual* for 1887 it caused barely a ripple – except from a another magazine publisher in America, the editor of *Lippincott's* who asked Doyle to write a second book for that magazine. Doyle duly produced *The Sign of Four*. This too attracted no particular interest and Doyle, unaware that the eye of fame was upon him, thought he would give up on Holmes and write the historical tales he preferred. (It has to be said that these first two Holmes novels are among Doyle's poorest works.) At least as a published author he had an agent, who sent the manuscripts for two other unpublished short stories to *Strand Magazine*.

The reception here was different. Smith, the editor, rushed to the office of his proprietor George Newnes: 'I at once realised that here was the greatest short-story writer since Edgar Allan Poe,' Smith said later. *Strand* ordered six stories, for which they paid two hundred pounds. The first of these, *The Adventure of a Scandal in Bohemia*, appeared in 1891 – while Doyle settled down to write his next historical novel, *The Refugees*. But Sherlock Homes was a success. *Strand*'s circulation leapt. The editor offered Doyle £300 for a further six stories and he, disappointed to put *The Refugees* aside, reluctantly agreed. In a sense, Doyle's reluctance foreshadowed the attitude he would have toward his creation for the rest of his life. Sherlock Holmes, he thought, was trivial, a mere entertainment, and what mattered were his historical novels. He was spectacularly wrong.

'Life is infinitely stranger than anything which the mind of man could invent. We would not dare to conceive the things which are really mere commonplaces of existence. If we could fly out of that window hand in hand, hover over this great city, gently remove the roofs, and peep in at the queer things which are going on, the strange coincidences, the plannings, the cross-purposes, the wonderful chains of events, working through generations, and leading to the most outré results, it would make all fiction with its conventionalities and foreseen conclusions most stale and unprofitable.'

Holmes, *in A Case of Identity*

The public devoured Sherlock Holmes. Before the last of the six stories had appeared their fame was such that people queued to snatch new issues of *Strand* magazine from news-stalls. Doyle meanwhile had written to his mother that the second six would complete the stories he would write: he would then kill off Sherlock Holmes and go back to writing novels 'You won't! You can't! You mustn't!' his mother replied. George Newnes echoed her; he wanted more. Conan Doyle said that in that case he wanted £1,000 for twelve – an impossible demand, he thought, to place on a mere magazine. Wrong again. But twenty-four stories, he determined, was all there should be. Despite the pleading of his agent and publisher, Doyle's twenty-fourth Holmes story was the one that he himself – he alone – had been looking forward to: *The Final Problem*. In this story came the famous 'death' of Sherlock Holmes, when the great detective tumbled together with his adversary **Moriarty** into the Reichenbach Falls. Holmes was dead.

The story appeared in the December 1893 edition of *Strand* and shocked the nation. Keen fans wore black arm bands. Hundreds of

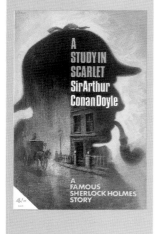

letters were written to Doyle and to his publisher. But Doyle remained adamant: Holmes was dead and he, Conan Doyle, would win a new public with historical dramas. Not until 1901 did he relent, when after continual demands for Sherlock Holmes to reappear, and (more importantly, perhaps?) with only moderate sales for his historical stories, Doyle 'resurrected' Holmes, first in the full-length novel *The Hound of the Baskervilles* set, Doyle emphasised, *before* the Reichenbach incident but then, as Doyle accepted the inevitable, in a true resurrection ('I think, sir, when Holmes fell over that cliff, he may not have killed himself ... ') in the 1903 short story *The Empty House*. But Holmes' finest day was past. Like an ageing, much-loved actor brought out of retirement for one last farewell tour and then one more, Sherlock Holmes continued to perform – rather frailer, not so fresh, lacking the sparkle and innovation that had set him above competitors – in further stories. Doyle himself dramatised one of his stories *The Speckled Band* for the stage in 1910.

> *It seems that a young lady has arrived in a considerable state of excitement, who insists upon seeing me. She is waiting now in the sitting-room. Now, when young ladies wander about the metropolis at this hour of the morning, and knock sleepy people up out of their beds, I presume that it is something very pressing which they have to communicate.*

Holmes, in *The Speckled Band*

Came the First World War and Holmes' career was surely over – but no: one last appearance, a collection of stories emphatically entitled *His Last Bow*, introduced as ever by the trusty **Dr Watson**: 'The friends of Mr Sherlock Holmes will be glad to learn that he is still alive and well, though somewhat crippled by attacks of rheumatism.' He was not so

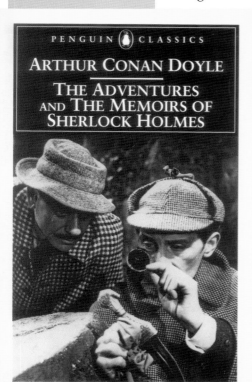

crippled that, among other exploits, he could not foil a German spy. Now, surely, Holmes could be laid to rest. In that apparently final tale – written in the middle of the interminable and terrible First World War – Watson described Holmes' departure from the stage in apocalyptic terms: 'One might have thought already that God's curse hung heavy on a degenerate world, for there was an awesome hush and a feeling of vague expectancy in the sultry and stagnant air. The sun had long set, but one blood-red gash like an open wound lay low in the distant west.' But it was not to be. A decade later came yet one more gathering of late short stories and, though they were weak, one still saw flashes of the ageing trouper's old appeal: this was *The Casebook of Sherlock Holmes*.

'It seems possible,' said Ian Ousby in *Bloodhounds of Heaven*, 'that Sherlock Holmes is the most famous character in English literature.' No fictional detective has had so much quasi-biographical research and documenting as has this great detective. Within

Doyle's own works we glean that Holmes was born in Yorkshire on 6 January 1854, the third son of a country squire. He is supposedly the grandson of a sister of the French artist Émile Jean-Horace Vernet, though despite Holmes' love for the violin there is no record of another musician in his lineage. He was educated at Christ Church, Oxford, where he never mixed much with fellow students. By 1881 he had become a successful detective, often consulted by the police, and it was in that year that he and Doctor Watson began to share lodgings at **221B Baker Street** (an address which never actually existed, despite the plaque today outside the reconstructed number 221).

> *It was a cold morning of the early spring, and we sat after breakfast on either side of a cheery fire in the old room in Baker Street. A thick fog rolled down between the lines of dun-coloured houses, and the opposing windows loomed like dark, shapeless blurs, through the heavy yellow wreaths. Our gas was lit, and shone on the white cloth, and a glimmer of china and metal, for the table had not been cleared yet. Sherlock Holmes had been silent all the morning, dipping continuously into the advertisement columns of a succession of papers, until at last, having apparently given up his search, he had emerged in no very sweet temper to lecture me on my literary shortcomings.*
>
> Watson, in *The Copper Beeches*

From Watson again we learn that the distinguished Holmes wrote a notable monograph, *Upon the Tracing of Footsteps*, and another *On the Polyphonic Motets of Lassus* which, according to Watson, was 'said by experts to be the last word upon the subject'. (It is actually a private joke by Conan Doyle, since a polyphonic motet is an obvious tautology.) Holmes also wrote *The Influences of a Trade upon the Form of a Hand* and his last known opus (written in his attempted retirement before the action of *His Final Bow*) was a *Practical Handbook of Bee Culture, with Some Observations upon the Segregation of the Queen*. Doyle clearly had his tongue pressed against his cheek, and Holmes fans have entertained themselves and each other since by expanding Holmes' history. Complete chronologies of his movements have been created, with ingenious excuses given for the inevitable inconsistencies in the tales.

These exercises are Holmes' devotees having fun; Doyle did not plan his short stories as a single interconnected narrative. Within the stories are numerous inconsistencies and bluffs which devotees have spent many hours teasing out. Books and monographs have been written on the subject, often amusing, always detailed, and a taste of this can be found in the Penguin edition that combines *The Adventures* and *The Memoirs* with 45 pages of deliberately finicky notes by Ed Glinert. Much of what we 'know' of Holmes comes from his devotees rather than from Doyle; even Holmes' trademark deerstalker hat is the invention of the original illustrator **Sydney Paget**. Our view of Holmes

Statue to the world famous detective in Switzerland.

himself is constructed partly from Paget's drawings and partly from the screen portrayals, of which the most lasting was from Basil Rathbone.

None of this should detract from the achievement of Doyle himself. He may have resented – even failed to understand – his own creation, but Sherlock Holmes really was the great detective. He had far more character than any detective before – and one is tempted to say, more than any detective since – his deductive method was revolutionary, his adventures were astonishing, original and brisk. This last should not be ignored. Conceived in the last years of the Victorian era, the Sherlock Holmes stories have little nineteenth century stodginess. When one reads the stories today they may recall hansom cabs and fog, high-born ladies and international villains, country houses and a vanished London, but their pace and sprightliness, their humour and ingenuity astound. There have been many pastiches of Sherlock Holmes, yet no pastiche is brighter than the originals. The stories, as Doyle wrote them, are as tight and easy to read as any crime stories written today. Compared to the laboured tales they competed with they are in a different league, and they still stand head and shoulders above the rest.

Sherlock Holmes was a man, however, who when he had an unsolved problem upon his mind would go for days, and even for a week, without rest, turning it over, rearranging his facts, looking at it from every point of view, until he had either fathomed it, or convinced

Jeremy Brett and Edward Hardwicke as Holmes and Watson outside the famous address.

Peter Cushing.

himself that his data were insufficient. It was soon evident to me that he was now preparing for an all-night sitting. He took off his coat and waistcoat, put on a large blue dressing-gown, and then wandered about the room collecting pillows from his bed, and cushions from the sofa and armchairs. With these he constructed a sort of Eastern divan, upon which he perched himself cross-legged, with an ounce of shag tobacco and a box of matches laid out in front of him. In the dim light of the lamp I saw him sitting there, an old brier pipe between his lips, his eyes fixed vacantly upon the corner of the ceiling, the blue smoke curling up from him, silent, motionless, with the light shining upon his aquiline features. So he sat as I dropped off to sleep, and so he sat when a sudden ejaculation caused me to wake up, and I found the summer sun shining into the apartment. The pipe was still between his lips, the smoke still curled upwards,

and the room was full of a dense tobacco haze, but nothing remained of the heap of shag which I had seen upon the previous night.

From *The Man With The Twisted Lip*

A Study in Scarlet (1888) and *The Sign of Four* (1890) are the first two novels, but if you are returning to Sherlock Holmes or, astonishingly, if you intend to read him for the first time, you should begin with the short stories. All collections are still in print, but they were originally issued as *The Adventures of Sherlock Holmes* (1892) and *The Memoirs of Sherlock Holmes* (1894) – these two are the finest – followed by *The Return of Sherlock Holmes* (1905), and later, *His Last Bow* (1917) and *The Case-Book of Sherlock Holmes* (1927). The other two full-length novels are *The Hound of the Baskervilles* (1902) and *The Valley of Fear* (1914).

There have been several portrayals on TV. In 1951 the BBC presented six of the stories, with **Alan Wheatley** playing Holmes and **Raymond Francis** as Watson. A 1965 series (following a 1964 one-off, *The Speckled Band*) saw **Douglas Wilmer** take on the Holmes role, with **Nigel Stock** as perhaps the most memorable Dr Watson. Stock kept the part for the 1968 series, when **Peter Cushing** took over as the great detective. **Jeremy Brett** was TV's most colourful Sherlock, neo-Byronic, complete with cocaine, insults and eccentricity, in a long-running series from 1984 to 1994, in which Watson was played first by **David Burke**, then from 1986 by **Edward Hardwicke**. In 2007 attention switched to the urchins Holmes occasionally employed to help track miscreants in the streets: *The Baker Street Irregulars* starred **Jonathan Pryce** as Homes and **Bill Paterson** as Watson. One might also mention *Young Sherlock* (ITV 1982), an 8-part children's series in which the 16-year-old 'tec was played by **Guy Henry**.

The cinema has always loved Sherlock Holmes – from the earliest days: *Sherlock Holmes Baffled* was an American short silent in 1900. **Viggo Larsen** may not have been the first Holmes but was the first actor to play Holmes repeatedly (between 1908 and 1919). **Georges Treville** played him in eight films around 1912 and 1913. Various early American actors tackled the part including **Francis Ford** (John Ford's brother), **William Gillette** and **John Barrymore**. The oddly named **Eille Norwood** made nearly fifty Holmes films in the early 1920s. **Clive Brook** played him. In Britain, **Raymond Massey** and **Arnold Wontner** led the way, till **Basil Rathbone** made the role his own (14 films, from 1939 to 1946). **Peter Cushing** stepped in for Hammer's 1959 *The Hound of the Baskervilles*, and perhaps inevitably, his sparring mate **Christopher Lee** played him three years later. **John Neville**, **Robert Stephens**, **Nicol Williamson**, **Christopher Plummer** and both **Peter Cook** and **Michael Caine** (as spoofs) have played him too. As Conan Doyle found, Sherlock Holmes has become immortal.

Ben Kingsley as Dr Watson and Michael Caine as Holmes.

An early silent movie Sherlock Holmes, William Gillette.

Gordon Harker.

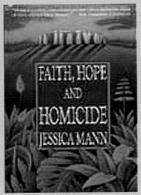

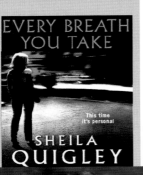

MARTY HOPKIRK TV series *Randall and Hopkirk (Deceased)*
See **Jeff Randall**

INSPECTOR HORNLEIGH
scripted by John P. Wynn (Hans Wolfgang Priwin)
Star of a popular pre-war radio series (from 1937), where he was played
by **S. J. Warmington**. His able sergeant was **Sergeant Bingham**,
played by **Ewart Scott**. A stage play followed, in 1938.

   Inspector Hornleigh was released in 1938, with **Gordon Harker** as
Hornleigh and **Alastair Sim** as Bingham. Follow-ups were *Inspector
Hornleigh Goes To It* (1939) and *Inspector Hornleigh on Holiday* (1940).
Despite their titles, each film was an improvement on the one before.

TAMARA HOYLAND
by Jessica Mann
An interesting example of a character taking over someone else's series.
Tamara Hoyland first appears as an archaeology student in a short-lived
series (two books) about her Edinburgh university tutor, **Thea
Crawford**, and did not branch out in her own story until 1981 with
Funeral Sites. Ex-tutor Crawford, though, was the initiator of Tamara's
second adventure in the follow-up, *No Man's Island* (1983), an
adventure indeed, with the plucky Hoyland dispatched to a remote
British island as an undercover agent in a murky dispute between
islanders and the government for the island's oil. The archaeological
slant continued through titles such as *A Kind of Healthy Grave* and
Death Beyond the Nile.
Funeral Sites (1981), *No Man's Island* (1983), *Grave Goods* (1984), *A
Kind of Healthy Grave* (1986), *Death Beyond the Nile* (1988) and *Faith,
Hope and Homicide* (1991).

LORRAINE HUNT
by Sheila Quigley
Detective Inspector Hunt might be excused if she thought her
Houghton-le-Spring patch would yield little in terms of major or
dramatic crime, but in that assumption, if in little else, she would be
wrong. This northern town, one that many southerners would be hard-
pressed to place on a map, is a hotbed of murderers and rapists. (Or it
is in Quigley's books, if not in reality.) In her first outing Hunt chases
down the 'Head Hunter' from an old case, and a violent
kidnapper from the present. In the recent *Every Breath You
Take* the local serial killer may have attacked the daughter of
Lorraine's partner, **DS Luke Daniels**. It's a living hell up
there.

   Much publicity was given to Quigley's being an ordinary
woman who turned to writing late. A grandmother and long-
time factory worker, her *Run for Home* came out in 2004, and
was followed by *Bad Moon Rising* (2005), *Living on a
Prayer* (2006), and *Every Breath You Take* (2007).

CETIN IKMEN
by Barbara Nadel

Cetin Ikmen is an **Istanbul** policeman, a Senior Homicide Detective Inspector in the Turkish National Police Force. Istanbul is a very different place: Cetin's mother was a neighbourhood witch – something not unknown in modern Istanbul – and his cases range from racist murder to the hunt for a serial killer in the gay community – another thing not unknown in modern Istanbul. Ikmen himself is shambolic, happily married with nine children (no longer all at home), he chain smokes, he likes the occasional drink and he is among those who firmly support the secular Republic. Though the Istanbul force is a modern force and well equipped, Ikmen likes to do a lot of walking and talking and getting out to where the action is. Accompanying Ikmen is Inspector Mehmet Suleyman, 17 years younger than Ikmen and from an old Ottoman family which has fallen on hard times. Younger than Ikmen, women generally find Mehmet irresistible. *Deadly Web* won the CWA Silver Dagger for 2005.

Titles include *Belshazzar's Daughter* (1999), *Deadly Web* (2005), *A Passion for Killing* (2007).

KATE IVORY
by Veronica Stallwood

An Oxford-based novelist – and jogger – who keeps running into trouble. Very **Oxford** in flavour (Stallwood was a librarian at the Bodleian), the plots revolve around stolen books and crucial papers found in libraries. An intelligent series.

Death and the Oxford Box came first in 1993, and it has been followed by a book every year, each with *Oxford* in its title.

KEN JACKSON
See **David Webb**

FRANK JACOBSON
by Iain McDowall

DCI Frank Jacobson may seem bleak and unsympathetically drawn, but to McDowall's fans, it is Jacobson's dark take on life and his black humour that appeal. Jacobson has a failed marriage behind him, one daughter, and a readiness to take a drink. (He prefers beer to spirits.) His politics, though kept in the background, are clearly left-wing, and his relationship with criminals is not automatically censorious. It is not difficult to detect the guiding hand of a left-wing author in these novels, but McDowall is an author who lets neither preaching, politics nor 'message' interrupt his story. Jacobson is assisted by **DS Kerr**.

The fictional English town of **Crowby** is portrayed as hard, but the viewpoint is softened by McDowall's injections of dark humour. Author Andrew Taylor described Crowby in a review as less a town than 'a state of mind'. It appears real, has its own consistency, but is based on no particular real-life locale – though is clearly within commuting

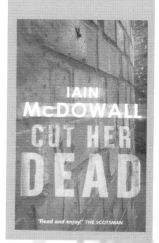

distance of Birmingham. Rather than serve as a mere background to the stories, Crowby the town appears in each book with as much personality as its inhabitants, and stands as a metaphor for the increasingly amoral and uncaring attitudes promoted and praised in modern British life.

The first book, *A Study in Death*, though published in 2000, was written and set five years earlier. Later books in the series are contemporaneous with when they were written. McDowall's style is unusual in that many scenes are seen through the eyes and perceived through the thoughts of specific, though different, characters – law abiding or law breaking. The crimes he writes about are equally untraditional: he features a 'family annihilator' in *Perfectly Dead* (2003), twenty-first-century arms dealers in *Making a Killing* (2001) and far-right racist killers in his fourth book *Killing for England* (2005). *Cut Her Dead* appeared in 2007.

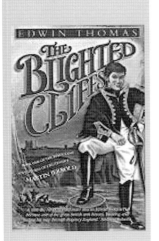

MR JELLIPOT
by Sydney Fowler
Crime-solving solicitor from a series which was quite successful in its time. Fowler is the pseudonym of the science fiction writer S. Fowler Wright. *The Bell Street Murders* came first, in 1931, and *With Cause Enough* was the ninth and last, in 1954.

MARTIN JERROLD
by Edwin Thomas
Back in the spirit-stirring days when Britain fought the French and Napoleon, there was one man who managed to emerge from Trafalgar without an ounce of credit. Through a weakness for rum and his bad luck, Lieutenant Martin Jerrold managed it. Bullied and harangued by his powerful uncle at the Admiralty, his career thereafter staggered from one near-disaster to the next: battling smugglers in Dover, chasing escaped French prisoners-of-war across England, and finally travelling to America to thwart a conspiracy that might have ended Britain's war against Napoleon for good. With cowardice and incompetence matched only by his knack for landing in trouble, Jerrold's misadventures remind one of **Flashman** and offer a sly counterpoint to the derring-do of his naval contemporary **Horatio Hornblower**.
The Blighted Cliffs (2003), *The Chains of Albion* (2004), *Treason's River* (2006).

JOHNSON JOHNSON
by Dorothy Dunnett
A hard-to-define character with a small but serious fan base: part spy, part detective; part professional painter, part amateur; part action hero, part silly ass. His upper class background and education allow him to turn up in an old jumper and baggy trousers, before appearing for dinner in a formal suit. He often wears bifocal glasses – a trait few women avoid commenting upon, and one which encourages a number of subtle jokes. Throughout the series the jokes, characters and plots

are subtly delineated, making the books fino sherry to others' Burgundy. But they leave a lingering sadness, which increases in later titles. Beneath the semi-comedy, tragedy lurks in wait.

His yacht is called *Dolly*. Hence the titles: *Dolly and the Singing Bird* (1968), *Dolly and the Cookie Bird* (1970), *Dolly and the Doctor Bird* (1971), *Dolly and the Starry Bird* (1973), *Dolly and the Nanny Bird* (1976), *Dolly and the Bird of Paradise* (1983), and the final *Moroccan Traffic* (1991).

MIKE JOHNSON
(see **India Kane**)

SAM JONES
by Lauren Henderson

Samantha Jones is a very 1990s creation, a sparky feminist, witty and assured, artistic and capable. She sculpts metal (designer jewellery) and goes anywhere she damned well wants. If a hunt takes her into the world of rubber fetishism, animal rights groups, art students, fringe theatre or merchant banking, it's all one to our Sam. Lauren Henderson is a founder member of a group of '**Tart Noir**' authors (all female) determined to stamp all over what a few diehards still see as male territory. Their quest comes about a hundred years too late, but it's still fun.

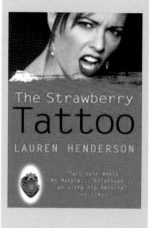

Dead White Female (1995) was an effective shocker that made critics sit up and take notice, and was followed by a succession of eye-catching titles: *Too Many Blondes* (1996), *Black Rubber Dress* (1997), *Freeze My Margarita* (1998), *The Strawberry Tattoo* (1999), *Chained!* (2000) and *Pretty Boy* (2001).

INSPECTOR JURNET
by S. T. Haymon

Ben Jurnet is a handsome man (his colleagues call him 'Valentino') working in **Norfolk** CID. One of the least aggressive cops, he hates to intrude. He is equally diffident about his love life: half-affianced to Miriam, who will marry him only if he converts to Judaism. Religion plays quite a part in these books, with Jurnet investigating a murder at a saint's shrine in the splendidly titled *Death and the Pregnant Virgin*, a dead choirboy in *Ritual Murder* and a splash of Druidism in *Death of a Warrior Queen*.

Haymon didn't write her first book till she was over 60 and she sadly died in 1995, so the complete range of Jurnet books is: *Death and the Pregnant Virgin* (1980), *Ritual Murder* (1982), *Stately Homicide* (1984), *Death of a God* (1987), *A Very Particular Murder* (1989), *Death of a Warrior Queen* (1991), *A Beautiful Death* (1993) and *Death of a Hero* (1996).

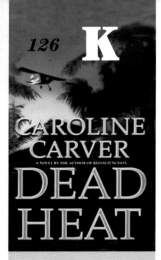

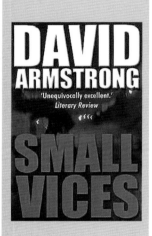

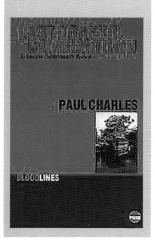

INDIA KANE
by C. J. Carver

India Kane is a features journalist whose investigations into criminal affairs have her working closely with Detective Sergeant **Mike Johnson** in a set of stories ranging from the **Australian outback** to the metropolis of Sydney. Described by reviewers as 'relentless page turners', they are contemporary novels involving love, greed, ambition and murder. The first, *Blood Junction*, won the coveted CWA Debut Dagger award and the pace, if anything, increased with the second, *Dead Heat*, concerning people-smuggling and Chinese villains whose pastimes included removing fingers with secateurs and leaving the victims to bleed to death. Carver threw in crocodiles, explosions and mysterious medicines to keep things hot.
Blood Junction (2001), *Dead Heat* (2003), *Black Tide* (2004).

DI FRANK KAVANAGH
by David Armstrong

We first meet Kavanagh as a forty-somethhing DI, recently divorced and recovering from a nervous breakdown. Seconded to London, he takes up with colleague **Jane Salt**, a streetwise Detective Constable, resilient and Jewish. They become lovers and crime-busters combined. Kavanagh's first appearance was in 1995's *Until Dawn Tomorrow*, his second was in *Thought For The Day* (1997), his third was *Small Vices* (2001) and his/their fourth outing, *A Kind of Acquaintance* (2007) the story runs on a tragic hit and run accident in 1986, the repurcussions of which are only fully felt twenty years later when a novelist disappears from her houseboat on the Grand Union Canal and is subsequently found murdered.

LENNOX KEMP
by M. R. D. Meek

An ex-solicitor turned private detective and later re-accepted as a solicitor, Kemp is a plump 40-something who doesn't marry until late in life (and late in the series). There is less blood and mayhem in this series than in many, but Meek might argue that the family troubles Kemp tends to handle are even more painful.

Mike Ashley complains that Meek's first book *With Flowers That Fell* (1983) is 'hard to find' but there have been plenty since – seven more in the 1980s, four in the 1990s, and two more since his *If You Go Down To The Woods* in 2001: *The Vanishing Point* (2003) and (ominously) *Kemp's Last Case* (2004).

CRISTY KENNEDY
by Paul Charles

Inspector Kennedy, though on a tough north London beat, is made deliberately different from other fictional cops in that he is milder. Where others are hard-drinking battle veterans with crumpled home lives, Cristy Kennedy drinks little stronger than tea (of which he drinks

almost as much as Tony Benn), and despite being in his late 30s and therefore born after 1960, is an ardent Beatles fan. Even the books' titles play with expectations: *Last Boat to Camden Town* is actually about the *first* boat. Music throbs through all the Kennedy books – but Paul Charles himself has been a roadie, a record producer and pop concert organiser.

Series includes *Last Boat to Camden Town* (1996), *The Hissing of the Silent Lonely Room* (2001), *I've Heard the Banshees Sing* (2003).

SUPERINTENDENT KENWORTHY
by John Buxton Hilton

Solid straightforward old-style copper, clever and determined, but whose career eventually fades. In the first books he is a mere Inspector, is promoted, but in the final books of a fairly long series Kenworthy takes early retirement and investigates cases privately. It's all very realistic in its way, but equally, a little dull. A library stand-by in the days when people went to the library to borrow books.

Death of an Alderman came first in 1968 and the series ended on the author's death with *Displaced Persons* (1987).

CONSTABLE KERR
by Peter Alding (Roderic Jeffries)

Young and surprisingly optimistic policeman who learns his trade from his older boss, the 'been there, seen that' **Inspector Fusil**. Against them are not only wily criminals but some unreliable witnesses. Why this particular *bête noir*? Author Jeffries had been a barrister in the 1950s.

The series ran from *The CID Room* (1967) to *One Man's Justice* (1983).

DS KERR
(see **Frank Jacobson**)

SAL KILKENNY
by Cath Staincliffe

Single-parent Sal Kilkenny juggles her work as a private investigator in the mean streets of the rainy city (**Manchester**) with the demands of home and kids. She lives in a shared house, enjoys the support of a close-knit circle of friends and escapes to her garden when in need of solace. Not the most hard-bitten PI, Kilkenny gets more involved in the plight of her clients than is good for her, and in consequence her fierce sense of justice leads her into jeopardy. The stories are an interesting contrast to those of the copper **Janine Lewis**, from the same author. *Looking For Trouble* (1994) starts the series, *Towers of Silence* (2002) is particularly recommended, and *Missing* came out in 2007.

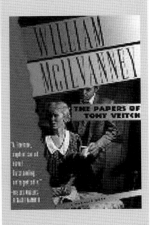

Natasha Cooper.

WILLOW KING

by Natasha Cooper

Lightly written but complex amateur sleuth drawn into cases via her part-time day-job auditing for the Department of Old Age Pensions and for Inland Revenue (which wouldn't make her the most attractive heroine to some readers). This dull day-job informs her other (one assumes equally part-time) job – as a successful romantic novelist 'Cressida Woodruffe'. Complications are inevitable. As the King series develops, romance gradually insinuates itself into her life in the shapely form of detective **Tom Worth** – but despite this, the crimes that she investigates are intriguing. Cooper also writes the **Trish Maguire** series.

Festering Lilies (1990), *Poison Flowers* (1991), *Bloody Roses* (1992), *Bitter Herbs* (1993), *Rotten Apples* (1995), *Fruiting Bodies* (1996) – in which she has a baby, and *Sour Grapes* (1997).

LAIDLAW

by William McInvanney

Laidlaw defines **Glasgow** in the same way Rebus defines Edinburgh. McIlvanney's prose is rock hard and angry, but funny with it – typically Glasgow, one might say. And Laidlaw is Glaswegian too: a strong man but not insensitive. Hard as he is, he has a brain. Jack Laidlaw reads and, a touch unconvincingly, keeps books by Camus and Kierkegaard in his office drawer. Despite that authorial concession, Laidlaw convinces as a cop, and we have no difficulty in believing that he can face up to and face down the mean city's notorious hard men. From within the Glasgow CID he strides from tough gang leaders to pathetic drunkards, from councillors to vagrants, without fear. He has seen it all and little fazes him – but some things, the most extreme, do touch him, and it is his deeply buried and masked humanity which makes Laidlaw real and his few tales worth reading. McIlvanney – who is a poet and writer of non-crime novels as well – has many fans among fellow crime writers (despite his tiny crime output); American crime writer Ross Macdonald went out of his way to praise the first book *Laidlaw* (1977), and Britain's Crime Writers' Association twice awarded him a Silver Dagger. *Laidlaw* (Silver Dagger, 1977), *The Papers of Tony Veitch* (Silver Dagger, 1983), *Strange Loyalties* (1991).

ARNOLD LANDON

by Roy Lewis

An **archaeologist** who seems to dig into crimes as often as into the ground, always looking for buried secrets, Landon has uncovered cases of modern-day drug-dealing, Chinese ganglords and corporate malfeasance while at the same time getting his hands dirty as he finds traces of Celtic bog people, Roman grave robbers and the Knights Templar. Some of the cases he discovers for himself, but on others he is called in as an expert witness. This quiet but effective series should soon reach its twentieth full-length novel.

STALKER
LIZA CODY

The series began in 1982 with *A Gathering of Ghosts*. Later titles have included *Men of Subtle Craft* (1987), *The Ghost Dancers* (1989), *Grave Error* (2005) and *Dragon Head* (2007).

JULIA LARWOOD
(see **Hilary Tamar**)

LORETTA LAWSON
by Joan Smith

As one would expect from this well-known feminist writer her heroine is a feminist investigator. Not a professional PI, Loretta Lawson is a university lecturer seemingly beset by examples of male chauvinism – though this is not to suggest that the books are grindingly polemical, because they are not: they are feminine but not aggressively feminist. Lawson is believable both as a lecturer and as an amateur but committed detective. Joan Smith seems to have had a lower opinion of her books than had her critics (who were generally more than favourable) since after the ominously named *Full Stop* she appears to have given up crime fiction for non-fiction and journalism.

A Masculine Ending (1987), *Why Aren't They Screaming?* (1988), *Don't Leave Me This Way* (1990), *What Men Say* (1993), *Full Stop* (1996).

A Masculine Ending was televised and shown in 1992, and *Don't Leave Me This Way* in 1993.

ANNA LEE
by Liza Cody

A female detective for whom the word 'feisty' could have been coined. She lives in a houseboat on the Thames, and in the books she is tough and fairly self-reliant (even if she does call on even tougher male friends when fists are needed), but she was made more feminine – too feminine, said many – on TV, which in the pilot found many opportunities to have Anna climb a ladder while the camera skulked about below to peep up her skirt. Anna wore denim jeans in the later, surprisingly short-lived series, but she remained softer than on the page. An ex-cop, Anna works for the Brierly Detective Agency where, as she herself would want, she is expected to handle the same cases a man would handle. Despite this, she remains a refreshingly feminine detective, able to empathise and bond with her contacts while never losing sight of her goal. She has a love life too, which in the books remains another part of her life and doesn't get in the way as she slips out to solve her cases.

Dupe (1980) won the John Creasey Memorial Dagger, and was followed by *Bad Company* (1982), *Stalker* (1984), *Head Case* (1985), *Under Contract* (1986), *Backhand* (1991).

Imogen Stubbs played Anna on TV in a 1994 series which achieved healthy viewing figures while annoying the books' fans. **Brian Glover** played her wrestler friend Selwyn Price.

Imogen Stubbs

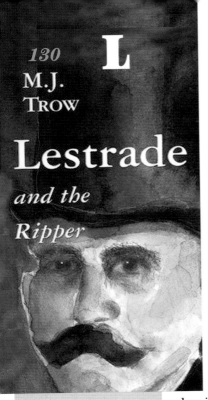

M.J. TROW

L

Lestrade

and the

Ripper

NELSON LEE

created by Maxwell Scott (John Staniforth)

Another **Sexton Blake** look-alike, whose boy companion is called **Nipper** and whose London office is in Gray's Inn Road. He first appeared in *Marvel*, a boys' paper, in 1894, and sleuthed on until the 1930s, although from 1917 he also worked as a schoolmaster at 'St Frank's'. In this latter and unlikely position he became even more famous. One of the main authors to continue the series was **Edwy Searles Brooks**, who also wrote **Dixon Hawke**.

INSPECTOR LESTRADE

by M. J. Trow

So many tricks and variations have been extracted from **Sherlock Holmes** that someone *had* to look again at Holmes' put-upon and surprisingly accommodating Inspector Lestrade. In Conan Doyle's stories Lestrade is usually a butt for Holmes' sarcasm, much like Watson, but like Watson and everyone else in the world Lestrade is not a fool: he is merely unable to match the great detective's mercurial mind. Trow brings him back in this series to solve mysteries often based on real-life crimes of the day, including Jack the Ripper inevitably, and those pesky suffragettes and goings-on in the royal household. Trow's Lestrade is sharper than Doyle made him and if he is still not quite up the master's level he has become a nicer man.

Trow produced sixteen of these fine stories in a decade, starting with *The Adventures of Inspector Lestrade* (1985) and ending with *Lestrade and the Devil's Own* (1996).

DCI JANINE LEWIS TV series *Blue Murder* (2003)

by Cath Staincliffe

TV series that developed from an unpublished novel (*Cry Me A River*) written by an established crime writer (see her **Sal Kilkenny**) in which **Caroline Quentin** plays Staincliffe's Manchester-based single mum cop who, though separated from feckless Pete (**Joe Tucker**), cast more than an eye over colleague Richard Mayne (**Ian Kelsey**). Since the show has been on air Staincliffe has written two novels about her police woman hero. In these she explores Janine's inner-life and reactions to her work in greater depth than could be done on screen. Janine Lewis contrasts with Staincliffe's other heroine Sal Kilkenny, who works outside the force and whose career is less obviously successful. The books are, *Blue Murder: Cry Me A River* (2004) and *Hit and Run* (2005). *Blue Murder* was piloted in 2003 and has since run to four series.

SERGEANT LEWIS TV series *Inspector Morse* (1987-2000)

See **Inspector Morse**

The *Morse* series was too successful to be allowed to pass away when its lead actor died, so in 2007 a spin-off, *Lewis*, began with **Kevin Whately** as the ever-reliable Detective Sergeant Robbie Lewis.

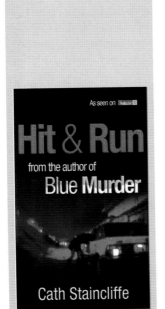

As seen on

Hit & Run

from the author of

Blue Murder

Cath Staincliffe

STONE LEWIS
by John Baker

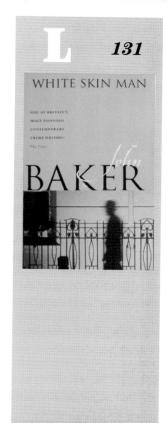

From the creator of **Sam Turner** comes another extraordinary private eye (are no detectives normal?). Stone Lewis is autistic and struggling to function in a world he finds perpetually confusing. Hard enough trying to live like that, let alone be a detective. Yet, to the credit of John Baker's writing, the character does just about work – and certainly his handicap adds an extra edge to the narrative. Lewis works in the grim city of **Hull**, a failing fishing port with high unemployment and a dearth of money. We meet him first in the excellent *The Chinese Girl*, a tale which mingles racism, drug dealing, gang warfare, mental illness and, fortunately, generous dollops of dark humour and empathetic writing. The second book, *White Skin Man*, is even more political: about racism again, in which Baker's message is that the villains are not only those who *are* racists but also those of us who see and don't react, the closet condoners. In Baker's book, by contrast, some of the villains (or members of the underclass, the skinheads and druggies) are portrayed sympathetically. Strong stuff: as far from cosy as one can get.
The Chinese Girl (2000), *White Skin Man* (2004), *Winged With Death* (2007)

DARINA LISLE
by Janet Laurence

Darina Lisle comes from the pen of a cookery writer who produced a weekly column for the *Daily Telegraph* and has written six cookery books, so it is no surprise that the series is enriched by gourmet recipes and juicy titbits from the world of high gastronomy. It began in 1989 with *A Deepe Coffyn* when Darina, an apprentice chef hired by the Society of Historical Gastronomes, helped prepare authentic feasts for their annual weekend. Two people died mysteriously – neither was poisoned – and suspicion fell on young Darina. The novel is as much a satire on the higher echelons of catering as it is a satisfying whodunit.

Seven more Darina Lisle titles followed at the rate of one a year, with a further two titles in 1998 and 2000. By the time of the tenth book (*The Mermaid's Feast*, 2002) Darina was married to the Detective **William Pigram**. For this adventure Davina dragged him away for two weeks on a luxury liner where her only duty was to advise the owners on the most suitable menus. Or so she thought. A lovelorn purser disappeared – and it wasn't suicide. Once again Darina and her husband had a succulent mystery on their hands.

LILA LISLE
by Adelie Ascott (John W. Bobin)

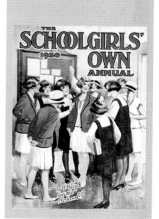

Teenage girl sleuth from the creator of **Sylvia Silence**, but for a rival magazine *Schoolgirls' Own*. Lila is the awkwardly named 'Girl Problem Investigator' and a slightly less physical, more empathetic detective than Miss Silence. To the envy of her teenage readers, Lila wore artificial silk stockings, a cloche hat and a fur-collared coat – which when duty calls

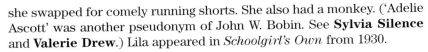

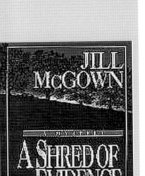

she swapped for comely running shorts. She also had a monkey. ('Adelie Ascott' was another pseudonym of John W. Bobin. See **Sylvia Silence** and **Valerie Drew**.) Lila appeared in *Schoolgirl's Own* from 1930.

LLOYD & HILL
by Jill McGown
Chief Inspector Lloyd gives little away – not even his first name. Presumably his sidekick **Judy Hill** learnt it, since she eventually became his lover. She is the more human of the two (beginning as Sergeant and later promoted to Inspector) but it's the dogged Lloyd who usually ploughs through to a 'result'. In most of the novels McGown gives them barely as much time on the page as she gives the victims, but this adds breadth and background and helps bring the reader into the story. *A Perfect Match* (1983) stood on its own for a while until *Redemption* (1988) but then the series got into its stride. Five novels later *A Shred of Evidence* (1995) was televised and although a TV series did not materialise, the books continued at a rate of nearly one a year.

   Philip Glenister and **Michelle Collins** made a pilot for a series, *Lloyd and Hill* in 2001.

SALLY LOCKHART
by Philip Pulman
Feisty Victorian young woman doubling as financial advisor and amateur detective in a short series of spirited stories made into a prime time occasional BBC TV series starring in 2007 and starring the indominatable if improbable Billie Piper as gorgeous Sally. Though the plots seem mainly teen fiction they also contain suprisingly dark patches and clever twists.

WILLIAM LORIMER
by Alex Gray

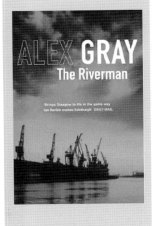

DCI Lorimer works in contemporary **Glasgow**, sometimes accompanied by a Jewish psychologist, **Solomon Brightman**, originally from London. Described as 'existential' by one reviewer, perhaps due to his ponderings on the deeper aspects of humanity and his appreciation of the arts, Lorimer (his first name is rarely used) is tall, dark and moody, totally absorbed in his work, but a restless spirit who prefers to be out and about during a murder hunt. His colleague Solly is quiet and bearded, and has fallen in love with his adopted city, Glasgow. He is an unworldly man who ponders the mysteries of human behaviour and is not afraid to cross swords with Lorimer, who often finds his friend, or his Jewish love of argument, irritating. Non-Glaswegians will expect the books to tell of bodies dumped all over the mean city but the stories also reveal the city's other side: the university, the business world and the Glasgow Royal Concert Hall. *Never Somewhere Else* was Scottish book of the month for both Waterstones and Ottakar's.
Never Somewhere Else (2002), *A Small Weeping* (2004), *Shadows of Sounds* (2005), *The Riverman* (2007).

LOVEJOY
by Jonathan Gash

Antiques dealer cum amateur detective whose books are ruder, more violent and sexier than his television series. In the books Lovejoy narrates in the first person and never reveals his first name. In both he is a shady, dodgy dealer, with one eye for a bargain and another for an attractive woman. Being more of a rogue than a detective he barely qualifies for inclusion here, but he does his share of sleuthing and to many TV viewers – especially women viewers – he was a hero.

The Judas Pair (1977) began the series which continued at the rate of about one a year into the twenty-first century. The book also won the CWA John Creasey Award for best first crime novel.

The first BBC TV series of Lovejoy in 1986 was followed by more from 1991 to 1994. **Ian McShane** played Lovejoy but his trademark leather jacket was never credited with a name. The show was also known (unofficially) as The Antiques Rogue Show.

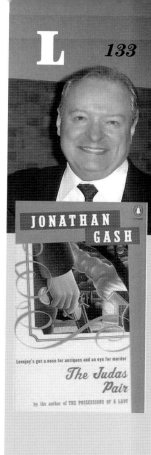

KAI LUNG
Ernest Bramah

An extraordinarily long-lived and, for quite a while, popular character created by his author at the age of 32 in 1900 who continued until his death in 1942. Lung is Chinese, with a western take on Chinese wisdom and sense of justice. His tales have a similarly westernised Chinese flavour, but will seem arch to modern readers. They were collected into seven volumes of short stories. (Bramah also wrote the **Max Carrados** stories.)

The Wallet of Kai Lung (1900) is the first collection. Kai Lung's Golden Hours eventually appeared twenty-two years later, to be slowly followed by four more ending with Kai Lung Beneath the Mulberry Tree in 1940. There was a re-selection, The Celestial Omnibus in 1963.

INSPECTOR LYNLEY
Elizabeth George

This quintessentially English policeman was created by an American, Elizabeth George, who, apart from a couple of minor blunders in the first book, managed to create and convey a convincing picture of England – urban, rural and provincial – and was even brave enough to discuss cricket in Playing for the Ashes. Detective Inspector Thomas Lynley is of noble birth, the Earl of Asherton, and his wife, before she married him, was **Lady Helen Clyde** (American authors don't do things by halves). The Lynleys live in Chelsea, at the smart end. Lady Helen is sister-in-law to Lynley's close friend **Simon Allcourt St James**, a forensic pathologist who was disabled in a car accident in which Lynley was the drunken driver. Such a tightly knit cast needs a commoner, and in one duly barges in the form of Sergeant **Barbara Havers** who, despite her aristocratic name, is a sharp-tongued working class girl with no time for the upper classes. With her arrival the stage is set for a series of long and complex stories (books can be anything up to 700 pages)

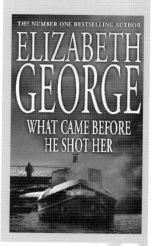

Nathaniel Parker.

which have been a popular success. The first book won an Agatha and an Anthony in America, as well as the French Grand Prix for literature, and the following titles won an even more important prize: big sales. They are well researched and classic mysteries.

The Inspector Lynley Mysteries began on BBC TV in 2001, with **Nathaniel Parker** playing Lynley and **Sharon Small** as Barbara Havers.

A Great Deliverance (1988), *Payment in Blood* (1989), *Well-Schooled in Murder* (1990), *A Suitable Vengeance* (1991), *For the Sake of Elena* (1992), *Missing Joseph* (1993), *Playing for the Ashes* (1994), *In The Presence of the Enemy* (1996), *Deception on his Mind* (1997), *In Pursuit of the Proper Sinner* (1999), *A Traitor to Memory* (2002), *With No One As Witness* (2005), *What Came Before he Shot Her* (2006).

HAMISH MACBETH
by M. C. Beaton

Amiable Scottish constable working his beat in and around his small home town of **Lochdubh** (pronounced Lockdoo) in the Highlands. The laid-back nature of the village bobby sets the tone for many gentle stories and is even more pronounced in his reincarnation on TV. Beaton writes persuasively and there are many who feel that, despite the popularity of the TV series, the pictures are even more charming in her books. (Beaton also writes the **Agatha Raisin** series.)

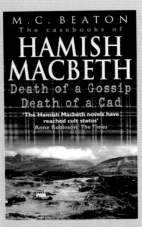

Death of a Gossip began the series in 1985 and like most of the titles which followed, the title gave the nature of the crime. Almost every title begins *Death of a ...* Hamish has investigated the deaths of a *Cad*, *Outsider*, *Perfect Wife*, *Hussy*, *Prankster*, *Glutton*, *Dentist* – even a *Scriptwriter* in 1998 – a *Dustman*, *Celebrity* etc. One exception was *A Highland Christmas* in 1999. The series continues.

Television avoided the temptation to make the series too much of a twee commercial for the Scottish Tourist Board and instead kept the stories both amusing and reasonably active. **Robert Carlyle** played Hamish (and was his first starring role). Among the colourful supporting cast his dog (**Towser** in the books) got most attention. The first, **Wee Jock** (real name Zippy), died in a hit-and-run accident and was replaced by Wee Jock Two, who was in fact played by two different dogs, Fraoch and then Dex. The series ran from 1995 to 1997 and has often been repeated.

TOM McCABE TV series *Badger* (1999)
created by Kieran Prendiville

Not only a straightforward Northumbria cop but a wildlife liaison officer with an additional remit to prevent cruelty to wildlife. The BBC TV series was made appropriately enough by *Feelgood Fiction*. Played by **Jerome Flynn**.

INSPECTOR MACDONALD
by E. C. R. Lorac (see **Ryvet**)

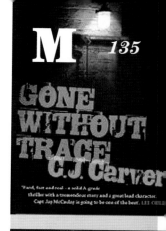

JAY McCAULAY
by C. J. Carver

Jay is 30, an ex-army captain who now works for TRACE, an international aid agency that helps to track and reunite families separated by conflict but, as if this were not enough, from time to time old friends call on her for help. In the first in the series, *Gone Without Trace*, Detective Inspector **Tom Sutton** is Jay's fiancé but when a friend goes missing in the Balkans, possibly trafficked into the UK, Jay teams up with the dangerous and enigmatic **Max Blake** from SOCA. The first book in the Jay McCaulay series, *Gone Without Trace* (2007).

LOGAN McRAE
by Stuart MacBride

Detective Sergeant McRae is the last outpost of sanity in the manic **Aberdeen** police department (doubtless fictionalised here while in real life a model of sobriety and diligence). Surrounded by squabbling, heavy drinking, cursing and frequently incompetent fellow officers, McRae – who is far from innocent himself and in any other force would be seen as a prime mover in the Awkward Squad – elbows others aside in his push to clear his casebook. His fellow officers are so overworked, hamstrung by procedures and plagued by unhelpful bureaucrats and defence lawyers, while at the same time caught up in interpersonal rivalries, hatreds and love affairs, that at times they are as out of their depth as an amateur rugger team playing the national squad at Murrayfield. These stories are not for the faint-hearted; they are outrageous, disgraceful and gobsmackingly glorious. Every one of the characters is a living, breathing, sweating, grunting, cursing, three-dimensional reality. If an American company crossed *Hill Street Blues* with the *Keystone Cops*, had the result scripted by the *Sopranos* team and set in Aberdeen, they might come near the scatological brouhaha that is a Logan McRae story. Even then, one feels, they'd struggle to keep up.

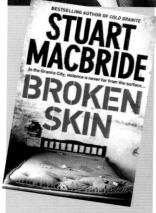

The books don't have to be read in sequence, but it's best if they are, if only to keep up with who is currently sleeping with whom. Then there was that grisly episode with the pincers ... First came *Cold Granite* (which won the Barry Award for the best first novel), then *Dying Light*, then the 2007 book, *Broken Skin*.

THE GREAT MERLINI
by Clayton Rawson

Connoisseurs of unusual detectives might like to hunt out the hard-to-find tales of this magician cum retailer of tricks and equipment to the conjuring trade, cum amateur but highly skilled detective. Naturally, the mysteries that confront him are of the 'impossible' type, including that other Golden Age favourite, the locked room.

Death from a Top Hat (1938) was followed by four more splendidly titled books (given the magic connection): *Footprints on the Ceiling*, *Headless Lady*, *Death out of Thin Air* and *No Coffin for the Corpse*.

ROSE McQUINN
by Alanna Knight

Daughter of Knight's **Inspector Faro**, Rose begins as a tragic figure, returning to her native Edinburgh after a tragedy in America, and finding herself soon caught up in an unsolved murder. It's a potentially interesting idea, done surprisingly seldom, to have a grown-up child continue an established, if fictional, family line. (It is not unique, though: consider **Paul Beck** the younger, son of Paul the elder and **Dora Myrl**.) Rose's **late nineteenth century series** now continues alongside that of her father.

The Inspector's Daughter (2000), *Dangerous Pursuits* (2002), *An Orkney Murder* (2003), *Ghost Walk* (2004), *Destroying Angel* (2007).

NICK MADRID
by Peter Guttridge

Comically wayward, attractively indolent journalist cum sometimes private eye Nick Madrid can't fail to bump into anything sinful in the neighbourhood. The real-life ocean-hopping journalist-author Peter Guttridge (who occasionally organises writer conferences) denies any resemblance between himself and his alter ego, but Madrid's first outing was to a comedy conference in Montreal where he and his fellow journalists were startled to encounter what looked like murder. It wasn't in their script, they cried. In subsequent novels Nick, usually together with his friend Bridget – 'the bitch of the broadsheets' as she is known (affectionately?) – stumble into a New Age orgy (tastefully done), block their ears at a rock music festival, fight the forces of big business and get sporty in *Foiled Again*.

No Laughing Matter (1997), *A Ghost of a Chance* (1998), *Two to Tango* (1999), *The Once and Future Con* (1999), *Foiled Again* (2001), *Cast Adrift* (2005)

TRISH MAGUIRE
by Natasha Cooper

An amateur detective maybe, but Trish Maguire is a tough hard-working **barrister** who specialises in gritty cases involving children. These cases inevitably lead her into dark places, and in the first of the series, *Creeping Ivy*, with Trish still a junior but on sabbatical, she becomes a suspect herself when her cousin's daughter disappears. Child abuse and unpleasant social issues loom large in this sometimes harrowing series – a contrast to Cooper's earlier series featuring the novelist-cum-clerk **Willow King**. *Fault Lines* begins with the rape and murder of a social worker, *Prey to All* has Trish working as legal consultant on a campaigning film looking into a possible miscarriage of justice, *Keep Me Alive* delves into the blood and guts of the meat industry, *Gagged and Bound* brings Trish into contact with a powerful politician alleged to have been involved in terrorism, and *A Greater Evil* tells of a troubled sculptor whose troubles increase when his wife is found beaten to death in his studio.

Creeping Ivy (1998), *Fault Lines* (1999), *Prey to All* (2000), *Out of the Dark* (2002), *Place of Safety* (2003), *Keep me Alive* (2004), *Gagged and Bound* (2005), *A Greater Evil* (2007).

MAIGRET
by Georges Simenon

One of the most loved and successful detectives ever, yet one of the most disparaged by his author. Simenon always claimed he wrote solely for money, he took no care about writing, and he 'tossed off' each story in a matter of days. This claim should be taken with the same scepticism that greets Simenon's claim to have slept with more than a thousand women – even if Simenon's literary output is variously estimated at over 300 or even 400 books! Maigret books are short. For some readers that is a fault, though to his fans it is their merit. Simenon was a famously fast writer and wasted no time on digressions and descriptive passages. 'Not a word wasted' is a cliché that could have been dreamt up for Georges Simenon.

Pierre Renoir in Maigret at the Crossroads.

Maigret was first conceived as just another character in one of Simenon's hack stories, and the first ten were collected into *M. Gallet, décédé* (translated as *The Death of Monsieur Gallet* and again as *Maigret Stonewalled*) in 1931. Maigret appeared in at least 80 stories until the final book *Maigret et Monsieur Charles* in 1972. For a detective who achieved world-wide success Maigret was not a pleasant man – short-tempered, irritable, paternalistic and Gallically chauvinist – and his family life was dull and conventional (although it supplied plenty of light humour in the stories) with the stern detective submitting to the rule of Madame at home. They lived in bourgeois harmony in a small Parisian flat (on the fourth floor of **130 Boulevard Richard-Lenoir**, in the eleventh *arrondissement*). He never drove, he loved Paris, and he hankered after a peaceful retirement in which to cultivate his *Candide* garden.

Maigret frequently used unpleasant methods to snare his villains. He was a solid, unromantic cop, dourly professional. A heavily built man, seldom seen without his pipe, bowler hat and heavy overcoat (an image which permeated French films), he personified the 'real' Paris. He stalked rain-drenched back streets, took his coffee at the *zinc*, sipped his gin in bars no tourist would ever find, spoke to everyone he met and owned his territory. It is often said that the stories are as much – if not more – about Paris as they are about Maigret, and although there is some truth in that it is more true to say that Simenon's sparse brutal style suited an image of Paris his readers recognised; Simenon supplied a canvas upon which one painted for oneself. Quite a number of the stories were in fact set outside Paris, in the flat unromantic scenery of northern France, and in these stories the Parisian imagery gave way to sketches of that area's dull rainy landscape, the slow muddy canals, the wet harbours.

130 Boulevard Richard-Lenoir, Paris

Jean Gabin.

A fine, cold drizzle was falling, and it was dark. The only light was towards the end of the street, near the barracks, where at half past five the trumpets had sounded, and now you could hear the noise of horses being taken to be watered. There the dimly-lit rectangle of a window could be seen: someone getting up early, or perhaps a sick person who had been awake all night.

The rest of the street was asleep. A wide, quiet street, newish with houses all much the same, one- or at the most two-storeyed, such as are found in the suburbs of most big provincial towns. The whole district was new, devoid of mystery; its inhabitants were quiet and unassuming; employees, commercial travellers, people of limited means, peaceable widows.

Maigret, coat-collar turned up, stood pressed into the corner of the entrance to the boys' school; he was waiting, watch in hand and smoking his pipe.

From *According to the Altar Boy*

But the settings were important; Maigret's technique was to become part of the landscape, to soak it up and, by becoming assimilated, understand. When he knew the *paysage* he knew the people; when he knew the people he knew it all. Maigret solved few crimes through deduction; he barely used instinct but relied on his sound if mildly disillusioned understanding of human nature. When he saw the crime he saw why it had been done. Knowing why led him to who. The books, the TV shows, the films – all had scenes in which Maigret took out his pipe and brooded: this is what happened, this must be why. If that is why, then... In part, this Delphic leap to a conclusion came less from Maigret's philosophy than from Simenon's haste to reach the end of a tale. He cared little for plot. He said more than once that he made up the stories as he went along, without pre-plotting (in which he is less alone among crime writers than he thought) and that to him all that mattered was to set out the story and solve the crime. But again, Simenon's

dismissive words cannot change the fact that the stories work, that their lack of literary artifice or superfluous decoration suits their subject. Literate crime stories work best when set in country houses and academe; Simenon's were on the streets. They were *of* the streets. His characters were not literate – some couldn't read. His gritty plots and gruff characters matched his fast no-nonsense style.

As there are over a hundred Maigret titles in English I can only suggest you read whichever takes your fancy. The various omnibuses are recommended, and the first two books in English (both being two novels in one volume) are *Introducing Inspector Maigret* and *Inspector Maigret Investigates* (both 1933). In truth, any title will do. The last new title to come out in Britain was *Maigret and the Coroner* (1980).

Maigret and Holmes must be the two most filmed classic detectives. Maigret was first filmed as early as 1932, played by **Pierre Renoir** in *La Nuit de Carrefour* (= *Maigret at the*

Crossroads) before several other French actors took on the part, including **Abel Tarride**, **Harry Baur** and **Michel Simon** before the quintessential screen Maigret, **Jean Gabin**, who starred first in *Maigret tend un piège* (= *Maigret Sets a Trap*) in 1958. (Gabin was the fan's choice. Simenon preferred Michel Simon.) The films themselves appear seldom now. Interesting ones include: *La Tête d'un Homme* (1933), (Harry Baur); *The Man on the Eiffel Tower* (1949); (Charles Laughton, made in Hollywood); *Brelan d'as* (1952) (Michel Simon) *Maigret tend un piège* (1958) (Jean Gabin).

Jean Richard was the first French TV Maigret (and poorly cast), before the surprise success of **Rupert Davies** on TV (a surprise because not only was this a British working of a classic French detective but because Simenon himself became a Davies fan). Davies took on and dominated the role in the 1960s. While in a sense he looked a typically middle class English gent he looked equally Parisian. The settings looked Parisian, the atmosphere was Parisian too. That 1960s TV *Maigret* was one of British television's greatest hits. There was a later series starring **Michael Gambon** but aficionados will always prefer Rupert Davies.

Rupert Davies.

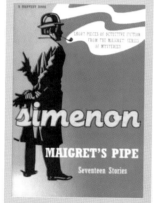

DAN MALLETT
by Frank Parrish (Roger Longrigg)
Literally a poacher-turned-gamekeeper, Dan Mallett was both a poacher and petty thief who in an 8 book series functioned as an unlikely amateur detective. An amusing and, beneath the humour, well observed series based around **country life**.

Fire in the Barley set the tone in 1977 and the series skipped along until *Voices from the Dark* (1993).

INSPECTOR (later Superintendent) MALLETT
by Cyril Hare
Almost forgotten now, except among a small but dedicated group of fans, the lightly written and amusing Mallett stories are a nostalgic souvenir of a more pleasant age. In later books (which continued until 1958) he sometimes appeared with Hare's other detective, **Francis Pettigrew**. *Tenant for Death* (1937) is the first, followed by *Death is no Sportsman* (1938), *Suicide Excepted* (1939) etc.

SUPERINTENDENT (Previously Inspector) MALLETT
by Mary Fitt
Not to be confused with Cyril Hare's policeman of the same name, Mary Fitt's officer is a huge Scot with a granite face and an aggressively ginger moustache, behind all of which lurks a sharp and cultured mind. His series extended to some 17 books between 1938 and 1959.

Two novels, *Sky Rocket* and *Expected Death*, came out in 1938 and most authorities give the former as the first. Unusual titles including *Murder of a Mouse*, *Death Starts a Rumour*, *The Banquet Ceases* and *The Man Who Shot Birds* continued until her final *Mizmaze* in 1959.

M

Roger Ormerod

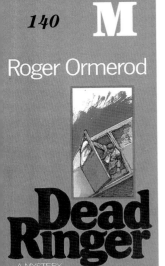

MALLIN & COE
by Roger Ormerod
David Mallin and George Coe are a pair of American-style private detectives but they are British and work in Britain. The books suffer the fate of other American-style stories transplanted here: despite their undoubted effectiveness they struggle for acceptance in a British market. Somehow these tales, and certainly these macho private eyes, seem more believable set in America. It's as if, to crime readers, Britain is a quiet and dozy little backwater. Ormerod dashed out an astonishing 16 Mallin & Coe books between 1974 and 1981, then gave up and switched to writing **Inspector Patton** stories instead.

First came *Time to Kill* in 1974 and the last title was *One Deathless Hour* in 1981. Mike Ashley recommends *The Weight of Evidence* (1978) and *Cart Before the Hearse* (1979) as being especially artful.

AUGUSTUS MALTRAVERS
by Robert Richardson
Gus Maltravers is a former journalist-turned-playwright/novelist who, along with his actress partner **Tess Davy**, has a curious knack of being in the vicinity when someone is found dead and of unearthing critical evidence. He makes little claim to be a detective and can be as emotional as he is rational; in *The Latimer Mercy* (which won the CWA John Creasey award) he breaks down and cries, which is not how amateur sleuths are meant to behave. Each book is an interesting variant on the classic detective story.
The Latimer Mercy (1985), *Bellringer Street* (1988), *The Book of the Dead* (1989), *The Dying of the Light* (1990), *Sleeping in the Blood* (1991), *The Lazarus Tree* (1992).

SIMON MANTON
by Michael Underwood
Initially an Inspector, later Superintendent, Manton's cases reflect his author's interest and experience in the courts of law. (Underwood worked in the Public Prosecutions Office for thirty years.) Suspicious deaths in these books tend to happen in the courts themselves.

Titles give a clue to the legal bias of the books, starting with *Murder on Trial* in 1954, continuing through such as *Death on Remand* (1956), *False Witness* (1957), *Death by Misadventure* (1960), *The Case Against Philip Quest* (1962) and the more blandly named final story: *The Anxious Conspirator* (1965).

SIR GEOFFREY MAPPESTONE
by Simon Beaufort (Susanna Gregory)
An **early twelfth-century crusader** (literally: his first 'case' happens in Jerusalem) who, despite the carnage around him in that religious age, determines to bring some of the perpetrators to book. Mappestone is a Norman knight who, after the crusades, lives in England and becomes a

reluctant agent for King Henry I. The books combine accurate historical detail with satisfying mystery.

The first two books, *Murder in the Holy City* (1998) and *A Head For Poisoning* (1999), were initially published only in America, but the next were published in the UK. They were *The Bishop's Brood* (2002), *The King's Spies* (2003) and *The Coiner's Quarrel* (2004).

MISS MARPLE
by Agatha Christie

The sweet old lady from **St Mary Mead** is one of the most formidable opponents a criminal could meet. Beneath those snowy curls lurks a fearsome intelligence. She flutters about the village, she gossips, she spies on neighbours, but as the vicar narrator to her first case *Murder at the Vicarage* declares: 'There is no detective in England equal to a spinster lady of uncertain age with plenty of time on her hands.'

Miss Jane Marple knows St Mary Mead; it is her world. That the village should become the country's number one crime spot is not her fault (not for nothing was St Mary Mead laughingly renamed Mayhem Parva); it was the unfortunate result of her stories becoming so popular that the audience called out for more – though, surprisingly, there was more than a decade between the first and second novels. St Mary Mead was a village which, its appalling crime rate aside, everyone recognised. Every reader knew the stock characters: the village bobby, the vicar, the district nurse, the spinster, the widower, the old colonel, the doctor, and that quarrelling family at the big house. Although few readers knew first hand a style of life which depended on cooks and scullery maids, with gardener and chauffeur, they were familiar with it from fiction and could slip into Miss Marple's world as easily as into the world of Hans Anderson. They understood that tea was taken in the drawing room at five o'clock and that the guest room must be aired.

Much of the series, in fact, was written and published after the war, when life had changed, when servants were unaffordable and tea came in tea-bags – but in St Mary Mead, life had barely changed. Neither had Miss Marple's crocodile skin handbag. But the modern world had to be incorporated; by the 1950s in *They Do It With Mirrors* the scene of the crime was a young offender's rehabilitation centre – though Miss Marple's attitude to the young inmates (an attitude shared by many of her readers) had been bonded firmly in the Thirties: they were not, she said regretfully, 'young people with a good heredity, and brought up wisely in a good home – and with grit and pluck and the ability to get on in life.' She was, in truth, out of her time, part of a world that did not exist, if it had ever existed. In part, that was the point: the world of St Mary Mead may never have existed but for the millions of Miss Marple readers it was a world that *should* have been, a world they wished had been, a world of enervating sameness made bearable, at one remove, by juicy crime. Like a fairy godmother, she would solve it. The evildoers would be brought to book, and life would be made perfect.

TV has served Miss Marple better than has the cinema. In 1956 there

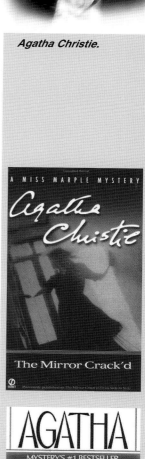

Agatha Christie.

A MISS MARPLE MYSTERY

Agatha Christie

The Mirror Crack'd

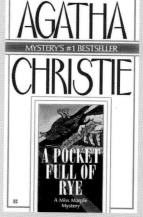

AGATHA

MYSTERY'S #1 BESTSELLER

CHRISTIE

A POCKET FULL OF RYE

A Miss Marple Mystery

Margaret Rutherford made an ideal female sleuth.

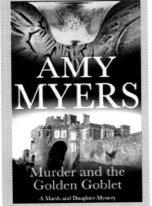

was a dramatisation of *A Murder is Announced* starring, of all people, **Gracie Fields** as Miss Marple. **Helen Hayes** played her in two TV movies in 1983 and 85 but her best adventures ran on BBC from 1984 to 1992, with repeats frequently since. In this series Miss Marple was portrayed perfectly by **Joan Hickson**, who invested the part with such credibility that it is now impossible to think of anyone else in the role, even the recent Geraldine McEwan. **David Horowitz** played the admiring but constantly out-of-his-depth Inspector Slack.

On film, the unforgettable Miss Marple has been **Margaret Rutherford**. Larger than life, lovable, stern and formidable when necessary, Rutherford made an ideal female sleuth – but she wasn't the mild and finicky Miss Marple that Christie created. Her films included *Murder She Said* (1961) based on *4:50 From Paddington*, then *Murder at the Gallop* (1963) based on *After the Funeral*, and the missable *Murder Ahoy* (1964), followed by *Murder Most Foul* (1965) based on the Poirot story *Mrs McGinty's Dead*. **Angela Lansbury** played Miss Marple in *The Mirror Crack'd* in 1980.

Books: *Murder at the Vicarage* (1930), *The Body in the Library* (1942), *The Thirteen Problems* (1942), *The Moving Finger* (1943), *A Murder is Announced* (1950), *They Do It With Mirrors* (1952), *A Pocket Full of Rye* (1953), *4:50 From Paddington* (1957). From here, the standard begins to slip: *The Mirror Cracked From Side to Side* (1962), *A Caribbean Mystery* (1964), *At Bertram's Hotel* (1965), *Nemesis* (1971, which continues from *A Caribbean Mystery*), *Sleeping Murder* (1976), *Miss Marple's Final Cases* (short stories, 1979)

PETER AND GEORGIA MARSH
by Amy Myers

It's hardly fair to call Peter Marsh an amateur since he is an ex-cop, though a wheelchair-bound one, having been shot on his last case. The nice twist in this series, allowing him and his daughter to continue investigating crimes, is that since leaving the force Marsh has started writing true crime books – which obviously need investigating, though they tend to be set way back in the past. Another plus point is that the father/daughter combination breaks away from the usual 'will they, won't they?' male/female bonding, and despite the daughter's ongoing love affairs elsewhere the series could run forever. Less certain to appeal to all crime readers is that the pair choose the crimes they will investigate according to a 'fingerprints on time' approach, based on the idea that violent crimes or crimes which have no closure can leave their impression on the atmosphere. All the novels are set in Kent.

The Wyckeham Murders started the series in 2004, with *Murder in Friday Street* in 2005, *Murder in Hell's Corner* in 2006 and the fourth, *Murder and the Golden Goblet*, in 2007.

ELIZABETH MARTIN
by Ann Granger

In the nineteenth century, Elizabeth Martin, known as Lizzie, was a doctor's daughter from a Derbyshire mining community, but alone and

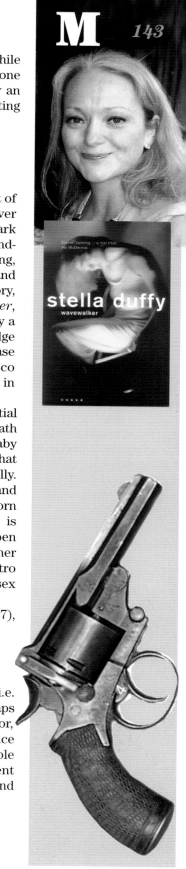

without funds and at the dangerous age for Victorian women, 29. While working as companion to a widowed aunt-by-marriage in Marylebone she re-meets a childhood acquaintance, Benjamin (Ben) Ross, now an inspector in the plainclothes division at Scotland Yard. Their meeting leads to a series of joint adventures and investigations.

A Rare Interest in Corpses (2006), *A Mortal Curiosity* (2007)

SAZ MARTIN
by Stella Duffy

Private investigator Saz Martin is a lesbian and her sexuality is a part of the stories – but Duffy does not preach, thump the barrel or deliver lectures on sexuality; she uses humour and warmth to enliven her dark but amusing tales. The first, *Calendar Girl*, explores the world of stand-up comedy in pubs and clubs, contrasted with the world of gambling, drug smuggling and high-class prostitution. 'A lot of lesbian lore and sex,' commented *The Times*, but 'a fast, witty and clever crime story, with cracking dialogue and exuberant characters.' *Wavewalker*, perhaps the best Saz Martin novel, came next, with Saz employed by a mysterious woman – the Wavewalker – who walks at the tide's edge where incoming waves cover footprints, and who leads Saz into a case that begins with an alternative lifestyle guru from 1970s San Francisco and spurts forward into Saz's hectic private and professional life in 1990s London.

Beneath the Blonde sees Saz investigating a stalker and potential murderer pursuing the female lead singer of the group called Beneath the Blonde. In *Fresh Flesh* Saz and her partner Molly are having a baby and Saz in consequence vows to take on no more dangerous cases. That vow, unsurprisingly, lasts a lot less time than do her vows to Molly. *Parallel Lies* is almost a cross-over novel between Duffy's crime and non-genre stories, despite the book's synopsis which has a Russian-born Hollywood legend (lesbian, of course) desperate to know who is sending her threatening and intimately well-informed poison pen letters. Duffy is one of the few overtly lesbian crime writers to make her books not only accessible but attractive to both homosexual and hetro homosexual readers. Her lesbians are exuberant and the same-sex relationships are central to the action.

Calendar Girl (1994), *Wavewalker* (1996), *Beneath the Blonde* (1997), *Fresh Flesh* (1999), *Parallel Lies* (2005).

HARRY MARTINEAU
by Maurice Proctor

DCI Martineau worked in the CID for the 'Metropolis of the North', i.e. **Manchester**, although in the books it was called Grantchester, perhaps in view of the many government grants it received, even then. Proctor, an ex-cop himself, placed Martineau in a particularly realistic police environment, and made his inspector an old-fashioned – i.e. believable – policeman, relying on old-fashioned techniques of persistent questioning and analysis. He walked the streets, knocked on doors, and hence understood his witnesses and suspects as people, rather than as today's yes/no boxes and 'clients'.

The 26-book series began with *No Proud Chivalry* in 1946, and continued to *The Dog Man* in 1969. *Hell is a City* (1953) is particularly recommended.

MASTERS AND GREEN
by Douglas Clark

A well-drawn pair of police officers who appeared in 27 novels in the 1970s and 1980s. Chief Inspector Masters (later Superintendent) and Chief Inspector Bill Green investigate their cases as real officers would and part of the pleasure in reading the books comes not only from the accurate police detail but also from the less often encountered detail on **poisons and pharmaceuticals**. (Clark worked for a pharmaceutical company.) The mysteries are old-style, in the best sense, in that they are genuine puzzle mysteries (there are even a couple of 'impossible' crimes) and the clues are cunningly provided in the classic manner.

The fine *Nobody's Perfect* (1969) was followed by titles among which particularly recommended are *Death After Evensong* (1969), *Table d'Hote* (1977), and *Shelf Life* (1982). The series ended with *Bitter Water* (1990).

ALEX MAVROS
by Paul Johnston

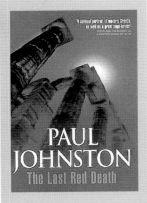

Private detective based in Greece, a country in which the author worked in the 1980s, first as a tourist guide, then later with a newspaper in Athens, thence to the small Aegean island of Antiparos in 1989, where he taught English to pay the bills. In the first book in the series, *A Deeper Shade of Blue*, Mavros sets out to trace a missing tourist, only to find she isn't the only tourist who has disappeared. *The Last Red Death* won the Sherlock for Best Detective Novel in 2004 and told of modern day and second world war terrorism, the memories and effects of which lie semi-dormant beneath hot Greek soil. Shortly after it was published, a real-life terrorist arrest occurred in Greece, apparently straight out of the book... The 2005 title *The Golden Silence* has been optioned for a film.

A Deeper Shade of Blue (2002), *The Last Red Death* (2003), *The Golden Silence* (2005), *The Fat Man* (2007) *The Death List* (2007)

PETER MAXWELL
by M. J. Trow

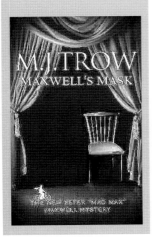

Quite how a teacher can become involved so often as amateur sleuth is a mystery in itself, but this is not a series that takes itself too seriously. The author, after all, wrote the fine pastiche series on Sherlock Holmes' patient foil **Inspector Lestrade**. Maxwell's first case was credible enough: one of his students was murdered and he himself became a suspect. In the second book a teacher is murdered and in the third a teacher and a student disappear. How many more combinations could there be? Plenty, as it turned out. A housemaster meets his doom, a

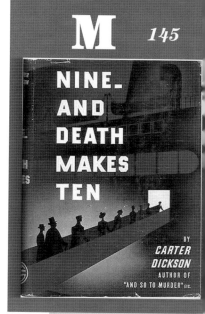

teacher drowns in a lake, a police inspector is found stabbed to death. Maxwell by this time has long been romantically close to another cop, **DS Jacquie Carpenter**, and more than once, as the bodies pile up around him, Maxwell's *real* concern has been the next OFSTED inspection. Now that *is* serious.

Maxwell's House started the fun in 1994. It was followed by *Maxwell's Flame* (1995), *Maxwell's Movie* (1997), *Maxwell's War* (1999), *Maxwell's Curse* (2000), *Maxwell's Ride* (2000), *Maxwell's Reunion* (2001), *Maxwell's Match* (2002), *Maxwell's Inspection* (2003), *Maxwell's Grave* (2004), *Maxwell's Mask* (2005), *Maxwell's Point* (2007) and *Chain* (2008).

SIR HENRY MERRIVALE
by Carter Dickson (John Dickson Carr)

'That was the day I first met Sir Henry Merrivale, under circumstances that will long be remembered in Lyncombe...' Thus (in *She Died a Lady*) are we introduced to another human grotesque from the creator of **Dr Gideon Fell**. Sir Henry (aka The Old Man) is large, bald, pigeon-toed and barrel-chested. He smokes too much, shouts, swears and scowls, and is a former Head of Counter-Espionage at the War Office. Despite his previous job, but perhaps because of his erratic personal behaviour, he is now a decidedly amateur detective. Coming from Carter Dickson (aka John Dickson Carr) the cases that Merrivale investigates are as astoundingly complex as one would expect, though they have a tendency to descend into farce (which is not unknown in the Gideon Fell stories also). Like a latter-day Mr Toad, Sir Henry poops and splutters his way through some twenty-three novels, though he is such a *bon vivant* he can be bothered with only two trifling short stories. His adventures bring him into contact with an abandoned condemned cell (*The Skeleton in the Clock*, 1948), a wheelchair race (*She Died a Lady*, 1943), a suitcase race (*The Night at the Mocking Widow*, 1950), an accident with a fruit barrow (*Death in Five Boxes*, 1938), his own libellous memoirs (*Seeing is Believing*, 1941), a house that has survived from the seventeenth century's Black Death (*The Plague Court Murders*, 1934), and an ancient Egyptian curse (*The Curse of the Bronze Lamp*, 1945).

Carter Dickson.

The Plague Court Murders came first, in 1934. Not mentioned above are *The White Priory Murders* (also 1934), *The Red Widow Murders* and *The Unicorn Murders* (both 1935), *The Magic Lantern Murders* (1936), *The Peacock Feather Murders* (1937), *The Judas Window* (1938), *The Reader is Warned* (1939), *Nine – And Death Makes Ten* and also *And So To Murder* (both 1940), *The Gilded Man* (1942), *He Wouldn't Kill Patience* (1944), *My Late Wives* (1946), *A Graveyard to Let* (1949), *Behind the Crimson Blind* (1952) and *The Cavalier's Cup* (his last, in 1953).

PENGUIN BOOKS

SHE DIED A LADY

CARTER DICKSON

COMPLETE UNABRIDGED

2/-

Ken Stott.

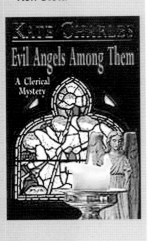

Ann Granger.

DCI RED METCALFE TV series *Messiah*

Following his success as **DI Pat Chappel** in *The Vice* **Ken Stott** landed an even darker part (filmed in a series more darkly lit) as a Detective Chief Inspector tormented by having turned in his own brother for murder years before. In the first story he is presented with a horrific series of brutal murders and a murderer who is clearly determined to continue killing – unless Metcalfe can find him first. He soon realises that the killer intends at least twelve murders, one for each of Christ's disciples: the victims share names with the disciples and in the mouth of each corpse is placed a silver apostle spoon. Their deaths are by crucifixion, beheading, being flayed alive, being sawn in half ... To what depths can this killer go? To what depths can the *series* go? Only the superb production values and Stott's agonised performance saved this from becoming gratuitous – and for some viewers it *was* gratuitous. Slick, compelling, dark, it seemed at the time about as far as TV could go. Yet before long, Ken Stott was back ... with *Messiah II*.

DAVID MIDDLETON-BROWN
by Kate Charles

David is a solicitor whose investigations (in the books at least) are into church matters – hence the overall series title *The Book of Psalms Series*. In the first book a priest is being blackmailed and in subsequent stories the plots are as much about church politics and intrigue as they are about crime. David's blossoming relationship with **Lucy Kingsley** is another major element. But it is the detailed and accurate study of things ecclesiastical that provides the real interest.

A Drink of Deadly Wine (1991), *The Snares of Death* (1992), *Appointed to Die* (1993), *A Dead Man out of Mind* (1994), *Evil Angels Among Them* (1995).

DETECTIVE CHIEF SUPERINTENDENT JAMES MILTON
(see **Amiss & Milton**)

SUPERINTENDENT MINTON
(see **The Sooper**)

MITCHELL & MARKBY
by Ann Granger

Meredith Mitchell is a former consular officer who returned to London to work at the Foreign and Commonwealth office, commuting from the fictional village of Bamford on the edge of the Cotswolds. She is in her middle to late 30s. Her friend Alan Markby started out as a Chief Inspector based at Bamford but was promoted to Superintendent in view of his astonishing clear-up rate (there are, after all, fifteen books in the series, and Markby succeeds in every one). He is divorced, in his mid-forties, and wants to marry Meredith. Their on-off relationship runs through the series, but even in the fifteenth and last book Ann Granger shies from letting them marry.

Say It with Poison (1991), *A Season for Murder* (1991), *Cold in the*

Earth (1992), *Murder Among Us* (1992), *Where old Bones Lie* (1993), *A Fine Place for Death* (1994), *Flowers for his Funeral* (1994), *Candle for a Corpse* (1995), *A Touch of Mortality*(1996), *A Word after Dying* (1996), *Call the Dead Again* (1998), *Beneath these Stones* (1999), *Shades of Murder* (2000), *A Restless Evil* (2002), *That Way Murder Lies* (2004)

LADY MOLLY OF SCOTLAND YARD

Baroness Orczy

Lady Molly Robertson-Kirk stars in a series of sly, tongue-in-cheek mysteries 'told' by her besotted companion/confidante **Mary Granard**. The idea of a titled lady having her own office within and being consulted by Scotland Yard is clearly preposterous, but it was the kind of absurdity Orczy delighted in. (Lady Molly's husband has been wrongly jailed for murder and is in Dartmoor – until she clears him.) Though the tales have dated – she can hardly have meant them to seem realistic – they have the deftness one expects from a born storyteller, and though set in their period they allow Orczy to bring in fashionable venues of the day such as Mathis' Vienna café in Regent Street, and to mention current West End shows like 'Trilby' or the sensational dancer Maud Allan at the Palace Theatre.

Lady Molly of Scotland Yard (1910) is a better read than is sometimes admitted.

Baroness Orczy.

WILLIAM MONK

Anne Perry

A substantial series from a best-selling author (see **Thomas Pitt**). The series began with *The Face of a Stranger* and ran to over 14 titles combining mystery and adventure, in which the **Victorian detective** fights an assortment of evil villains and is assisted by the no-nonsense **Hester Latterly**. Monk himself is a complex character – he could hardly not be as, following an accident, he has lost his memory – and the stories delve into the heart of the nineteenth-century legal system.

It begins with *The Face of a Stranger* (1990) and continues on an annual basis.

PHYLLIDA MOON

by Eileen Dewhurst

We first meet Phyllida Moon in *Now You See Her* when, as an actress approaching forty, she prepares for her latest role as a TV detective by temping at the Seaminster detective agency. Asked to check on a man accused of molesting a teenage girl, Phyllida casts herself as a parent visiting the girl's school and is there conveniently when a boy is strangled. Before long, now in a different disguise, the plucky actress is at the school again when another girl student falls – or was she pushed? – from a high window. This concept, of the actress whose real life is as dramatic as her roles, has been repeated in a series of 8 entertaining books to date. Expect lots of disguises.

Now You See Her began the series in 1995 and was followed by

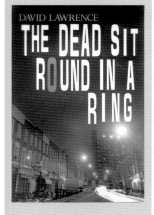

Verdict on Winter (1996), *Alias the Enemy* (1997), *Roundabout* (1998), *Double Act* (2000), *Closing Stages* (2001), *No Love Lost* (2001), *Easeful Death* (2002), and *Naked Witness* (2003).

DS STELLA MOONEY
by David Lawrence

David Lawrence is the pseudonym of the poet David Harsent. He is also a TV script writer. The startling opening to his first Stella Mooney novel gives us four dead bodies sitting in a ring in a room in Notting Hill Gate, three of whom appear to have committed suicide while the fourth has been professionally dispatched. How exactly did they die? To sort this out comes DS Stella Mooney, a realistically drawn and flawed policewoman whose private life is crumbling. The case involves a turf war between London and Bosnian gangs fighting to control a lucrative trade in imported prostitutes. Next in the series, *Nothing Like the Night* sees Stella and her colleagues out to find and stop a pair of particularly vicious serial killers. Behind both tales lies the mess that is Stella's love life. In *Cold Kill* Stella works on her own, unconvinced by the young man who confesses to the slaying of a young woman. *Down into Darkness* maintains the tone. In each book the poet's hand is evident, adding atmosphere and depth to stories which are already strong.*The Dead Sit Round in a Ring* (2002), *Nothing Like the Night* (2003), *Cold Kill* (2005), *Down into Darkness* (2007).

THE HONOURABLE CONSTANCE MORRISON-BURKE
by Joyce Porter

Comic butch lesbian detective who barged through the 1970s with gay abandon, trampling sensibilities and clues and dragging her put-upon and permanently anxious chum Miss Jones in her wake. Noisy, nosey and dramatically direct, her only technique is to march in, cause chaos, and smash through the subterfuge till the culprit is exposed. It's hell for the suspects but great fun for the reader. **The Hon Con** (as she's known) finds Miss Jones a tad dull and is often distracted by other attractive young women on the scene. But unrequited love is her lot, and if that side of life is duff, why shouldn't she duff up some suspects? *Rather a Common Sort of Crime* (1970), *A Meddler and her Murder* (1972), *The Package Included Murder* (1975), *Who the Heck is Sylvia?* (1977), *The Cart before the Crime* (1979).

BEV MORRISS
by Maureen Carter

Birmingham-based hard-nosed female cop. Or, as one critic wrote (meaning it as a compliment): Bev Morriss has a gob on her. A modern woman she may be, but politically correct she ain't: she shoots from the lip. Her boss **Bill Byford** tries but usually fails to keep her in line, because Bev's big mouth and quick wit talk her into trouble as often as they talk her out. The stories are as hard and earthy as her dialogue. *Working Girls* (2004), *Dead Old* (2005), *Baby Love* (2006), *Hard Time* (2007), *Bad Press* (2008).

INSPECTOR MORSE
by Colin Dexter

By the time the TV series began in 1987 the Morse books were already a success. The books had begun in 1975 and by 1987 Dexter had won two Silver Daggers and was to win a Gold in 1989 and 1992. His Oxford-based Inspector epitomised the town; each book could, in part, be taken as a reliable guide, though to get the full A to Z of Oxford one would need to read the entire series. Morse walks the streets, drinks in many of the pubs, shops there, lives there, occasionally (very occasionally) loves there, and unlike his numerous Oxford predecessors he doesn't spend the bulk of his time dreaming in Oxford quadrangles. Colleges do play a part (how could they not, in Oxford?) but they are simply a part, albeit an important part, of this bustling town.

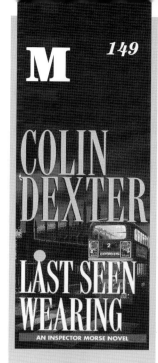

Morse himself is an intelligent policeman; not only does he do *The Times* crossword but he competes with himself to solve it in record time. (Dexter, it is well-known, was a *Times* crossword compiler.) Morse applies that same intelligence to the crimes set for him to solve, often making more of them, expecting solutions more complex than they are and being disappointed when they turn out to be the sorry result of basic human nature, rather than as deviously complex as he might have hoped. With basic human nature, in truth, Morse finds himself a little lost. He is a long-term bachelor – unmarried, in his 50s – attracted to and occasionally wooed by worthy women, and once or twice losing his heart to them. (There was, of course, one great love in his life, long ago...) But the ins and outs of Morse's sex life are not revealed to us. Much of his private life is closed. We do know he does crosswords, because he fits them in at work. We know he drinks Hook Norton, because he takes his lunch at work. We know he likes opera (particularly Wagner) because he sometimes mentions that to Lewis.

Ah, Lewis. **Sergeant Lewis** is Morse's foil. No one would call Lewis an intellectual. But then, no one would expect Morse to enjoy the plod and thump of everyday policing. Where Morse might stand outside a suspected hideaway to look for clues, Sergeant Lewis will kick the door down. With your permission, sir. Asked afterwards. Lewis respects his inspector's intellect but doesn't share it. He knows what he knows and to him that's that.

Oxford streets, background to the successful book and TV series.

But the two men need each other. The Morse of the books is less detached than he is on screen, more likely to be caught off duty attending to a piece of mundane DIY, and the Lewis of the books is, in truth, more colourless than he is on screen. Morse is described as an ordinary-looking man, not tall, rather plainly dressed, distinctly gruff. Lewis is more affable, till roused. Both men, in the books, have to tackle crimes dressed up as puzzles (one remembers Dexter's background: crossword compiler, national crossword competition champion, holder of an MA in

M

Classics – from Oxford, naturally). The books are a combination of police procedural and puzzle mystery. Sometimes Dexter lets the ingeniousness of the puzzle run away with him, surrendering reality for the sake of an outrageous but intellectually satisfying explanation – yet few readers complain. The books are conspicuously clever, and we are glad of that. We ourselves may not be clever enough to spot the solutions in advance, but we are happy to sit with the book in our hands and watch.

Many Morse fans, it must be said, only watch. ITV ran *Inspector Morse* from 1987 to 2000, even though Dexter had, to public consternation, killed Morse off in his book *The Remorseful Day* in 1999. (There was even greater consternation later when the non-reading public learned the same would happen to their television hero, resulting in one of TV's great brouhahas when the 'offending' episode was aired.) On TV Morse's rueful love-life was played up a little, and the visual splendours of Oxford were exploited via walkabouts and shots of Morse easing through Oxford's notoriously traffic-unfriendly streets in his red 1960 Mark 2 Jaguar. John Thaw, though he doesn't look like the Morse described on the page, was correctly gruff and tetchily fastidious, while Whately's Lewis, the gentle Geordie (though he was Welsh, and older, in Dexter's books) stuck by the inspector closely like a best man at a wedding which he suspects may soon go wrong. The TV adaptations kept to, and perhaps improved on, Dexter's concept of an intelligent policeman given to over-intellectualising his cases and having to be discreetly bailed out by his unintellectual but more practical companion.

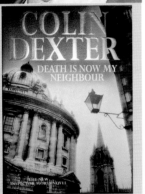

John Thaw.

To say the TV series ran from 1987 to 2000 is correct but a touch misleading, since the series proper ended in 1993, to be followed by intermittent one-off specials leading to the audience-pulling finale of *The Remorseful Day* in 2000. Dexter's book series could not supply all the story-lines, though it supplied a good number, and inevitably some of the episodes had to be 'based on characters created by' him. Dexter himself, like Alfred Hitchcock, wangled himself a walk-on part as an extra in every episode. Another neat touch was that the theme tune was based on the beat created by the Morse code letters MORSE. Chief Inspector Endeavour Morse was played by **John Thaw**, an actor one would have thought already typecast from earlier roles, and the steady Detective Sergeant Robbie Lewis was played by **Kevin Whately**. In the original series, regular appearances were made by **James Grout**, as Morse's boss Chief Superintendent Strange; **Peter Woodthorpe** as Max (a pathologist); and **Amanda Hillwood** as Doctor Grayling Russell (another pathologist). Several years after John Thaw died Whately earned a **Lewis** series of his own.

Last Bus to Woodstock (1975), *Last Seen Wearing* (1976), *The Silent World of Nicholas Quinn* (1977), *Service of All the Dead* (1980), *The Dead of Jericho* (1981), *The Riddle of the Third Mile*

(1983), *The Secret of Annexe 3* (1986), *The Wench is Dead* (1989), *The Jewel That Was Ours* (1991), *The Way Through the Woods* (1992), *The Daughters of Cain* (1994), *Death is now my Neighbour* (1997 – this book reveals Morse's extraordinary first name), *The Remorseful Day* (1999). Short stories: *Morse's Greatest Mystery* (1993).

DORA MYRL
Matthias MacDonald Bodkin QC
Wilful, all-action Edwardian lady detective, one of the first. She carries a small hidden revolver, can pick a lock and can cycle like the wind in pursuit of villains. Sadly, she met Bodkin's other hero **Paul Beck** and, Reader, she married him. In a doomed attempt to prolong the series Bodkin had them produce a son (also Paul) who would continue in the business.
Dora Myrl: The Lady Detective (1900), *Young Beck: A Chip Off The Old Block* (1911).

Denise Mina.

NATASHA NEVKORINA
(see **Birdseye & Nevkorina**)

INSPECTOR GUY NORTHEAST
by Joanna Cannan
From his name you'd guess he was a parody, as he is, of Inspector West and of all those village bobbies summoned by aristos to the big house to sort out the tedious little murder that threatens to put a damper on the weekend. By no means an aristocrat, though a son of a farmer, the fact that his social standing is lower than some he must question is a deliberate source of humour in the books, allowing him to stand in ironic contrast to the forelock-tugging police detectives of Cannan's better known Golden Age rivals.
They Rang up the Police (1939), *Death at 'The Dog'* (1940).

Joanna Cannan.

MAUREEN O'DONNELL
by Denise Mina
In a grim trilogy largely based in **Glasgow** O'Donnell is dragged reluctantly into murder cases that have distressing echoes of her own broken life. She has herself been in intensive psychiatric therapy after being a victim of child sexual abuse, her mother is a drunk and her brother a drug addict. Things haven't improved much since she grew up. It's not given to O'Donnell to meet many well-balanced human beings or to spend her days in decently furnished middle-class surroundings. Instead she picks her way through dark tenements, ill-lit streets, refuge shelters and dingy drug dens.

The first book in the trilogy, *Garnethill* (1999), won the CWA John Creasey Award for the best first crime novel. It was followed by *Exile* (2000) part set in London, and the trilogy closed with a third murder and shattering confrontations in *Resolution* (2001).

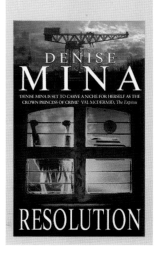

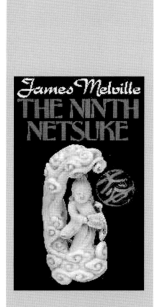

THE OLD MAN IN THE CORNER

Baroness Orczy

The first armchair detective sits at his favourite table in a Lyons ABC café and by deduction alone solves cases usually brought to him by the narrator/journalist Miss Mary or sometimes Polly Burton. In an early *Royal Magazine* story, *The Mysterious Death on the Underground Railway* he did admit to having earlier attended court but one wonders why, since he has his own cavalier attitude to justice. Impressing young ladies with his cleverness seems his prime concern, solving crimes an interesting second, and seeing the criminal brought to justice merely an option, often dispensed with altogether. Orczy amused herself by creating a rather repulsive old man, endlessly fiddling with a piece of knotted string and dressed as unattractively as only an old man can dress. She describes him through her female narrators' eyes as 'grotesque', 'the old scarecrow', etc., though his name is eventually revealed as **Bill Owen**. The stories are typically clever and brightly told.

The stories start from 1901, and the best are collected in *The Old Man In The Corner* (1909), though other collections are *The Case of Miss Elliott* (1905) and *Unravelled Knots* (1926).

JOHNNY ONE-EYE

by David Stuart Davies

Johnny Hawke is a private detective working in London during the war. He is 'One Eye' because when war broke out he left the police force to enlist but, during training, a rifle back-fired and he lost his eye. He is not a tough guy and these are light pleasant tales. Johnny first appeared in short stories, then in novel form, and to date has proved more popular in America than Britain.

Forests of the Night (2005), *Comes the Dark* (2006), *Without Conscience* (2008).

THEA OSBORNE

by Rebecca Tope

A peripatetic housesitter, Thea, in the company of her cocker spaniel Hepzibah, is engaged to work in a succession of Cotswold houses which seem to attract foul deeds like flies in summer. The series is set in named and identifiable **Cotswold villages** and is less cosy than the titles suggest. *Death in the Cotswolds* for example, has Thea and her detective boyfriend confronted with a murder in a Cotswold village (Cold Aston), a murder besmirched by paganism and Freemasonry.

The series begins with *A Cotswold Killing* (2004) and continues with *A Cotswold Ordeal* (2005), *Death in the Cotswolds* (2006) and *A Cotswold Mystery* (2007).

TETSUO OTANI

by James Melville

Interesting and accurately drawn Japanese detective (hence the books having been translated into Japanese) by an author who spent some years as a cultural diplomat there before returning to this country to write crime novels and work as a nationally known crime critic. Superintendent Otani works in the Hyogo Prefecture Police where the cases he deals with are a match for any our own country throws up. Behind the fine crime stories lie a fascinating portrait of **modern Japan**.

The series began with *The Wages of Zen* (1978). *The Chrysanthemum Chain* (1980) is also recommended, as is *Sayonara, Sweet Amaryllis* (1983) and *The Reluctant Robin* (1988).

BILL OWEN
See **The Old Man in the Corner**

CAPTAIN GARETH OWEN
See **Mamur Zapt**

FRANK PALMER
See **Riley Gavin**

GEORGE PALMER-JONES
by Ann Cleeves
Bird-watching amateur detective who, along with his wife **Molly**, combines his hobby with solving occasional human crimes. Sounds unlikely? But before George retired from the civil service he wrote a manual for the police on interviewing techniques. Perhaps that doesn't give him all the qualifications he needs to go sleuthing on his own but it does at least make him semi-professional, and explains why the police regard him kindly and are willing to work with him. Be that as it may, the real interest in these pleasant stories lies in the **bird watching and rural interest**. (The author once worked on a bird observatory on Fair Isle, so she's hardly an amateur at this.) To add more credibility later in the series, the couple set up an ad hoc enquiry service helping to find missing teenagers. (Molly used to be a social worker.)
A Bird in the Hand (1986), *Come Death and High Water* (1987), *Murder in Paradise* (1998), *A Prey to Murder* (1989), *Sea Fever* (1991), *Another Man's Poison* (1992), *The Mill on the Shore* (1994), *High Island Blues* (1996).

MRS PARGETER
Simon Brett
A more amusing version of Miss Marple, appearing in half a dozen full-length books. Although the emphasis is on light humour her cases are nevertheless deft and intricate.

The series began in 1986 with *A Nice Class of Corpse*.

CHARLES PARIS
Simon Brett
Hero – though that's seldom an accurate description – of an amusing series of theatrical detective stories from this accomplished author, Paris struts and stumbles his way through

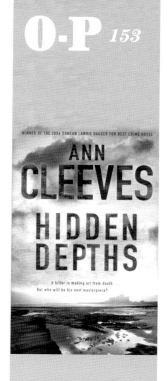
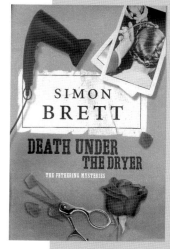

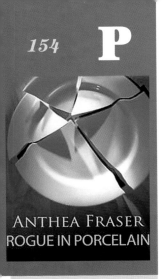

ANTHEA FRASER
ROGUE IN PORCELAIN

a number of bizarre and sometimes deliberately creaking mysteries like a tipsy but talented leading man in a long-established weekly rep. The stories should be read for their humour and fizzy descriptions of theatrical life, rather than as serious crime novels

Books from 1975 to date, starting with *Cast, in Order of Disappearance*. One can start anywhere as the books are of an even standard, though perhaps *A Series of Murders* (1988) stands out.

RONA PARISH
by Anthea Fraser
Biographer and freelance journalist on a glossy magazine, but also an occasional amateur detective – even if her enquiries are usually into matters within her own family. An innocent enough pastime, you would think, but lurking in those ancestral trees are some curious discoveries – enough to have spawned a whole series of light adventures.

The present-day series began with *Brought to Book* in 2003 and the fifth, *Rogue in Porcelain*, came out in 2007.

INSPECTOR PARKER *(Lord Peter Wimsey* stories)
(See **Wimsey**)

JACK PARLABANE
by Christopher Brookmyre
Investigative journalist of dubious ethical standards (well, he is a journalist) whose work plunges him up to the nostrils in dodgy and dangerous goings-on. Louder and more frenetic than most journalist-cum-detective series, these very Scottish stories are a riot of savage laughter, violence and dizzy pace. At the heart of most crimes Parlabane investigates is a large dollop of political shenanigan – largely because corrupt politicians (indeed, politicians of any sort) are high on the Parlabane hate list. Brookmyre is the court jester of **Tartan Noir**, and his creation was voted best Comic Detective in 2001.

Quiet Ugly One Morning (1996) won the Critics' First Blood award for the best first crime novel. It was followed by *Country of the Blind* (1997), *Boiling A Frog* (2000), *Be My Enemy* (2004) and *Attack of the Unsinkable Rubber Ducks* (2007).

PARRY & LLOYD
by David Williams
A **Welsh** duo comprising DCI Merlin Parry and his assistant DS Gomer Lloyd whose patch is a mix of town and valley in South Wales. Decent cops and a worthy little series but never as commercially successful as the author's **Mark Treasure** series.
Last Seen Breathing (1994), *Death of a Prodigal* (1995), *Dead in the Market* (1996), *A Terminal Case* (1997) and *Suicide Intended* (1998).

MRS PASCHAL
anonymous but perhaps by W. S. Hayward
Fiction's **first woman detective**, appearing in a short story collection

REVELATIONS OF A LADY DETECTIVE

in 1861. A widow, aged about 40, clever, something of an actress, she is offered work as a detective upon the death of her husband and agrees to take it as she feels it will be 'remarkable, exciting and mysterious.' Her adventures have dated.

The Revelations of a Lady Detective (1861).

RICHARD PATTON
by Roger Ormerod

Patton is not the only retired cop who turns detective but he is one of the few who hangs around in the station doorway, never sure whether to continue down the steps or turn round and go back inside. On his first appearance Detective Inspector Patton is a mere three days away from retirement, and, never one to keep things simple, he gets involved with the wife of the man he is supposed to be looking for. In later books he spends much of the time when he should have his feet up being called back in to help with cold cases that turn out not to be cold at all. A well-plotted and underrated series.

Face Value (1983), *Still Life With Pistol* (1986), *An Alibi Too Soon* (1987), *An Open Window* (1988), *Guilt on the Lily* (1989), *Death of an Innocent* (1989), *No Sign of Life* (1990), *When an Old Man Died* (1991), *Shame the Devil* (1993), *Mask of Innocence* (1994), *Stone Cold Dead* (1995), *The Night She Died* (1997).

PC 49   radio show
created by Alan Stranks

In the late 1940s and early 1950s, on the wireless, the serial *PC 49* told the relatively peaceful and reassuring adventures of Police Constable Archibald Berkeley-Willoughby, an ordinary bobby on the beat, working for Q Division of the Metropolitan Police. **Brian Reece** played PC 49, **Joy Shelton** was his girlfriend Joan Carr, **Leslie Perrins** was Detective Inspector Wilson and **Eric Phillips** appeared as Detective Sergeant Wright. The series comprised 112 episodes, beginning in 1947 and ending in 1953. There were various comic strip spin-offs.

   A Case for PC 49 was a forgettable British film of 1951.

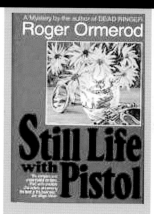

CHARLIE PEACE
by Robert Barnard

The Charlie Peace series comes out at the gentle rate of about one every two years, a pace that reflects the gentle tone of the stories themselves, which combine mystery with police procedural. Peace is a decent man, father to a young child, a **black Detective Sergeant** attached to Scotland Yard but more often than not working on cases set around **Leeds** in the north of England. His name is not actually Charlie, although practically everyone calls him that; he was born Dexter Peace but was nicknamed Charlie after a famous (real life) Victorian murderer. Though each book stands alone, Peace's family life forms a continuous strand, and various other characters recur. (Superintendent

Robert Barnard.

Mike Oddie works with Peace.) Charlie tends to work on cases involving broken families: *A Fatal Attachment* tells of a biographer who tries to *attach* himself to his subject's children, *No Place of Safety* explores the world of homeless kids for whom no family life remains, and *The Bones in the Attic* teams Peace with **Matt Harper**, a retired footballer and now local radio broadcaster, who has discovered a child's bones in his attic. The bones are old but the investigation uncovers a grim story of children who disappeared in the 1970s. *A Hovering of Vultures* is rather different, in that the contemporary murder mystery is set against the murder cum suicide of a well-known literary couple in the 1930s. Charlie Peace solves both.

Peace also makes an appearance in the earlier *Bodies* (1986) alongside another Barnard series character, **Perry Trethowan.**

Death and the Chaste Apprentice (1989), *A Fatal Attachment* (1992), *A Hovering of Vultures* (1993), *The Bad Samaritan* (1995), *No Place of Safety* (1998), *The Corpse at the Haworth Tandoori* (1999), *Unholy Dying* (2001), *The Bones in the Attic* (2001), *A Fall From Grace* (2007).

HENRY PECKOVER
by Michael Kenyon
DCI Henry Peckover, **the Bard of the Yard** (so-called for his habit of composing instant doggerel), was born in Stepney, remains a cockney, wears dreadful clothes and, despite being a Deputy Chief Inspector, has been demoted twice. His cases are serious enough but the books are essentially comic. Good fun.

The series started with *Zigzag* (1981) and ended with the eighth, *Peckover and the Bog Man* (1994).

Michael Kenyon.

INSPECTOR PEL
by Mark Hebden
A reasonably successful attempt to create a latter-day Maigret. Hebden was well established as a writer before he created Pel in 1979, both as a thriller writer (under his own name John Harris and a pseudonym Max Hennessy) and for his short series of books about the spy Colonel Mostyn. But his Inspector Pel is **French**, a dyspeptic career police detective whose morose attitude adds a piquancy to his many adventures. The books are light but entertaining police procedurals, and their Burgundy setting is a bonus. Idyllic though that setting might be to some, it doesn't stop Inspector Pel complaining. Indeed his complaints are a large part of the books' character: he complains about his fellow officers, his health, his housekeeper, and anything which gets in the way of solving a case. He even complains about his own name – and on that he might have a point, since his parents saddled him with quite a mouthful: Evariste Clovis Desiré Pel.

He appeared first in *Death Set To Music* in 1979 and the books streamed out until *Pel and the Sepulchre Job* in 1992. Sadly, Hebden had died the previous year. For a while his daughter continued the series, writing as Juliet Hebden. Appropriately enough, her first title was *Pel Picks up the Pieces* (1993).

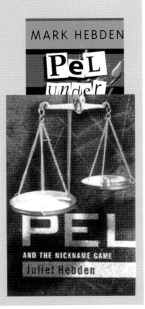

MARK HEBDEN

PeL
under

PEL
AND THE NICKNAME GAME
Juliet Hebden

SUPERINTENDENT PEMBERTON
by Peter N. Walker, then by Nicholas Rhea

The prolific Walker/Rhea (they are the samen person) is more famous for his *Constable* series (see **Nick Rowan**) and for **Carnaby** but his Pemberton is a higher-ranking officer, again from the north of England. Pemberton is a top man in the North Yorkshire CID and his complex cases suit his high position.

The first two books, *False Alibi* (1991) and *Grave Secrets* (1992), were written as by Peter N. Walker, and the rest by Rhea. Those are *Family Ties* (1994), *Suspect* (1995), *Confession* (1997), *Death of a Princess* (1999), *The Sniper* (2001), *Dead Ends* (2003). *Murder Beneath the Midnight Sun* (2008).

WESLEY PETERSON
by Kate Ellis

Detective Inspector Peterson tackles unusual cases, in that each that he handles is shadowed by a **parallel historical mystery**, whose periods range from Viking to Regency. He himself is unusual, in that he is **a black cop working in rural Devon** – both his parents are doctors, born in Trinidad – and his Devon beat is in towns with names such as Morbay and Tradmouth, whose real-life equivalents Devonians won't find too hard to decipher. Peterson is married, with a young family, but this doesn't mean there is no sexual tension between Wesley and the occasional female colleague (one of those relationships eventually goes further). But basically, he is a straight, decent cop. The historical strand running through the books involves Wesley's regular contact and friend, the archaeologist **Neil Watson**. (The author herself is an amateur archaeologist.) To keep the parallel time theme going for an entire series ought to be tricky but Kate Ellis writes with such ease that she makes it seem simplicity itself. The stories have a comforting blend of police work, history and archaeology.

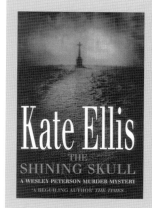

The Merchant's House (1998), *The Armada Boy* (1999), *An Unhallowed Grave (*1999), *The Funeral Boat (*2000), *The Bone Garden* (2001), *A Painted Doom* (2002), *The Skeleton Room* (2003), *The Plague Maiden* (2004), *A Cursed Inheritance* (2005), *The Marriage Hearse* (2006), *The Shining Skull* (2007).

DI (later Chief Inspector) PETRELLA
by Michael Gilbert

For his time Patrick Petrella is a particularly realistically drawn policeman – honest, painstaking and at times even plodding, often put upon and not always successful. Though he generally solves his cases his criminals are not necessarily put away; their lawyers, victims and circumstances all conspire to keep the felons from imprisonment, and sometimes they succeed. Petrella is London-based, working out of **Gabriel Street** police station. He lives alone and spends a lot of useful time on the street, in local pubs and small shops, building contacts – despite which, the stories are light and amusing. Petrella can be found

not only in full-length novels but in numerous short stories in magazines such as *Argosy*.

Books and short stories run from the 1950s to the 1980s. Try *Blood and Judgement* (1959).

FRANCIS PETTIGREW
by Cyril Hare

A barrister and occasional detective, sometimes in the more professional company of **Inspector Mallett**, he features in a brief series of light and amusing crime stories. But despite the comic tone of the stories the man himself is a more serious figure, sensitive to the awfulness of the crimes – and, in the case of the ultimate penalty, of the punishment too. This makes him both human and credible.

Tragedy at Law (1942), *With a Bare Bodkin* (1946), *When the Wind Blows* (1949), *That Yew Tree's Shade* (1954) and *He Should Have Died Hereafter* (1958).

SUPERINTENDENT PIBBLE
by Peter Dickinson

His name gives you a clue. Jimmy Pibble is a far from serious crime creation. Everything about him and the plots is a poke in the eye for the conventionalities of top-selling mysteries. Pibble is too old (well, so is Rebus), dull and grey (so were several Golden Age policemen) and the crimes he investigates are bizarre. Take his first case, in *Skin Deep*, where the leader of a New Guinea tribe is ensconced in a fine London house so he can be studied by an anthropologist who is in turn the daughter of a missionary who converted the tribe to Christianity. The Chief is murdered. Or take *A Pride of Heroes* in which although it's not the butler who dunnit, the butler gets mauled to death by a lion. Take *The Seals* where Dickinson creates another weird religious sect – who kidnap a scientist and hold him on their remote Hebridean island. These are clever, well-written stories, though not to everybody's taste.

Skin Deep (1968), *A Pride of Heroes* (1969), *The Seals* (1970), *Sleep and his Brother* (1971), *The Lizard in the Cup* (1972) and *One Foot in the Grave* (1979 and no connection to the television comedy series).

JOANNA PIERCY
by Priscilla Masters

Disorganised but committed, forever on the go, Detective Inspector Piercy charges full tilt at her cases, set in the **Staffordshire moorlands**. Attractive as the countryside may be, the crimes she deals with are far from pleasant. The books reveal a part of England and a range of attitudes and problems unfamiliar to most readers, all of which adds to their appeal. Piercy herself has a gruff appeal and is convincingly professional. As happens in many crime series with female leads she faces continual lurking sexism, but rather than fight back strongly, she usually concentrates on the job in hand and ignores the prejudice, from whomsoever it comes. In that fight and more

Peter Dickinson.

Priscilla Masters.

importantly in her cases she is supported by Detective **Mike Korpanski**, a half Polish body-building fan.

Although Masters introduced Joanna Piercy with her first book, *Winding Up the Serpent* in 1992, it was another four years before the second Piercy book, *Catch the Fallen Sparrow*, was published. (The non-series book *A Wreath From My Sister* came in between.) The Piercy and non-Piercy books then continued in roughly equal numbers at the rate of one a year. Among them *Scaring Crows* (1999), fifth in the Piercy series, can be picked out for the interesting light it sheds on the uneasy coexistence of incomers and locals in rural Staffordshire. Recent titles include *Endangering Innocents* (2003) and *Wings Over the Watcher* (2005).

PRISCILLA MASTERS

WINGS OVER THE WATCHER

'More than a match for Rendell and Christie'
Hampstead and Highgate Express

MISS PINK

by Gwen Moffat

From an author who mountaineers in real life comes this **mountaineering amateur detective**. Miss Melinda Pink is an author too: she writes gothic novels. As if scaling the heights were not dangerous enough she finds murderers up there. But she's a tough lady; she can handle it. (She's no Miss Marple; she doesn't knit. She is a magistrate.) These are bracingly straightforward, no nonsense stories, in which the no nonsense heroine comes up against rather more erratic characters. The worldwide settings are exhilarating.

Lady with a Cool Eye began the series in 1973. Later titles include *Miss Pink at the Edge of the World* (1975), *Die Like a Dog* (1978), *Grizzly Trail* (1984), *The Stone Hawk* (1989), *Rage* (1990), *The Lost Girls* (1998) and *Retribution* (2002).

LADY WITH A COOL EYE

The first work of fiction by an author well known for mountaineering and autobiographical books, that is set in the North Wales she knows so intimately

Gwen Moffat

Gollancz Detection

THOMAS PITT

Anne Perry

From this best-selling author (see **William Monk**) comes a **Victorian policeman** working for the nineteenth-century Bow Street Police. A solid and realistic policeman, often helped by his high-minded and high-born wife Charlotte, Pitt's investigations take him into and across a wide variety of social classes. The series began with *The Cater Street Hangman* (1979) and continued at the rate of almost one a year till *Southampton Row* (2002).

The Cater Street Hangman was made into a pilot in 1998 for a series which was never made.

GWEN MOFF...

DIE LIKE A DOG

At last!
A new Snowdonian detective story featuring
Miss Pink

Gollancz Detection

MONTAGUE PLUKE

by Nicholas Rhea

A curious police officer, Detective Inspector Pluke is a small-town cop, perhaps not surprisingly, since although he solves his crimes he is an oddly superstitious man whose behaviour is unlikely to commend him to more mundane superiors. Despite working in a backwater he gets some mainstream cases. (The author is more famous for his *Constable* series (see **Nick Rowan**) and for **Carnaby**.)

The *Pluke* books are: *Omens of Death* (1996), *Superstitious Death* (1998), *A Well-Pressed Shroud* (2000), *Garland for a Dead Maiden* (2002), *Prize Murder* (2006).

HERCULE POIROT
by Agatha Christie

> *It has been said of Hercule Poirot by some of his friends and associates, at moments when he has maddened them most, that he prefers lies to truth and will go out of his way to gain his ends by means of elaborate false statements, rather than trust to the simple truth.*
>
> From *Five Little Pigs* (1942).

Given that he had a career of over 50 years it is hardly surprising that Poirot changed. For some he is the Poirot portrayed on film by Finney or Ustinov, for others he is the television Poirot of David Suchet. Most *readers* will think of the supreme Poirot of the middle-period novels. Certainly the late novels show a falling off; certainly the short stories are poorer than the novels; certainly again the early Poirot was quite different from the one most casual readers (and all Poirot *viewers*) know. *The Mysterious Affair at Styles*, one should remember, was a first novel – not just the first Poirot novel but Christie's first of any kind. She may have hoped to create a series, she may have hoped to produce a good puzzle mystery, but she can have had little expectation that her first lead character would go on to become **one of the twentieth century's most famous fictional detectives.**

The original Poirot was bizarre – so bizarre that one wonders why. Unlike fictional detectives before, Christie's creation was not good looking, not athletic, not commanding, not in any way endearing; he wasn't even British. Why a Belgian? One could look to the year. A book published in 1920 would have been penned in 1919, the year after the First World War, when in the view of many British civilians their country had gone to war, at least in part, to come to the aid of plucky Belgium, overrun by the Kaiser's hordes. In 1919 there was little of today's unjustly dismissive attitude to that country, and Christie's Poirot was, honourably enough, a wounded refugee. It's clear that she deliberately created a character against the mould, but she went so far that, had she been an established writer, one might have thought she wanted to see how far she could push the barrier. But she was not established; she wasn't even published. (*Styles* was rejected by the first six publishers to see the manuscript.) So ought one to assume that her motive was to create a detective as unlike his predecessors as she could make him? Some have said so; I think not.

The early Poirot (and this is particularly clear in the short stories) is a thrown-together assemblage of bizarre traits: a short man with an egg-shaped head; a vain man whose vanity is expressed both in his disdainful speech and his absurd waxed moustache; a strutting showman who cannot resist theatrical effects. Despite all this, he is not original. Those early stories – before her first big sales success with *The*

Murder of Roger Ackroyd in 1926 – show all too clearly the debt Christie owed to Conan Doyle. Take just one of those stories as an example: the earliest, *The Affair at the Victory Ball*. Here we meet the great detective sharing quarters in London with his Watson surrogate, a pleasant if characterless foil called **Arthur Hastings**. To their apartment clients come – as will, on the second page, a baffled officer from Scotland Yard. It's hard to believe we are not in Baker Street. (We are actually in 14 Farraway Street. In the mid-1930s Poirot moves to 203 Whitehaven Mansions and replaces Hastings with an iron lady secretary called **Felicity Lemon**.) Hastings, in the early stories before he is shunted to the background, is a blurred carbon copy of Doctor Watson. Like Watson he is an ex-military man, and like Watson again he is Boswell to Poirot's Johnson. 'Since I have a first-hand knowledge of most of his cases,' he tells us in the first paragraph, 'it has been suggested to me that I select some of the most interesting and place them on record.' Christie steals Doyle's trick of increasing plausibility by having the narrator make reference to other cases and stories in the press:

> *I refer to the affair at the Victory Ball. Although perhaps it is not so fully demonstrative of Poirot's peculiar methods as some of the more obscure cases, its sensational features, the well-known people involved, and the tremendous publicity given it by the Press, make it stand out as a cause célèbre and I have long felt that it is only fitting that Poirot's connection with the solution should be given to the world.*

From *The Affair at the Victory Ball*.

This is pure Sherlock Holmes. When Inspector Japp appears on the second page, Poirot predictably 'had a good opinion of Japp's abilities, though deploring his lamentable lack of method.' Sherlock Holmes again. One could go on. Indeed, the second short story, *The Adventure of the Clapham Cook* uses a subterfuge to decoy away the cook that seems suspiciously like that in Doyle's *The Red-Headed League*. In this story too, as in many Holmes and Watson stories, the two bachelors are interrupted from their perusal of the morning papers in their London rooms:

> "That was a ring at the bell. You have a client."
> "Unless the affair is one of national importance, I touch it not," declared Poirot with dignity.

From *The Adventure of the Clapham Cook*

The indebtedness to Holmes continues when, in order to find the Clapham cook, Poirot places advertisements in the papers – a device which Holmes uses several times, always with surprising success. One would think that people had nothing better to do in those days than read the personal columns in the popular press. Poirot lacks Holmes' knack of brilliant observation and deduction. He may say waspishly (in the *Waverly* story), 'If you must wear a tie pin, Hastings, at least let it be in the exact centre of your tie,' but Holmes, we know, would have named the stone and gone on to deduce from it that Hastings had inherited the pin from his father – who had served, of course, in Afghanistan – that he

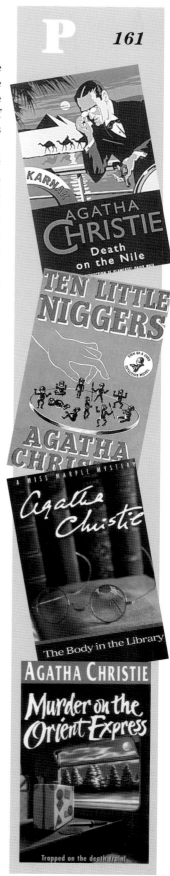

David Suchet.

hadn't worn it for several years, and that when he had affixed it that morning he had pinned it left-handed because he had nicked his right forefinger shaving, but when he was getting dressed the bleeding had not ceased. Not even Holmes would have needed the ludicrous coincidence, in *The King of Clubs*, of that very card (already significant) being left inside its box later from an entirely different pack of cards.

But in her novels Christie would not have needed such a ham-fisted coincidence, because the Poirot novels are much better than the short stories. For many crime writers the reverse is the case; a puzzle can be neatly set out and cleared in a few thousand words, and to make the story longer simply pads it out. But Christie, for all her deficiencies as a mistress of prose, gains in strength as her tales get longer. A short story may have three or four suspects, each of whom has one or two scenes, and whoever turns out to be guilty is no great surprise. In a novel, the longer the story the more she baffles us with twists and turns. It is quite possible in a Poirot novel to approach the end feeling that at one time or another you have suspected everyone in the book, and when Poirot draws everyone together for his final denouement you *still* don't know who he will denounce. Those climactic scenes – in the library, or in the state-room of a luxury liner – are rightly regarded as Christie's own. There is no debt to Conan Doyle there. Book after book ends with such a scene. As a reader one sees it coming – but that's *all* one sees coming: one knows there will be a grand revelation but one doesn't know who or what will be revealed – so one approaches this scene with delight and anticipation, for it is here that the Poirot novels are superb: every time she gives you an intriguing ride, at the end of which she guarantees a satisfying climax.

> "Ah, mon ami, you know my little weakness! Always I have a desire to keep the threads in my own hands up to the last minute. But have no fear. I will reveal all when the time comes. I want no credit – the affair shall be yours, on the condition that you permit me to play out the denouement my own way."

From *The Affair at the Victory Ball.*

The Mysterious Affair at Styles (1920), *The Murder on the Links* (1923), *Poirot Investigates* (short stories, 1924), *The Murder of Roger Ackroyd* (1926), *The Big Four* (1927), *The Mystery of the Blue Train* (1928), *Peril at End House* (1932), *Lord Edgware Dies* (aka *Thirteen at Dinner*, 1933), *Murder on the Orient Express* (1934), *Three Act Tragedy* (aka *Murder in Three Acts*, 1935), *Death in the Clouds* (aka *Death in the Air*, 1935), *The ABC Murders* (1935), *Cards on the Table*, (1936), *Murder in Mesopotamia* (1936), *Death on the Nile* (1937), *Dumb Witness* (1937), *Murder in the Mews* (1937), *Appointment with Death* (1938), *Hercule Poirot's Christmas* (1939), *One, Two, Buckle My Shoe* (1940), *Sad Cypress* (1940), *Evil Under the Sun* (1941), *Five Little Pigs* (1943), *The Hollow* (1946), *The Labours of Hercules* (12 stories, 1947), *Taken at the Flood* (1948), *The Underdog & other stories* (1951), *Mrs McGinty's Dead* (aka *Blood Will Tell*, 1952), *After the Funeral*

(1953), *Hickory Dickory Dock* (1955), *Dead Man's Folly* (1956), *Cat Among the Pigeons* (1959), *The Adventure of the Christmas Pudding* (1960), *The Clocks* (1963), *Third Girl* (1966), *Hallowe'en Party* (1969), *Elephants Can Remember* (1972), *Poirot's Early Cases* (short stories, 1974), *Curtain: Poirot's Last Case* (posthumous, 1975). Short stories continued to be issued in various collections.

Poirot has appeared on TV less than one imagines, largely because the repeats come around so often. **Peter Ustinov** reprised his film successes (see below) with *Thirteen at Dinner* in 1985 and *Dead Man's Folly* the following year. The year 1986 also saw **Ian Holm** play Poirot in *Murder by the Book*. **David Suchet** played him admirably in an occasional series of feature-length episodes in 1996 and 1997, and again in 2000 and 2002. In that series **Hugh Fraser** was Hastings, **Philip Jackson** was Inspector Japp, and **Pauline Moran** was Felicity Lemon.

Austin Trevor was the now-forgotten first film Poirot, in *Alibi* and *Black Coffee* (both 1931), and *Lord Edgware Dies* (1934). Later, in 1966, **Tony Randall** was miscast as Poirot in *The Alphabet Murders*, in which **Margaret Rutherford** had a cameo appearance as Miss Marple. (It didn't save the film.) **Albert Finney** made surprisingly heavy work of his portrayal of Poirot in *Murder on the Orient Express* (1974), perhaps feeling he had to out-act the rest of the star-studded cast. **Peter Ustinov** was far too large for Poirot but could and did reproduce all the man's idiosyncrasies in *Death on the Nile* (1978), again with a star-studded cast, and he appeared again in *Evil Under the Sun* (1982) in which the cast was almost as strong.

Peter Ustinov.

TOM POLLARD
by Elizabeth Lemarchand

From the cosy corner of Scotland Yard comes happily married Inspector Pollard (later Superintendent) and his wistful companion **Sergeant Toye** (later Inspector Toye). Both are amiable – Pollard always concerned for the comfort of his art teacher wife Jane and their young twins, and Toye liable to occasional murmurings about his twin obsessions, cowboy films and cars. Their investigations usually take them away from London's hurly-burly: to private schools in *Death of an Old Girl* (1967, their first appearance) and there again in *Let or Hindrance* (1973) or *Light Through Glass* (1984); to archaeological digs in *Suddenly While Gardening* (1978) or *Buried in the Past* (1978); to a stately home in *Death on Doomsday* (1971) and to yet more local history sites in *The Affacombe Affair* (1968), *Troubled Waters* (1982) and *The Wheel Turns* (1984).

Including the titles shown above Lemarchand wrote seventeen well-constructed detective novels and a number of short stories.

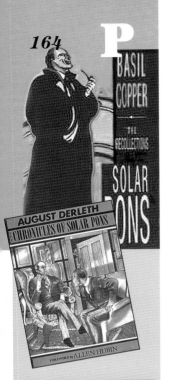

SOLAR PONS
by August Derleth, then Basil Copper (1976 to date)
Conceived as an Edwardian detective who assumed the identity of **Sherlock Holmes** to solve a crime, the idea was successful enough for the stories to continue, first from Derleth (19-years-old when he wrote the first story) and then, after his death, from the prolific Basil Copper (see **Mike Faraday**). Pons lived at 7B Praed Street (rather less salubrious than Baker Street) and his 'Watson' was **Dr Lyndon Parker**.

Derleth's first two collections acknowledged the Holmes anthologies by being titled *The Adventures* and then *The Memoirs of Solar Pons* (1945 and 1951). His last, posthumous title was *The Chronicles of Solar Pons* (1973). From many others in the series, Copper's *Some Uncollected Cases of Solar Pons* (1976) is as good as any. (There are also the *Dossier*, the *Secret Files*, the *Exploits*, the *Recollections*, etc.).

KATE POWER
by Judith Cutler
Kate Power, a young 30-something, started out as a detective sergeant in a West Midlands CID team based in central **Birmingham** and was in time promoted to Inspector. As befits a heroine carving out a career in what used to be seen as a man's world Kate Power is tough, no-nonsense, and a powerful woman.
Power on her Own (1998), *Power Games* (2000), *Power Shift* (2003).

Judith Cutler.

GEORGINA POWERS
by Denise Danks
That Georgina Powers is a techie-journalist and **computer specialist** means that the investigations she logs on to are thoroughly modern and up-to-date – at times, indeed, so leading edge they sound futuristic. It's no mean trick in an age when computer technology changes so fast that what may be leading edge one year is *passé* when the book is published. But Danks knows her stuff (she was a computer journalist herself) and far from rehashing source material she practically creates it. Georgina is no computer nerd. She's a modern metropolitan woman whose experience of sex is as complex and diverse as is her knowledge of computers. The Powers plots includes internet porn, drug-addicted rock stars, alternative reality, sado-masochism and financial scams.

The Pizza House Crash came out in 1990, followed by *Better Off Dead* (1991), *Frame Grabber* (1992), *Wink a Hopeful Eye* (1993), *Pheak* (1998), *Torso* (1999) and *Baby Love* (2001).

Denise Danks.

LORD FRANCIS POWERSCOURT
by David Dickinson
Towards the end of Queen Victoria's reign and into the **early years of the twentieth century** there were matters affecting the highest in the land, either concerning politics or of a personal nature, that were so delicate they had sometimes to be handed to the discreet Lord Powerscourt for sensitive disposal. One overlooked the fact that he was

too old and Irish: the man was an aristocrat, dammit, and utterly reliable. His investigations might involve Victoria herself or, when she died, her dissolute heir; they would take Powerscourt into the grandest country houses; he had access to the cabinet; and on occasions he was even summoned to help the government of a friendly state. The stories are marked by historical accuracy and detail, as well as by intriguing plots.

Clues to what Powerscourt is investigating each time can be gleaned from the books' titles: *Goodnight, Sweet Prince* (2002), *Death and the Jubilee* (2003), *Death of an Old Master* (2004), *Death of a Chancellor* (2005), *Death Called to the Bar* (2006), *Death on the Nevskii Prospekt* (2007), *Death on the Holy Mountain* (2008) – that's Ireland's holy Croagh Patrick.

CHARLIE PRIEST
by Stuart Pawson

Yorkshire-based Detective Inspector who made his appearance in *The Picasso Scam* in 1995 and has been delighting readers since, especially if they've had the pleasure of hearing the author read his text. A soft **Yorkshire** accent (there are such things) brings out the humour running through these tales of a laid-back, unorthodox copper who does things his own way and gets results. Not that this brings him much thanks from his superiors, who are more concerned for him to behave himself than catch pesky thieves. By the time we reach the eleventh book, *Shooting Elvis*, Charlie has acquired a new girlfriend, a former world-class athlete known as La Gazelle – but this being a crime book, what does she do? Gets herself kidnapped. So who'll have to rescue her? *The Picasso Scam* (1995), *The Mushroom Man* (1995), *The Judas Sheep* (1996). *The Last Reminder* (1997), *Deadly Friends* (1998), *Some By Fire* (1999), *Chill Factor* (2001), *Laughing Boy* (2002), *Limestone Cowboy* (2003), *Over the Edge* (2005), *Shooting Elvis* (2006), *Grief Encounters* (2007).

Stuart Pawson.

Dr PRIESTLEY
by John Rhode (John Street)

'Scientific' detective in the mould of **Dr Thorndyke**, an expert on mathematics, who for many of his investigations barely moves from his armchair in a Westbourne Terrace apartment. For a while in the noontime of his career he does stir himself rather more, but since doing so only lands him in dangerous situations it is no surprise that in later books he goes back to his armchair. The series begins with *The Paddington Mystery* (1925) and survives for an extraordinary 55 full-length novels untill *The Vanishing Diary* in 1951.

John Rhode.

LAURA PRINCIPAL
by Michelle Spring

A modern take on the 'detective in academia', Laura Principal is a private eye working in **Cambridge** and her cases, although not confined

exclusively to the university and people attached to it, cannot fail to be coloured by them. Her cases are a far cry from the donnish mysteries of the Golden Age, and are more likely to involve stalkers, migrant workers and students who turn to semi-professional prostitution. Yet the stories are far from sensationalist; Spring writes intelligently, as a Cambridge-based writer should, and has created in Laura Principal an adult and believably human private eye. Laura's relationship with **Sonny Mendlowitz**, her partner in both the personal and professional senses, becomes increasingly edgy as the series progresses, and she turns for moral support to a trio of close female friends, including **Detective Inspector Nicole Pelletier**.

Every Breath You Take (1994), *Running For Shelter* (1995), *Standing in the Shadows* (1998), *Nights in White Satin* (1999), *In the Midnight Hour* (2001).

MR PRINGLE
by Nancy Livingston

You might think there was little mileage in having a **tax inspector** as the running hero in a series, but at eight books, the Pringle series seems rather short. (It would have been longer but sadly the author died of cancer aged 58.) Mr G. D. H. Pringle isn't even a maverick; he is exactly what you'd expect a tax inspector to look like, and his attitudes are exactly what his superiors would expect in turn. He is a quiet, self-effacing man but beneath his diffident manner lies a suspicious and attentive mind. The cases he becomes engaged in involve money but he probes much deeper. In his first appearance he investigates a murder at a French health farm. Indeed, he often slips abroad, even as far as Australia in *Death in a Distant Land*. His travels bring him up against a host of odd and fascinating characters, when we find that he is not such a dry old stick as he first appears. His near-permanent companion, for example, is **Mavis Bignell**, by whom he was first smitten when she was a nude model at an art class. The succession of eccentric characters and complicated plots lead us to suspect that Miss Livingston was writing with her tongue pressed lightly in her cheek. But she writes so well that we don't mind.

The eight books are *The Trouble at Aquitaine* (1985), *Fatality at Bath and Wells* (1986), *Incident at Parga* (1987), *Death in a Distant Land* (1988, which won the *Punch* award for most comic novel), *Death in Close-up* (1989), *Mayhem in Parva* (1990), *Unwillingly to Vegas* (1991) and *Quiet Murder* (1992).

INSPECTOR PURBRIGHT
by Colin Watson

Purbright is by no means always the leading character in the **Flaxborough** books but he is an agent of calm at the heart of the funniest series in the mystery genre. These are outrageous, laugh-out-loud books, and to call Purbright a comic policeman would be accurate but too dismissive. Purbright's task is to attempt to restrain the squirming inhabitants of Watson's magnificent creation 'Flaxborough', the Gomorrah of East Anglia, a town whose sins are wonderfully comic though, some would say, accurately East Anglian. Reality is replaced by satire here. Watson made no secret of his low opinion of British 'cosy' mysteries, and his Flaxborough, which ought to have been the sort of quiet seaside town that cosy writers thrive on, turns their world of comfort upside down. Watson mocked the setting – but he mocked the cosy crime plot also, deliberately parodying established and conventional devices. In each book it seems that the town grows crazier and Inspector Walter Purbright more and more bemused. Crime writers reacted well, shortlisting *Hopjoy Was Here* for the CWA Gold Dagger.

Coffin, Scarcely Used began the series in 1958, followed by *Bump in the Night* in 1960 and *Hopjoy Was Here* in 1962. After a pause till *Lonelyheart 4122* (1967) the series continued fitfully (but always spiritedly) through 7 more titles to the last, *Whatever's Been Going On In Mumblesby* in 1982, the year of Watson's death. Watson also wrote his much-praised exposé *Snobbery With Violence: Crime Stories and their Audience* in 1971.

Murder Most English, based on the Flaxborough stories, was shown on TV in 1977.

SIMON PUTTOCK
by Michael Jecks

That **a fourteenth-century Stannary Bailiff on Dartmoor** should also be an amateur detective might seem odd, till one has read the books. But Simon, younger and rather more fearless companion to **Sir Baldwin de Furnshill**, finds the remote medieval countryside about him racked by crime: rape and murder, impersonation, theft and deception of many kinds. If the crimes don't concern him directly they concern his friends and family. And if the crimes don't affect them Sir Baldwin drags him into the investigation anyway. These are rumbustious tales of laughter and detection.

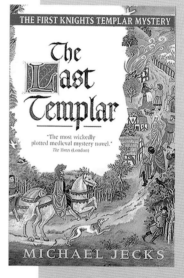

Try *The Last Templar* (1995), *The Dispensation of Death* (2007), *The Templar, the Queen and her Lover* (2007).

MISS PYM
by Josephine Tey

Miss Pym is of the sweet old lady school, though she is in fact only middle-aged. A psychology scholar, she puts her specialist knowledge to good use in *Miss Pym Disposes* (1946) when she sets out to discover who caused a fatal 'accident' in the school gym. More by luck than psychological judgement she solves the mystery – but she sympathises with the killer and won't turn her in. 'I am quite incapable of sending anyone to the gallows. I know what my plain duty is and I can't do it.' Which is all very well for a psychology scholar but of no use at all to a potential sleuth. Understandably, Josephine Tey had more luck with her other detective, Inspector **Alan Grant.** Miss Pym should not on any account be confused with **Mrs Pym**.   *Miss Pym Disposes* (1946).

MRS PYM

by Nigel Morland

Diametrically opposed to **Lady Molly of Scotland Yard** was the Yard's thuggish lady detective Palmyra Pym, who, in the words of Julian Symons, 'is a figure straight out of the *Beano* or the *Dandy*, tearing about London in a preposterous hat, indulging in dangerous driving, snarling at her subordinates, coming up slap against gangsters with WHAMS and THUDS.' In her first book she turned on the crooks with a Thompson sub-machine-gun. Staggeringly original as she seems to us for a character created in the 1930s, she was in fact, admitted Morland, inspired by one of Edgar Wallace's minor characters, the bulky **Mrs Ollorby**, who in his *Traitor's Gate* (1926) said, 'I'm not sensitive. If I were, I should be dead.' Over her 40 years of aggressive sleuthing Mrs Pym, in a reverse of the social patterns around her, moderated her behaviour and became more feminine. She did not end up a sweet old lady, but by the 1970s it might at least have been possible to sit and finish your tea at the same canteen table.

The Moon Murders* and *The Phantom Gunman* (both 1935) launched a series of more than 20 books, with titles such as *The Clue of the Bricklayer's Aunt* (1936), *The Clue of the Careless Hangman* (1940) and *A Corpse on the Flying Trapeze* (1941). Of the many titles *A Rope for the Hanging* (1938) best typifies her early bludgeoning manner, while *The Lady Had a Gun* (1951) finds her quite respectable. The dulling slide stopped there, and by her final *Mrs Pym and Other Stories* (1976) she had lost her patience again: 'This is my case and I'll damn well handle it Pym fashion.'

QUIRKE

by Benjamin Black

Dublin-based pathologist in the 1950s with a highly developed sense of curiosity that tempts him out of the mortuary onto the trail of potential murderers. (Quirke appears not to have a first name. Certainly no one uses it.) He has made a successful life for himself despite a hard upbringing in a succession of grim orphanages (they were grimmer in the '50s, grimmer still in Ireland) and benefits from having, as his creator, the Man Booker Prize winner John Banville as his pseudonymous author – an open secret that helped ensure that the first book, *Christine Falls*, would be noticed. As you'd expect, the books are noticeably well written but, as you might *not* have expected from a 'literary' writer, the stories are strong and the main charater convincing. *Christine Falls* (2006), *The Silver Swan* (2007).

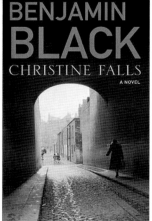

IMOGEN QUY

by Jill Paton Walsh

Redoubtable nurse cum detective in St Agatha's college, Cambridge. This is an interesting modern-day series from an author usually thought of as mainstream but whose output has been wide and consistently good.

The latest title, her fourth in the series, *The Bad Quarto*, is a fine place to start.

MAISIE RAINE TV series *Maisie Raine*
Breaking away from the usual clichés of TV cops, perhaps because the tales are based on the memoirs of a real-life policewoman (played by **Carol Bristow**), Raine is a balanced and domesticated East End widow, never happier than when gardening, and conscientious at work. She even gets on with her boss, Jack Freeman, (**Ian McElhinney**) – though less so with some faster-track colleagues. Being East End born and bred does bring her a few problems, most notably in the form of her dodgy brother Kelvin (**Paul Reynolds**), a small-time thief. But humanity and reality remain the cornerstone of this series, partly from their real-life origin but mostly from the solid performance by the ever reliable **Pauline Quirke**.

Pauline Quirk.

AGATHA RAISIN
by M. C. Beaton
Old lady detective – less dodery than she looks – whose Cotswold village rivals St Mary Mead for Mayhem. Agatha ran her own public relations company before retiring to what appears to be an even more active life solving crime. Though the village mysteries may begin quaintly – in an amateur gardening society, at a fete, on a healthy country walk, or at a jam making competition – they soon segue into classic crime territory. (Beaton also writes the **Hamish Macbeth** books.

Back in 1992 the fun began with *Agatha Raisin and the Quiche of Death*, to be followed with an annual succession of *Agatha Raisin and...* titles, including *...The Vicious Vet* (1993), *...The Terrible Tourist* (1997), *...The Wizard of Evesham* (1999) and the variant title (her 19th) *Badly Preserved* in 2008.

PRECIOUS RAMOTSWE
by Alexander McCall Smith
An unlikely detective who became an enormous success – perhaps because the idea seemed so implausible. Precious Ramotswe runs a female detective agency (which is fairly unlikely) and she runs it in **Botswana** (which is extraordinary). She is practically the entire establishment. Her casebook, unsurprisingly, includes investigations into every kind of marital mishap – betrayal, adultery, serial philandering and foolhardy money mismanagement. Not for Precious the first world's techniques of lonely vigils, tapped phones and credit references; this is Botswana, they do things differently there. Hers is not a First World agency:

> *"These were its assets: a tiny white van, two desks, two chairs, a telephone, and an old typewriter. Then there was a teapot, in which Mma Ramotswe – the only lady private detective in Botswana – brewed redbush tea. And three mugs – one for herself, one for the secretary, and one for the client. What else does a detective agency really need?"*
>
> From *The No 1 Ladies Detective Agency*, 1998.

R

Alexander McCall Smith.

Her cases, her clients and her opponents are not First World either, and that is what makes them such a delight. McCall Smith may not be African but he was born in Zimbabwe, lived in Botswana and lectured at university there. Few white men, especially in what is essentially a set of comedies, could produce such a touching and uncondescending portrait of the country and its people. The writing is deft, the tales amusing and the characters rapidly become part of the readers' life. If one were in Botswana and in trouble there – as one might well be, one imagines – one would want Mma Ramotswe on one's side. Her methods are simple, but they work, as in this example from the first book in the series:

> *She crept up behind the boy and raised her Bible into the air. Then she brought it down on his head, with a resounding thud that made the children start.*

It's best to start this series at the beginning: *The No 1 Ladies' Detective Agency* (1998), though *Morality for Beautiful Girls* (2003) and *The Kalahari Typing School for Men* (2004) can be recommended.

STEPHEN RAMSAY
by Ann Cleeves

Inspector Ramsay is a lonely man, and not just because he is stationed in **Northumbria**. Indeed, in his first book he seems a secondary character but as we come to know him we find that although Ramsay is reserved and remote he is thorough and persistent. All of which makes him particularly fit for his isolated patch among the former pit villages and the bleak but haunting landscape. He reveals his secrets slowly, from his barely visible presence in *A Lesson in Dying* through *Murder in my Back Yard* when we learn a little about his failed marriage, then on, slowly, until in the fourth book appears a wary romance. Here too he treads a careful path: will he settle down a second time, with a single mother who has a teenage daughter?

Clearly, these are books that have to be read in sequence – although you might skip the first, *A Lesson In Dying* (1990) and begin with *Murder in my Back Yard* (1991). The fourth, *Killjoy* (1993) introduces Prue, his future lover, and this book must be read before the sixth, *The Baby Snatcher* (1997).

JEFF RANDALL TV series *Randall and Hopkirk (Deceased)*

Randall and Hopkirk (Deceased) was one of those silly ideas that worked. When Marty Hopkirk was killed in a car crash it seemed the end of the detective agency he ran with partner (in the business sense) Jeff Randall. Or so Jeff thought. Then, amazingly, he was visited by Marty's ghost – who not only was still around but wanted to continue in the agency. From then on the pair scampered through a run of scrapes and investigations. Everyone else saw only Jeff, but for him – and for us, who 'saw' Marty as if he were really there (one of the

Mike Pratt as Jeff Randall, Kenneth Cope as Marty Hopkirk.

least expensive effects on television) – they worked as a pair. Marty could go where Jeff could not and, more entertainingly, could give Jeff more advice than he'd ever want to hear – telling him to stop mistreating his old car, and even giving advice on Jeff's relationship with his widow. That this nonsense not only worked but was fun was a testament to the scripts, production and fine cast. Inexplicably, there was only a single series. An American version failed, and about the recast British version with **Vic Reeves and Bob Mortimer** in 2001 the least said the kindest for all concerned. The original and greatest starred **Mike Pratt** as Jeff Randall, **Kenneth Cope** as Marty Hopkirk, and **Annette Andre** as Jean Hopkirk.

JOHN RAWLINGS
by Deryn Lake
John Rawlings actually did exist, though you might suspect otherwise from these lively escapades. He was in reality and in the books an **eighteenth-century apothecary**, a close friend of **John Fielding** who founded the Bow Street Runners. For Deryn Lake that was too good an opportunity to miss, and she paired Rawlings and Fielding in a set of well-researched **Georgian adventures**, generally but not always set in London, more dangerous and lively in that century than in our own.
Death in the Dark Walk (1994), *Death at the Beggar's Opera* (1995), *Death at the Devil's Tavern* (1996), *Death on the Romney Marsh* (1998), *Death in the Peerless Pool* (1999), *Death at the Apothecaries' Hall* (2000), *Death in the West Wind* (2001), *Death at St James's Palace* (2002), *Death in the Valley of Shadows* (2003), *Death in the Setting Sun* (2005), *Death and the Cornish Fiddler* (2006), *Death in Hellfire* (2007).

REBUS
by Ian Rankin

**Ken Stott.
Rebus 2007.**

Ian Rankin.

Any budding crime writer searching for a character who might turn out sufficiently attractive to stay at the top of the best-seller list year after year would be mad to come up with John Rebus. He's a Detective Inspector, but how did he cling to his job? He drank too much, ate the wrong food, his private life was a mess. He was ex-army, an old-style cop, too old to progress further in a New Labour styled, endlessly mucked about police force – not that he was better when he was younger. Too bolshy. His face didn't fit – and as for his attitude! The only reason **St Leonard's Division** kept him on was that despite his occasional mistakes and stumbles, despite his ability to irritate, Rebus latched on to his cases like a terrier and wore them down. Tenacious, he was that. He might look washed up but he solved too many cases for the higher-ups

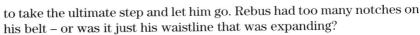

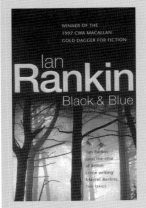

to take the ultimate step and let him go. Rebus had too many notches on his belt – or was it just his waistline that was expanding?

Rebus, then, was unpromising material. A book publicist would have wanted to tidy him up, to add social graces – and to move him, for Heaven's sake, away from out-of-the-way **Edinburgh** to somewhere more saleable down south. No surprise, perhaps, that he wasn't an immediate success. Only after several books had come out and, perhaps, the first television adaptation had been aired, did John Rebus begin to move from the steady mid-list to big sales. Readers recognised that here was a real cop, faulty, full of foibles, superbly drawn and working in a real town. Edinburgh looms large, grim and dirty in the books, but the author's love for the city is plain. Though he never rhapsodises. In *Let it Bleed* he writes:

> *It was another grim day. No snow or ice, but a freezing wind and gusts of rain, the sky oppressively weighted with cloud. It was like the city was in a box, and someone had pushed the lid on too tightly.*
>
> From *Let It Bleed*

The stories, complicated and multi-layered as they seem, are unlike other police procedurals, and the characters, one realises, are equally well drawn. Ian Rankin can write. A major figure now, it was obvious from his early books that he was a novelist of stature. Not only has he become Scotland's leading crime writer, he is probably their leading writer of any kind. He has made Edinburgh 'Rankin's Edinburgh' and has immortalised **The Oxford Bar**. He has allowed readers who have never strolled more than a hundred yards from Princes Street to feel they know the city.

Rebus himself lives in real time. As the years pass Rebus ages, and the series has lasted long enough for him to have reached that certain age – one that some forecast he would never make – dragging him from active service into retirement. He has lived *through* real times: the early years of Scottish devolution and the country's distancing of itself from a semi-colonial past. The creation of a new Scottish Parliament – its buildings, equipment, opportunities for graft – have supplied rich material for his books to plunder. In the fourth novel, *Strip Jack*, a populist MP, Gregor Jack, is compromised following a police raid on an Edinburgh brothel. But he is a strong man and faces down the accusations. As he tries to shrug them off he is faced with more revelations. Then his wife disappears. There is also that matter, the police remind him, of two unexplained bodies – and an inmate from an asylum who has tales to tell. Jack's protective layers are being stripped away. Apparently unrelated in Rebus's workload is the curious case of some books stolen from the Professor of Divinity at the University of Edinburgh. One of the books is *Tristram Shandy*:

> *Only that particular title had meant anything to Rebus. He owned a paperback copy of the book, bought at a car-boot sale on The Meadows for tenpence. Maybe the Professor would like to borrow it...*
>
> From *Strip Jack*

In a Rebus tale, as in most crime stories, nothing is unrelated. In *Dead Souls* the matter that grabs everyone's attention is the deportation from America to Edinburgh of a multiple murderer. That surely can have nothing to do with the re-emergence of an old case of abuse within a children's home? Or with the unexpected suicide of a colleague? No Rebus tale can deal with one thing at a time. Few of the stories leave out politics. The tales may be set in a time of New Labour and the New Scottish Parliament but politics remains the same dirty old game. In *Let It Bleed* the Lord Provost's daughter disappears. She appears to have been kidnapped, or has she simply run away? Has this domestic affair any link to the apparently separate matter of a prominent Edinburgh councillor and a years-old fraud? Why, incidentally, should the Scottish Office's Permanent Secretary take a sudden interest in Inspector Rebus?

Whichever politicians rule Scotland, Edinburgh remains wreathed in mist and murk. The economy booms but the smart hip restaurants are yards away from dank dour pubs. The swirling mix of past and present, together with uneasy questions of national identity, is explored further in *Set in Darkness*. But some of the books ease back from politics to move into familiar crime fiction territory. When Rankin wrote a serial killer story he added trademark authenticity by basing his killer, Johnny Bible, on a real-life Scottish serial killer from decades earlier, Bible John, whose body, people said, was not the one buried in the grave which bore his name. In *Black and Blue* Rankin's Johnny Bible is not the real-life Bible John – but what if a serial killer did return, apparently from the grave? What if he contacted John Rebus? Could Rebus stop him or is the flawed inspector already on his own road to self-destruction?

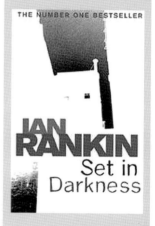

In *A Question of Blood* the killer is not a serial killer, though this is another case with disturbing echoes of real-life tragedies. The facts seem simple enough, but Rebus, seldom satisfied, wants to know why an ex-soldier would, for no clear reason, shoot two 17-year-old schoolboys. Everyone else thinks the case is cut and dried. They are more concerned with another death: that of a stalker found burnt to death at home – a stalker who had been plaguing Rebus's colleague **Siobhan Clarke**. When the book opens Rebus is in hospital with burnt hands. Scalded, he insists, but even Siobhan has doubts. No one would put it past Rebus to take the law into his own hands – even if he burnt his hands in doing so.

"*I can give you some paracetamol?*" *the nurse suggested.*
"*Any chance of a beer to wash them down?*"

From *A Question of Blood.*

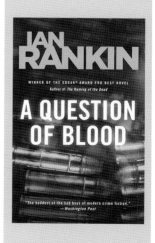

Siobhan is Rebus's younger colleague, introduced well into the series as Rebus approaches retirement, possibly to extend the life of the series after he moves on. She seems tough, she uses the gym, but the taxing life and broken hours of a working cop have told on her. Unbeknownst to colleagues she gets panic attacks:

The first time she'd suffered a panic attack, she'd felt as if she

John Hannah.
Rebus 2001.

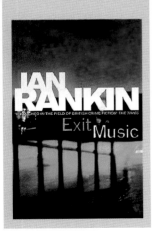

was going into cardiac arrest: heart pounding, lungs giving out, her whole body surging with electricity. Her doctor had said she should take some time off.

From *A Question of Blood*

There are no unblemished heroes in the Rebus books. There are no simple crimes. But the darkness and complexity of the stories, the warmth and vulnerability of the characters and the bitter humour, have drawn millions of readers to buy the books. Characters and city are strongly drawn, but this has not stopped television from putting its own visual take on them.

Rebus was first filmed for TV in 2001 with **John Hannah** in the title role. He was an unlikely choice – too young by decades, too good looking – but he played it well. The complex storylines had to be simplified and could not be easily converted into a weekly serial format (though Hannah did not want to appear in a weekly serial) so the stories came out as isolated one-offs. Then, surprisingly, TV had a rethink (responding perhaps to a chorus of recommendations from viewers that there was a more obvious man for the part) and *Rebus* was reborn with **Ken Stott** in the title role. Stott was older, more battered, more suitable than Hannah, though by then the books had garnered such an enormous following that among the crowd were many readers for whom even Stott was not how they 'saw' their man. But which actor *would* be right? The argument ran on.

Rebus tried to stop listening. He knew his drinking was a problem these days precisely because he'd learned self-control. As a result, few people noticed that he had a problem. He was well-dressed at work, alert when the occasion demanded, and even visited the gym some lunchtimes. He ate lazily, and maybe too much, and yes, he was back on the cigs. But then nobody was perfect.

From *Let It Bleed*

Black and Blue won the CWA Gold Dagger in 1997, and *Resurrection Men* the Edgar for best novel in 2004.

Knots And Crosses (1987), *Hide And Seek* (1991), *A Good Hanging: And Other Stories* (1992), *Tooth And Nail* (aka *Wolfman* 1992), *Strip Jack* (1992), *The Black Book* (1993), *Mortal Causes* (1994), *Let It Bleed* (1995), *Black And Blue* (1997), *The Hanging Garden* (1998), *Dead Souls* (1999), *Rebus: The Early Years* (omnibus, 1999), *Set in Darkness* (2000), *The Falls* (2001), *Rebus: The St Leonard's Years* (omnibus, 2001), *Three Great Novels: Strip Jack/The Black Book/Mortal Causes* (omnibus, 2001), *Resurrection Men* (2002), *A Question of Blood* (2003), *Rebus: The Lost Years* (omnibus, 2003), *Capital Crimes* (omnibus, 2004), *Fleshmarket Close* (aka *Fleshmarket Alley* 2004). *The Naming of the Dead* (2006), *Exit Music* (2008).

CHRISTOPHER REDMAYNE
by Edward Marston

In a series of **Restoration** mysteries set in England in the 1660s Redmayne is an architect in his 20s helping to rebuild London after the Great Fire. Despite the disaster the city finds plenty of time to rejoice in the happier times that have followed the restoration of Charles II. But crime still stalks the streets. And Charles II's crown is not necessarily safe. Redmayne becomes involved in investigations with his parish constable friend **Jonathan Bale**.
The King's Evil (1999), *Amorous Nightingale* (2000), *The Repentant Rake* (2001), *The Frost Fair* (2003), *The Parliament House* (2006), *The Painted Lady* (2007).

J G REEDER
by Edgar Wallace

The little man with an enormous brain. He knows everything. He knows everyone. Reeder looks the type of man who steps off the train in the morning rush hour in the company of thousands of identical dull drones, each carrying their furled umbrella, and each with their pince-nez tucked into the top pocket of their pin-striped suits worn daily beneath slightly worn frock coats and sombre bowler hats. But Reeder's umbrella has a knife blade in the handle. And he has a revolver in his pocket. He is a dangerous man – to criminals, for he works in the public prosecutor's office, where his extraordinary memory and his ability to think like a criminal makes him their deadly foe. Of the mild-mannered, apparently inoffensive little man who is in fact an ice-cold professional, there is no finer example than J. G. Reeder. His memory is prodigious and his calmness in a crisis is invaluable. Even when trapped with a pretty young woman in a cellar rapidly flooding with water that the criminals intend will drown them both, you know that if there is one person who can save her from any mishap graver than a severely dampened skirt, it is the excellent Mr Reeder. Wallace is often written off as a hack journalist who wrote pot-boilers. This is wrong. He was indeed successful; his sales were massive; but reading these tales in the twenty-first century, 80 years after they were published, one finds that the Reeder tales – they are all short stories – are amusing, sprightly written, and hold up far better than most others written at the time.

Mr Reeder's smile was one of self-depreciation.
"One picks up odd scraps of information," he said apologetically.
"I – I see wrong in everything. That is my curious perversion – I have a criminal mind."

    From the short story *The Poetical Policeman*.
Room 13 (1924) was technically the first Reeder book, though *The Mind of Mr J G Reeder* (1925) was the first proper collection (and the best). He reappeared in *Terror Keep* (1927), *Red Aces* (1929) and *Mr J G Reeder Returns* (1934). Some later titles were written by J. T. Edson.
    The Mind of Mr J G Reeder was a thoroughly enjoyable series shown

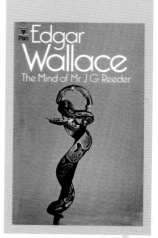

Jack Regan was played by John Thaw and George Carter's role by Dennis Waterman.

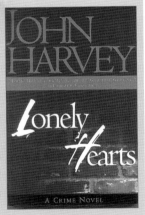

Tom Wilkinson played Resnick.

on ITV from 1969 to 1971 with **Hugh Burden** ideally cast as Mr Reeder. **Willoughby Goddard** played his boss Sir Jason Toovey.

The Mind of Mr Reeder was a 1939 film starring **Will Fyffe**.

JACK REGAN
created by Troy Kennedy Martin
Leather-jacketed new-style Scotland Yard detective from the hugely popular series *The Sweeney* which ran from 1974 to 78, in which he was played by **John Thaw**. The show broke new ground with its realistic (?) portrayal of tough no-nonsense police officers and tactics, leaping forward from the breakthroughs of *Z-Cars* and *Softly Softly* a decade before. Regan would cut any corner to get a villain banged up and was himself eventually charged with taking bribes. His sidekick was the initially clean **George Carter** (played by **Dennis Waterman**) who became enthused of his teacher's tactics. A rough and raw series, laced with fights and humour, it was lovingly looked back to three decades later in the TV series *Life on Mars*.

Novelisations of the TV series followed, all with the name *Regan* in their title.

CHARLIE RESNICK
by John Harvey
Brooding, conscientious cop working mainly in **Nottingham**. Of Polish ancestry, fond of Polish food – and jazz; there is always jazz, but then, the author is a jazz saxophonist – Resnick has a deep bond with his city and its inhabitants, including a number of villains and victims, and that empathy helps him understand what drives them, and thus it helps him solve the crimes. As well as series characters in the local force, the books occasionally feature a would-be Raffles character, **Grabianski**, almost a friend to Resnick, but against whom he reluctantly is set. Grabianski appears in *Rough Treatment* and *Still Water*, both of which are recommended, and *Still Water* is an example of how Resnick can become personally involved with his cases: his lover, Hannah, was a friend of the murdered woman. Violence by men on women is a recurrent theme; Harvey's first book, *Lonely Hearts*, has the police arrest a man with a record of violence on the understandable suspicion that he killed his common-law wife. But there's a second murder while he's in custody. Resnick, never a one to jump to easy conclusions, has similar doubts in *Off Minor* during a frantic, perhaps too hasty, hunt for a child killer. The series was brought to an end with *Last Rites* and Harvey, who has written a number of stand-alone novels, introduced a new series character, **Frank Elder**, in 2006. John Harvey has been dubbed the 'King of Crime' by *The Times* and in 2007 won the **Cartier Diamond Dagger** for lifetime achievement.

Lonely Hearts (1989), *Rough Treatment* (1990), *Off Minor* (1991), *Cutting Edge* (1991), *Wasted Years* (1993), *Cold Light* (1994), *Living Proof* (1995), *Easy Meat* (1996), *Still Water* (1997), *Last Rites* (1998). *Now's The Time* (1999) comprises the complete Resnick short stories.

Resnick was a short, much-praised but commercially unsuccessful series of five episodes (a 3-parter followed by 2 singles) scripted by John Harvey and based on two of his novels (*Lonely Hearts* and *Rough Treatment*) in 1992 and 1993. **Tom Wilkinson** played Resnick. Harvey has scripted some Resnick stories for radio.

SUKEY REYNOLDS
by Betty Rowlands

Sukey Reynolds first appears as a Gloucestershire SOCO in *An Inconsiderate Death* (1997) on a case where a businessman's wife has been strangled; in later books similarly nasty deaths continue. *Deadly Obsession* (2004) finds a corpse with a broken neck below a garden staircase, and in *Party to Murder* (2005) a pregnant estate manager is discovered strangled with a necklace. Her employer made her pregnant, but did he kill her? The series charts Sukey's progress from the ranks, and in later books she leaves the Gloucester area for Bristol. In *Alpha, Beta, Gamma ... Dead* (2007) she achieves her ambition of joining the CID. From which point, anything can happen!

Though the books stand alone they are better read in sequence. First is An *Inconsiderate Death* (1997) and the series is still running.

MERLIN RICHARDS
by Keith Miles

Set in the late 1920s and early 1930s, Richards is a young Welsh architect who emigrates to work for the famous **Frank Lloyd Wright** in America. Lloyd Wright is by now in his 60s while Richard is in his 20s. Richards is less of an amateur who can't help delving into matters which ought to be left to the professionals than he is a man who finds himself unwillingly at the heart of things. In *Murder in Perspective* while he works on the building of the Biltmore Hotel in Arizona in 1928 a female designer is killed and Merlin becomes a main suspect. He thus has to solve the murder to exonerate himself. Similarly in *Saint's Rest* when a man is found hanged in the Chicago house being built for a meat baron, Merlin again finds himself under fire from all sides, including from the killer who stalks him in the meat factory.
Murder in Perspective (1997), *Saint's Rest* (1999).

RICKMAN & FOSTER
by Margaret Murphy

Margaret Murphy.

After a string of stand-alone thrillers, Murphy began a series based in **Liverpool** featuring Detective Chief Inspector Jeff Rickman and Detective Sergeant Foster. Rickman's face bears a few battle scars, and at 6 foot 4 he towers over most men. But though the hard men of Liverpool's criminal world are intimidated by him, the women respond warmly. 'Some big men are intimidating,' one woman says. 'Others make you feel safe. Rickman makes me feel safe.' He's a team player, respecting the contributions of his team as well as the scientists integral to modern policing. These fast-paced novels evoke the gritty reality of

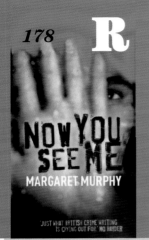

crime in one of Britain's most vibrant and brutal cities.
The Dispossessed (2004), *Now You See Me* (2005).

INSPECTOR RIVERS
See **Inspector Ryvet**

SOPHIE RIVERS
by Judith Cutler
Feisty amateur sleuth Sophie Rivers is in her mid-30s and like her
creator is a former English lecturer at an inner-city college of further
education somewhere unmissable in the Midlands, but she has latterly
been ranging further afield as a professional caterer. Fortunately she is
an excellent cook, despite which she strayed from the kitchen in her
debut novel, *Dying Fall*, when she was *dying* to right wrongs.

Titles include *Dying Fall* (1995), *Dying to Score* (1999), *Dying to
Deceive*(2003)

ROBERTS & BRANT
by Ken Bruen
Inspector Roberts and Detective Sergeant Brant are known as the R&B
of the Metropolitan Police, as rough and sleazy a pair of cops as you
could ever hope not to meet, hung over from the Seventies, you might
say, let alone from the night before. Vigilantes in uniform they may be
but when the series begins they've gone too far, and what they need is a
'white arrest', a major, headline-grabbing success to wash their sins
away and leave them sparkling clean. They raise their sights for the
second book, hauling themselves off to Dublin and New York in search
of ever more interesting lowlife, and in the third book things get
personal: someone has killed Roberts's brother. Not that Roberts liked
his brother – but you can't let that sort of thing go unpunished, can you?
And while they're at it, they'd better catch the Clapham rapist. These
three books – the 'White Trilogy' – are very tough and utterly pared
down chillers.
A White Arrest (1998), *Taming the Alien* (1999), *The McDead* (2000).

ROGER THE CHAPMAN
by Kate Sedley
Though a chapman was a roving pedlar, a medieval travelling salesman,
the eponymous Roger is also a lapsed Benedictine monk and friend to
the future **Richard III** (he of the 'Winter of our discontent' and 'My
kingdom for a horse' speeches). This Richard is rather less villainous
than is Shakespeare's version, and Roger is his personal spy and
amateur sleuth, a character unaccountably missing from my edition of
the play. Kate Sedley's recreation is probably more accurate than
Shakespeare's and her books are entertaining mysteries while at the
same time they improve our knowledge of an exciting period.

Death and the Chapman came out in 1991 and the series has
continued at the rate of roughly one a year.

GEORGE ROGERS
by Jonathan Ross

Inspector Rogers (later Superintendent) is a realistically drawn police officer whose portrayal owes much to his author having served as a policeman for some 30 years. (He does not introduce TV chat shows.) Accompanied by his companion **Lingard**, Rogers solves his cases by genuine old-fashioned police methods rather than by astonishing feats of deduction or lucky chance. This is what gives the series its special feel. Few other police series are as convincing in their detail or as revealing in telling how the police really operate.

Though the books are vanishing from the bookshelves the series lasted some three decades, beginning with *The Blood Running Cold* in 1968 and ending with *Murder, Murder Burning Bright* in 1996. Standout titles are *Diminished by Death* (1968), *A Rattling of Bones* (1979) and *Dark Blue and Dangerous* (1981).

CONSTABLE NICK ROWAN
by Nicholas Rhea

Constable Nick is known mainly from the TV series *Heartbeat* although he began in book form and his creator has written some novelisations of the TV character as well as working on the scripts. The Nick Rowan stories are based on Rhea's own early career in the police back in the **1960s**, and are at least as much about the day-to-day life of a young policeman as they are about crime.

Nick Berry.

First came *Constable on the Hill* in 1979 and the series has continued at an astonishing pace to date, with titles such as *Constable on Call* (1993), *Constable in Control* (1994) and the thirty-fifth (!) *Constable on the Coast* in 2006.

The long-running TV series *Heartbeat* began in 1992. **Nick Berry** played Rowan, with **Niamh Cusack** (originally) as his wife Kate and **Juliette Gruber** as Jo Weston. When Rowan moved to Canada (to become a Mountie) a new village bobby, Mike Bradley (played by **Jason Durr**) took on a major role, although Sergeant Craddock (played by **Philip Franks**) was Rowan's official replacement.

Dr SAM RYAN TV series *Silent Witness* from 1996 (creator: Nigel McCrery)

Amanda Burton.

Following the success of female pathologists in books (after P. D. Cornwell *et al*) BBC TV had an immediate success on their hands with *Silent Witness*. Its storylines were dour and uncompromising, and actress **Amanda Burton** took an appropriately stern unsmiling stance in her role, thereby adding verisimilitude. Ryan had the requisite tortured background, hailing from Northern Ireland, her father murdered by terrorists, her mother decayed by Alzheimer's and even her sister sour and resentful. Burton bowed out in 2006 but the series carried on.

A WHITE CIRCLE CRIME CLUB

A POLICEMAN AT THE DOOR

CAROL CARNAC

CRIME CLUB

INSPECTOR RYVET
by Carol Carnac

Solid, decent cop of the 1930s, 1940s and 1950s, Ryvet is another version of the policeman this author introduced under different names in different books; as Inspector Rivers and Inspector MacDonald (MacDonald came first, being seemingly the same man a few years younger). Ryvet plays with the author's real name, Edith Caroline Rivett (1894-1958) and 'Carol' relates to her other pen-name E. C. R Lorac, being Carol backwards, using her own initials. 'Lorac' is the name she used for the MacDonald series.

Triple Death (1936) features Ryvet, while A Double for Detection (1945) introduces and A Policeman at the Door (1959) is the last book to feature Rivers. MacDonald can be found in the earlier The Murder on the Burrows (1931) and the MacDonald series ran through nearly 50 titles to Dishonour Among Thieves published posthumously in 1960.

THE SAINT (SIMON TEMPLAR)
by Leslie Charteris

Known as '**the Robin Hood of modern crime**' the archetypical schoolboy's hero gained an enormous number of adult readers who identified their favourite from his 'stick man' logo on the covers of (usually) Gollancz yellow and black crime books. Impossibly debonair, carefree and witty, Templar approached his many escapades much as a schoolboy knight might approach the latest joust. He wasn't always honest; depending on little more than whim he'd skip between being a detective, a righter of wrongs (especially for mistreated maidens), or a thief (only from the rich and nasty). For his earliest readers, even the settings Charteris chose (skipping effortlessly between London and New York) seemed glamorous. In the books Templar's wit delighted a succession of entrancing ladies, his fists floored numerous villains and his intelligence (both his own and from well-placed contacts) thwarted any number of dastardly opponents. Light-hearted but laced with action, the books remained best-sellers for decades. They spawned a long but so-so TV series that nevertheless launched the career of Roger Moore, and some equally indifferent films. The books have dated, of course – certainly the humour has, because humour always dates – but they are still fun to read.

Saint books began in 1928 and continued to the 1960s. Though Enter the Saint appeared in 1930, his first actual appearance was in Meet the Tiger in 1928. In the 1930s the books came out at the rate of more than one a year. There were four books in the war, two more in the post-war 1940s, then after a long break in which only short story collections appeared, Vendetta for the Saint came out in 1964 and finally, The Saint in Pursuit in 1970 and (probably not by Charteris) Salvage for the Saint in 1983. It is rumoured that most post-1960 novels were not actually written by Charteris. Those from the 1930s are the best. The comic-strip Saint Mystery Magazine ran from 1958 to 1967.

Several actors have attempted this part. **Louis Hayward** was first

Louis Hayward.

George Sanders.

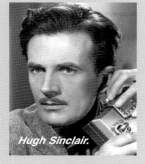

Hugh Sinclair.

(*The Saint in New York* in 1938); **George Sanders** made five fairly forgettable appearances (*The Saint Strikes Back* in 1938 to *The Saint in Palm Springs* in 1941); **Hugh Sinclair** made two (*The Saint's Vacation* in 1941 and *The Saint Meets the Tiger* in 1943); Louis Hayward came back for *The Saint's Return* in 1954, and after a long absence **Val Kilmer** had a try with a feeble *The Saint* in 1997.

TV produced the one successful adaptation: **Roger Moore**, in a long-running series, brought suavity and humour to the role and remains **the quintessential Saint**. At the end of the 1970s the series was reprised with **Ian Ogilvy** in the role.

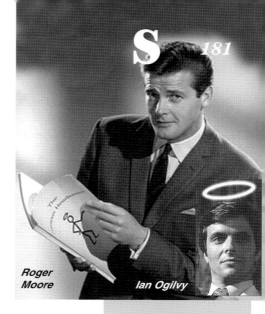

Roger Moore

Ian Ogilvy

JOE SANDILANDS
by Barbara Cleverly

An interesting historical variation: – his career extends from the late nineteenth century into the 1920s – Commander Joe Sandilands, ex-army, ex-Military Intelligence, is now part of Scotland Yard but often seconded on foreign missions. This allows Joe to demonstrate his expertise in exotic frontier lands such as Kashmir, Simla and Afghanistan and, in *Tug of War*, the First World War battlefields of northern France. Cleverly's third book *The Damascened Blade* (2003) won the CWA Ellis Peters Historical Dagger Award, and her next book *The Palace Tiger* was shortlisted for it. Each of the books is colourful and dramatic.

The Last Kashmiri Rose (2001), *Ragtime in Simla* (2002), *The Damascened Blade* (2003), *The Palace Tiger* (2004), *The Bee's Kiss* (2006), *Tug of War* (2007).

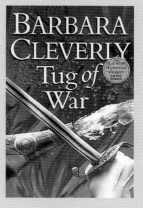

ALAN SAXON
by Keith Miles

A professional golfer in his early 40s, Saxon manages to run into serious trouble in whichever country his sport takes him to – and being a top golfer he gets to visit top resorts in top places. Helped at times by **Clive Phelps**, a golf writer, Saxon tees off by proving his innocence at St Andrew's when a female hitchhiker is found dead in his motor caravan. In the more recent *Honolulu Play-Off* he is best man at a wedding where the groom is murdered and whoever killed him seems to want Saxon dead as well. Extraordinary, really, that they keep inviting him to play.

Bullet Hole (1986), *Double Eagle* (1987), *Green Murder* (1990), *Flagstick* (1991), *Bermuda Grass* (2002), *Honolulu Play-Off* (2004).

THE SCARLET PIMPERNEL
by Baroness Orczy

They seek him here, they seek him there – and if you're wondering how he pops up in a compendium of detectives it's because he *was* a detective; his creator certainly thought so and Ellery Queen himself

dubbed him one of the *great* detectives. During the Reign of Terror in the aftermath of the **French Revolution** the Scarlet Pimpernel was the assumed name of **Sir Percy Blakeney**, who most of the time masqueraded as an irritatingly useless English aristocrat, while at times of crisis (frequently at night) he emerged as the dashing secret agent and scourge of Robespierre, the Jacobins and the Committee of Public Safety (this last being even more ghastly than the Health and Safety committees we have today). We cheer on the Pimpernel as he rescues fellow aristocrats from the guillotine (his author was a baroness) and we marvel at his brilliant disguises, his way with women and the way he is able to open any door. Against him looms the might of Robespierre's bureaucracy and especially his henchman **Citizen Chauvelin**. But they are no match for Percy. One should not forget that, despite his irritatingly effete mannerisms, he was happily married to the spirited and gorgeous **Marguerite Blakeney**.

This hugely successful series began with *The Scarlet Pimpernel* in 1905 – it is still a great read – and continued through another ten full-length adventures including the *Elusive*, the *Triumph*, the *Adventures*, the *League* and the *Way of*, as well as *Lord Tony's Wife*, *Sir Percy Hits Back* and *Sir Percy Leads the Band*. Finally came *Mam'zelle Guillotine* in 1940.

The Scarlet Pimpernel in 1934 stared **Leslie Howard**, generally recognised as *the* Pimpernel. **Merle Oberon** was Marguerite. Later versions had **Barry K Barnes** in the role (*The Return of the Scarlet Pimpernel*, 1937) and **David Niven** (*The Elusive Pimpernel*, 1950), when **Margaret Leighton** played his wife. Leslie Howard returned to play an updated version set in the Second World War (*Pimpernel Smith*, 1941).

In 1954 **Marius Goring** (who had played Sir Percy on radio) starred in a BBC TV serial version, and in 1983 **Anthony Andrews** played him in a TV movie, with **Jane Seymour** as his wife. More recently (1999 and 2000), **Richard E. Grant** strode through six feature-length episodes accompanied by **Elizabeth McGovern** as Marguerite and **Martin Shaw** as Chauvelin.

Richard E Grant.

JACK SCOTT
by John Paxton Sheriff

Amateur PI in the unlikely guise of a toy soldier maker from Liverpool, now living in Snowdonia. Sheriff is a prolific author of Westerns, under several pen-names.

Jack Scott novels: *A Confusion of Murders* came out 2005, followed by *A Bewilderment of Crooks* (2006), *The Clutches of Death* (2006), *Deathly Suspense* (2007), and *An Evil Reflection* (2008).

MISS SEETON
by Heron Carvic, then Hampton Charles, then Hamilton Crane
Dotty but amusing ultra-cosy, long-lived series of books written by at
least three different authors over time, about a little old lady amateur
detective who in print, at least, appears immortal. (Perhaps she wasn't
as old as she seemed, because she still taught art. But rumour has it she
has finally retired.) The books remained set in the Golden Age, the
1930s, although in the later Hamilton Crane adventures they crept, with
a shudder of genteel distaste, into the Second World War. Miss Seeton
was always helped by her Scotland Yard friend **Chief Superintendent
Delphick** (aptly named), though when war finally struck she became
attached to the Ministry of Information. Heron Carvic created Miss
Seeton, but after his death 'Hampton Charles' (actually James Melville:
see **Tetsuo Otani**) picked up the mantle, to be followed in turn,
although Melville was still very much alive, by Sarah J Mason (see
Trewley and Stone) as 'Hamilton Crane'.

Heron Carvic titles ran from 1968 (*Picture Miss Seeton*) to 1976
(*Odds on Miss Seeton*). Hampton Charles wrote (or published) three in
1990. Hamilton Crane began with *Miss Seeton Cracks the Case* in 1991
and continued through the decade at the rate of about two a year.

SIMON SERRAILLER
by Susan Hill
From a mainstream novelist who began her crime series late in her
career, comes DCI Serrailler, part of the North Riding Police, who after
leading a serial killer hunt is considered an expert by his peers. A
sensitive man, he lives alone, and his more interesting sister Cat, a
doctor working with the deprived, has a shaky marriage. These rather
depressing stories tell *about* crime rather than guve us mysteries to be
unravelled.

The Various Haunts of Men (2003) was followed by *The Pure in
Heart* and *The Risk of Darkness* before *The Vows of Silence* in 2008.

SIR ROGER SHALLOT
by Michael Clynes (= Paul Doherty)
From the pen of this prolific author comes a lovable
rogue and, when the mood takes him, amateur
investigator, Shallot, private agent to Cardinal Wolsey
in the time of **Henry VIII**. In this series Shallot looks
back over the murders and mysteries he has
investigated. His first foray is an amusing locked room
mystery. That book, *The White Rose Murders* (1991)
started a short series running to *The Relic Murders*
(1995).

MATTHEW SHARDLAKE
by C. J. Sansom
To be a lawyer in **Tudor England** can be dangerous

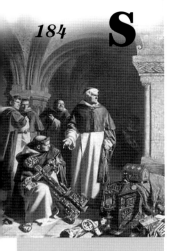

and Shardlake's position is not made safer by the predilection of those in power to use him to achieve their often warped idea of 'justice'. With paymasters like Henry VIII and Thomas Cromwell, Shardlake has more to worry about than whether he'll be paid: disappointing those two is not an option. He is first engaged during the dissolution of the monasteries to discover why Cromwell's Commissioner was found decapitated. It is but the first of Shardlake's reluctant involvements in the dramas of troubled times. The second book has a series of brutal murders and in the third book he becomes embroiled in an uprising against Henry by his angry northern subjects. The Shardlake stories are superior historical fare.

Dissolution (2003), *Dark Fire* (2004), which won the Ellis Peters prize *Sovereign* (2006) and *Revelation* (2007).

NICK SHARMAN
by Mark Timlin

Few British authors can transplant the American-style private investigator to our less gun-strewn country, so it's interesting to see how Timlin does it. Largely, it seems, by ignoring the supposed restrictions on gun ownership and our equally imagined reluctance to use shooters.

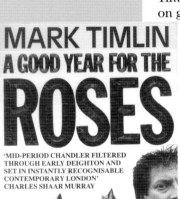

When Timlin started writing the exciting Sharman stories back in 1988 the distance between real life and his London might have seemed enormous but today, especially since the government banned guns for everyone except cops and criminals, his violent world seems everyday. Nick Sharman was a right-minded but renegade cop invalided out of the service moments before he would be busted on drugs charges. In *A Good Year for the Roses* he set himself up as a south London private eye, using the work in part to give himself something to think about other than his tangled love life. Assuming he'd be into little more than debt collection he picked and stumbled his way through the mayhem (missing girl, drugs, corrupt cops) much as, to be honest, the author picked his way through this first book. It's a curious thing about the series that after an uncertain start (the first book needed cutting) the stories got better and better and the style more honed and sharp. Sharman's private life added enormously to the astringent flavour; where other writers throw in some troubled background, Timlin created a painfully believable broken family (present and past women, his adolescent daughter) and allowed his tough-guy hero – and his women – to suffer the scars and bruises of a violent life.

> *The doctor didn't take long to examine the body. A blind man with a good sense of smell could have told him the girl was dead. He mumbled softly to the detectives as he peeled off his rubber gloves. He left as slowly as he had come. Only when I heard the front door slam behind him did it occur to me that I should have had him look at the wound on my head.*
>
> From *A Good Year for the Roses*.

A Good Year for the Roses sets the scene. In 1990, 1991, 1992 and 1993 there were two books each year, yet despite their frequency the books soon settled into a strong and compulsive rhythm, *Falls the Shadow* (1993) being particularly powerful. Among those that followed, *Pretend We're Dead* (1994) and *Paint it Black* (1995) can be recommended. Sharman last appeared in *All the Empty Places* (2000).

In 1995 five Sharman stories, beginning with his 1991 title *The Turnaround*, were adapted to make a short but impressive TV series starring the then almost unknown **Clive Owen**.

ROGER SHERINGHAM
by Anthony Berkeley

One of the great detectives of the Golden Age, though little read today, Roger Sheringham was a journo-novelist turned amateur detective. His adventures began in 1925 with *The Layton Court Mystery* (originally published anonymously), and in his introduction to the book the author described Sheringham as a gentleman and no wizard sleuth: 'I have never believed very much in those hawk-eyed, tight-lipped gentry who pursue their silent and inexorable way straight to the heart of things without ever once overbalancing or turning aside after false goals.' Sheringham is fallible, at times bumbling – a trait he was to lose over the years as he moved from his initial 'well bred amateur' persona to one more credible for harsher times. The Sheringham of the first books is a loud, self-centred, quite arrogant man, and his evident intelligence is not always wisely applied. He drinks beer and smokes a large pipe. Despite these seemingly fatal flaws, the mystery was good and the book succeeded, encouraging a second book the following year. This, *The Wychford Poisoning Case* (1926), showed clear signs that the author was not content to write routine whodunits. The ingenious novel revisited the real-life Victorian *cause célèbre* of **Florence Maybrick** and, rather than have Sheringham simply solve the crime, Berkeley proposed several alternative solutions. The third book, *The Vane Mystery* (1927), was a psychological crime mystery, the fourth straightforward, but the fifth novel, *The Poisoned Chocolates Case* (1929), saw Berkeley gently lampoon his own Detection Club. (In this famous story, rather than have the case solved by a master detective, Berkeley served a collation of cases swarmed over by six investigators, among whom Roger Sheringham came up with the wrong answer.) The following year's *The Second Shot* was equally bizarre: Sheringham identified the culprit but shielded her from prosecution, and only at the end of the book did we learn that she didn't do it. (Sheringham was quite likely to play about with the evidence and to act unprofessionally. But then, he wasn't a professional.) The Sheringham stories were memorable more for their originality than for their characterisation, and Berkeley never seemed to make up his mind whether his hero was a hero or a clown.

The Layton Court Mystery (1925), *The Wychford Poisoning Case* (1926), *The Vane Mystery* (1927), *The Silk Stocking Murders* (1928), *The Poisoned Chocolates Case* (1929), *The Second Shot* (1930), *Top Storey Murder* (1931), *Murder in the Basement* (1932), *Jumping Jenny*

(1933) and *Panic Party* (1934). There were also half a dozen separate short stories.

EDDIE SHOESTRING

created by Robert Banks Stewart

Radio hack cum amateur private eye who spices up his radio programme by solving listeners' mysteries. Long-haired, mournful and shambolic (and recovering from a nervous breakdown) he somehow stumbles his way through to solving the fairly ordinary crimes given him. He works for 'Radio West' in **Bristol**, so the crimes he tackles take place there and in the west country. **Trevor Eve** played Shoestring but would only do so for two series (1979 to 80). 'Radio West', though fictional in the series, became the name of the local independent radio station later in real life. Robert Banks Stewart also devised **Bergerac**.

JEMIMA SHORE

by Antonia Fraser

Despite her upbringing – she was educated at a convent – Jemima Shore became a savvy TV journalist with her own TV programme: 'Jemima Shore – Investigator'. No surprise, then, that her old school called her in to help investigate a suspicious death at the convent – even if, during her investigation, she herself had to be rescued (by a nun with a gun!). On her second case (the second book) she forgot all the convent had taught her and went to bed with one of the suspects. Bad practice: is she a convent girl or a modern miss? A brief pause for due reflection followed, but three years later Jemima was back, taking orders for the first of five books to span the decade. Then came another pause, for four years this time, broken with *Political Death* in 1994, when she retired again.

Quiet as a Nun (1977), *The Wild Island* (1978), *A Splash of Red* (1981), *Cool Repentance* (1982), *Oxford Blood* (1985), *Your Royal Heritage* (1987), *The Cavalier Case* (1990), *Political Death* (1994).

Quiet As A Nun was an *Armchair Thriller* TV production in 1978, with Jemima played by **Maria Aitken**, and in 1983 ITV ran a short series called *Jemima Shore Investigates* in which **Patricia Hodge** played the leading role.

SYLVIA SILENCE

by 'Katherine Greenhalgh'

This 15-year-old detective emerged from the pages of *Schoolgirls' Weekly*, where with a typical lack of imagination she was called **The Girl Sherlock Holmes**. To be fair, her father is a detective and he does wear a dressing gown and play the violin. (He doesn't take cocaine.) Dad is relegated to the background for most of Sylvia's exploits in which the beautiful, plucky, slender, winsome and very English heroine leaps at adventure and seizes it with both hands. She can claim to have been **the first schoolgirl sleuth**. ('Katherine Greenhalgh' was a pseudonym of John W. Bobin, who also created **Lila Lisle** and **Valerie Drew**.) She

appeared in *Schoolgirls' Weekly* magazine from its very first issue, October 1922 till around 1933.

MISS SILVER

by Patricia Wentworth

Second only to **Miss Marple** in crime detection's hall of fame comes Miss Silver. Like Miss Marple, Miss Silver dresses to deceive. Her clothes are out of date, she carries a brightly coloured chintz knitting bag – and she appears this way deliberately, knowing that, as she puts it, 'To be considered negligible may be the means of acquiring the kind of information which only becomes available when people are off their guard.' Maud Silver gossips, she parades her knitting patterns; she would put anyone off their guard.

But she is a professional detective, not one of those little old ladies who just happen to be in the right place at the right time. To be called a 'Detective' she might find repugnant: on her business cards it says merely: Private Enquiries. Earlier in life she had been a teacher but just as she began to reconcile herself to a quiet future in retirement a stroke of luck brought her sufficient means to allow her to establish herself in her new profession. It was a curious profession for her to choose, since at heart she is a gentlewoman. Miss Silver may be one of the last survivors of the breed but when on duty she is nosy, surreptitious, a dangerous guest. She is also – a touch of realism – unable to close a case: she is a private enquiry agent; she cannot arrest. To do so she must invoke the aid of the real police, usually in the shape of **Chief Inspector Lamb** and **Inspector Abbott** from Scotland Yard. These two men respect her, and they have cause to. From time to time they call on her services to help them solve a crime. (This perhaps is less realistic – but how else can she become involved in so many crimes? It's only fiction.)

Though her investigations are meticulously undertaken Miss Silver does rely on a whiff of intuition, coupled with her keen sense of other people's character. This acuity helps her recognise when they are *out* of character. She is more intuitive, less deductive, than Jane Marple. Her stories are less puzzling; they veer at times toward romance – not that she herself is ever involved in romance, but in many of the stories a young couple can be glimpsed acting out their courtship beneath Miss Silver's benevolent gaze. Sitting primly in a quiet corner with her knitting in her lap she quietly watches how people behave and listens to what they say. Sometimes the fact that she doesn't have to join in the conversation helps her concentrate; she sees what others don't see, she hears what they don't hear. For she is easy to ignore. Small, trim and practically nondescript – old, of course: who pays attention to old ladies? – she seldom wears makeup and what conversation she has is likely to be liberally sprinkled with quotations from the Bible or from Tennyson. Oh, she is easy to ignore. When she wants to be.

Grey Mask, her first book, in 1928, had a potentially lurid plot involving a criminal who wore an India-rubber mask to hide his features from his gang. It appeared to be a stand-alone title, since nothing

followed until *The Case is Closed* in 1937. *Lonesome Road* came two years later and *Danger Point* in 1942, but from that point on the books appeared at the approximate rate of one a year, ending with *Miss Silver Detects* and *The Girl in the Cellar* in 1961.

TIM SIMPSON
by John Malcolm

To call Tim Simpson an **antiques expert** is an understatement, and to confuse him with **Lovejoy** a bad mistake, for he is far more knowledgeable and utterly law-abiding. A specialist in the intricacies of art investment, Simpson is engaged by banks and wealthy collectors on an absorbing series of cases concerning stolen artworks, fakes and murder. The stories are clever and at the same time educational, since the author is similarly expert: he founded the Antique Collectors' Club.

Simpson first appeared in *A Back Room in Somers Town* in 1984 along with, that same year, *The Godwin Sideboard*. *The Gwen John Sculpture* (1985) was followed by the excellently titled *Whistler in the Dark* (1986) and eight more into the mid-1990s. *Simpson's Homer* came in 2001, followed by *Circles and Squares* (2003), *Mortal Instruments* (2004) and *Rogues' Gallery* (2005).

THE SINGING DETECTIVE
by Dennis Potter

Dennis Potter.

A bizarre but successful experimental drama from one of Britain's foremost TV playwrights in which a hospitalised crime writer (Philip E Marlow, played by **Michael Gambon**) lies in his hospital bed drifting between hallucination, memory and reality, all the while suffering from a severe form of psoriasis – a condition he shared with Dennis Potter, as most of the audience knew. Marlow's own fiction is an assemblage of pulp fiction stereotypes which rely heavily on Raymond Chandler and Chandler's Philip Marlowe (note Potter's deliberately misplaced E), who come before us on screen as characters in – we are never sure which – either the latest book Marlow is working on, his feverish fantasy, or something actually happening in real life. The same characters appear (with different names) in a parallel set of memories from Marlow's childhood, memories which, again as most of the audience were aware, drew heavily on Dennis Potter's own childhood memories and his previous TV dramas. The six episodes were beautifully filmed, intriguing, and laced with sex and 1930s and 1940s music. Probably no one but Potter could have drawn a mainstream audience to stay with such a convoluted experiment. But he pulled it off.

BBC screened the drama over six weekly episodes, first in 1986 and then as a tribute soon after Potter's death in 1994. **Michael Gambon** played Philip E Marlow, while **Patrick Malahide** played his wife's lover (and his mother's, years before). **Jim Carter** was Marlow's father, rooted in the Forest of Dean. **Alison Steadman** was Marlow's mother (and an imagined good-time girl years later), **Janet Suzman** played his wife, and **Joanne Whalley** raised several million male temperatures as

a sexy nurse. The 2003 Hollywood film, starring **Robert Downey Jr**, couldn't match the TV original.

JOE SIXSMITH
by Reginald Hill

Bald and black and London-based, Joe is a good-hearted decent man who by some strange quirk has turned private eye. Though something of an occasional series from the author more famous for his **Dalziel & Pascoe** novels, these are entertaining books, and the first in the series, *Blood Sympathy*, is especially amusing.

Blood Sympathy (1993), *Born Guilty* (1995), *Killing the Lawyers* (1997), *Singing the Sadness* (1999)

BOB SKINNER
by Quintin Jardine

Another fictional **Edinburgh** cop, this one being senior to the more famous **Rebus** and, by the strange rules of fiction, unaware of him. Skinner starts out in the series as Assistant Chief Constable and achieves success enough to later become Deputy Chief Constable. None of this prevents him from getting his hands well and truly dirty in the many violent and nasty crimes covered in the books. These are gritty and realistic urban stories.

The first books all had *Skinner* in their title. There were his *Rules* (1993), his *Trail* and *Festival* (1994), then his *Round, Ordeal, Mission* and *Ghosts* (1998). *Murmuring the Judges* was the slightly odd title chosen to break the pattern in 1998, and the series continued with titles such as *Autographs in the Rain* (2001) and *Head Shot* (2002).

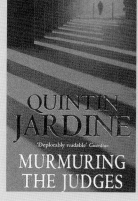

BILL SLIDER
by Cynthia Harrod-Eagles

Police Detective first met in *Orchestrated Death* (1991) investigating a naked female corpse, a Stradivarius and an over-size can of olive oil. You sense the flavour? In the first books Slider seems to be a middle-aged cop going nowhere, annoyed by red tape and government guidelines, and by the third book, *Nerochip*, he is further burdened with a boss he cannot stand. *Blood Lines* sees him looking for a serial killer within the BBC. Harrod-Eagles's wry humour permeates and the books impress with sharp pace, expert plotting and clever resolutions.

A good introduction to this well-established series is *The Bill Slider Omnibus* (1998).

C D SLOAN
by Catherine Aird

The early middle-aged Detective Inspector C. D. Sloan (known as 'Seedy' to his colleagues) works alongside the younger – and one fears, never to grow older and wiser – Detective Constable **W. E. Crosby** (the 'Defective Constable') in an extensive series of contemporary books beginning with *The Religious Body* (1966). The two detectives are an old-fashioned pair, and their stories are

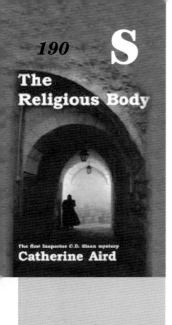

The Religious Body

The first Inspector C.D. Sloan mystery

Catherine Aird

less police procedurals than wry English village mysteries with a modern twist. Far from mere 'cosies' these tales are ironic and at times wildly funny, with extraordinarily ingenious plots. One such is a welcome return to the locked room mystery (*His Burial Too*), while another leaps up to date with DNA. In *The Religious Body* a nun is murdered (how many villages have their own convent?), but in Aird's seemingly peaceful villages we may stumble across a mysterious hologram, a maze, or a series of unethical medical drug trials. Village people – of the old-fashioned sort – abound, as do strange goings-on around the golf course, the local planning authority, and so forth. Bodies turn up in a locked church, on an archaeological site, or beside the road, and each time the brighter-than-he-looks Inspector Sloan solves the crime.

Recommended titles include *The Religious Body* (1966), *Henrietta Who?* (1968), *The Complete Steel* (1969), *His Burial Too* (1973), *A Late Phoenix* (1971), *Harm's Way* (1984), *Stiff News* (1998), *Little Knell* (2000), *Losing Ground* (2007). *Henrietta Who?* was made into a film, but why in the Netherlands?

> *"If you can't be a good example, then you'll just have to be a horrible warning."*
>
> Inspector Sloan, in *His Burial Too.*

Rebecca Tope.

DREW SLOCOMBE
by Rebecca Tope

If one is looking for an amateur detective with a credible reason for becoming involved in more than one suspicious death, what better profession than an undertaker? Slocombe is one such (as was the author in a previous existence when she was an assistant undertaker for seven years). As with Tope's **Den Cooper** series, the stories also have a farming interest.

Dark Undertakings (1999), *Grave Concerns* (2000), *The Sting of Death* (2002), *A Market for Murder* (2003).

THE SOOPER
by Edgar Wallace

To get into my compendium on the strength of one full-length novel is an achievement, but the Sooper, **Superintendent Minter**, is an extraordinary policeman. Awkward and ungainly, he assumes a mantle of unconvincing unintelligence wrapped up in slovenly speech and lugubriousness, but he is, of course, feared and respected throughout both the Yard and the criminal fraternity. His one novel-length appearance, in *Big Foot*, has him threshing his way through a field of bizarre occurrences and misleading clues as he investigates the case of a solicitor, his housekeeper and an attractive young woman all threatened (at first by letter, then with death) by a mysterious killer who signs his missives 'Big Foot' and leaves correspondingly big shoeprints wherever he goes. The plot is mad, the action frantic, the jokes and impossible twists frequent, and as you approach the end of the tale you

Death lurks in the dark where his footprints are found

BIG FOOT
EDGAR WALLACE

realise it will be impossible for Wallace to tie it up. But he does. Even if you guess the guilty person you'd never expect Wallace to sort out all the tangles. He does that too. The Sooper himself is great company and it was a shame that he appeared in only this one novel – plus fortunately a few short stories.

Big Foot appeared in 1927 but paperback reprints went on for years. Short stories can be found in *The Sooper and Others* (as late as 1984) and *The Lone House Mystery* (1927) in which the title story is the longest and the worst – of an otherwise great bunch.

VERA STANHOPE
by Ann Cleeves

Interesting and believable variant on the modern police detective: Inspector Stanhope is a plain, overweight, single and lonely professional cop making her considerable presence felt in the north of England. Fictional women police officers usually have to put up with condescending sexism from their colleagues but Vera is too tough and forthright for that. Not that many in her **Northumberland** patch would try: she has a deserved reputation for fierce efficiency. At home, though, we see a different Vera: lonely, wishing there was a man in her life but knowing there won't be, and consoling herself too often with junk food and beer. Perversely, this helps her empathise with the ordinary people she meets on her cases – even if the crimes, as in most crime fiction, are far from ordinary.

First in the series was *The Crow Trap* (1999) in which three women friends meet in a lonely North Pennines cottage to undertake an environmental survey. But one appears to commit suicide. *Telling Tales* (2005) has Vera investigate the ten-year-old murder of a 15-year-old girl. The supposed killer had been in jail for years but kills herself rather than face the people who so easily accepted that she was a killer. *Hidden Depths* (2007) is about the linked ritual murders of a young man and young woman who appear never to have met. In each book the surrounding countryside is as much a presence as is Vera.

HAGAR STANLEY
by Fergus Hume

A contender for **the earliest female *amateur* detective**, Hagar is a 'Gypsy Detective', beautiful in a dark Romany way, sensuous and intelligent, who runs a Lambeth pawnshop she inherited from her uncle where she solves crimes brought to her by her customers. She solves her crimes more by common sense than by detection, but it's a great way to build customer loyalty. (Hume also wrote the

massively successful *The Mystery of a Hansom Cab*, 1886.)
Hagar of the Pawn-Shop: The Gypsy Detective (1898).

NIGEL STRANGEWAYS
by Nicholas Blake

'The outstanding British private detective of the 1930s' says the late critic T. J. Binyon, pointing out that Strangeways is named after the famous Manchester prison. Not that Strangeways resembles any of that house's inhabitants. No old lag he. Nigel is tall, slim and well-educated (though he was 'sent down' from Oxford for answering his examination paper in limerick form, a rather harmless if not meritorious prank, one would have thought, though educational expectations have changed since the 1930s). He is a believable character nevertheless, gifted, intelligent, almost as fond of cups of tea as is Wedgwood Benn, with an inability to sleep unless covered by a comforting weight of blankets. (He bummed around the world after being sent down.)

Nicholas Blake is, of course, the pseudonym of the Poet Laureate C. Day-Lewis and his newspaper-man detective was based on fellow poet W. H. Auden (who admitted being addicted to detective fiction). Although the Strangeways books have a literary tone they are less burdened with unlikely and tedious quotes than are some from less literary authors. Blake/Lewis brings an unmistakably left-wing point of view to the books (unusual for the Golden Age) and was perhaps the only Golden Age writer to dare make a national hero turn out to be the murderer, as he does in his second book *Thou Shell of Death* (1936). Nowadays it is almost *de rigueur* for crime writers to be left wing (I know some exceptions but am pledged to keep their secret) and by some standards the amount of politics in Blake's books is hardly noticeable. His left-wing slant shows more in contrast to pro-authority competitors at the time.

But when was Blake's time? It is easy to think of him as 'Golden Age' – i.e. from the 1930s – but the Strangeways books span four decades, from 1935 to 1966. The idea of a gentleman detective, non-professional, is Golden Age, as is his habit (under reasonable control) of dropping quotes – and indeed the Strangeways type of book, the puzzle mystery, is Golden Age too. But had the books been stuck there, locked in the amber paperweight of the 1930s, they would not have remained popular for so long – certainly not into the know-everything 1960s. The emphasis in his books changed as public taste moved from puzzle to psychology. The books could not be called psychological crime stories but they did display a real interest in who people were and what made them behave as they did. Blake's villains were never cardboard villains, any more than his hero was a cardboard man.

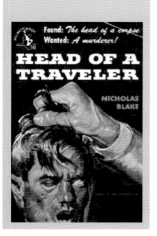

Earlier titles are generally best. The first four are *A Question of Proof* (1935), *Thou Shell of Death* (1936), *There's Trouble Brewing* (1937) and the excellent *The Beast Must Die* (1938). His post-war *Minute for Murder* (1947) is fine, as is his penultimate title *The Worm of Death* (1960). By then, Blake's interest was on other works and it was six years before the final Strangeways book, *The Morning After Death* (1966).

Two years later he would write the superb non-Strangeways *The Private Wound* (1968).

BERNARD SUTTON
by Max Pemberton
Narrator of a number of short stories in the series *Jewel Mysteries I Have Known* published in the handsome *English Illustrated Magazine* of the 1890s. He is a detective who specialises in solving jewel robberies, and the setting for the stories is accordingly high society.

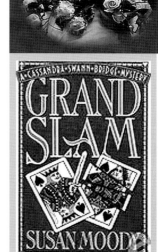

CASSIE SWANN
by Susan Moody
Mild-mannered, overweight bridge expert – she both teaches and plays the game – who brings her vulnerability to the fore in a series of pleasant puzzle mysteries, carefully arranged to suit what ought to be a large audience: those intelligent but sedentary types who play bridge and enjoy mysteries. Far from being a mere player, untouched by reality, Cassie had to investigate the mysterious death of her father and has herself been the victim of a hit-and-run 'accident'.

The appeal to bridge lovers was clear from the titles: *Takeout Double* (1993), *Grand Slam* (1994), *King of Hearts* (1995), *Doubled in Spades* (1996), *Sacrifice Bid* (1997) and *Dummy Hand* (1998).

PROFESSOR HILARY TAMAR
by Sarah Caudwell
He or she? Caudwell never made Tamar's gender clear. An **Oxford don**, lecturing on legal history, called upon from time to time to help a team of barristers from Lincoln's Inn, Tamar is a particular taste – revered by some crime fans, unappealing to others. Caudwell's style strikes some as impossibly arch, while others see it as witty and sophisticated, and it is your own take on this that will decide whether you love or loathe these stories. (Most crime writers fall into the 'love them' brigade.) Either way, it is hard to deny that the stories are well-crafted and ingeniously plotted. A significant supporting player is the Lincoln's Inn team's beautiful but fluffily incompetent tax lawyer **Julia Larwood**. Tamar likes her, but then...

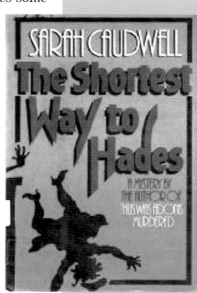

Thus Was Adonis Murdered (1981), *The Shortest Way to Hades* (1985), *The Sirens Sang of Murder* (1989), *The Sybil in her Grave* (2000). There was only one short story: *An Acquaintance with Mr Collins* (1990).

SUSAN TAYLOR TV series *Touching Evil* (1997)
(creator: Paul Abbott)
Ambitious cop in the Organised and Serial Crime Unit, working alongside DI Dave Creegan (**Robson Green**) on a series of cases with plenty of pace and action. Actress **Nicola Walker** brings welcome femininity to an all-male team,

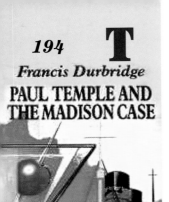

Francis Durbridge.

John Bentley.

though she's as ready to get stuck in as they are.

SIMON TEMPLAR
See **The Saint**

PAUL TEMPLE
by Francis Durbridge

So popular was the **radio series** that many fans were barely aware the books existed. The radio series ran from the 1930s to the 1960s and its *Flying Scotsman* theme tune was one of the most familiar of all time, and the sound of the clickety-clack opening bar was enough to have thousands of listeners humming along in anticipation. Paul Temple and his wife **Steve** live in Mayfair but own a country home in the vale of Evesham (that's Worcestershire, for London readers) between which residences they dash up and down in splendid cars. The Temples themselves are graciously middle class, effortlessly elegant and spend their lives in constant equanimity. Not content with solving crimes and living off an unearned income they each have well-paid jobs: Paul is a best-selling novelist and Steve a successful journalist. (Apparently, it takes Paul only three months to write a best-seller, leaving him the rest of the year to indulge in sleuthing. Ah, me.) Paul investigates for 'research' and Steve comes hoping for a scoop. When not on the trail with her dashing husband she shops in fashion houses or waits in the lounge with a restorative cocktail poised. Naturally, they have a manservant (Pryce) to look after the housekeeping. But none of this should conceal the fact that many of the stories are cleverly thought out and deftly written. The books were better than they might sound and the radio couple were loved throughout the land. During its incredibly long run on radio Temple was played by no less than six different actors, **Hugh Morton** being the first. **Peter Coke** played him from 1954 to 1968. **Marjorie Westbury** remained Steve throughout. (Though she sounded tall and elegant she was only 4 feet 10 inches in real life. The joy of radio.)

Send For Paul Temple appeared in 1938 and the first novelisation of one of their radio stories, *Paul Temple and the Front Page Men*, came in 1939. *News of Paul Temple* and *Paul Temple Intervenes* were followed by the lazily titled *Send for Paul Temple Again*. *Paul Temple and the Kelby Affair* and *Paul Temple and the Harkdale Robbery* were both as late as 1970, then hard on their heels came *The Geneva Mystery* (1971) and *The Curzon Case* (1972). Durbridge and Douglas Rutherford collaborated to produce two earlier novels supposedly written 'by' Paul Temple: *The Tyler Mystery* (1957) and *East of Algiers* (1959).

Paul Temple was a successful BBC series from 1969 to 1971 (one of their earliest colour productions) in which the perfectly mannered and perfectly cast **Francis Matthews** played Paul, and the beautifully dressed **Ros Drinkwater** was Steve.

John Bentley starred in three Temple films: *Calling Paul Temple* (1948), *Paul Temple's Triumph* (1950), and *Paul Temple Returns*

(1952). Where these three are concerned, *Paul Temple Vanishes* would be a more appropriate title.

CONSTABLE THACKERAY
See **Sergeant Cribb**

MICHAEL THACKERAY
by Patricia Hall
DCI Michael Thackeray is a countryman who finds his high-flying police career stalled in the grimy manufacturing town of Bradfield in **West Yorkshire**. Added to his troubles is a family tragedy for which he blames himself. Time passes. Later, as a cop, perhaps he should know better than to get involved with a headstrong girlfriend, **Laura Ackroyd**, a reporter on the local paper. The series deals with contemporary issues – prostitution, people smuggling, drugs – in the context of a run-down town desperate for regeneration.

Death by Election (1993) started the series and *Death in a Far Country* (a tangled tale of cup fever, bungs and exploited women at the local football club) came out in 2007. *Deep Freeze* (2001) is recommended.

THANE & MOSS
by Bill Knox
DCI Colin Thane and Inspector Phil Moss appear in a long series of two dozen full-length crime novels set in and around **Glasgow** where the officers work. Thane is the thinker of the pair, while Moss relies more on hard work and research. The books too are well-researched: their author was a lifetime crime reporter for both newspapers and TV. Plots vary from high-tech crime to the brutal murder of a modern-day white witch.

Deadline for a Dream began the series in 1957, which continued till *The Lazarus Widow*, completed by Martin Edwards after the author's death in 1999. Other titles include *Little Drops of Blood* (1962), *Live Bait* (1978), *Death Bytes* (1998), *To Kill A Witch* (1971, reissued 2006).

LUKE THANET
by Dorothy Simpson
Detective Inspector Thanet and his colleague Sergeant **Mike Lineham** operate in and around the fictional Sturrenden in **Kent** in an extensive set of novels set in the 1980s and 1990s (some locations are real, some imaginary). Though their adventures at first seem traditional and cosy, when the pair investigate they uncover murky sub-fauna beneath the stones. From unhappy marriages through missing persons to murder itself the stories sit snugly between

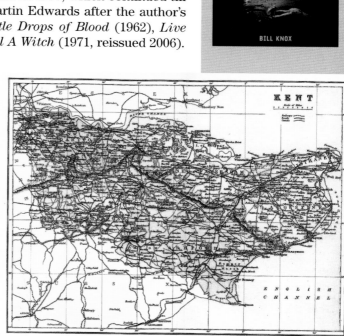

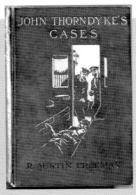

the genres of police procedural and psychological, and when the guilty are unmasked they are believable and human. In the series of some fifteen books, each novel is a separate story. They are whodunits which are whydunits as well.

The Night She Died (1981) began the series, which continued at the rate of one a year through the Eighties, including *Close Her Eyes* (1984) and *Dead on Arrival* (1986), and with *Last Seen Alive* winning the Silver Dagger in 1985. *Doomed to Die* kicked off six books in the Nineties including *Wake the Dead* (1991) and *A Day For Dying* (1991) leading finally to *Dead and Gone* in 1999. The books have also been issued in five omnibus volumes.

DR THORNDYKE
by R. Austin Freeman

Thorndyke has the best claim to be **the first scientific detective**. Fictional detectives claimed to use science before him (Holmes is one of several to wave test-tubes in the air and make impressive-sounding pronouncements that would fool no scientist) but Freeman himself was a keen amateur scientist, and in his novels and short stories he explains the experiments and scientific tests Thorndyke uses to solve mysteries. The credibility this adds to the stories allows Freeman to have Thorndyke appear equally credible when he cracks 'impossible' ciphers or reconstructs documents thought destroyed. Nicknamed '**The Great Fathomer**', Thorndyke is a lecturer in medical jurisprudence at London's St Margaret's Hospital and also works as an investigator for an assurance company. He resides in chambers at 5A King's Bench Walk in the Inner Temple, and his 'Watson' is another doctor, **Christopher Jervis**, who works self-effacingly as his secretary and laboratory assistant.

In a number of the Thorndyke stories there is, for the reader, no mystery to be solved: we have seen the crime committed and we know who did it. What we don't know, and what the story will be about, is how the perpetrator will be brought to book. This is the '**inverted**' crime story, a style Freeman is usually credited with having invented (specifically, in the stories of *The Singing Bone*). If that seems too generous, it is certainly true that Freeman extended and established the form. He described it thus: 'The usual conditions are reversed; the reader knows everything, the detective knows nothing.' Actually, there is often one vital fact the reader does *not* know, which Doctor Thorndyke discovers and uses to solve the crime.

Innovative as the Thorndyke stories are, it cannot be denied that he himself is rather dull, with no endearing idiosyncrasies and little wit. But the use of forensic science makes up for any lack of human interest. Since Freeman himself was a scientist, the tests and experiments in his stories are genuine and in many cases are fully explained to the reader. The stories are best read in their original form in *Pearson's Magazine* where they were often illustrated with laboratory photographs. Thorndyke's use of science is better than that of any other detective of

On the negative could be seen the grotesque transparency of a colossal thumb-print.

his day; his superiority to Holmes in this respect is such that he wouldn't have engaged the great detective even as assistant to his man Jervis – yet, decent as the Thorndyke stores are (and they *are* decent, above the general standard of their day) the Great Fathomer can't hold a candle to Sherlock Holmes. But who can?

Thorndyke appears first in *The Red Thumb Mark* (1907), and continues in *John Thorndyke's Cases* (short stories, 1909), *the Eye of Osiris* (1911), *The Mystery of 31 New Inn* (1912), *The Singing Bone* (short stories, 1912), *A Silent Witness* (1914), *Helen Vardon's Confession* (1922), *The Cat's Eye* (1923), *Dr Thorndyke's Casebook* (short stories, 1923), *Mystery of Angelina Froud* (1924), *The Shadow of the Wolf* (1925), *The Puzzle Lock* (short stories, 1925), *The D'Arblay Mystery* (1926), *The Magic Casket* (1927), *A Certain Dr Thorndyke* (1927), *As a Thief in the Night* (1928), *Mr Pottermack's Oversight* (1930), *Pontifex, Son and Thorndyke* (1931), *When Rogues Fall Out* (1932), *Dr Thorndyke Intervenes* (1933), *For the Defence: Dr Thorndyke* (1934), *The Penrose Mystery* (1936), *Felo De Se?* (1937), *The Stoneware Monkey* (1938), *Mr Polton Explains* (1940) and finally *The Jacob Street Mystery* in 1942.

THE MAGIC CASKET
R.AUSTIN FREEMAN

www.ClassicCrimeFiction.com

H&S

TOM THORNE
by Mark Billingham

Thorne is a Detective Inspector with the Metropolitan Police and has more than his fair share of grisly cases including serial killers, psychotics and the seriously weird. Despite which – and redeemingly for what might otherwise have been a grim series – Thorne holds on to his humanity. Despite all Fate can throw at him he remains tenaciously fond of country music and Tottenham Hotspur: two sad cases, as he himself admits, which bring only heartache and put him on the receiving end of mockery. Good as he is at solving cases he is less able to understand himself: to know when he isn't wanted or (rather more sadly) when he is, and this failing mars his relationships at home and at work. As the series develops we see an essentially good man pushed further and further into himself, but Billingham's easy style makes the journey more than bearable. Colleagues **Dave Holland** (a Detective Sergeant) and pathologist **Phil Hendricks** join Thorne on his dark and tense investigations.

The first book *Sleepyhead* (2001) was a best-seller and the second, *Scaredy Cat* (2002) won the Sherlock Award and was nominated for the CWA Gold Dagger. These were followed by *Lazybones* (2003), *The Burning Girl* (2004), *Lifeless* (2005), *Buried*

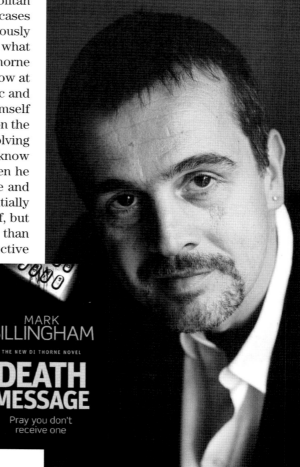

MARK
BILLINGHAM

THE NEW DI THORNE NOVEL

DEATH
MESSAGE

Pray you don't
receive one

(2006) and *Death Message* (2007).

Television adaptations are on the way.

INSPECTOR THORNHILL
by Andrew Taylor

The **Lydmouth series** is set in and around a fictional town on the Anglo-Welsh borders in the years after the Second World War. Detective Inspector Thornhill and the journalist **Jill Francis**, linked in an uneasily adulterous relationship, are the central characters in this well-regarded series. Each book is an independent crime novel, but taken as a whole the series sets out to build a picture of provincial life and provincial mores in a forgotten decade of British history.

An Air That Kills (1994), *The Mortal Sickness* (1995), *The Lover of the Grave* (1997), *The Suffocating Night* (1998), *Where Roses Fade* (2000), *Death's Own Door* (2001), *Call The Dying* (2004), *Naked to the Hangman* (2006).

HENRY TIBBETT

by Patricia Moyes

Chief Inspector Tibbett clearly draws a good salary, since most of his adventures occur when he is holidaying abroad with his wife **Emma** – skiing in the Alps, sailing in the Caribbean, sojourning in America. His wife is as good a detective as he (no, she's better) and at times her knowledge is more relevant – as in *Johnny Under Ground* where her wartime work helps shed light on a more recent crime. (The title is a reference to a famous wartime poem, *Johnny Head in Air*.) Henry, in fact, is no great shakes as a detective; simply a nice man in the right place at the right time with a more than useful right-hand woman.

There are eighteen books in the series, starting with *Dead Men Don't Ski* (1959) and continuing to *Black Girl, White Girl* (1989). *Who Saw Her Die?* (1970) and *Falling Star* (1964) are particularly recommended.

THE TOFF

by John Creasey

Alias the Honourable Richard Rollison, the Toff was an adventurer detective in the mould of **The Saint** though, frankly, not as funny or inventive. Like Templar, he is cool, rich and debonair. He mixes with upper crust Mayfair friends or the lower orders down in Bow, and though he can use a gun or his trusty fists he prefers to use his wits. He has a liking for the kind of high living, beautiful women and ocean cruises his readers could only dream about in the 1940s.

Introducing the Toff (1938) led to many similar titles: *Here Comes the Toff*, *The Toff Proceeds*, *The Toff on Board*, etc. until *Call the Toff* in 1953, with one much later title, *Vote for the Toff* in 1971.

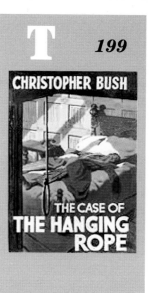

Unremarkable low-budget British films include *Salute the Toff* (1951) and *Hammer the Toff* (1952).

TOMMY & TUPPENCE
See **Beresford**

LUDOVIC TRAVERS
by Christopher Bush

Almost totally forgotten now, despite having appeared in some 80 stories, Travers is a writer and gentleman of leisure who, through his relationship with his uncle, a commissioner at Scotland Yard, is able to blag his way into an extraordinary number of criminal investigations. In these he is often assistant to or assisted by the long-suffering **Superintendent Wharton**. Eventually, after the Second World War, Travers finally founds his own detective agency.

The long line of books began with *The Plumley Inheritance* in 1926. Most titles began *The Case of the...*, including *The Case of the Green Felt Hat, the April Fools, the Hanging Rope, the Fourth Detective, the Silken Petticoat*, and the final *Case of the Prodigal Daughter* in 1969.

MARK TREASURE
by David Williams

A successful merchant banker who nevertheless finds time for amateur detective work, Mark Treasure is as sharp-minded as you'd expect, given his profession, but is also humane and likeable. His mysteries are not necessarily bank-related and are certainly not dull. In his first, for example, he investigates a murder which seems linked to the discovery of what might be a Shakespearian manuscript. Any suspicion that a **merchant banker detective** must be a short-lived concept was dispelled when the series ran to 17 full-length books.

Unholy Writ came first, in 1976, and the fourth book, *Murder for Treasure* (1980) was shortlisted for the CWA Gold Dagger. Most books have *Treasure* in their title, apart from the first and *Murder in Advent* (1985), *Prescription for Murder* (1990) and the final two: *Planning on Murder* (1992) and *Banking on Murder* (1993).

PHILIP TRENT
by E. C. Bentley

Many a Golden Age detective is given to joking but Trent was a joke personified. Conceived as a parody, his first adventure was *Trent's Last Case* (1913), a title which ought to have given the game away. An archetypal amateur, Trent was a dishevelled and handsome artist engaged for no logical reason by a newspaper editor to investigate the murder of a millionaire. Trent stumbled gaily through his mission, identifying the wrong culprit – twice – and falling in love with the chief suspect. Recognising his own incompetence he finally vowed never to touch a case again. Hence Trent's *last* case. Unfortunately, Bentley had made him far too funny (for his time; it's less easy to laugh at the man

E. C. Bentley.

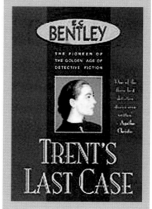

Michael Wilding.

Margaret Lockwood.

Orson Welles.

today) and sequels were demanded. It was typical of the professionally comic Bentley (he invented the clerihew) to begin a crime series with such an inappropriate title. He might also have enjoyed hearing **Martin Jarvis** play Trent on radio (in 1986).

If you enjoy *Trent's Last Case* (1913), continue with *Trent's Own Case* (1936) – the time-gap tells its own story – and *Trent Intervenes* (short stories, 1938); but if you find this humour excruciatingly dated, don't go near them.

Trent's Last Case was a Herbert Wilcox film of 1952 in which Trent was played by the debonair **Michael Wilding**. (**Orson Welles** and **Margaret Lockwood** also appeared in it.) A 1929 version directed by Howard Hawks is unlikely to resurface.

PERRY TRETHOWAN
by Robert Barnard

This 1990s Scotland Yard Detective Inspector appears in an occasional but popular series from this accomplished author in which he gently sends up the 'gentleman amateur sleuth' novels of the Golden Age. Less straightforward than their synopses suggest, the tales have an offbeat air, plenty of wry humour and more than a trace of the author's deep knowledge of literature ranging from Emily Bronte to Agatha Christie. Trethowan is no Christie hero, being 6 feet 5 and a one-time shot-putter and weightlifter. *Sheer Torture*, which begins the series, is a deliciously crackpot story in which Trethowan investigates the death of his own father. Given the inspired lunacy of the ancestral household (fascists, would-be artists, ego maniacs) and given that Perry's father met his doom while playing with his new S&M torture device, it's a relief to find Perry himself to be sane.

The books comprise *Sheer Torture* (1981), *Death and the Princess* (1982), *The Missing Bronte* (1983 (Barnard has also written a much-praised biography of Emily Bronte), *Bodies* (1986) which also features **Charlie Peace**, and *Death in Purple Prose* (1987).

TREWLEY & STONE
by Sarah J. Mason

A curious pair, this, from an author who specialises in artful dottiness (see **Miss Seeton**). Superintendent Trewley is a relatively conventional older officer teamed with a bright young thing, Sergeant Stone. They are more father and daughter than potential lovers. Their cases are peculiar: when they find a corpse in ice on the fish counter of a shop, it's an indication of what you should expect. (This book is called *Frozen Stiff!*) Shopkeepers beware, because in another book a baker is suffocated in her own rising dough and in yet another an optician who can't see danger is kidnapped. Clues to the crimes sometimes come from the titles:

Murder in the Maze (1993) has a body found just there, then came

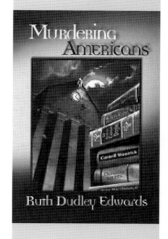

Frozen Stiff (1993) and *Corpse in the Kitchen* the same year, followed by *Dying Breath* (1994), *Sew Easy to Kill* (1996), *Seeing Is Deceiving* (1997), *Corpse in the Case* and *Deep-frozen Death* (both 1999).

IDA (JACK) TROUTBECK

by Ruth Dudley Edwards

Outrageous lady detective who joined and, in truth, took over the author's existing **Amis and Milton** series. Far larger than life, more macho than most men, she stamps through these witty political and social satires with all the indelicacy of Gladys Mitchell's **Mrs Bradley**. She joined the series in the fifth book, *Matricide at St Martha's*, became a baroness in *Ten Lords a-Leaping*, and has since shown no evidence of good behaviour in any book including the gloriously titled *Murdering Americans*.

Matricide at St Martha's (1994) remains a classic, *The Anglo-Irish Murders* (2000) pokes fun where few other authors dare, *Murdering Americans* (2007) is topical – but all the books are wickedly amusing.

SAM TURNER

by John Baker

Private investigator Sam Turner is a very British creation, a reformed (he hopes) alcoholic burdened with a strong social conscience and with colleagues who are as much a liability as an aid. Like many fictional PIs, especially British, Sam champions hopeless causes and old rock music – but gets his man. The tales are set mainly in the city of **York**, known normally for its history, its architecture and its year-round throng of tourists. But Sam Turner's York has a darker underside, evident from titles such as *King of the Streets*, *Poet in the Gutter*, *Death Minus Zero* and *Walking With Ghosts*. This last has a 'master of disguise' villain who could have taken the plot into comic-book territory were the book's strong theme not the difference between what the media says happened in a case and what actually did. *Shooting in the Dark* (perhaps the best Sam Turner book) explores voyeurism, blindness and the different ways we see the world, while *The Meanest Flood*, although set in York at a time when the River Ouse reached its highest level, shares its main crime plot with intelligent writing about magic and dreams and sleight of hand. After six books in the Turner series Baker switched his sombre gaze to the less glamorous town of Hull, and to a new hero, **Stone Lewis**.

Poet in the Gutter (1995), *Death Minus Zero* (1996), *King of the Streets* (1998), *Walking With Ghosts* (1999), *Shooting in the Dark* (2001), *The Meanest Flood* (2003).

VAN DER VALK

Nicolas Freeling

Piet Van der Valk is a deliberately awkward and mistrustful Dutch police inspector (based in **Amsterdam**) who wanders slowly through his well-ordered terrain (sometimes stepping out into Belgium) to solve

W

Barry Foster.

distinctly European crimes. (In one book he investigates a case of butter smuggling!) His dogged persistence usually solves the case, though at times he does need the help of his smart French wife **Arlette** – who after Piet's death in *A Long Silence* had a short series of her own. Today's readers may prefer the television series – though even they were made at a leisurely pace, with blond and curly star **Barry Foster** fitting each series in between other filming contracts. Both the books and the TV series are a particular taste: you tend to love them or find the character so exasperating you won't go near. Some love the books but can't stand Foster; some love him but can't take the books. But that, as Piet himself might say, is how life is.

Love in Amsterdam (1962), *Because of the Cats* (1963), *Gun Before Butter* (1963), *Double Barrel* (1964), *Criminal Conversation* (1965), *The King of the Rainy Country* (1966), *Strike Out Where Not Applicable* (1967), *Tsing Boum* (1969), *Over the High Side* (1971), *A Long Silence* (1972). *Sand Castles* (1989) has Piet investigate a case earlier in his career. Two later books, *The Widow* (1979) and *One Damn Thing After Another* star Arlette, who also appears with **Henri Castang** in *Lady Macbeth* (1988).

There have been three television series, widely spaced, each with **Barry Foster** as Van der Valk. **Susan Travers** played Arlette in the first series (1972-73), **Joanna Dunham** took over for the 1977 series, and **Meg Davies** came in for 1991-92.

Love in Amsterdam was filmed as *The Amsterdam Affair* in 1968 with **Wolfgang Kieling** as Van der Valk.

JOHNNY VALLON
by Peter Cheyney

From one of the most prolific authors of the 1930s and 1940s came this ex-Military Intelligence operative, now demobbed, strong as an ox although carrying an unhealed stomach wound from the war (which didn't stop him drinking a truly astonishing amount of liquor, at that time when even to *find* so much alcohol was a feat). Vallon's adventures reek of post-war austerity, and at a time when most British crime stories either clung to pre-war bumbling amateurs or tried the new concept of police procedural, Cheyney's stories were comparatively hard-boiled. His big sellers in other books had been **Lemmy Caution** and **Slim Callaghan**, but among the many characters he created, Johnny Vallon may be one of the better to read today, partly for the books' historically interesting wartime attitudes but also for their amoral darkness.

You Can Call It a Day (1949), *Dark Bahama* (1950), *Lady, Behave!* (1950).

EUGENE VALMONT
by Robert Barr

'The first humorous detective of any standing,' said Peter Haining. Journalist and prolific author Robert Barr joined the turn-of-the-century detective boom with both serious detective stories and parodies, some of which told of Eugene Valmont, a detective as foreign as Hercule Poirot. (Others told of a parodic Sherlock Holmes, called Sherlaw Kombs, in *Detective Stories Gone Wrong* within *The Idler* magazine.)

HARRIET VANE
See **Lord Peter Wimsey**

FRAN VARADY
by Ann Granger

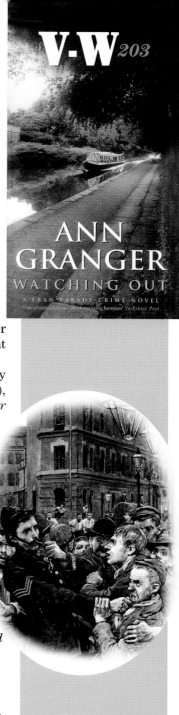

London-based amateur detective from a writer better known for her **Mitchell & Markby** novels. Varady wants to be an actress and like many with these dreams spends most of her time in fill-in jobs while waiting for work. Strangely enough, those jobs, borderline and temporary as they are, cause Fran (and sometimes **her dog Bonnie**) to be dragged into all kinds of illegal activities. When nasty things happen to a girl's friends, what can she do but try to help? One friend is **Ganesh Patel**, who first works in his parents' greengrocer's in Rotherhithe before he and Fran slip off to Camden. Fran has another friend in the police in the form of **Inspector Janice Morgan**. A light and pleasant series.

Asking For Trouble began the series in 1997, followed immediately by *Keeping Bad Company* (1997), then *Running Scared* (1998), *Risking It All* (2001), *Watching Out* (2003), *Mixing with Murder* (2005), *Rattling the Bones* (2007).

SERGEANT VERITY
by Francis Selwyn (Donald Thomas)

William Verity is very much a **Victorian policeman**: stern and moralistic. The crimes he investigates combine authentic nineteenth-century backgrounds (slum streets, steam trains, etc.) with classic 'impossible crime' situations, and the Victorian period allows for exciting train robberies and jewellery robberies – again authentic, as the author is a historian who specialises in the nineteenth century.

The train robbery occurs in the first book, *Cracksman on Velvet* (1974), while the second, *Sergeant Verity and the Imperial Diamond* (1975) is set in India. Later books, set in London, include *Sergeant Verity and the Blood Royal* (1979) and *The Hangman's Child* (2000).

HILDA WADE
by Grant Allen

Probably **the first nurse-detective**, a useful device at the time, allowing a woman to dirty her hands in detective work. In her first case she has to clear the name of her dead father, wrongly accused of murder. She adopts the Wade pseudonym to mask her real identity – her real name, Maisie Yorke-Bannerman, not having the same ring. The plucky and beautiful 'Hilda' storms off on a world-wide quest to clear Dad's name and even when shipwrecked is undefeated. She's beautiful but over-fond of hunches and intuition.

Her adventures in *Strand* magazine were interrupted by Grant Allen's untimely death but the story was completed by another *Strand* writer, Arthur Conan Doyle.

PENNY WANAWAKE
by Susan Moody

At times, Penny is hardly an investigator at all. She is rich, black, hardly needs to earn a living, but is a freelance photographer who, freed from the need to keep the money coming in, finds time to become involved in whatever adventures take her fancy. Penny's money comes in part from her ambassador parents but, unlike previous rich British detectives, she has a strong and active social conscience. Her first outing, in *Penny Black*, sees Penny and her then lover as modern-day Robin Hoods, stealing jewellery from the rich and using the money thus realised to aid the third world. Later in the series we see her rescuing or investigating the death of sundry friends. Although a lightweight series, the tales were brightly told and Penny was a cheerful companion.

All titles have Penny in them. *Penny Black* (1984) was followed by *Penny Dreadful* (1984), *Penny Post* (1985), *Penny Royal* (1986), *Penny Wise* (1988), *Penny Pinching* (1989) and finally, *Penny Saving* (1990). – What happened to *Penny Farthing*, *Penny Whistle*, *Penny Worth* and *Penny-a-Liner*? We'll never know.

INSPECTOR WANG
by Christopher West

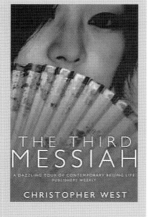

Inspector Wang is **a present-day Chinese policeman**, very effectively created by a British writer who lived there. We first meet Wang (real name Wang Anzhuang) in 1991 Beijing when his night at the People's Opera is interrupted with a murder, which in turn leads him into the secret world of Beijing's Triads and Communist Party politics. In *Death on Black Dragon River* he encounters another murder when he revisits the village of his birth, a murder which, as in the third book, will have uncomfortable links to China's past. The fourth book, *The Third Messiah*, has the sister of Wang's wife **Rosina Lin** caught up in the cultish New Church of the Heavenly Kingdom. When the cult's mystical leader is reported dead, Wang investigates. Again, the case presents the reader with a new view of contemporary China. It seems a shame that this fine series did not catch on.

Death of a Blue Lantern (1994), *Death on Black Dragon River* (1995), *Death of a Red Mandarin* (1997), *The Third Messiah* (2000).

MERRILY WATKINS
by Phil Rickman

Merrily Watkins is officially known as the Deliverance Consultant to the Diocese of Hereford, and is an **unconventional vicar** whose dedication to her calling prompts her to do whatever she thinks fitting, including, where necessary, carrying out the odd exorcism. She's a single mum with a daughter who grows from teens to young adulthood in the series, and she serves a large rural parish, partly real, partly imaginary, stretching across southern **Herefordshire** and north-west **Gloucestershire**. If this makes the books sound cosy they are a long way from that. Her past boyfriend, who crops up from time to time, carved out a career elsewhere as a rock star with a strongly mystical bent, and Merrily's patch includes the old stamping grounds of real-life serial killers Fred and Rosemary West. In *The Lamp of the Wicked* she pursues a creepy case in which it seems West's spirit has lived on to inspire others to follow his evil path. Similarly mystic and semi-supernatural threads run through all the stories, giving them a haunting quality beyond crime fiction. In *The Prayer of the Night Shepherd* a TV producer wants to prove that his house inspired *The Hound of the Baskervilles*. Meanwhile, a local legend tells of a ghostly black dog whose appearance foreshadows death... These are long but deftly written novels, rich in atmosphere and practically unique.

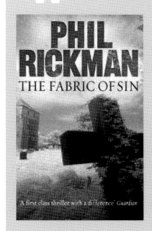

Merrily first appeared in *The Wine of Angels* (1998), then continued in *Midwinter of the Spirit* (1999), *A Crown of Lights* (2001), *The Cure of Souls* (also 2001), *The Lamp of the Wicked* (2002), *The Prayer of the Night Shepherd* (2004), *The Smile of a Ghost* (2005) *Remains of an Altar* (2006) and *The Fabric of Sin* (2007).

CHIEF INSPECTOR JOHN WATT
See **Charlie Barlow**

DAVID WEBB
by Anthea Fraser
Detective Chief Inspector Webb is in his late 40s. A competent amateur water-colourist and a brilliant cartoonist, he uses cartoons to help solve his cases, by sketching first the background, then the characters in the case, putting people in the positions they claimed that they were in when the crime was committed. To his colleagues at the station this practice is known as 'the Governor drawing conclusions'! Webb is helped on his cases by the happily married, ever hungry Detective Sergeant **Ken Jackson**.

First in this present-day series was *A Shroud for Delilah* (1984) and the last, *The Twelve Apostles* (1999). Within the series it's also worth looking for *Six Proud Walkers* (1988) and *The Ten Commandments* (1997).

MARTIN WEBB
by Sally Spedding
Martin Webb appears in a new series of crime novels set in the brooding Malvern Hills. From the one book to appear so far it promises to be a darkly wrought series. In *Come and be Killed* we see Webb, whose relationship with his own father was uneasy, sense family tensions behind an apparent disappearance and suicide. The dead woman's sister, a single mother, looks after a vulnerable woman in her large house near Malvern – but she has a secret: she wants to seek out the mother who abandoned her as a baby. Webb is suspicious. He doesn't

Ruth Rendell.

believe the sister committed suicide.

The series will see Webb move to South Worcestershire Division and rise from Detective Constable to Detective Inspector.

Come and be Killed (2007).

JOSIE WELFORD
by Judith Cutler

Exmoor-based gastro-publican Josie Welford is a successful Weightwatcher of a certain age and widow of one of the UK's most wanted criminals. Blessed or cursed with a strong sense of justice, she now operates strictly on the right side of the law — when it suits her — often in the company of local ex-cop **Nick Thomas**. Shades of Martina Cole, one would think, but a lot less bleak and in your face.

The Food Detective (2005, *The Chinese Takeout* (2006) — best read in sequence.

INSPECTOR WEST
by John Creasey

Roger West (also known as 'Handsome' West) was a straightforward Scotland Yard detective who sold on the author's name and, despite the humdrum nature of the plots, went on to appear in a long string of crime novels. They were a mix of detection and thriller.

How Creasey managed to turn out so many books is a greater mystery than occurs in any in his books — and while they are not great books they are not bad books. Inspector West was only one of John Creasey's creations, and there over forty titles in this series alone. First came *Inspector West Takes Charge* in 1942, but then, in uncharacteristic vacillation came *Inspector West Leaves Town* (1942) followed by *Inspector West At Home* (1943). We had *West's Regrets* in 1945, his *Holiday* in 1946 and both a *Triumph and a Battle* in 1948. On and on he went, eventually dropping the words Inspector West from the titles, till *Alibi* in 1971, *The Extortioners* in 1974 and finally in 1978, *A Sharp Rise in Crime*. Perhaps the rise was too much for him.

INSPECTOR WEXFORD
by Ruth Rendell

Reginald Wexford comes from the quieter side of one of Britain's darkest and most able crime writers – but coming from Rendell's pen he cannot be cosy. Relatively rural (relatively for Rendell, whose metier is metropolitan), he deals with fairly domestic cases and is himself married and well into his fifties. A Chief Inspector in the (fictional) Kingsmarkham, his frequent sidekick is the more uptight Inspector **Mike Burden**, a true policeman who became a widower early in the series and remains sour and distrustful of the civilian world. Burden – unhappy, his life a wreck, a man given to skeetering dangerously off the rails (until … but that would be giving too much away) – would for many crime writers be the main character, with the dependable Wexford trailing behind. But

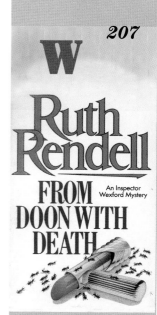

by placing the focus on the man most of us would like investigating *our* cases (assuming we were innocent!) Rendell is able to keep her distance from Burden and to avoid the fault common among many fellow writers: of wallowing in her character's gloom. We might have tired of Burden if we had not seen him through Wexford's critical but tolerant eyes.

The 'domestic' cases Wexford investigates are far from cosy: no cardboard characters, no vapid victims. Into the comfortable market town Rendell brings transvestites, manipulators, dead children, families at war and, most frightening of all in a Rendell novel, couples who appear to love each other. As Dilys Winn once famously quipped: 'In a Rendell novel, a couple is not a happy thing to be.'

This long-running series began back in 1964 with a superb starter, *From Doon With Death*, and has continued with a new title every two years or so. *Not in the Flesh* came out in 2007. All are good, and they are best approached in sequence. (It's not essential but does help put Mike Burden, and to some extent, Wexford's family, into context.) The best Wexfords are probably those written in the Seventies, but if you read in sequence you'll become an addict anyway.

The TV dramas are softer than the books – even, dare one say, cosier – but Burden remains a properly gloomy man and **George Baker's** Wexford is as solid and believable as he ought to be. His accent, too, seems more pronounced on TV, largely because, on the page, one is unaware of it. And the countryside looks fine. **Christopher Ravenscroft** is Burden (deliberately and aptly named) and **Louie Ramsay** plays Wexford's supportive wife Dora.

George Baker.

LORD PETER WIMSEY
by Dorothy L Sayers

> *She perceived a young man, attired in a mauve dressing-gown of great splendour, from beneath the hem of which peeped coyly a pair of primrose silk pyjamas.*
> Mrs Ruyslaender meets Lord Peter
> *The Unprincipled Affair of the Practical Joker*

Love him or loathe him, Wimsey is the ultimate toff turned 'tec. Not merely a lord, but one given several pages of bogus pedigree by his doting author, Wimsey chortled onto the scene in 1923 in *Whose Body?* A sporty, lightly-learned young man with a monocle and more than enough money to preserve him from ever having to earn a living, Wimsey lives in Piccadilly, partnerless apart from his able manservant **Bunter** (a usefully virile ex-sergeant Wimsey met in the war, though the thought of Wimsey dirtying himself in the mud of Flanders defies rational belief) from which comfortable abode he pootles out in a dashing Daimler Twin Six, often in search of a country house but just as likely to find an unsolved crime instead.

> *Lord Peter emerged from Bunter's hands a marvel of sleek brilliance. His primrose-coloured hair was so exquisite a work of art that to eclipse it with his glossy hat was like shutting up*

the sun in a shrine of polished jet; his spats, light trousers, and exquisitely polished shoes formed a tone-symphony in monochrome.

From *The Entertaining Episode of the Article in Question.*

Any amateur detective faced with a series of crimes needs both a justifiable reason for finding them, plus at least one contact in the real police. Wimsey's contact (later his brother in law) is **Inspector Parker of Scotland Yard**. A less essential adjunct is a romantic partner and Wimsey's, **Harriet Vane**, debuts in *Strong Poison* (1930), but takes another seven years to wed him, which she finally does in *Busman's Honeymoon* (1937). Courtship can settle a man, and after meeting Harriet, Wimsey does become a slightly less fatuous character (perhaps because Vane is supposedly a crime writer and thus sane). Whether Wimsey becomes more interesting is a question which has divided critics ever since, though that division is essentially between those who thought him engaging before he met Harriet and those who found him tedious from the start. Readers beginning to gag on the sickly courtship scenes in *Strong Poison* revived a little with the best book in the series, *Murder Must Advertise* (1933), only to sigh in despair at Sayers's pretentious (or gorgeous, depending on your point of view) *Gaudy Night* in 1935. Such heartless souls would not have responded to the wedding invitation extended in *Busman's Honeymoon*. But all would have agreed that behind Lord Peter Wimsey lay a set of ingeniously thought-out mysteries with teasingly unlikely but possible solutions — even if sometimes, as at the end of *The Five Red Herrings*, Sayers needed over thirty pages to explain whodunit and how. Oh, my giddy aunt, as Lord Peter might say.

I'm not denying that the body was in the coffin when the coffin was placed in the chapel. I only doubt whether it was there when it was put in the ground.

Lord Peter Wimsey:

The Undignified Melodrama of the Bone of Contention

Books: *Whose Body?* (1923), *Clouds of Witness* (1926), *Unnatural Death* (1927), *The Unpleasantness at the Bellona Club* (1928), *Strong Poison* (1930), *The Five Red Herrings* (1931), *Have His Carcase* (1932), *Murder Must Advertise* (1933), *The Nine Tailors* (1934), *Gaudy Night* (1935), *Busman's Honeymoon* (1937).

Sayers produced several volumes of short stories, through which were scattered her 21 Wimsey stories plus even more non-Wimseys, but *Lord Peter Views The Body* (1928) is the only book to comprise only Wimsey stories, twelve in all.

Between 1972 and 5 BBC TV screened five Lord Peter novels in *Lord Peter Wimsey*. **Ian Carmichael** played Lord Peter, **Glyn Houston** played Bunter and **Mark Eden** played Inspector Parker. The novels chosen were *Clouds of Witness*, *The Unpleasantness at the Bellona Club*, *Murder Must Advertise*, *The Nine Tailors* and *The Five Red Herrings*. Carmichael played Lord Peter faithfully, though either he or the scripts made him seem a little more intelligent, with his twitishness a mere façade. More than a decade later, in 1987, BBC2 screened *Strong Poison*, *Have His Carcase*

Robert Montgomery and Constance Cummings

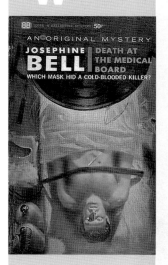

and *Gaudy Night* with **Edward Petherbridge** as Peter, **Richard Morant** as Bunter, **David Quiller** as Parker and **Harriet Walter** as Harriet Vane.

Busman's Holiday (1940) may be the most enjoyable Wimsey film, with **Robert Montgomery** portraying Lord Peter and Constance Cummings as Harriet Vane.

DAVID WINTRINGHAM

by Josephine Bell

Wintringham is a doctor and this allows Bell to incorporate plenty of medical detail into the stories, which are more *Doctor in the House* than *Casualty*, being crammed with comic incident, misbehaving medical students and complicated murders. Recurring cases of romance keep the pulse rate throbbing healthily, and in most books **Inspector Mitchell** provides the necessary second opinion.

Murder in Hospital (1937) was a duller title than was the book. It was followed by titles such as *Death on the Borough Council, From Natural Causes, Bones in the Barrow* and the final *The Seeing Eye* in 1958.

VALERIA WOODVILLE

by Wilkie Collins

In his 1875 novel *The Law and the Lady* Collins created a model amateur detective, the woman who has to solve a murder mystery to clear her husband's name. When the book was written this high motive was enough to excuse a woman's excursion into 'man's business', and for that reason many a later writer used the same device. But Valeria Woodville could be seen as **an early feminist hero**. Collins invests her with intelligence and determination (in contrast to her spineless husband) and has her undertake a methodical step investigation despite an array of obstacles. In the view of Craig and Cadogan in their book *The Lady Investigates* 'she is the first woman detective whose investigative exploits are built on step-by-step deduction; she knows when to proceed painstakingly and when to take off and follow a hunch.' The case seems hopeless, her uncle ridicules her ('a lawyer in petticoats') and the sinister cripple **Miserrimus Dexter** dares to lecture her on woman's inadequacies and inferiority to men. Collins makes Dexter such a gothic horror that no reader could agree with him.

The Law and the Lady (1875)

HANNAH WOLFE

by Sarah Dunant

Sarah Dunant.

Wolfe starred in a short-lived series of three books which promised more. A sharp and adventurous journalist detective who never forgot her femininity and hence vulnerability in a fight (or her deceptive appeal for certain men), Hannah plunged into cases far from usual and refreshingly up to date. Animal rights activists and dodgy health farms

accompanied missing daughters and mysterious deaths. The stories were told with plenty of pace – and too many quips for some readers – but the jokes didn't subvert the deliberately nasty undertones.

Birth Marks (1991) was the first Hannah Wolfe story, to be followed by two more: *Fatlands* in 1993 (the most successful of the series and winner of a CWA Silver Dagger) and *Under My Skin* in 1995.

DAPHNE WRAYNE
by Mark Cross

Ex-barrister, now self-appointed head of the 'Adjusters', a team of four rich but active philanthropists who seek to put right the wrongs the law will not. No fee is charged but clients are asked to donate to charity. Though the novels started in the early 1920s it's an idea with echoes today: that of benevolent business repaying its dues and assuming the responsibilities of an ossified state. The Adjusters do what the state cannot: in their first outing, for example, they capture the villains, whip and drug them, then place them comatose in coffins to be found by the police. It is an ideal concept, as Daphne is an idealised woman: feminine but tough, modest but intelligent, logical but intuitive. The stories are simple, delightfully cosy, and in their time were a great success. Guaranteed to delight every *Daily Mail* reader.

The Shadow of the Four began a series of (incredibly) 46 books, the first 11 of which all have Four in their title. Highlights among those which followed were *Murder As Arranged* (1943) and *The Mystery of Joan Marryat* (1945). The series climaxed with two books in each of its six final years, the last of which being *Perilous Hazard* (1961).

SUPERINTENDENT WYCLIFFE
by W. J. Burley

Serious, almost stolid police detective whose **Cornish** beat attracts all kinds of offbeat incomers attracted by the vision of an alternative life on the long peninsula, though many of them find the place does not bend to their whims and is not what they hoped it might be. Meanwhile the locals carry on as they have for centuries, masters of fishy enterprise. Charles Wycliffe patrols with a canny patience; though not a Cornwall native he knows the people and is prepared to take time to get to know the incomers – even if they might prefer he didn't. His cases are interesting, and Cornwall, with its wild coast and remote rural areas, is an ideal setting.

He was not a good driver; he enjoyed no rapport with the internal combustion engine nor, indeed, with the age which had deified it. He often told himself that he had been born out of due time, that he should have muscled in on the age of steam and grown old while, among other things, it was still possible to be a Fabian Socialist and believe in the perfectibility of man.

Wycliffe described in *Wycliffe's Wild-Goose Chase*

The series began with *Three-Toed Pussy* in 1966, followed four years later with *To Kill A Cat* and 6 more in the 1970s, 7 in the

1980s, 6 in the 1990s, and with titles continuing this decade. *To Kill A Cat* (1970) – also called *Wycliffe and How To Kill a Cat* – and *Wycliffe and the Redhead* (1997) are recommended.

The LWT TV series *Wycliffe* ran from 1993 to 1998, with repeats on one channel or another practically ever since. **Jack Shepherd** plays Wycliffe.

SUPERINTENDENT YEADINGS
by Clare Curzon

Yeadings is the lead player in Clare Curzon's **Thames Valley Mystery series**, the valley comprising a triangle of Bucks, Berks and Oxfordshire. Mike Yeadings is married and his elder child has Down's Syndrome. Also in his team are DCI **Angus Mott**, who is married to a defence barrister, and DI **Walter Salmon**, a cold and unsympathetic character, along with two Detective Sergeants, **Beaumont and Zyczynski**, who vie with each other for seniority. The interplay between these characters, and between the police work and their family life, is a part of every story.

The series started with *I Give You Five Days* in 1983, continued (after a fashion, since the lead characters were relegated to minor parts) with *Masks and Faces* (1984), then it stabilised with three more in the Eighties, nine in the Nineties, and one a year since the millennium. Recent titles include *Body of a Woman* (2002), *A Meeting of Minds* (2003), *Last to Leave* (2004), *The Glass Wall* (2005), *The Edge* (2006), *Payoff* (2007).

SERGEANT YELLICH
See **Chief Inspector Hennessey**

PRINCE ZALESKI
by M. P. Shiel

The most bizarre detective of them all, against whom Holmes with his liking for cocaine and the occasional trance seems unadventurous. Zaleski, conceived at the height of the Decadent movement and sharing Holmes' intuition and Poe's Gothic mania, is permanently stoned and seldom strays from the darkened lair in which he lies surrounded by exotic Orientalia. He himself is an exiled Russian nobleman who lives in a lonely castle where he is attended by a black servant. There are only three stories: the first portraying an aristocrat destroyed by syphilis, the second the theft of a magic jewel, and the third an enquiry into a mysterious society dedicated to the greater use of eugenics.

Collectors fight to obtain a first edition of the book which contains those three stories: *Prince Zaleski* (1895) published by the crown prince of Decadent publishing, John Lane (publisher of the notorious Yellow Book).

MAMUR ZAPT
by Michael Pearce

M. P. Shiel.

Prince
Zaleski

M.P. Shiel

Tartarus Press

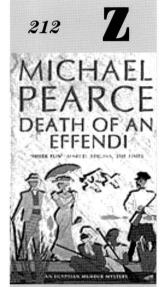

Before the First World War, the Mamur Zapt was the name for the Chief of the Secret Police in Cairo, actually an Englishman, **Captain Gareth Owen**, there to supervise British interests in the **Anglo-Egyptian Sudan** – a description not without its complications, since the French thought they had greater rights to the area. This description suggests a weighty read but the Zapt books are deft and great fun, although extremely well-informed on the complex world of British, French and Egyptian interests of the time. 'As fertile as your favourite oasis', remarked the *Literary Review*.

From *Mamur Zapt and the Return of the Carpet* (1988) till *The Point in the Market* (2005) which is set after the First World War has begun, this has been a consistently entertaining series, whose highlights include *The Mamur Zapt and the Spoils of Europe* (1993) which won the CWA Last Laugh Award, and *Death of an Effendi* (1999) and *A Cold Touch of Ice* (2000) which were both shortlisted for the CWA Ellis Peters Historical Dagger.

AURELIO ZEN
by Michael Dibdin

An Italian policeman realistically portrayed in a series of darkly authentic Italian settings, Zen exists in a compromised, often corrupt police force, where an officer's success is measured more by his ability to manipulate the system and help fellow officers than by the number of criminals he brings to book. When we first meet Zen (in *Ratking*, 1988) he has yet to learn these lessons, but as the series continues he changes from a well-intentioned innocent to a world-weary, bitterly experienced cop – not without upsets along the way. Initially he is shunted aside and almost kicked out of the force, but he is then made directly accountable to the Interior Ministry with an innocent-sounding brief to ensure the Italian police follow correct procedures – a one-man mission, if ever there was one, not helped by the devious motives of his employers. His work takes him to a number of Italian cities, with a change of location in every book. Zen remains well intentioned, but throughout the series his methods become increasingly devious and thus suited to the world he works in. He is under no illusions about his brief: do a bad job but please the right person and you get promotion; expose a villain that someone above you wants protected and you get put down. Somehow, within all this, try to remember you're a lawman. This is a series that should be read in sequence, to live with Zen as the hard knocks give him experience and to watch him learn the necessary adjustments.

Ratking (1988) starts the series, which continued until Dibdin's untimely death in 2007.

FURTHER EVIDENCE

Also Known As
Crime Writers' *Pseudonyms*

Pseudonym	*Also Known As*
Conrad Allen	*Keith Miles*
Andrew Arncliffe	*Peter N Walker*
Clifford Ashdown	*R Austin Freeman*
Gordon Ashe	*John Creasey*
Simon Beaufort	*Susanna Gregory*
Anthony Berkeley	*Anthony Berkeley Cox*
Nicholas Blake	*Cecil Day Lewis*
Jolyon Carr	*Edith Pargetter*
P F Chisholm	*Patricia Finney*
Michael Clynes	*Paul Doherty*
Hamilton Crane	*Sarah J Mason*
Edmund Crispin	*Robert Bruce Montgomery*
Mark Cross	*Archibald Thomas Pechey*
Nicholas Freeling	*F R E Nicholas*
Paul Harding	*Paul Doherty*
Jack Harvey	*Ian Rankin*
Francis Iles	*Anthony Berkeley Cox*
Martin Inigo	*Keith Miles*
Michael Innes	*J I M Stewart*
Dan Kavanagh	*Julian Barnes*

Will Kingdom	*Phil Rickman*
John Le Carre	*David Cornwell*
Robert Markham	*Kingsley Amis*
J J Marric	*John Creasey*
Edward Marston	*Keith Miles*
Jennie Melville	*Gwendoline Butler*
Anthony Morton	*John Creasey*
Frank Parrish	*Roger Longrigg*
Ellis Peters	*Edith Pargeter*
Patrick Quentin (also Q Patrick)	*R W Webb & H C Wheeler*
Nicholas Rhea	*Peter N Walker*
John Rhode	*Cecil John Charles Street*
Patrick Ruell	*Reginald Hill*
Andrew Saville	*Andrew Taylor*
Peter Tremayne	*Peter Beresford Ellis*
Barbara Vine	*Ruth Rendell*
Patricia Wentworth	*Dora Amy Elles*
P B Yuill	*Gordon Williams & Terry Venables*

Just how good a detective are you?

A ten number combination will unlock this safe; the numbers are scattered throughout the Directory section. Once you have found all ten numbers visit the publisher's website and follow the instructions. Should you have uncovered the correct combination and opened the safe, you will discover a sellection of prizes that will be awarded to the first ten Great Detectives.

Cinema: films with a strong detective element

Anatomy of a Murder
Otto Preminger, 1959
James Stewart, Lee Remick,
Ben Gazzara, George C Scott
*One of the best courtroom dramas,
where the attorney's investigations
outside the court decide the case.*

Brelan d'as
Henri Verneuil, 1952
Michel Simon
*Is Simon a better Maigret than Jean
Gabin? Discuss.*

Bunny Lake is Missing
Otto Preminger, 1965
Laurence Olivier, Keir Dullea,
Carol Lynley
*Did the missing daughter really exist?
Fascinating quest and strong
resolution.*

Chinatown
Roman Polanski, 1974
Jack Nicholson, Faye Dunaway,
John Huston
*Over-confident detective and his
untrustworthy clients. A must for
any director manqué.*

Devil in a Blue Dress
Carl Franklin, 1995
Denzel Washington,
Tom Sizemore, Jennifer Beals,
Don Cheadle
Fine realization of Walter Mosley's first Easy Rawlins novel.

Farewell My Lovely
Adrian Scott, 1944
Dick Powell
Possibly the best Chandler film, with the least likely but successful casting.

Note how the publicity artist 'added 'umph' to this 'still' for the Farewell My Lovely *poster.*

Father Brown
Vivian A. Cox, 1954
Alec Guinness, Peter Finch,
Joan Greenwood
Well played and a delightful oddball comedy.

Gorky Park
Michael Apted, 1983
William Hurt, Lee Marvin,
Brian Dennehy
As revealing about a cop's life in Moscow as was the book, plus an intriguing mystery.

Gumshoe
Stephen Frears, 1971
Albert Finney, Billie Whitelaw
A wonderful pastiche of the hard-boiled detective story.

Harper
aka **The Moving Target**
Jack Smight, 1966
Paul Newman, Lauren Bacall
Ross MacDonald's Lew Archer cried out to be filmed, and Newman was ideal.

The Hound of the Baskervilles
Sidney Lanfield, 1939
Basil Rathbone,
Nigel Bruce
Rathbone's first and unforgettable appearance as Sherlock Holmes.

L. A. Confidential
    Curtis Hanson, 1997
Kevin Spacey, Russell Crowe, Kim
Basinger
*James Ellroy's paranoid take on
L.A.'s corrupt cops and complex
social mores.*

Maigret Sets a Trap
    Jean Delannoy, 1958
Jean Gabin
The best of Gabin's Maigret films.

The Maltese Falcon
    Henry Blanke, 1941
Humphrey Bogart, Sidney
Greenstreet, Peter Lorre, Elisha
Cooke Jr, Mary Astor
*The best crime film ever? Bogart
had to be good to top this brilliant
cast.*

The Name of the Rose
    Jean-Jacques Annaud, 1986
Sean Connery
*Historical detective stories rarely
make it to the screen (or work
when they do). This one does.*

Night Moves
    Arthur Penn, 1975
Gene Hackman, Jennifer Warren,
Melanie Griffith
*Brilliant example of a dark and
complex film noir.*

The Scarlet Claw
    Roy William Neill, 1944
Basil Rathbone, Nigel Bruce
*Probably the best of Rathbone's
Sherlock Holmes films.*

The Silence of the Lambs
    Jonathan Demme, 1991
Anthony Hopkins,
Jodie Foster
*Don't overlook the detective
element in Clarice
Starling's frustrated
attempts to track the serial
killer.*

The Usual Suspects
    Bryan Singer, 1995
Kevin Spacey, Gabriel
Byrne, Stephen Baldwin,
Pete Postlethwaite
*An enigma wrapped in a
puzzle wrapped inside a
flashback.*

Day Jobs of the Amateur Detective

Where did amateur detectives really earn their money? Some were toffs, and didn't need to worry (too much) about where the next meal was coming from, and some had a sufficiently full casebook to live on their sleuthing earnings, but many of our amateur detectives needed a day job. Here are some of them.

Detective (Author)	Where the money came from:
Johnny Ace (Ron Ellis)	*Disc Jockey*
Robert Amiss (Ruth D Edwards)	*Civil Servant*
Jonathan Argyll (Iain Pears)	*Art Dealer*
Bertie (Peter Lovesey)	*Prince of Wales*
Mrs Bradley (Gladys Mitchell)	*Consultant psychiatrist at the Home Office*
Theodora Braithwaite (D. M. Greenwood)	*Deaconess*
Nell Bray (Gillian Linscott)	*Suffragette*
Miles Bredon (Ronald Knox)	*Investigator (Indescribable Life Insurance Co)*
Father Brown (G. K. Chesterton)	*Roman Catholic Priest*
Keith Calder (Gerald Hammond)	*Gunsmith*
Albert Campion (Margery Allingham)	*Gentleman of leisure (possibly of royal blood)*
Canaletto (Janet Laurence)	*Artist*
Melissa Craig (Betty Rowlands)	*Crime Novelist*
Auguste Didier (Amy Myers)	*Master Chef*
Montague Egg (D. L. Sayers)	*Commercial Traveller*
Dr Gideon Fell (J. D. Carr)	*Lexicographer & Historian*
Gervase Fen (Edmund Crispin)	*Oxford Professor of English & Clumsy Motorist*
Flash the Alsatian (John W. Bobin)	*Dog*
Reginald Fortune (H. C. Bailey)	*Pathologist*
Antony Gillingham (A. A. Milne)	*Gentleman of Leisure*
Lindsay Gordon (Val McDermid)	*Noisy Journalist*

Francis Hancock
(Barbara Nadel) — *Anglo-Indian Undertaker*
Dido Hoare (Marianne MacDonald) — *Antiquarian Book Dealer*
Mr Jellipot (Sydney Fowler) — *Solicitor*
Arnold Landon (Roy Lewis) — *Archaeologist*
Lovejoy (Jonathan Gash) — *Antiques Dealer*
Miss Jane Marple (Agatha Christie) — *Spinster*
Peter Maxwell (M. J. Trow) — *Teacher*
Phyllida Moon (Eileen Dewhurst) — *Actress*
Charles Paris (Simon Brett) — *Heavy Drinking Actor*
Francis Pettigrew (Cyril Hare) — *Barrister*
Miss Pink (Gwen Moffat) — *Mountaineer*
Dr Priestley (John Rhode) — *Mathematician and Scientist*
Mr Pringle (Nancy Livinston) — *Tax Inspector*
Roger Sheringham (Anthony Berkeley) — *Novelist*
Tim Simpson (John Malcolm) — *Antiques Expert*
Nigel Strangeways (Nicholas Blake) — *Journalist and Poet*
Dr Thorndyke (R Austin Freeman) — *Medical Jurist/Amateur Scientist*
Ludovic Travers (Christopher Bush) — *Gentleman of Leisure*
Mark Treasure (David Williams) — *Merchant Banker*
Philip Trent (E. C. Bailey) — *Artist*
Merrily Watkins (Phil Rickman) — *Deliverance Consultant*
Lord Peter Wimsey (D. L. Sayers) — *Gentleman of Leisure*
David Wintringham (Josephine Bell) — *Doctor*

Laugh Lines

'I tell you there's been some funny business, George. My God, George, there's been some funny business.'

Vintage Murder (1937) by Ngaio Marsh

From its earliest beginnings, crime fiction lightened its load with humour, bringing us a splendid succession of wise guys and wisecracks. Most crime novels have at least a sprinkling of jokes, but here are some detectives by writers who seem to invented their sleuths purely for fun.

Sleuth	Creator
Amiss and Milton	Ruth Dudley Edwards
Fitzroy Maclean Angel	Mike Ripley
Tommy & Tuppence Beresford	Agatha Christie
Birdseye and Nevkorina	Nancy Spain
Mrs Bradley	Gladys Mitchell
Auguste Didier	Amy Myers
Inspector Dover	Joyce Porter
Marcus Didius Falco	Lindsey Davis
Gervase Fen	Edmund Crispin
Reggie Fortune	H. C. Bailey
Inspector Hanaud	A. E. W. Mason
Miss Hogg	Austin Lee
Nick Madrid	Peter Guttridge
Constance Morrison-Burke	Joyce Porter
Charles Paris	Simon Brett
Charlie Priest	Stuart Pawson
Mrs Pym	Nigel Morland
Precious Ramotswe	Alexander McCall Smith
'Seedy' Sloan	Catherine Aird

Ruth Dudley Edwards.

Mystery Magazines

In their heyday, from the last quarter of the nineteenth century till the outbreak of the First World War, magazines of general interest, both fiction and non-fiction but with detective fiction to the fore, sold in their hundreds of thousands. For over a century, from the mid nineteenth till the last quarter of the twentieth, magazines cried out for short stories to attract more readers. Those stories, although interspersed between (allegedly) factual articles, were often the mainstay of the magazine and prominently advertised on their covers. The most popular stories were romance, adventure and detection. Women wanted romance, men adventure, but everyone read detective fiction.

Detective fiction works particularly well (many say it works best) in short story form. Many of the nineteenth century's detectives first appeared in short stories – initially in 'Penny Bloods' – and the king of all detectives made the fortunes of *Strand* magazine.

(Not that *Strand* was unsuccessful before Sherlock Holmes: its first issue sold 300,000 copies, but Holmes took it to over half a million.) Readers' love of detective stories caused *Strand* to quickly snap up Arthur Morrison's Martin Hewitt stories and to run tales by other great names until the magazine's demise in 1950.

Among *Strand's* early rivals for crime fiction, *Windsor Magazine* was the main contender. *Windsor* also ran Martin Hewitt stories, along with tales by other stalwarts including Arnold Bennett. Detectives appeared in *The Boys' Herald*, *Penny Pictorial* and *Halfpenny Marvel*. *Harmsworth* and *Illustrated* ran adventure and romance but few detective stories, while other newsstand rivals veered towards humour, literary or domestic matters. Boys' comics featured detectives among their swashbuckling heroes and two hugely successful detective series, the *Sexton Blake Library* and the *Nelson Lee Library*, were launched during the First World War. Among adult magazines *Argosy* held a useful niche as a compendium of short stories in which crime and detection were ever present, and in the late Thirties a few detective short stories cropped up in

racier new entrants such as *Lilliput* and old favourites like *Punch*. But compared to American magazines (whose 'Pulps' included the *Black Mask* series, *Murder Mystery Monthly, Clues and Thrilling Detective* among others) British magazines looked respectable – even if they weren't always to the taste of vicars, schoolmasters and guardians of public decency. Concentrating less on the sex and violence unashamedly offered by their US rivals, Britain's magazines put the stress on mystery and shrewd detection. In Britain's shops lurid American pulps were obtainable from beneath the counter and only one or two US magazines such as *Ellery Queen* and *Alfred Hitchcock's Mystery Magazine* were deemed sufficiently respectable to go on general display.

Why is it then, that even if we extend our definition of 'detective' magazine to include any magazine which carries detective stories, that the story of British detective magazines is of noble decline? In Britain, detective magazines have all but disappeared. Story magazines have always been bought more by women than by men. The magazines that men do buy tend to be specialist (sport and motoring, hobbies and girls) and only in the biggest-circulation 'girlie' magazines has there been any permanent call for fiction. *Playboy* frequently ran pieces by 'serious' names – though curiously, it seldom felt the urge for detective fiction. (Perhaps, in its Sixties heyday, Hefner wanted no taint of pulp fiction.) Here in post-war Britain, detective writers found their outlets dwindling: short stories could be submitted either to American magazines (mainly *Ellery Queen* and *Hitchcock*) or to small-circulation specialist British titles such as *Sherlock, Crime Time, Shots, Crimewave* or CAD.

Sadly today (as this book is printed) it seems that none of these fine British magazines is easily available in a newsstand version. For some years they were almost unavailable outside London and existed almost entirely by subscription. Then even those sales dwindled. *Sherlock*, as the name suggests, was mainly about the great detective, although it did run reviews of modern-day crime fiction and a number of pastiches and pieces to

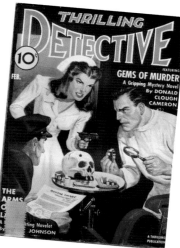

attract other crime fans. *Crime Time* had a wider range, covering the whole gamut of crime fiction from the earliest classics to the latest releases in print or film. *Shots* (formerly *A Shot in the Dark*) was in the *Crime Time* mould but threw in its hand earlier to move from paper to entirely internet production. (*Crime Time* has followed and is also available online.) *Crimewave* was the most beautifully produced of the magazines, devoted exclusively to crime short stories, but has struggled to find a wide audience. The more learned CAD (*Crime and Detective Stories*) – academic and amusingly homemade in feel – may not survive long beyond its fiftieth issue, despite the desperate loyalty of its few readers. Given the huge popularity of detective novels and TV series, it seems unbelievable that this book should pronounce a eulogy for detective magazines.

Olden Time Detectives

Old Times have come upon us fairly recently. A hundred years ago, a reader would struggle to find any mysteries set in ancient times, but over the last two decades that tiny sub-genre has become a substantial movement on its own. One of the first — certainly one of the first historical crime novels of note — came from the Queen of Crime, **Agatha Christie**, who in 1944 set *Death Comes As The End* in ancient Egypt. (Her husband was an archaeologist.) In 1959, **Josephine Tey** re-examined the mystery of the Princes in the Tower in her fine novel, *The Daughter of Time*, into which she incorporated her twentieth century hero Inspector Grant. (He was ill in bed, looking at history for relief.) But the kick-start came in 1977 when **Ellis Peters** brought out her first Cadfael story, *A Morbid Taste for Bones*. Here was a detective novel that broke a fundamental tenet of crime-writing: it was old hat. (One of the attractions of the genre for many readers is that detective stories are bang up-to-date and set in a world they recognise.) Cadfael wasn't even a detective; he was an amateur who wasn't a toff. He was a monk! How on earth could a medieval monk be a detective?

That, of course, was his appeal. The first book, intended by Peters as a one-off, was swiftly followed with a new title almost every year. The series was, and still is, one of the most successful series in detective fiction, both in book form and on TV (twelve 90-minute dramas). Success bred imitation: the history-mystery fan today is spoilt for choice, especially if their taste is medieval. For those interested in other eras, there is hardly a period in history which does not have its sleuth:

Ancient Rome	Falco	*by Lindsey Davis*
7th century	Sister Fidelma	*by Peter Tremayne*
Medieval	Owen Archer	*by Candace Robb*
	Brother Athelstan	*by Paul Harding*
	Matthew Bartholomew	*by Susanna Gregory*
	Brother Cadfael	*by Ellis Peters*
	Hugh Corbett	*by Paul Doherty*
	Crowner John	*by Bernard Knight*
	Gill Cunningham	*by Pat McIntosh*
	Delchard & Brett	*by Edward Marston*
	William Falconer	*by Ian Morson*
	Sir Baldwin de Furnshill	*by Michael Jecks*
	Abbess Helewise	*by Alys Clare*
	Sir Geoffrey Mappestone	*by Simon Beaufort*
	Simon Puttock	*by Michael Jecks*
	Roger the Chapman	*by Kate Sedley*

Tudor & Elizabethan

	Simon Ames	*by Patricia Finney*
	Ursula Blanchard	*by Fiona Buckley*
	Nicholas Bracewell	*by Edward Marston*

Peter Tremayne .

	Sir Robert Carey	*by P. F. Chisholm*
	Simon Forman	*by Judith Cook*
	Sir Roger Shallot	*by Michael Clynes*
	Mathew Shardlake	*by C. J. Sansom*
17th century	Thomas Chaloner	*by Susanna Gregory*
	Christopher Redmayne	*by Edward Marston*
18th century	Canaletto	*by Janet Laurence*
	John Rawlings	*by Deryn Lake*
Early 19th century	Roger Brook	*by Dennis Wheatley*
	Martin Jerrold	*by Edwin Thomas*
	The Scarlet Pimpernel	*by Baroness Orozy*
Victorian	Robert Colbeck	*by Edward Marston*
	Sergeant Cribb	*by Pete Lovesey*
	Jeremy Faro	*by Alanna Knight*
	Thorpe Hazell	*by V. L. Whitechurch*
	Elizabeth Martin	*by Ann Granger*
	Rose McQuinn	*by Alanna Knight*
	William Monk	*by Anne Perry*
	Thomas Pitt	*by Anne Perry*
	Sergeant Verity	*by Francis Selwyn*
Edwardian	Bertie	*by Peter Lovesey*
	Nell Bray	*by Gillian Linscott*
	Inspector Brunt	*by John Buxton Hilton*
	Auguste Didier	*by Amy Myers*
	George Dilman	*by Conrad Allen*
	Solar Pons	*by Basil Copper*
	Lord Francis Powerscourt	*by David Dickinson*
	Joe Sandilands	*by Barbara Cleverly*
	Mamur Zapt	*by Michael Pearce*
Between the wars	Corinth & Brown	*by David Roberts*
	Bernie Gunther	*by Philip Kerr*
	Merlin Richards	*by Keith Miles*
	Miss Seeton	*by Hamilton Crane*
Second World War	Francis Hancock	*by Barabara Nadel*
1940s & 1950s	Inspector Thornhill	*by Andrew Taylor*

Sidekicks

In the model for the fictional detective outlined by Auguste Dupin and set in stone by Sherlock Holmes, one essential was that the detective should have an assistant, the intelligence of whom, said Ronald Knox, should be 'slightly, but very slightly, below that of the average reader.' Writers soon eased up on that over restrictive definition and brought us many colourful sidekicks and assistants – including:

Detective:	*Sidekick:*
Dick Barton	***Jock Anderson*** *Distinctive accent for radio*
Van der Valk	***Arlette*** *Smart French wife and eventual successor when Piet died*
Scarlet Pimpernel	***Marguerite Blakeney*** *Spirited, rich and gorgeous*
Lord Peter Wimsey	***Bunter*** *Useful strong-arm ex-army manservant*
Inspector Wexford	***Mike Burden*** *Dour professional cop who might easily have taken the starring role*
Max Carrados	***Louis Carlyle*** *The 'eyes' for the blind detective*
Sexton Blake	***Yvonne Cartier*** *Glamorous Australian adventuress*
Rebus	***Siobhan Clarke*** *Attractive female aide who comes into the later books presumably to replace him*
Inspector Sloan	***PC W. E. Crosby*** *The 'defective constable' who never learns*
Albert Campion	***Amanda Fitton*** *Aircraft engineer, later his wife*
Inspector Alleyn	***Inspector Fox*** *The 'common man'*
Ben Cooper	***Diane Fry*** *The copper's stern female boss*
Modesty Blaise	***Willie Garvin*** *The handsome hunk*
Thea Crawford	***Tamara Hoyland*** *Took over her boss's series*

Dr Thorndyke	**Christopher Jervis** *'Watson' to the scientific detective*
Inspector Morse	**Sergeant Lewis** *Stolid legman to the mercurial Morse — but outliving him on TV*
Albert Campion	**Magersfontein Lugg** *Reformed burglar turned manservant*
Inspector Dover	**Sergeant MacGregor** *Reasonable and capable, unlike his boss*
Jeremy Faro	**Rose McQuinn** *Copper's daughter who branched out in a series of her own*
Paul Beck	**Dora Myrl** *Rival detective who becomes his wife*
Nelson Lee	**Nipper** *Facsimile of Tinker*
Inspector Hanaud	**Julius Ricardo** *Wine-lover and patron of the arts*
Inspector Lynley	**Simon Allcourt St James** *Aristocratic forensic pathologist, disabled in a car accident*
Sergeant Cribb	**Constable Thackeray** *Stolidly Victorian foil*
Sexton Blake	**Tinker** *Healthy young lad always getting into scrapes*
Inspector Alleyn	**Agatha Troy** *Society artist and eventually his wife*
Tom Barnaby	**Sergeant Troy** *Manly, down-to-earth cop*
Lord Peter Wimsey	**Harriet Vane** *Crime writer, later Wimsey's wife.* *Probable projection of the author.*
Sherlock Holmes	**Dr Watson** *The archetype, who exactly matches Knox's specification for a sidekick*
Charlie Barlow	**Chief Inspector John Watt** *The more tolerant and lighter of the realistic police duo*
Dick Barton	**Snowy White** *Updated version of the loyal valet*

TV Detectives

Here are your favourite shows, the detectives, and the year the programme was first aired.

Agatha Christie's Partners in Crime (1983)
Tommy Beresford *James Warwick*
Tuppence Cowley *Francesca Annis*
Albert *Reece Dinsdale*

Agatha Christie's Poirot (1989)
Hercule Poirot *David Suchet*

The Alleyn Mysteries (1990)
Inspector Alleyn *Simon Williams*

Inspector Alleyn Mysteries (1993)
Inspector Alleyn *Patrick Malahide*

Anna Lee (1993)
Anna Lee *Imogen Stubbs*

Ashes to Ashes (2008)
DCI Gene Hunt *Philip Glenister*
DC Alex Drake *Keeley Hawes*

The Avengers (1961)
(see also The New Avengers)
Dr David Keel *Ian Hendry*
John Steed *Patrick Macnee*
Cathy Gale *Honor Blackman*
Emma Peel *Diana Rigg*
Tara King *Linda Thorson*

Badger (1999)
Tom McCabe *Jerome Flynn*

Baker Street Irregulars (2007)
Sherlock Holmes *Jonathan Pryce*
Dr Watson *Bill Paterson*

Barlow at Large (1971) & Z-Cars (1962) & Softly, Softly (1966)
DCS Charlie Barlow *Stratford Johns*

Beiderbeck Affair (1985),

Beiderbeck Tapes (1987), Beiderbeck Connection (1988)
Trevor Chaplin *James Bolam*
Jill Swinburne *Barbara Flynn*

Bergerac (1981)
Jim Bergerac *John Nettles*

The Bill (1984)
Frank Burnside *Chris Ellison*
DI Neil Manson *Andrew Lancel*

Blue Murder (2003)
DCI Janine Lewis *Caroline Quentin*

Mrs Bradley Mysteries (1998)
Mrs Adela Bradley *Diana Rigg*

Budgie (1971)
'Budgie' Bird *Adam Faith*

Bulman (1985) & Strangers (1978)
George Bulman *Don Henderson*

Cadfael (1994)
Father Cadfael *Derek Jacobi*

Campion (1988)
Campion *Peter Davison*

C.A.T.S. Eyes
DI Maggie Forbes *Jill Gascoigne*

Chandler & Co (1994)
Elly Chandler *Catherine Russell*

The Chinese Detective (1981)
DS Johnny Ho *David Yip*

City of Vice (2008)
Henry Fielding *Ian McDiarmid*
John Fielding *Iain Glen*

Colonel March of Scotland Yard (1956)
Colonel March *Boris Karloff*

Cracker (1993)
Edward Fitzgerald *Robbie Coltrane*
Jane Penhaligan *Geraldine Somerville*

Jonathan Creek (1997)
Jonathan Creek *Alan Davies*
Maddy Magellan *Caroline Quentin*

Cribb (1979)
Sergeant Cribb *Alan Dobie*

Dalziel and Pascoe (1996)
DI Peter Pascoe *Colin Buchanan*
Det Supt Dalziel *Warren Clarke*
DS Edgar Wield *David Royle*

Dangerfield (1995)
Dr Paul Dangerfield *Nigel le Vaillant*

Dempsey and Makepeace (1985)
Jim Dempsey *Michael Brandon*
Harriet Makepeace *Glynis Barber*

Department S (1969)
Jason King *Peter Wyngarde*

Detective (1964, then 1968)
Maigret (*see below*) *Rupert Davies*

The Detectives (1993)
(a comedy send-up)
Bob Louis *Jasper Carrott*
Dave Briggs *Robert Powell*
Frank Cottam *George Sewell*

Dial 999 (1958)
DI Mike Maguire *Robert Beatty*
DI Winter *Duncan Lamont*
DS West *John Witty*

The Expert (1968)
Professor John Hardy *Marius Goring*

Fabian of Scotland Yard (1954)
Inspector Robert Fabian *Bruce Seton*

A Touch of Frost (1992)
Inspector Jack Frost *David Jason*

Foyle's War (2002)
DCS Christopher Foyle *Michael Kitchen*
Sam Stewart, chauffeuse *Honeysuckle Weeks*
Sgt Paul Milner *Anthony Howell*

Fraud Squad (1969)
DI Gamble *Patrick O'Connell*
DS Hicks *Joanna Van Gyseghem*

The Gentle Touch (1980)
DI Maggie Forbes *Jill Gascoigne*

Gideon's Way (1965)
Commander George Gideon *John Gregson*

Hamish Macbeth (1995)
Hamish Macbeth *Robert Carlyle*

Hazell (1978)
James Hazell *Nicholas Ball*

Heartbeat (1992)
Nick Rowan *Nick Berry*
Sergeant Blaketon *Derek Fowlds*
Mike Bradley *Jason Durr*
Sergeant Craddock *Philip Franks*
PC Rob Walker *Jonathan Kerrigan*

Hetty Wainthropp Investigates (1996)
Hetty Wainthropp *Patricia Routledge*

Sherlock Holmes:

**The Adventures (1984),
The Return (1986)
The Casebook (1991) &
The Memoirs (1994)**

Sherlock Holmes *Jeremy Brett*
Dr Watson (Adventures) *David Burke*
Dr Watson (the rest) *Edward Harwicke*
Inspector Lestrade *Colin Jeavons*

Inspector Lynley Mysteries (2001)
Thomas Lynley *Nathaniel Parker*
DS Barbara Havers *Sharon Small*

Jonathan Creek (1997)
Jonathan Creek *Alan Davies*
Maddy Magellan *Caroline Quentin*

Juliet Bravo (1980)
Insp Jean Darblay *Stephanie Turner*
Inspector Kate Longton *Anna Carteret*

Martin Kane, Private Investigator (1959)
Martin Kane *William Gargan*

Kingdom (2007)
Kingdom *Stephen Fry*

The Last Detective (2003)
Dangerous Davies *Peter Davison*

Lewis (2007)
DI Robert Lewis *Kevin Whately*
DS James Hathaway *Laurence Fox*

Life on Mars (2006)
DI Sam Tyler *John Simm*
DCI Gene Hunt *Philip Glenister*

Lord Peter Wimsey (1972)
Lord Peter *Ian Carmichael, then Edward Petherbridge*

Maigret (1960)
Maigret *Rupert Davies*
Mme Maigret *Helen Shingler*
Lucas *Ewen Solon*

Maisie Raine (1998)
Maisie Raine *Pauline Quirke*

The Man From Interpol (1959)
Anthony Smith *Richard Wyler*
Supt. Mercer *John Longdon*

The Man in Room 17 (1965)
Oldenshaw *Richard Vernon*

Colonel March of Scotland Yard (1956)
Colonel March *Boris Karloff*

Mark Saber (1957)
Mark Saber *Donald Gray*

McCallum (1995)
Iain McCallum *John Hannah*

Messiah (2001)
DCI Red Metcalfe *Ken Stott*
DCI Joseph Walker *Marc Warren*

Midsomer Murders (1997)
DCI Tom Barnaby *John Nettles*
DS Gavin Troy *Daniel Casey*

Mind to Kill (1995)
DCI Noel Bain *Philip Madoc*

Miss Marple (1984)
Miss Marple *Joan Hickson followed by Geraldine McEwan*

Inspector Morse (1987)
Inspector Morse *John Thaw*
Sergeant Lewis *Kevin Whately*

Murder Rooms (2000)
Dr Joseph Bell *Ian Richardson*

The New Avengers (1976)
John Steed *Patrick Macnee*
Purdey *Joanna Lumley*

New Scotland Yard (1972)
DCS John Kingdom *John Woodvine*
DI Alan Ward *John Carlisle*
DCS Clay *Michael Turner*
DS Dexter *Clive Francis*

New Tricks (2003)
Jack Halford *James Bolam*
Brian Lane *Alun Armstrong*
Supt Sandra Pullman *Amanda Redman*
Gerry Standing *Dennis Waterman*

Nick of the River (1959)
Det Inspector Nixon *George Baker*

No Hiding Place (1959)
Supt Lockhart *Raymond Francis*

The Persuaders (1971)
Danny Wilde *Tony Curtis*
Lord Brett Sinclair *Roger Moore*

Pie in the Sky (1994)
Henry Crabbe *Richard Griffiths*

Agatha Christie's Poirot (1989)
Hercule Poirot *David Suchet*
Capt. Arthur Hastings *Hugh Fraser*

Prime Suspect (1991)
Jane Tennison *Helen Mirren*
DS Boll Otley *Tom Bell*

The Professionals (1977)
Ray Doyle *Martin Shaw*
William Bodie *Lewis Collins*

Public Eye (1965)
Frank Marker *Alfred Burke*

Randall and Hopkirk (Deceased) (1969)
Jeff Randall *Mike Pratt*
Marty Hopkirk *Kenneth Cope*

Resnick
DI Charles Resnick *Tom Wilkinson*

Rosemary and Thyme (2003)
Rosemary Boxer *Felicity Kendall*
Laura Thyme *Pam Ferris*

Ruth Rendell Mysteries (1988)
CI Wexford *George Baker*
Mike Burden *Christopher Ravenscroft*

Saber of London (1959)
Mark Saber *Donald Gray*

Sally Lockhart (2006)
Sally Lockhart *Billie Piper*

Sergeant Cork (1963)
Sergeant Cork *John Barrie*

Sexton Blake (1967)
Sexton Blake *Laurence Payne*

Shadow Squad (1957)
Vic Steele *Rex Garner*
Don Carter *Peter Williams*

Shoestring (1979)
Eddie Shoestring *Trevor Eve*

Silent Witness (1996)
Dr Samantha Ryan *Amanda Burton*
Nikki Alexander *Emilia Fox*

The Singing Detective (1986)
Philip E Marlow *Michael Gambon*

Softly, Softly (1966), Barlow at Large (1971) & Z-Cars (1962)
DCS Charlie Barlow *Stratford Johns*
CI John Watt *Frank Windsor*

South of the Border (1988)
Pearl Parker *Buki Armstrong*
Finn Gallagher *Rosie Powell*

Special Branch (1969)
DCI Alan Craven *George Sewell*
DCI Tom Haggerty *Patrick Mower*
DI Jordan *Derren Nesbitt*

Spender (1991)
DS Spender *Jimmy Nail*

The Strange Report (1969)
Adam Strange *Anthony Quayle*

Strangers (1978) & Bulman (1985)
George Bulman *Don Henderson*

The Sweeney (1975)
Sgt George Carter *Dennis Waterman*
Inspector Jack Regan *John Thaw*

Taggart (1983)
DC Mike Jardine *James MacPherson*
CI Jim Taggart *Mark McMannus*
DCI Matt Burke *Alex Norton*
DS Jackie Reid *Blythe Duff*

The Third Man (1959)
Harry Lime *Michael Rennie*

A Touch of Frost (1992)
Insp. Jack Frost *David Jason*
George Toolan *John Lyons*

Trial and Retribution (1997)
Supt Michael Walker *David Hayman*
Det Insp Pat North *Kate Buffery*
DCI Roison Connor *Victoria Smurfit*

**An Unsuitable Job for a Woman
(1997)**
Cordelia Gray *Helen Baxendale*

Van der Valk (1972)
Piet van der Valk *Barry Foster*

The Vice (1999)
DI Pat Chappel *Ken Stott*

**Hetty Wainthropp Investigates
(1996)**
Hetty Wainthropp *Patricia Routledge*

Waking the Dead (2000)
DCI Peter Boyd *Trevor Eve*

Inspector Wexford (1988)
CI Wexford *George Baker*

Wire in the Blood (2002)
Dr. Tony Hill *Robson Green*
DCI Carol Jordan *Hermione Norris*

Wolcott (1981)
Winston Churchill Wolcott
George William Harris

Wycliffe (1993)
D Supt Charles Wycliffe *Jack Shepherd*

**Z-Cars (1962) and Softly, Softly
(1966)**
CI John Watt *Frank Windsor*
DCS Charlie Barlow *Stratford Johns*

Detective (1964, then 1968) is a
show that deserves special mention.
Introduced by Rupert Davies in his

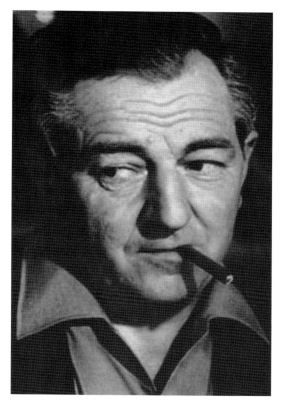

*Rupert Davies, as Maigret, introduced
a series of detective dramas in the
1960s.*

Maigret guise, this was a series of one-
off dramas about other fictional
detectives. In various episodes
Roderick Alleyn was played by
Geoffrey Keen, then Michael Allinson
Father Brown by Mervyn Johns
Albert Campion by Brian Smith
Sergeant Cluff by Leslie Sands
Inspector Dover by Paul Dawkins
Auguste Dupin by Edward Woodward
Gervase Fen by Richard Wordsworth
Reggie Fortune by Denholm Elliott
Inspector Ghote by Zia Mohyeddin
Sherlock Holmes by Douglas Wilmer
Roger Sheringham by John Carson
Nigel Strangeways by Glyn Houston,
then Bernard Horfall
Dr Thorndyke by Peter Copley
Philip Trent by Michael Gwynn

A Timeline of Detection

1753 Bow Street Runners founded
1780 Novels priced at around 2/-
      a volume
1794 Caleb Williams published
1812 Vidocq made Chief of Sûreté
1821 Price of a novel fixed at 1½
      guineas
1828 Mémoires de Vidocq published
1829 London Metropolitan Police
      founded
1841 The Murders in the Rue Morgue
      published in Graham's
      Magazine
1848 W. H. Smith establishes its first
      book and news stand, at Euston
      Station
1850 Pinkerton National Detective
      Agency formed in Chicago
1853 Inspector Bucket appears in Bleak
      House
1859 The Woman in White published
1863 The Ticket-of-Leave Man staged
1865 The Notting Hill Mystery
      serialised
1868 Sergeant Cuff appears in The
      Moonstone
1870 The Mystery of Edwin Drood
      serialisation begins
1878 CID formed at Scotland Yard
      First detective story written by a
      woman: The Leavenworth Case
      by Anna Katharine Green
1886 First transvestite detective story:
      My Lady the Wolf by Baron
      Skottowe
1887 In Beeton's Christmas Annual the
      first appearance of Sherlock
      Holmes, in A Study in Scarlet
1890 Britain's first literary agents set up
      Conan Doyle's The Sign of Four
      published
1891 First Strand Magazine Sherlock
      Holmes story: A Scandal in
      Bohemia

1892 Anarchist bomb outrages in Paris
      'Death' of Sherlock Holmes at the
      Reichenbach Falls
1893 Independent Labour Party
      founded
      First appearance of Sexton Blake
1894 The 6/- novel comes in to destroy
      the 1½ guinea 'three-decker'
      Martin Hewitt, Investigator
      published
1898 Deaths of Gladstone & Bismark
      Radium discovered
1900 British Labour Party founded
      Commonwealth of Australia
      established
      Mafeking relieved
      The first Holmes film (silent):
      Sherlock Holmes Baffled
1901 Queen Victoria dies
1903 Mrs Pankhurst forms WSPU
      Wright brothers' first air flight
      Sherlock Holmes returns! The
      Adventure of the Empty House
      in Strand Magazine
1905 Automobile Association formed
      A printer founds Sinn Fein
      First Edgar Wallace novel: The
      Four Just Men
1906 Liberals landslide election victory
1907 First ever blood transfusion
      First appearance of Dr Thorndyke:
      The Red Thumb Mark
1908 The FBI founded, within the US
      Dept of Justice
1910 Dr Crippen arrested at sea
1911 Siege of Sidney Street
      Coronation of King George V
      First Father Brown book: The
      Innocence of Father Brown
1914 August: First World War begins
      The last full-length Sherlock
      Holmes novel: The Valley of Fear
1916 Easter Rising in Dublin

Lloyd George becomes Prime Minister
1917 *Tsar of Russia abdicates*
America joins the First World War
His Last Bow appears to be the end of Sherlock Holmes
1918 *November: First World War ends*
1920 *Prohibition introduced in America*
Irish Home Rule Bill passed
IRA killings escalate
Bull-Dog Drummond published
First appearance of Hercule Poirot: The Mysterious Affair at Styles
1921 *Larson invents the lie detector*
1923 *Hitler addresses first Nazi rally*
German currency collapses
First appearance of Lord Peter Wimsey: Whose Body?
1924 *Britain's first Labour government*
The 'Zinoviev Letter'
First appearance of Inspector French: Inspector French's Greatest Case
1925 *Parliament establishes 'Daylight Saving Summer Time'*
First appearance of Roger Sheringham: The Layton Court Mystery
1926 *The Murder of Roger Ackroyd published*
General Strike
1927 *Lindbergh's solo flight across Atlantic.*
'The Jazz Singer' becomes the first talking picture.
British Broadcasting Corporation established
Truly the last appearance of Sherlock Holmes: The Case-Book of Sherlock Holmes
1928 *Central London floods in January.*
Women over 21 get the vote
Fleming discovers penicillin
The Detection Club founded
First appearances of Ashenden, Miss Silver and The Saint
1929 *First British woman cabinet minister: Margaret Bondfield*

The Wall Street Crash.
Britain has 22 public telephone boxes
First appearance of Albert Campion: The Crime at Black Dudley
First appearance of Inspector Grant: The Man in the Queue
First talking film of Holmes (with Clive Brook): The Return of Sherlock Holmes
1930 *Amy Johnson flies solo from Britain to Australia.*
Uruguay win first soccer World Cup
Conan Doyle dies
First appearance of Miss Marple: Murder at the Vicarage
1931 *Moseley forms fascist 'New Party'*
National Coalition Government
The pound devalues
First appearance of Maigret, in M. Gallet, décédé, trans. as The Death of Monsieur Gallet in 1933 (UK).
Malice Aforethought published
1932 *Hunger marches in British cities*
Unemployment reaches 2.7 million
First appearance of Maigret on film: La nuit du carrefour
1934 *Hitler becomes President & Chancellor of Germany*
Bonnie & Clyde killed in America.
First appearance of Roderick Alleyn: A Man Lay Dead
1935 *1st Penguin paperback: cost 6d*
First appearance of Nigel Strangeways: A Question of Proof
1936 *Germany occupies the Rhineland*
Jarrow March
Abdication crisis
First appearance of John Appleby: Death in the President's Lodging
1937 *Coronation of George VI*
Duke of Windsor marries Wallis Simpson.

Final Peter Wimsey book:
Busman's Honeymoon.

1938 'Peace in our time' claims
Chamberlain.
Germany invades the Sudetenland.
First episode of radio serial Paul
Temple (the last of which was
in 1968)

1939 World War Two declared in
Europe
First screen appearance of Basil
Rathbone as Sherlock Holmes:
The Hound of the Baskervilles

1943 Germans defeated at Stalingrad.
Allied forces gain upper hand
in war. (Only now) the first
appearance of Holmes on BBC
radio, played by Arthur Wontner

1945 World War Two in Europe ends

1947 Al Capone dies in America

1949 Haigh executed for the Acid Bath
Murders

1951 The Festival of Britain
Winston Churchill becomes PM
again
First appearance of Holmes on
British TV, played by Andrew
Osborne

1952 King George VI dies
First stage production of The
Mousetrap
First James Bond novel: Casino
Royale

1953 Coronation of Elizabeth II
Hillary & Tensing conquer
Everest
The murderer Christie hanged
John Creasey founds the Crime
Writers' Association

1954 Bannister runs first 4-minute mile
Food rationing ends.
Holmes & Watson played on BBC
radio by John Gielgud & Ralph
Richardson.

1955 Eden succeeds Winston Churchill.
Ruth Ellis is the last woman to be
hanged in Britain.
ITV launched in September.

CWA establishes the Crossed Red
Herring Award for the year's
best crime novel. (Since
renamed the Gold Dagger, and
in 2006 the Duncan Lawrie
Dagger.)

1956 The Suez crisis
Hungarian uprising is crushed by
Soviet Union

1958 Manchester United team air
crash
Parking meters introduced in
Mayfair
First screen appearance of Jean
Gabin as Maigret: Maigret tend
un piége
First screening of Dial 999

1959 The 'Mini' launched to much
acclaim
First screening of No Hiding Place

1960 Macmillan makes 'Wind of
Change' speech
Kennedy wins US election
Lady Chatterley's Lover brought to
trial
First TV screening of Z-Cars,
which continued till 1978
First of 52 TV episodes with
Rupert Davies as Maigret

1962 Cuban Missile crisis
Marilyn Monroe dies of overdose
Beatles first hit: Love Me Do
London Airport Bullion Robbery
First screening of Z Cars
First appearance of Inspector van
der Valk: Love in Amsterdam,
and of Adam Dalgliesh: Cover
Her Face

1963 The 'Profumo affair'
Martin Luther King's 'I have a
dream' speech
President Kennedy assassinated.
The Great Train Robbery

1964 Power cuts greet launch of BBC2
Nelson Mandela sentenced to life
imprisonment

*First appearance of Inspector
    Wexford: From Doon With
    Death, and of Inspector Ghote:
    The Perfect Murder*

1965 *Winston Churchill dies
US troops into Vietnam
First screening of Public Eye*

1966 *Ian Brady & Myra Hindley
    jailed for the 'Moors Murders'
England wins soccer World Cup
First screening of Softly, Softly*

1969 *Man first walks on the moon.
British troops deployed in N Ireland
MPs vote to end hanging (343 to
    158)
First screening of Department S
    and of Special Branch*

1970 *The Beatles split up
'New English Bible' launched: sells
    1m in first week
First appearance of Dalziel &
    Pascoe: A Clubbable Woman*

1971 *Britain switches to decimal
    currency*

1972 *Britain signs up provisionally to
    EEC
'Bloody Sunday' riot in Londonderry
Government introduces 90-day
    pay and dividend freeze
Nixon re-elected as US President
Vietnam war approaches its end
First appearance of Cordelia
    Gray: An Unsuitable Job for a
    Woman
Last appearance of Maigret:
    Maigret et Monsieur Charles
First screening of New Scotland
    Yard and of Van der Valk*

1973 *Ceasefire in Vietnam
The Watergate affair*

1974 *Lord Lucan disappears
Nixon resigns*

1975 *Margaret Thatcher becomes first
    woman leader of Conservative
    Party
Inflation reaches 25%*

*Last appearance of Hercules
    Poirot: Curtain (a book actually
    written in the '40s)
First appearance of Inspector
    Morse: Last Bus to Woodstock
First screening of The Sweeney*

1976 *Britain's hottest summer of the
    century
Harold Wilson resigns
Punk Rock & culture pushes to
    fore
Agatha Christie dies
Last appearance of Miss Marple:
    Sleeping Murder (actually
    written in the '40s)*

1977 *Elvis Presely dies
Virginia Wade wins Wimbledon
    title
First appearance of Cadfael: A
    Morbid Taste for Bones, and of
    Jack Laidlaw: Laidlaw
First screening for The Professionals*

1978 *Inflation down to 10%
First screening of* **Hazell**

1979 *Margaret Thatcher becomes Prime
    Minister.
Iran Embassy siege*

1980 *Mugabe becomes PM of Zimbabwe,
    and Nixon President of USA.
John Lennon is shot in New York.
First screening of Juliet Bravo*

1981 *Prince Charles marries Lady
    Diana Spencer
First screening of Bergerac*

1982 *IRA bomb Horse Guards
Iraq bombs Iran.
Britain wins Falklands war*

1983 *Iranian forces invade Iraq
HIV virus identified
First screening of Taggart*

1984 *IRA bomb Tory party conference
First screening of The Bill*

1985 *Year-long miners' strike ends
First screening of Dempsey and
    Makepeace*

1986 *US space shuttle Challenger
    explodes*

US bombs Libya
Chernobyl nuclear disaster
Jeffrey Archer resigns
Ruth Rendell's first Barbara
    Vine novel: A Dark Adapted
    Eye
First appearance of Inspector
    Rebus: Knots and Crosses

1987 Zeebrugge ferry disaster
King's Cross underground fire
    disaster
Black Monday shares disaster
First screening of Inspector
    Morse

1989 George Bush succeeds President
    Reagan
Tiananmen Square protest
Berlin Wall comes down
Georges Simenon dies, in
    Lausanne

1990 The first Gulf War begins

1991 Soviet Union collapses
Helen Sharman is first British
    astronaut
5,000 year old frozen body
    discovered in the Alps
Gulf War ends
First screening of Prime Suspect

1992 Killings in Sarajevo begin war
    in Yugoslavia
Phil Collins plays Great Train
    Robber Buster Edwards in
    'Buster'
First screening of Prime Suspect
    2, of Heartbeat, and of A
    Touch of Frost
First appearances of Kate
    Brannigan and of Commissario
    Brunetti

1993 Human Genome Project launched
    in San Diego
Queen Elizabeth II is first British
    monarch to pay income tax
First screening of Prime Suspect 3
    and of Cracker

1994 Channel Tunnel opens
First screening of Cadfael and of
    Chandler & Co

1995 26-year old Nick Leeson brings
    down Britain's oldest bank,
    Barings, losing £620 million
First screening of Hamish
    Macbeth

1996 NASA announces 'proof' of life-
    forms in Martian asteroid
First screening of Dalziel and
    Pascoe and of Hetty Wainthropp
    Investigates

1997 Roslin Institute clones Dolly the
    sheep
New Labour wins election
Princess Diana killed in car
    crash
First screening of Midsomer
    Murders

1999 NATO air attacks on Serbia
First screening of The Vice

2001 9/11 attack on Twin Towers
Denis Tito pays $20m to become
    first space tourist
First screening of Messiah

2002 Terrorist bombings in Bali
First screening of Wire in the
    Blood

2003 US-led invasion of Iraq
International Criminal Court
    established.
Dolly the sheep dies.
First screening of New Tricks

2004 Asian tsunami kills 300,000

2005 UN authorises International
    Criminal Court to try Darfur
    war criminals
July: London bus & tube bombings
Hurricane Katrina hits New Orleans

2006 Floyd Landis wins Tour de France
    –but fails drug test
First screening of Waking the Dead
Final, 2-part episode of Prime
    Suspect

2007 Saddam Hussein executed
Tony Blair finally resigns

2008 First publication of Great
    Fictional British Detectives

Acknowledgements

I am fortunate to have many friends in the **Crime Writers'
Association** who have provided data for this book. Further
information has come from the internet, using crime writers' own
sites and the following general resources:

Fantastic Fiction (www.fantasticfiction.co.uk)

the *Crime Writers' Association* (www.thecwa.co.uk)

the *Custard Online TV Guide* (www.thecustard.tv.co.uk)

Screen Online (www.screenonline.org.uk).

Much of the information and many of the pictures here come from
books and magazines in my own collection, and from those loaned
me by the **Oxfam** Bookshop in Cheltenham.

Among the **reference books** I have consulted the following stood
out:

100 Great Detectives edited by Maxim Jakubowski (Xanadu 1991)

Bloodhounds of Heaven by Ian Ousby (Harvard University Press 1976)

Bloody Murder by Julian Symons (Papermac 1992 revised edition)

Boys Will Be Boys by E. S. Turner (Michael Joseph, 1948)

Companion to Literature in English edited by Ian Ousby (Cambridge, revised 1992)

The Crime and Mystery Book by Ian Ousby (Thames & Hudson 1997)

Elementary My Dear Watson by Graham Nown (Ward Lock 1986)

Imaginary People by David Pringle (Grafton 1987)

The Lady Investigates by Craig & Cadogan (Victor Gollancz 1981)

Mammoth Encyclopedia of Modern Crime Fiction by Mike Ashley (Robinson 2002)

Movie and Video Guide by Leonard Maltin (Plume 2002)

The Murder Book by la Cour and Mogensen (George Allen & Unwin 1971)

Murder Will Out by T J Binyon (OUP 1989)

Mystery by Peter Haining (Souvenir Press 1977)

Novels and Novelists edited by Martin Seymour-Smith (Windward 1980)

Oxford Companion to Edwardian Fiction by Kemp, Mitchell & Trotter (OUP 1997)

Penguin TV Companion by Jeff Evans (Penguin 2003 revised edition)

Sequels compiled by M E Hicken (London Assoc of Asst Librarians 1982)

Acknowledgements continued

Thanks also to the editors of and contributors to *Crime Time*, *CADS* and *Sherlock* magazine, with special thanks also to David Stuart Davies of *Sherlock* for providing a number of rare screen shots and photographs, to Ali Karim and Mike Stotter of *Shots* magazine for author photos, to Roni Wilkinson and the production team at Pen and Sword and to my friend and editor, Fiona Shoop. Every effort has been made to trace the appointed owners of the material still covered by copyright, but where any accidental infringement has occurred please contact the author care of the publishers.